JASON ANSPACH   NICK COLE   WALT ROBILLARD

ORDER OF THE CENTURION

CALLSIGN VALKYRIE

GALAXY'S EDGE

ISBN: 978-1-949731-96-5

Edited by David Gatewood
Published by Galaxy's Edge Press

Cover Art: Tommaso Renieri
Cover Design: M.S. Corely
Formatting: Kevin G. Summers

Website: www.GalaxysEdge.us
Facebook: facebook.com/atgalaxysedge
Newsletter (get a free short story): www.InTheLegion.com

·

Dedicated to John Chapman

The Order of the Centurion is the highest award that can be bestowed upon an individual serving in, or with, the Legion. When such an individual displays exceptional valor in action against an enemy force, and uncommon loyalty and devotion to the Legion and its legionnaires, refusing to abandon post, mission, or brothers, even unto death, the Legion dutifully recognizes such courage with this award.

98.4% of all citations are awarded posthumously.

1

Mack drove all his strength into shutting the cab door. Again. He was struggling to shut it so much he had to close it twice. "*Bal hah tek voo amok vo.*"

The hulking, hairy Drusic behind the wheel laughed at the human blundering his way at trying to be polite in his language. "Oh man. Okay. I can't take anymore. That was good. I speak Standard. All good here guy."

Mack gave a slight scowl. "Wait. then why'd you let me blunder around like that?"

"Figured you need the practice!" The ape-like alien slapped the wheel with a guttural laugh. "Hey, listen. Here's my holocard. You need a ride while you in *Damyagora*, you ping my comm. I like you, off-worlder. I take care of you."

The Drusic resembled gorilla-like humanoids with musculature several times stronger than that of humans. To make matters more interesting, they had testoster-one-producing glands throughout their body. The joke around the galaxy was that the males had eighteen tes-ticles, so no matter where you hit them, you were at least guaranteed a sucker shot. While some part of the specu-lation was true, the glands accounted for the race's rep-utation for being more powerful than many other races and easily provoked to anger.

Mack pulled a stack of credit chits from his pocket, and dialed in one to match the fare. He passed it to the driver and took the alien's holocard in return.

"I'm serious," the Drusic pressed. "Call my comm. I'm the best driver around. At least the best one you're likely to get—ha!"

"Thanks. Bet you say that to all your fares."

"No way. Most humans come to *Damyagora* and never even try to learn *Apothin*. Them, I don't like. You, I do."

Mack caught the inflections in his accented Standard. When the Drusic growled low in *Apothin*, the regional dialect for this hemisphere, it was usually understood to be sarcastic.

"I'm honored," Mack said, waiting for the driver to give him the okay despite knowing that the credit chit carried the full fare and could be used as credits in that amount or emptied into a larger wallet or chit.

"The good ones always try to at least say thank you in the local lingo, ya know?" The slow processor built into the Drusic's cab pinged. "Huh." The alien fished out another credit chit, spun it to load up a set amount, and offered it back. "You overpaid."

Mack waved him off.

The cab driver grabbed Mack's wrist, engulfing it completely in his massive ebony palm and then pushed the chit into the middle of the human's palm so hard that he felt like it might go right on through to the other side. The Drusic wasn't trying to hurt him; their natural strength was just incredible. "Mister. I can't keep this. It's too much and I would be indebted to you."

With a flick of his hand, Mack said, "Think of it as an apology for all those human fares who never knew how to say *mangara no*."

The enormous simian slapped the steering wheel nearly hard enough to pound it from its housing. "You are welcome, Mister. I look forward to driving you again."

Mack hoisted his bag from the dusty ground, making his way through Market Street in the multicultural city of *Damyagora*. While the Drusic race had developed a reputation for hyper-aggressive negotiations over anything they could get their paws on, the rest of the galaxy recognized their home planet Drusar as a world of opportunity. The Drusic had embraced modern technology much sooner than most other predatory races, allowing for cosmopolitan cities and resorts to spring up from the planet's gorgeous landscape. While other races were strongly encouraged to remain within the safe zones, it was common enough for the Drusic to dispatch recovery teams to rescue thrill seeking aliens trying to experience the wild side of the planet.

Damyagora was a tourist trap for those who liked things a little bit dangerous. Set in the badlands just inland from the Dread Sea, the metropolis was carved into the walls of a canyon that ran for miles with multiple forks dividing the city into different neighborhoods. The Diamond District, named for the light reflecting off the Hagimada River, was the most lavish, reserved for core world upper crusters and clan elders who could afford such a view. Mack walked onto Market Street in the center of the Cultural District, where Drusic and all other races met for commerce on and off the street.

The smell of cooking meats, various smokes and vapor, and sparking repulsors from a first local attempt at making speeders—these bad glitchy pulse regulators—dominated the streets Mack meandered through.

He aimed his nose over a food cart where a vendor was cooking some sort of lizard meat. "*Halda mok cho?*"

"*Savgada. Hav neh?*" the older Drusic barked. He was shorter than most of his kind Mack had encountered. His fur had turned ash-gray, and his face didn't have the hard edge most Drusic had, but was round, pleasant, and wizened in age. Likely the old man had avoided many of the aggressive pastimes favored by his kin, living to an age where smiling was taken for what it was, the simple enjoyment of life. Mack also hoped that "wizened" meant knowing that selling a foreigner tainted mok cho would be bad for business, and thus a problem he wouldn't have with the aged alien.

"I'll take, yes, that. On the... noodles with the... pepper-looking things. Thank you. *Mangara, no,*" Mack said, blundering through the language.

The gray Drusic seemed happy the foreigner was at least attempting to speak in Apothin. He patted Mack on the shoulder and ladled a bowl full of noodles, stewed vegetables, and the mok cho lizard meat. The steam coming off the bowl was tangy, smelling of citrus and something like grilled chicken.

The next man in line then asked for the same. "*Taku mishta no habin, sobray.*"

The aged cart purveyor nodded, handing a bowl to the second human. The diner greeted the bowl with hungry gratitude, paying for his meal with a hastily produced chit.

"Hey," Mack said, still holding out his own credit chit and waiting for the vendor to take it. "Don't forget about me."

The Drusic vendor pretended not to hear, and finally the stranger nudged Mack with an elbow.

"Kind of a tradition we have around here. New guy gets his first meal paid for and then owes his debtor a favor," the stranger said.

"Is that right?" Mack asked skeptically. He had his hand positioned near his pocket, ready to pull a folding knife from it in one smooth motion.

"Sure is. *Kodra*, this is really good today. *Jahibi nok lagova shee.*" The stranger's accent and inflections were almost native, using breathy, near coughing sounds to show enthusiasm. "My name's Ryan Lahm, by the way. You Banes?"

Mack angled himself against the bar to use his peripheral vision to watch the passersby. "You sword and wreath?"

The stranger smiled through a mouthful of noodles. "Me? A legionnaire? No, man. I couldn't handle that level of structure. I'm more of a broken rhythm type of guy."

"I see that. So you're an Alpha Section liaison or admin?" Mack asked, mirroring the way Lahm was talking and chewing at the same time.

"Neither. I'm the Knife."

Mack stopped chewing, fixing his glare on the other man. Alpha Section sending their infiltration specialist to greet him sent up all sorts of red flags to the veteran legionnaire. Normally, a pickup like this was done by an admin specialist or a liaison officer if the Legion section was deployed. Having a tier-one special warfare agent pick up the new guy was highly irregular.

With a mouthful of chow, Mack asked, "Is the threat level that high that we have the Knife scooping me up from the pavement?"

"Old boss heard about you. Knew your last tour on the wing was more than rough. He wanted you to have an easy first day at school," Lahm answered nonchalantly.

Mack slurped in another mouthful of noodles. "That works. So, we going to hang around here all day and slurp, or are you going to take me to the lodge?"

Lahm handed his empty bowl back to Kodra. "Perfect as always, sir. *Mangara no.*"

Mack slurped the rest of his meal and followed his not-quite-a-liaison into the city. Carved into cliffs, the homes and businesses were elegantly minimalist, building upon building soaring up into the sky. Handholds and brachiation points, which natives used to swing from place to place, spread through dense plant life growing between structures. Walking through Market Street was a chaotic endeavor at most times during the day. At present, Mack forced himself to walk naturally while keeping his hands close enough to his pockets to discourage anyone looking to take help themselves to their contents, and not jostling anyone with his bulky shoulder bag.

Wet earth petrichor drifted to Mack's nostrils as they rounded a corner into a covered bazaar. Streaking vines wove themselves into the dense vegetation penetrating every corner of the overhead, making one forget the city was built into a dusty canyon. Giant Drusic merchants snapped long fingers to get their attention. One pushy female tapped Lahm on the shoulder, and he threw out his arms.

"How many times do I have to tell you, Hana? I don't need a sash!" the Knife protested.

"Bah!" Drusic spat through flapping lips. "You know you want it. Your girl will love you for it."

Lahm thumbed back toward Mack as if in apology. "My only companion is this one. He's new and doesn't like scarves."

Hana cast Mack an appraising look, who tried his best not to look like he wanted to be part of the conversation, which was true. "He is more of a turquoise, I think. For you, pretty one."

Mack held the scarf at arm's length, trying to decide whether he should be offended by her comment. "*Mangara no?*"

Chuckling, she said, "I like this one, Lahm. He is polite."

"*Shashoa va,*" Lahm said, waving the merchant away.

As they slipped through the market, Mack asked, "Do you know everyone here?"

"Bah." Lahm gave him the same gesture he'd given Hana.

They entered a shop off the main bazaar, the door opening with a tinkling bell. Antique teapots, a large assortment of tea, and handcrafted display pieces were meticulously arranged. The shop's purveyor, a middle-aged Endurian, wore a long dress over combat boots. An odd fashion choice, but functional. She wore a deep hooded shawl over her head, covering the tendrils underneath. As she approached, she brought with her a myriad scents from about the room, powerful and fragrant.

"Nissa, this is Malcolm Banes. Mack, Nissa."

Mack attempted to reach for her hand to shake it, but Lahm touched the side of his arm to keep it from coming forward. He flinched back, knocking a tangle of herbs drying over his head.

Nissa reached forward, catching the bundle before it hit the floor. He was close enough to see her eyes were white. Burn marks tracked around her orbits. Her shawl shifted and he could see the scarred remains of her hair-like tendrils, cut into ruins raked into her scalp. It was times like this that Mack regretted some of the time he spent being a legionnaire on the edge. He knew the signs of torture at the hands of the Gomarii slavers.

"It's a pleasure to meet you, ma'am," Mack said.

"He the new hard stripe for the Valkyr—"

Lahm interrupted the woman's question. "They don't call them that anymore, Nissa."

The woman laughed, taking Malcolm's hand in her own. "Rough hands, typical of the Legion. Oh, this is interesting."

Mack withdrew his hands, clutching the shoulder strap of the bag he carried instead. When that didn't seem to be enough of a way to reclaim his dignity, he wiped his palms into his pockets.

The abrupt withdrawal didn't faze Nissa. "I like the old name better. Stupid House of Reason and their oversensitive inclusivity mandates mucking up the place, as if they knew what would offend someone and what wouldn't. And what happens if that does happen? Oh, no. Someone was offended. The universe will end now that they're offended. Valkyries. Who cares?"

Lahm stood behind her, flicking a finger into the air every time she used the word "offended." She kicked back, striking him in the shin.

"Ow! You sure you're blind?"

"Mr. Banes. Please accept my greetings to our humble shop. Tea is promptly at fifteen-hundred local standard time. You are welcome to sample at your leisure."

Trying not to laugh at Lahm's misfortune as the man had bought him lunch, he managed a reserved, "Much obliged."

Lahm motioned him into the back. Mack took the herb bundle from her, replacing it on its ceiling hook. "Sorry about that."

Nissa tapped him on the forearm. "No problems, Mr. Banes. I appreciate a polite man about the shop, even if your size makes you a tyrannasquid in a terrarium."

With a chuckle, Mack followed Lahm into a storage closet.

"Stand here. Just taking some biometrics," Lahm instructed.

"In a closet?"

The agent gave a *you-must-be-new* look and then swept aside a rug hanging on the back wall. He pushed his hand through the wall, exposing a sliding hatch leading to a set of stairs going down.

"Torrid," Mack said of the hard light hologram hiding the door. "Is it really necessary with the rug hanging like that?"

Lahm nodded. "You'd be surprised what Drusic kids get into."

The two descended the narrow stairs, ending in a room that was the antithesis of the one they'd just left. Clean and orderly, there were six stations with techs moving back and forth, pouring over holo screens and real paper maps laid out on tables. Above the maps was a holographic projection of the same terrain represented in ink on the perishable and expensive substance. Leaning on the table was a man in his early to middle age. He was thin, with hard eyes and white hair in stark contrast to his tan skin.

Mack stopped dead in his tracks. He couldn't help but stare at the man's face, a visage he'd seen over and again whenever the Legion's victory in the Savage Wars was taught, remembered, or written about. General Tyrus Rex, the Legion Commander who won the ultimate victory for the Republic, only to betray it years later. Depending on whose version of the story you believed—the House of Reason's or the old NCO's who served with Rex.

Quirking a grin, Lahm snapped his fingers at a curly-haired woman standing next to the man. "Pay up!"

Glaring, she cried, "Every time. Just once I'm going to beat you!" She pounded the table, her emerald eyes flashing.

"Not until we get another CO there, chief," Lahm corrected.

The thin man walked around the table, reaching out to shake Mack's hand. "No. I'm not him. Uncanny resemblance, though, right? Gotten me in trouble more than once when we operated on a core world. Nathan Gallagher. Top Cat, Team Commander, or TC for short."

"Ahem!" came from the mop of curls.

"Either way, it's nice to meet you, Master Sergeant Banes," TC said.

Mack shook himself clear of the surprise. "You look just like him."

"You'll get over it," TC said. "Did you read up on us?"

"Yes, sir. I'm just not used to dealing with the Alpha Section directly. Did Repub Intel implement a change?"

"Nope. They still run the same boring shop. I like to be a little more open with the Legion element."

One of Mack's eyebrows flicked up. "I don't know how to behave around regular folks. This is going to be an all-new ride."

"Don't worry. Neither do we," the Team Commander said. He nodded to the woman beside him and picked up his things to leave. "Listen, your CO is out with the boys at the moment for a training event. Grab a cup of kaff and make yourself at home. Just don't let Nissa know you're drinking coffee or it'll be hell to pay for all of us."

"Is she an asset or an agent?" Mack asked.

The mop of curls bounced from her spot at the table to meet the new arrival. "Since TC is going to continue to ignore me, I'm Ladonna Cantrell. Nice to meet you, Sergeant. I'm the A-SEC XO."

Mack took her hand, marveling at the strength of her grip. She was short and curvy, not someone he would expect to do pull-ups for fun. "Now, that's a grip, Chief!"

"You're damn right it is," she said with a wink. "And to your question, Nissa is our psyops specialist. She has a doctorate in exoethnographic psychology, another in human behavioral sciences, and a master's degree in I-beat-you. That is a lady you do not want to cross."

"Good to know," Mack said.

Chief Cantrell deactivated the hologram over the table. "Tell ya what, Sergeant. TC is going to be busy with today's intel reports. How about I show you around? Give you the ten-credit tour."

"Sounds like a plan. Just one question. What was that not-so-friendly wager between you and Lahm?"

"Ah. He bets me that every leej who walks in the door is going to rocket propel their jaw to the floor when they see our CO. One of these days I'm going to get the one that hits the handshake and cool breezes right on by."

Mack shook his head in the resoundingly negative. "Not likely. The guy looks exactly like General Rex."

2

Generations of special warfare operators in the Legion had come up through the Savage Wars and into a time of relative peace, at least for the Core Worlds. As Mack sat at a spare workstation in the Alpha Section's basement ops-center, he wondered what had held up legion R&D over the past few years from producing a faster way for him to sign for everything. R&D couldn't use the Savages as an excuse anymore. That was had ended a long time ago.

"That's the non-sexy part of being in any military unit," Mack muttered to himself. When you got past a certain rank, the powers that be heaped more responsibility on you than just your blaster and bucket. Unit oversight coming all the way from the lofty House of Reason demanded their spreadsheets be maintained from the lowliest private to the highest ranking general. There was no escaping signing for your issued gear, and as the incoming senior team sergeant for this particular REC-Team, he got to sign for more than most.

What bothered Mack most of all was simply being here. He'd been a legionnaire for his entire military career, spending a decade plus as a Valkyrie leej in a recovery and rescue unit. That meant he noticed when things didn't quite line up.

Somehow, over the last several conflicts, Legion doctrine had determined the Valkyries worked best as a split force made up of varying services. Legion Command worked in tandem with the Republic's Department of Security to make the REC-Teams comprised of a logistical element, the Alpha Section, and a Bravo Section of Dark Operations legionnaires full of doctor grade medics who doubled as sappers. Considered a matter of section security, the two units were supposed to operate out of separate locations.

Maybe that system would ultimately be better than the one Mack knew and loved, but for now, he huffed at having to wait in the middle of smart-guy central with all the "movers." His last unit had called the Alpha Section guys by that particular flavor of slang, as if the A-Sec agents were just there to haul the Bravos from A to B.

To be fair, it was more than that. Even as Valkyries inserted into hostile territories to recover lost Repub personnel or perform asset denial missions, the A-Sec agents procured needed transport and equipment while trying to keep the Bravo section's presence under wraps via alternative measures, much of which would be considered illegal on most Republic worlds.

Mack found all of the cloak and virbo-dagger stuff to be insanely boring. Then again, he didn't see any of the "movers" have to continue checking off boxes on a spreadsheet.

Trapped in a room with multiple techs and the team's intel specialists wasn't doing wonders for Mack's ability to finish his homework. The dank, musty basement echoed all the noise coming from the bullpen full of keyboard cowboys surrounding him. The worst being the kid claiming to be the senior tech, slurping from a straw hard enough to turn himself inside out.

The head tech adjusted the floating holo screens over his desk. With his free hand, he sipped on a metal straw stuck in an impervisteel tumbler.

Ladonna Cantrell, the leader of the A-Sec movers walked up to the senior tech with a smirk. "Hey, Martin. You know drinking that garbage out of repurposed hull plating is going to give you cancer, right?"

"Hey, Chief. Everything gives you cancer. Luckily, Utopion's got a pill for that," Martin countered.

"Sure they do. But you're a DOS employee. That's not covered by the health plan," Chief Cantrell said, shaking her finger. "So you better start saving."

The tech set the cup down. "On another happy note—hey, TC! Raptor's back."

An immense human sporting a high and tight haircut, riding leathers, and a set of saddlebags over his shoulder strolled in from the tea shop entrance. The legionnaire strode over to Martin's desk, dropping a fizz water soda in front of the tech. "New flavor. Adrena-Berry."

"Thank you, sir. That's great!" Martin poured the drink straight into the tumbler and patiently waited for the fizz to settle. "They told me drinking out of this would give me cancer."

"Pansies," Raptor said.

The Team Commander strode over to shake his hand. "Who's the kid upstairs being accosted by Nissa?"

"Corpsman out of the Repub navy, just passed Legion selection. I picked him up on the way in," Raptor confirmed.

TC pointed to Mack. "Cool. I got you a new team sergeant while you were out. Where's Rocco?"

Raptor reached into his bag and produced a chrome bottle. A couple of swigs from it, and he closed his eyes and steadied himself with a breath. "He's putting the team down. Figured I'd come into the shop to grab the new guy, roll him through the talk on the way out."

Chief slapped the powerful leej on his jacketed sleeve. "You just got back!"

A half smile in the chief's direction made the normally unshakable agent blush. "Oba created me to stare into the ugly side of life and beat it beautiful. There's already too much of that here. You don't need me."

Martin tipped his cup in Raptor's direction. "Careful, Captain Rashad. The House of Reason is going to send down a tech to administer a harassment briefing with talk like that."

"Doubtful. The last one put a restraining order on me for harassment during the harassment briefing." The leej walked through the consoles and their techs, high-fiving and patting them on the shoulders. He came to Mack. "You Sergeant Banes?"

Mack stood, reaching out for the man's hand. "Call sign Mack. You the team sergeant?"

"Negative. That would be my guy, Rocco. He's over-seeing team gear turn in and AAR at the crew cages after today's training. I'm Captain Emilio Rashad. LS-190, call sign Raptor."

"Sorry, sir. I had my comm going when you walked in, didn't hear your rank. I was—"

"Don't care. You dive rated?"

Mack wasn't used to meeting with the team CO in front of everyone like this. Usually, they'd meet in an office where the two could hash out the other's style, ask questions they already knew the answers to, and feel out whether the two would be close or have to avoid each other. This was unusual. Mack straightened himself into attention, not sure what to expect. The Legion had a certain vibe to it, and the captain was acting more like a Dark Ops commander than a regular legionnaire. "Dive rated. Yes, sir. We going to—"

Raptor interrupted again. "See Martin over there for some fins. He'll get you rigged in plunger armor. Meet me up top in thirty. Bring the new kid from upstairs and kit out for deep squeeze."

The Team Commander interrupted the captain's roll. "I didn't get a rescue order. What's going on, Rap?"

"Local Saber unit out of Nosh Kitahn lost a crew on a deep dive to recover a sat-team trying to repair some infrastructure from the last hurricane. A close contact we have for them reached out and wanted to know if Repub had any assets in the area they could send. I'm not going to waste time waiting for Utopion to respond, so I cleared it through Captain Dawson, who's acting sector commander, just to have her tell me to do it, anyway. Going to use the op to break in the new kid and see if Sergeant Mack has the required amount of profanity for the job."

Raptor didn't wait for Mack to respond. He hooked the Team Commander by the arm and led both him and the chief into an office.

When the door shut, Mack whirled around in search of a friendly, helpful face. All he found was Martin, who seemed amused by the entire ordeal. "He always swoop in like that?"

The lead technician shrugged. "Now you know why they call him Raptor."

Mack, Raptor, and a junior legionnaire floated in the suspension chamber wearing their deep sea rated armor, specifically designed for the Legion Recovery Rescue Teams to secure pilots and crew from starships that were forced down over deep seas. The bulky armor resembled the standard kit if it had been stung by mummy bees, growing swollen and ungainly. Endoskeletal struts within the plates gave near bionic strength to the legionnaires operating at extreme depths.

The leejes submerged in the tank for nearly forty-five minutes to satisfy Legion doctrine concerning acclimation to both gear and pressure. Nanotechnology had revolutionized deep sea exploration for nonaquatic races as well as those not capable of traveling to extreme depths. The suits used a type of rebreather to feed viscous fluid into the lungs. The oxygen-rich solution also contained nanites which exerted or released pressure within the body to help regulate the diver against adverse conditions. Unlike the saturation divers of humanity's past, the micronized robots more rapidly adjusted the body's blood gasses so that sitting in a pressure chamber took minutes instead of hours.

Raptor's icon jumped into the other leejes' HUD. "This is Raptor to all Pelican elements. Stand by for systems check."

"Raptor, this is Pelican Alpha," came a voice over L-comm. "We read you Lima Charlie. Translator bots are function forward and alpha one alpha. Send systems check."

Each diver read out their Legion ID number along with current suit chamber pressure, vital signs, and function check for all exoskeletal operations. The info screen in the helmet display jumped from one side of the screen to another, testing visual acuity and lucidity. If the solution mixture was off or the diver's blood gasses were out of range with those in the liquid delivery system, he could feel a sense of disorientation which would make a simple radio check more than difficult. The call-in would also let the command-and-control station judge whether the nanite-infused fluids were reading lung micro pushes, mouth movement, and jaw vibrations to translate that mess into intelligible speech.

"This is Pelican Alpha. We have you green on systems check. You are go for lift. Stand by for LARS."

"This is Raptor. Go for LARS."

The Liquid Adaptive Restraint System light flickered onto Martin's screen in the control room. He toggled the holo, sending the command through orbital track into the tank kilometers away at the Legion compound on Camp Chapman. The energy surge from the tank turned the liquid inside into a gelatin, effectively locking the three legionnaires in place.

"Alpha, this is Raptor. We are sitting pretty in LARS. Deploy KDRV for delivery to Drop Zone Saber."

The newly assigned Legion corporal in the tank tried to raise his hand as though either of them could see what he was doing. Pressure sensors in the tank gel transmitted his motion to the other leejes.

"Did you just try to raise your hand, Cherry?" Mack called into the comm.

Mack had only seen the kid for a minute while they suited up in their plunger armor. It was easy for the incoming team sergeant to forget that not only had the young leej passed rescue selection, but was also a junior NCO himself. Olive complexioned with a mismatched mouth where one side smiled, and the other side frowned, the corporal had the overly cocky look of someone who just got assigned to a REC-Team on the first try. As a former team sergeant with other Valkyrie units, Mack had seen the type before. Highly skilled and highly convinced of his own ability, which was a hallmark of an aggressive leej. It also had the potential to get out of hand unless the team boss had a good grip on the kid's leash.

"Yes, Sergeant. Rookie move on my part, but the only other time I sat in one of these was in the Wrecker Course. Also, my call sign is—"

Raptor snorted into the comm, an approximation by the nanites translating what he would have said if his lungs weren't pushing fluid past his vocal cords. "Your name is Cherry until it isn't, rook."

"Yes, sir. Sorry to interrupt, but what is a KDRV?"

Chief Warrant Officer Frank Demura, Callsign Snowball laughed into the L-comm. "KDRV is a Kelhorned Driven Rescue Vehicle, thank you very much."

"Snowball, this is Raptor. We're all tucked in and ready to ride."

"Roger that, Raptor," Snowball called into the radio. "I'm on approach, clearing the locks and pulling you up now." The pilot's voice was all raspy and slick, like how a sled dealer might talk on late-night holos while trying to sell you a new car at twenty-eight percent interest.

The tank rose into the sunshine from a containment pod set onto the center of the VTOL landing pad. The Legion compound was five fabricated buildings, surrounded by a large motor pool. Leejes in various states of dress and senses of purpose watched as a three-man recovery team from a REC-R, or Wrecker unit, trapped like flies in amber, locked into place.

Snowball chimed into the L-comm. "I have you on the hook. Going to feel a little tug."

The crysteel bucked and shook as grav cables locked onto the outsides of the case. The three leejes were hoisted against the modified SLIC body where rapid-fire *KATHUNK*s shook the outside of the enclosure.

"Chapman CoC, this is Legion Rescue Vehicle Bouncer-Two-Bravo," Snowball called into the net. "I am three leejes heavy for deployment on recovery order 1241-772-Alpha-niner. I am outbound on bearing two-twenty-one local magnetic, looking to clear sector defense your POS. How copy? Over."

The legionnaire that answered had all the right vowels and consonants together with full call signs read back in all the right places like a good appointed officer should. "Legion Rescue Vehicle Bouncer-Two-Bravo, this is Chapman CoC. You are clear to proceed on two-two-one local magnetic in accordance with your recovery order. Good hunting and good luck."

"I hear that one's a Point," Snowball came over their private comm.

"You guys get them out here on the regular?" Mack asked.

"Not that I could remember," Raptor answered. "We had one show up four months ago, but he got shined and they moved him."

"Shined?" Cherry asked.

"Someone noticed him for his grand accomplishments of making sure security cam footage was properly cataloged, and got promoted into a cushy position off this rock. That's what they call the shine, Cherry."

Lucky for Cherry, the nanites translating his pushing on the liquid as speech could do *disappointed*. "I was totally thinking of something else."

"Don't sweat it, Cherry," Snowball said. "Tracking on course to Drop Zone Saber. Lighting it up!"

The SLIC's nose dipped and the repulsors' whine turned over to the thrusters. Jumping through the space, the aircraft sent up a tumultuous dust cloud at the leejes watching from the ground. The vehicle roared past the camp's observation tower, rattling the building and any dental work on the personnel inside.

"How many times do I have to tell you not to buzz those guys, Snow?" Raptor asked over the operation's channel.

"Sorry, sir. I get so excited I just can't help myself," Snowball admitted.

Raptor's next snipe sounded more jovial than demeaning. "Snowball, would another knock down to porto-fresher engineer help you?"

"I can't promise I wouldn't buzz the fab-freshers on the way out if you did, sir."

The laughter that came over the L-comm sounded like they had a studio audience. Mack figured the Alpha Section was listening in, as were any of the Wreckers not on duty, which presented him with a leadership moment. The tricky part for any senior NCO coming into an established unit was to strike a balance between being the leader the team needed, while still taking the time to learn the culture. Other than the two leejes with him, Mack didn't know most of the other players, which didn't absolve him from doing his job. The Valkyries, by nature of being a highly specialized subset of the Legion, were a tight community where in leejes knew most of the major personalities by word of mouth, if not directly. It was like a small town. For good or bad, everyone knew a bit about everyone. And if they didn't, they were about to find out. "This is LS-341. Clear comm for op traffic. Three-four-one, out." The nanites were doing a good job approximating his voice to sound like a judge's gavel pounding home a verdict.

"Wow, usually that would have erupted into full-blown hysterics from the Alpha Section. Figure they don't want to test the new top stripe before they can find out how leej he is," Raptor said.

"I was kind of hoping my on-the-job training extends to more than just being turned into a legionnaire-and-jelly sandwich flying over the Hassica Ocean," Mack said dryly.

"That it does, Sergeant," Raptor agreed.

Snowball pitched in over the comm. "Raptor, I have a flotilla at five klicks above Drop Zone Saber. Gonna be hard to put you straight over, in the event one of them tries to adjust position. Three plungers in a jelly mold on rapid descent is four metric tons traveling at three-point-nine meters per second per second. Any of those craft get in the way, they're gonna get smooshed."

"Snowball, this is Mack. We haven't officially met, so I gotta ask, is *smooshed* a Legion designation for smashed beyond all hope of repair?"

"Roger that, Sergeant."

"Just making sure," Mack added. "I can't wait to use that term during our first PT together."

"LS-eleven-fifteen, call sign Snowball, shutting down vocal operations to secure total concentration for delivery of rescue demons—divers! I meant divers—to Drop Zone Saber."

It was Mack's turn to laugh over the comm. While the action of the goop coursing through his mouth and lungs felt alien, the sensation of being able to laugh, even in this situation, was like coming home again. He wasn't riding a desk to wait out his fiftieth psyche eval or hoping to take another physical readiness test to prove he was mobile, agile, and tactically cold-blooded. He was ready to serve with real leejes doing the jobs only the Legion could do.

Serving on a REC-R unit had a habit of making one the butt of many jokes in the Legion. Star Dusters, Laser Fairies, and Rescue Rickies were his favorites among the callouts by his fellow leejes. But none of that bothered those who actually *served* on a Wrecker team. Legion assessment had a forty-two percent failure rate, with another twenty-seven percent dropping out after being assigned to Legion expeditionary units because training for it and living it every day weren't the same thing. During training, REC-R dropped half a class... among *legionnaires*. Appointed officers couldn't be assigned to a unit because they couldn't pass the proficiency exams for even a tenth of the equipment they fielded. It would be like having someone watch a quick holochit tutorial before diving into brain surgery.

Being suspended above open water with nothing between him and the crushing depths except some plate armor and mini bots in his veins felt like coming home. The locking clamps snapped away from the tank, dropping them into the drink with a heady *whoosh*. The enclosure splashed into the ocean several hundred meters away from the flotilla of Drusic rescue vehicles, news agencies, and military vehicles, all looking to get screen time showing them "helping."

"Mack, Cherry, this is Raptor. Status, and plot me a new course to the drop zone."

"Raptor, this is Cherry. Sensor bots to deploy once LARS goes liquid, over."

"Roger, out," Raptor said.

The trio hit the bottom of the ocean floor. Nanotech infusers rushed to compensate for the lighter pressure of their current depth, adjusting on the fly as the LARS gel turned to liquid.

Free from the semi-solid restraint system, Mack raised his gauntlet to fire a spike into the ground with a floating bulb on the end. Striking the ocean floor, it pinged with a red strobe. "Switching to icon mapping over L-comm. Signal strobe out. Snowball, call it."

"Roger, Sergeant. Good flash. Good flash. I see strobe to the following grid. I am dropping rescue payload on your strobe," Snowball called into the net.

Small pictographs of the legionnaire faces popped into view whenever someone was talking, making it easy to identify who broadcast. The ghostly blue image of a square-jawed Mack filled the HUD in Snowball's interface in the SLIC. "Execute drop."

The trio exited the suspension tank, using plasma cutters on their gauntlets to break apart the panes. One pane went to Cherry's armor, attached to a suspension arm on its back. Raptor thrust one into the stony ground, using the torch to melt it into place. He slammed home a clip on the top of the pane, which started scrolling data across the surface like smart glass. Fifty meters from the captain, Mack slotted two panes across from each other. He placed another at the head of the bracket he'd made.

"Waypoint marker's up," Raptor called.

"Launch point's up," Mack responded. "I have vis-con on rescue pod at four-one mark two-seven."

The other two Wrecker leejes adjusted the gain on their sensor suite to pick up the cylindrical rescue pod descending at a steady plot.

"Mack, with me on the puller. Cherry, get those drones up," Raptor ordered.

There was no response, only action. Powerful hydro jet pack intakes cycled up and shot Raptor and Mack up toward the falling tube. As they neared the vehicle, micro-thrusters kept the rescue pod level and aimed at the strobe pulsing on the ocean floor.

Small spherical bots disconnected from their housing on the exterior of Cherry's armor, pushing into the depths ahead of the team. The metallic balls with a red central ocular lens flared to life, illuminating the ocean floor. Sea creatures flashed away, slinking back in the shadows, escaping the light. Active sonar and spatial awareness mapping combined to provide digital renderings of the rescue site.

"Pups are out," Cherry said.

Mack and Raptor guided the descending recovery pod in between the panes of crysteel they'd disassembled from their KRDV for use as a recovery zone. Once the pod was under their control, they guided it with the thunderous jets in their armor supporting the vehicle's weight until it touched down on the bottom in a puff of silt. Programming routines done in holographic displays cascaded across the panes, turning the simple barriers into an undersea workstation. The two went to work on the screens, setting life support routines, pressure regulation, and powering shields.

"Life support set," Raptor said.

Mack touched the board on his side. "Shields are set."

"Raptor, the pups are detecting large predators in the vicinity of Drop Zone Saber," Cherry announced.

"Define large," Raptor said.

"We have two whales hovering above us, acting curious about what we're doing. Those are roughly ten meters in length and weighing over twelve metric tons. Suit AI is identifying them as naxa whales. Curious about humanoids but usually not threatening to us, unless there's a calf, which we don't have. Near the trapped workers and rescue team, we have something that is either twice the length of the whales or is two creatures of equal size. Debris at the bottom is making it difficult for the AI to lock onto a creature type."

Raptor thrust a knife hand at Mack. The Wrecker leej worked over the interface in his HUD, reconfiguring modular rescue gear into improvised weapons if the need arose. "Armor set."

"Snowball, this is Raptor. Send the second vehicle to my beacon."

"Copy that. Rescue payload number two is ready on your call," Snowball confirmed.

"Execute drop."

The leejes repeated the process with the first pod, placing it in line with the first. The crysteel panels locked onto the vehicle systems for the second pod the instant the duo dropped it to the floor. Swirling dust hid the displays, but they didn't need to see them. The AI globes at the top of each panel were set to mirror the settings from the first craft.

"Snowball, this is Raptor. We're set for long fall."

"Raptor, this is Snowball. I copy long fall. Bouncer-Two-Bravo will stay on station until mission complete.

Execute long fall in three, two, one—execute, execute, execute."

Cherry jumped to the top of the rescue cylinder, bringing the drones around him in a halo of light. Mack and Raptor grabbed reinforced handrails on the exterior of the decompression and recovery chamber, igniting their armor's thrusters to bring them away from the sea floor, gliding toward a cliff, meters to their front.

"Cut jets in three, two, one," Raptor ordered.

The three leejes drifted out of sight into a colossal canyon along the sea floor, following a pipeline containing bundles of cabling the local Drusic workforce had failed to repair. The shining halo gradually vanished into the abyss, forcing its light up ahead for the leejes attaining their objective.

3

Lights from the incandescent halo surrounding the rescue pod highlighted the particulates riding undersea
tides along the trio's deep descent.

"Where we at, Cherry?" Raptor asked over L-comm.

"Passing three hundred meters, sir. On target for six-
twenty-five at trench floor," Cherry confirmed.

"Roger. Hover here for two. Anyone got any ghost stories?" Raptor asked.

Mack huffed into the comm, "There once was a leej
from Kharduckett..."

Raptor wasn't impressed. "Heard that one. I want
ghost stories, Leej. Not dirty limericks."

"All I got, sir," Mack said.

Raptor abandoned his request for the moment.
"Cherry, bring us to five hundred and cycle for two."

"Roger that, sir," the junior legionnaire said. He flicked
several toggles across a holographic HUD only he could
see, syncing their armor under his control. The water jets
flared to life, working with ballast bladders in the suits to
continue their drop into the trench.

"How 'bout it, Malcolm 'Mack' Banes?" Raptor said, returning to his original request. "You sure you don't have
any ghost stories?"

The senior NCO chewed on what the CO was asking. There was the nagging thought that, in joining the new team, at some point, he'd have to talk about his old one. He just didn't think he'd have to do it at a crushing depth of five hundred meters below sea level, with his commanding officer on one side of the comm and his most junior trooper on the other. Flaring his head to either side, Mack stretched his neck as though he were going to step on the mat. Everything made sense there. When pressure was against a trigger or a collar choke, the decisions were easy. Life on the line with a regular Legion reconnaissance company wouldn't involve all this touchy-feely stuff.

"You want all the grim and gory about my last hop to Kabillon."

Translator nanites did a pretty good job of rendering the no-nonsense, "let's have it," with a simple, "Mmm-hmm," from Raptor.

"Need me to switch off the comm for this, Raptor?" the new guy asked.

"Negative, Cherry. We all share. Please continue, Sergeant."

Mack cycled the chalky taste of the breathing fluid several times. It felt like breathing syrup. Each inhale going down his throat as though he were taking a drink to quench a never-ending thirst. There wasn't any real swallowing. The real trick was forcing your throat to breathe instead of swallow. Still, Mack wished he could've had this conversation topside where a deep inhale got his dissatisfaction across better than by translator bot. With the fluid in his lungs straining his voice box, he'd have to get to the point.

"Got the Rescue Order from Fleet. Sector official shot down over Rho Neem. We pulled the ambassador, but my team got dusted in the process. I only made it out because I was riding the SLIC."

Raptor seemed fine with the short version because he moved on to the Cherry. "Story time, kid."

"No ghost stories here, sir," Cherry said apologetically.

"So, nothing involving being a former member of the Marikano crime syndicate turned state's evidence in return for a spot in the Legion?" Raptor asked.

Cherry was silent until their depth gauges reached five hundred meters. They came to rest on a shelf along the cliff they were diving past. "Cycling for two. Yes, sir. I got a lot of the family dusted by a leej kill team sent to do the work. Won't ever lose sleep over it, either."

"So, you're good with getting in the Legion by way of your family's corpses?" the captain prodded.

If there was any anger over the line of questioning, the Cherry didn't put it into his answer. "No sir. My deal was for a spot in selection. I still had to pass."

Mack was curious. "How'd you end up on a REC-Team?"

"My family is a pack of jackals. I wanted to do something to throw karma the other way. I started as a corpsman in the Fleet. Figured helping people was a good place to start. Once I got into the Legion as a medic, Wreckers seemed like a natural fit, so I tried out."

"You got a ghost story, Captain?" Mack felt a twang in his stomach, a slight twinge of fear that let him know he'd overstepped.

If that was the case, Raptor didn't seem to mind. "Cancer. Probably terminal."

Both men fell silent. Cancer was one of the great plagues of the human condition there to remind everyone just how mortal they still were. Several attempts to purge it from the gene pool had resulted in more harm than good. There were treatments on inner core worlds where doctors sorted the illness in an afternoon. A quick visit to the doctor's office for a nap in a medi-bed, and suddenly, you were part of the social elite that had stared down the abyss looking to claim you. Common were the movie stars, beloved by everyone throughout the core worlds, who posed—or licensed their image—for late-night info-coms that scrolled across everyone's media feeds when insomnia struck. *"Join us in the battle to bring life-saving technology to the mid-core and worlds on galaxy's edge. For one credit a day, you can sponsor..."*

But those cures were not easily obtainable on a Legion salary, even a captain's. If they stationed someone on a mid-core world, the Legion could get their people re-gression meds to keep the cancer from spreading. Every once in a while, the Legion would hear of some LS num-ber becoming a media darling after finding favor with a pro-military House of Reason delegate. In a whirlwind of fame and fortune being broadcast on the info-com and talk show circuits, the leej was whisked away to show Utopion's progressive fight against the horrid disease. Of course, those instances only occurred during election cy-cles, and Mack figured there wasn't one in sight, or some-one like Raptor would have discovered how to leverage it.

"Sorry, sir," Mack said. The nanites extrapolating his voice through the soup in his larynx did a fair interpreta-tion of sympathy.

"Don't be," Raptor said. "We all have our ghosts. Legion's full of 'em. Cherry, give me depth to hard contact."

"One hundred and sixty-one meters, sir," Cherry confirmed.

Raptor used the tongue toggle in his helmet to su-perimpose the topographic map of the Kajofa Abyss with the grid coordinates for where their targets rested. "We're at forty-one meters straight ahead. Give us a green light when the pressure is handled."

Unlike the long fall, the ocean floor was teeming with life. Slender macoffi sharks glided on unseen currents while alien-looking sabba fish, with their tentacled faces, sifted through the rocks and sea vegetation for some tasty morsel. One naxa whale was almost half a klick above them, rotating itself periodically to study them on the seabed below them. As the trio moved forward, plants along the floor glowed to a spectacular brilliance in the shadowy depths of the Kajoffa. Carnivorous narka worms punched from their tuberous homes in the coral to slam into the recovery pod with no effect, retreating to their lairs to wait for more succulent fare. From the deck of a boat, the Hassica Ocean was a dark, forlorn place of storms and alien monsters gliding beneath its depths. On this side of the extreme pressure, Mack pitied those who never got to experience something like this. Never got to see the Shangri-La of harmonious death that all sea creatures shared.

Raptor broke the spell of the luminous refuge as they landed on the bottom of their long drop. "Cherry, what's the read on that creature?"

"It's just ahead, sir. Definitely a large animal of some type hiding behind the wreck site."

Mack piped in, "Sir, I'm getting a weak signal on line with our target. Boosting now."

"Send it, Mack," Raptor said.

"This is—*squawk*—broadcasting from grid—*SKREEEEE*..." Even with the signal-devouring algorithms of their enhanced buckets, the Wreckers couldn't get a clean read on the signal. Despite being broken and unreadable, they were broadcasting in both Drusic and Galactic Standard.

"Cherry, deploy a pup forward to catch that signal and feed it to us. Dim the light to twenty lumen and have it send out TENS-Wave pulses every fifteen seconds to keep interested creatures away," Raptor said.

"Roger that, sir," Cherry confirmed. The tiny globe dimmed its shine considerably, moving away from the group at a startling speed. The rest of the orbs closed in, forming a triangular formation around the leejes.

Mack whispered his goop-filled voice into the comm as though any of the nasty wildlife at this depth would hear them, "The naxa whales are circling, but they're not aiming toward us. Something on our target has them upset."

"Break. Break. Break. Raptor, this is Cherry. I have comms to survivors!"

"Patch 'em through, kid," Raptor said.

"Any station this net, this is Hagim Construction, broadcasting from grid—"

"Hagim Construction, this is Republic rescue mission Rusty Pelican. I have divers inbound to your location with rescue vehicles. What is your status? Over," Raptor broadcast.

"May the Mother of Trees bless and keep you, sir! We have twenty-two techs recovered from our cable mission here in Kajofa. Four of our thirty-three techs are confirmed dead. That leaves seven missing. The storm was set to pass us by, but it damaged our rigging platform and slammed into us. When we went to repair it, we were attacked!"

Raptor typed into a holo interface, attaching missions notes for future equipment recovery while taking pictures of the terrain he slowly drifted through. Resting in the sandy trench was a broken Drusic kython submersible with a squad's worth of broken Saber Special Forces, scattered and limp. Sharks and other scavengers feasted on their remains.

"We found the Sabers," Mack called out. "Looks like someone put them through a food processor."

"Thanks, Sergeant. Now you've ruined my special alone time in the kitchen," Cherry remarked.

A shadow passed along the ocean floor.

Keeping the comms channel to the workers away from Cherry on the team net, Raptor asked, "What attacked you, Hagim?"

Far above them, a new duo of naxa whales joined the agitated pair who'd hovered over the rescue site since the legionnaires arrived. Mack had done a quick search on the local sea life before jocking up for the REC. The info search pegged the circling tactic joined by ever increasing numbers of whales as an aggression display. Mack was about to signal his new boss they had more animals lining up to watch them work, when the myriad scavengers picking at dead Drusics disappeared into the inky dark water beyond the lights.

The sea current flopping the corpses, and the sudden retreat of animals giving up a free meal, sent memory-induced shivers into the pit of Mack's stomach. When he was a line legionnaire patrolling a village, the one thing you could count on was the locals always knew when trouble was coming. Animals were no different. The small fish always scattered to make way for bigger sets of teeth.

As the thought sunk in, Mack's enhanced sensor suite in his bucket tracked a silt cloud forming over the rig. Mack broke into the conversation. "Raptor! You and the kid go max thrust to the repair rig! I'll act as bait!"

"What?" Raptor barked.

Mack activated the strobes on his armor, blinking twice with a neon green flash. The second pulse changed to hyper adaptive luxicron white lights patterned into the seams of the armor. He sped off at max push via his water thrusters, shooting off like a torpedo while lighting the space around him for ten meters.

"Cherry! Light that wayward pup!" Raptor yelled into the comm.

The glowing sphere sent ahead of them illuminated a creature equal to the size of the rigging platform, hovering under it along the stony depths of the abyss. Its rocky hide helped it to blend into the terrain, confusing the mapping software in their HUDs. Along the stony outcroppings of its hide were eel-shaped fish, with vaguely humanoid torsos and demonic heads. Taloned arms, where their ventral fins should be, pulled them along the surface of the mountainous creature. The serpentine mermen flitted along the creature like pilot fish beside a shark.

"What in Oba's crew cut is that?" Cherry cried.

Raptor screamed into the L-comm, "Punch it!"

Mack rocketed by its face, taxing the drive thrusters to their limits and blinking another searing green flash with the strobes in his armor. The creature roared at the luminescent morsel evading its maw, its cry one part whale song, nine parts nightmare, and powerful enough to raise the temperature in the cold ocean depths.

With an earth-heaving pull from cyclopean arms ending in a forest of tentacles instead of fingers, the monster catapulted into a chase to swallow the tiny, armored tidbit. The white flare of the armor's seam lights came back on, giving the creature a clear target to follow.

Inside the confines of the armor, warning indicators, combat sensors, tactical advisory algorithms, and a host of other specialized tech devised by the best minds at Republic SOAR-Dev screamed at Mack that, other than his first marriage, this was the stupidest thing he'd ever done.

Oba, would he have loved to have had this tech when he met that woman. It would've saved him the aggravation it took to get free of her. If he ever saw that shrink aboard the *Reliant* again, he'd share how this monster dredged from a thousand Drusic nightmares was analogous to his amorous encounters as a young legionnaire.

All he'd have to do was survive this one first.

"Rescue pod is air locked. Venting water and establishing seal," Cherry declared.

"Good copy," Raptor said, switching the comms to the cable company's feed. He was careful to keep his tone steady as more than a few rescues had been fouled by a frantic Valkyrie leej shouting over the channel. After all, the only thing he had to worry about at the moment was hundreds of tons of angry sea beast about to turn them into breakfast. "Hagim, this is Rusty Pelican. We are matching your atmosphere to our rescue pod."

"Thank you, Rusty Pelican. How many can we fit?"

"I can fit you for half," Raptor said with finality. He didn't want to waste time arguing with people willing to beg, bargain, or break under the stress of how many could fit in the first run.

"I read you. Fitting half. How long until second vehicle?" There was desperation in the Drusic's tone.

"Twenty standard minutes." Raptor waited for the response. If there was panic in the Drusic's voice, that meant his crew was experiencing a breakdown over the accident and the sight of the creature. He wouldn't be able to get them in the pod quickly enough for a fast turnaround.

"I understand twenty standard minutes. We are putting the most injured among us in first. Thirty seconds until we are full up," the cable diver said.

"Good copy, Hagim. Locking them in and ready for departure." Raptor keyed in the stabilization protocol and activated the pod's shields. At least with those in place, the vehicle could withstand a nibble from the monstrosity chasing Mack. "Kid?"

Above the ongoing rescue, a mob of eel men had detached from the mother creature to swim toward the Drusics transferring into the rescue pod. Several times they got close enough to poke at the shield, only to be reviled by the   electrostatic pushback of the barrier negating any damage or attempt to intrude. One swam close enough to Raptor for him to see glass-like globular eyes all too accustomed to life in the crushing depths. To ensure they understood each other, Raptor punched the eel thing in its bulbous eye, sending it on a rampant swim away from the legionnaire's attention

Off to his flank, Cherry flew into the dust and silt at his feet, engulfed by the wide flat tail of the eel man formerly darting around the beast. The merman was almost three meters in length, covered in spiky armor, ending in a face straight out of Oba's junk drawer. Long needle-like teeth flashed in a mouth wide enough to swallow a human head whole. They were semi-translucent, as though they were made of a hyperplastic instead of bone. White milky eyes locked on to Cherry, then searched the plunger battle armor for any cracks to get at the chewy flesh underneath. Rapid fire strikes with its bite repeatedly slammed home against the hardened battle armor. Even if its wicked teeth couldn't pierce the hard plates, it was only a matter of time before it found a crease or crack to suck the legionnaires through.

"Raptor! What the kelhorned tea party is this thing?" Cherry screamed.

"Pilot organism from the kython," Raptor shouted back.

Four more swam in, two ramming Raptor with the speed of a pro-seamball player diving for the end plate. They enveloped him with their wide flat tails, slamming him against the rescue pod, right up against the viewing port. Wide, flat Drusic faces, rife with concern, slammed on the crysteel to gain the leej's attention to more eel men bearing down on him.

"From the sub?" Cherry said, confused.

"No!" Raptor shouted. One of the eel men had his helmet in a vice-like grip. It slapped his head against the shielded hull of the pod, causing a rippling effect from the energy barrier with every impact. "They named the sub after the myth!"

"Someone needs to tell them two things! One! *That* is not mythological!"

Search and rescue lighting built into the seams of the armor flared to life, temporarily blinding the attacking beasts.

"And two, my tag ain't Cherry. It's Thresher!"

Thresher forced his power strut reinforced hand armor around the eel man's side, tearing out a handful of gills flapping in hurried gasps. It released its tail from him, thrashing about the silty floor beneath the rigging platform. A furious thrust from the plunger's jets catapulted the leej into an oncoming murderous duo of eel men. Thresher punched through the first, using his momentum along a rocky jut to rip the monstrosity free. Turning in mid-glide, Thresher latched onto the remaining attacker, desperate to get away from him. Pulling an obscenely large hand cannon from a strap along his leg, Thresher punched it towards the monster's chest. Crushing the trigger in his armored glove, the kid discharged the round, displacing water in nearly a meter-wide bubble. The gyrojet projectile launched from the barrel at near crawling speed until a pico-second later, the nano-rocket in the back of the round fired, sending it slamming through the eel with enough force to turn it inside out.

Raptor pulled his own pistol, downing two more serpentine attackers. He keyed his comm. "Thresher-Cherry! Let's move!"

"On it, sir." The Wrecker leej fiddled with a setting in his HUD. "TENS-Wave round out!"

The pistol spat another miniature torpedo into the expanse between the rapidly closing mob of symbiotic pilot eels. The darting, spasmodic hunters were nowhere near the round when it detonated. But it didn't matter. The high-yield warhead rent the water with a transcutaneous, electro-shock nerve saturation pulse. Six hundred times more powerful than those occurring in nature, the electrocution pulse arced through the water, using each target as a conductor to pass the shock on to the next. Water molecules burst, sending an ear-crushing hydrostatic shock into the surrounding targets not caught in the blast.

Raptor and Thresher grabbed the drag handles for the pod, pushing their drive motors to propel them through the water at max speed.

"Can't we just float this up to the surface?" Thresher asked.

"Negative. That kython might bat it around or swallow it. Until Mack deals with Fido, we go back to the launch point and get it done."

"And what about Mack?" Thresher asked.

While military contractors chose "soothing" warning systems voices, hearing them never was.

"*Thruster Warning. Right dorsal thruster experiencing drive malfunction. Sixty seconds to critical failure without reset.*"

"Yeah, yeah!" Mack shouted at the plunger suit AI. He darted into a cavern in an underwater ridge. The kython's tentacled arms slammed into the entry, coiling and writhing into the fissure to capture its elusive snack. The leej sergeant pulled his gyro pistol from its dock, programming the warhead with a vocal command. "Burner round!"

The projectile screamed through the water, burying itself into the giant creature's armored flesh. The aquatic demon didn't seem to notice it—that is, until the warhead reached critical mass, turning into a white-hot miniature sun. A swath of tentacled fingers sheared off from its limb caught in the explosion, like fingers brought too close to bandsaw. With the creature distracted, Mack shot out from the crag into open water.

The beast recoiled in pain, withdrawing the damaged limb in horror as if it had never experienced pain before. It peered at its ruined limb in abject fascination, its place as the lord of the deep now in doubt. Bringing its attention back toward the green strobing little water wasp, the creature was further confused that its tormentor was charging straight at it.

Now that he'd gotten the chance to calibrate his thruster, Mack rocketed toward the beast. In the distance, Raptor and Cherry were lugging the first pod to the cliff wall. If Mack could find a way to keep Mister Tall, Dark, and Creepy occupied, his team would have no problem ascending the cliff wall.

An idea struck him and just as quickly flitted away when the angry titan opened its giant maw. It roared like a water dragon of old, its man-sized teeth glinting. A writhing, tangled mass slipped past its fangs in a stream as wide as a light freighter and easily as long, resolved itself into a school of eel men.

For newly vomited men, they looked pissed.

They hit him like a hurricane, gnashing, clawing, and slapping. They buffeted him, seeking a way to tear into his armor like hungry seagulls would a crab. Meanwhile, the kython floated in wait.

Here was an interesting evolutionary development. The kython spit out a mouthful of eel goons. They softened the target, and it swallowed what was left. A strange digestive symbiosis.

"*Warning. Warning,*" the AI warning more soothed than bellowed. "*Power shield failing. Right thruster offline. Gyro pistol offline.*"

"Shut up and listen! Put remaining power into defensive countermeasures and fire TENS-Wave at max yield," Mack shouted.

HUD warnings scrolled through his vision even as the slapping claws pounded his visor.

"*Warning! Max yield TENS-Pulse could disable life support and render pilot deceased.*"

"Do it!" Max screamed, as the mob tried to twist him out of his suit like meat from a cracked crab leg. They tried their best to get the tender bits of him out of his shell. The armor wouldn't hold much longer. Already the power capacitors along the armored skin whined, climbing in intensity, while his weapon slowly charged. Normally the plunger's TENS-Pulse was for scaring away an interested shark or handsy octopus. Looking on his long-range feed, he spotted his team cycling up the next rescue pod.

"Fire!" Mack roared.

The mega-pulse tore through the water. An explosive wave of electricity burned its way through the mob, which exploded like super-heated corn kernels. Pop-hisses followed flashes of detonating water as the pressure wave from the pulse ruined what remained of the gastric mob, slamming them into their master. Outraged, the kython reared back, then swam upward to get away from the expanding shock wave.

Mack's world faded to black, his suit creaking around him. His HUD failed, the screen cracking from pressure it could no longer withstand.

"Swallow that, you smug kelhorned puddle jumper," was the last thing he said to no one in particular, before the darkness took him.

4

The inside of Mack's mouth tasted like he'd licked the top of a battery someone had dipped in an ashtray. Then there was the smell. It was wet dog mixed with desperation, or possibly a briny pungency permeating everything it touched in a confined space.

Mack opened his eyes to the concerned stares of several Drusic males. An assortment of blood and grime stained their coveralls, no doubt the remnants from the last harrowing hours of being submerged while awaiting rescue.

"I speak the Standard tongue. I will talk with you," said one of the hulking beings.

"That's good, because my Apothin sucks," Mack said, rubbing the back of his skull. He was sitting in a rescue pod, surrounded by a half crew of Drusic saturation divers.

The one who spoke translated Mack's joke got chuckles from the rest of the crew. "My name is Kendobar Nalhoa. Ken for short. You are the rescuer named Mack, yes?"

"Who told you that?" Mack asked.

"The rescue commander. He told us to take care of his good buddy, Mack. We assumed that was you."

Set out on the floor, Mack's armor had been savaged by eel men and deep oceanic pressure alike. The rescue pod's bilge system slowly pumped out a considerable puddle of reddish, viscous fluid through the grating under the plunger armor. Seeing the ruined state of his kit soaked in pressure adaptive breathing fluid, Mack asked in a raspy voice, "Did all that juice come out of me?"

Ken patted him on the back. "Oh yes. We were very impressed you could hold so much."

Checking over his bucket, Mack asked, "How did they get me in here?"

Frowning, Ken puzzled through the question. "Ah. The rescue commander is quite clever. He adjusted the energy shield to act as a pressure equalizer, turning the pod into a moon pool. Once he had it set, all he had to do was push you through."

Mack switched from rubbing the back of his head to rubbing his temples. "No wonder I feel like I've been in a hovercar crash. Where are we?"

"On top of the cliff overlooking the Kajofa Abyss."

"And the kython?" Mack asked.

At the mere mention of the word, the Drusics coughed out a slew of curses, pounding their chests rhythmically. Chanting and thumping, they worked themselves into a frenzy until Ken raised his paws. "They respect your fight with it. Several of them want to adopt you as a brother, to add your strength to their family."

Mack nodded his appreciation. "Is that good?"

"A big honor for a non-Drusic," Ken said. "Although not something to undertake without alcohol."

Eyebrows raised, Mack said, "Good to know."

Ghostly metallic pings echoed behind Mack's head, drawing the attention of his benefactors in the pod. Raptor was outside in his plunger armor, tapping against the energy-shielded rescue vehicle. It didn't take a PhD in astro-navigation to figure his boss, who was pointing at his bucket, wanted a chat.

Without being secured into his armor, the plunger helmet was heavy. You could wear it without the neck servos stabilizing the heavy bucket, but you wouldn't want to run an obstacle course in it. Not that Mack would be running one, not in this small pod crammed with a dozen Drusic divers.

The HUD flicked on, using internal batteries for the bucket since it was deprived of the suit. "Nice of you to call. Been a while. How's things on your side of the screen?" Mack said as he answered Raptor's comms request.

"Oh, you know. Just out for a stroll and wanted to see what you were up to," Raptor replied.

"Roger that. I have you to thank for the rescue?"

"Nah. New guy scared off the rest of the vomit goblins mobbing your plunger. Nanites in the suit and goop had just enough juice to maintain pressure and oxygenation to keep you alive until we got you in the can. Downside is you're going to have to ride out the depressurization with your hosts."

Mack nodded, instantly regretting the motion while wearing the boulder's worth of tech on his skull. "Ain't so bad. They're cool dudes. One guy liked my bout with the kython so much I think he wants to go steady. He looks like marriage material—that dive union offers great benefits, I hear—but I don't think I can take him up on it. I hate being the little spoon."

"And now I'm uncomfortable," Raptor said in that bland tone soldiers used, just to confuse civvies.

"What happened to the kython?" Mack inquired.

"Beat feet. The vomit goblins were going to bring you to their papa, all shucked and ready to be slurped, but the kid showed up. You gave them such a hard time, they probably figured they couldn't handle the newer, younger model. They swam back to the trench when the kid charged them, and the kython's gone."

With a scratchy laugh, Mack said, "Yeah, next time, send the kid in first. I'll bat cleanup."

"Deal. You've been out for a minute, but nothing to suggest serious injury. Nanites broadcast a bio-sign update for you before they went offline. Pressure and the shock wave from the TENS-Pulse put you out. You should be fine once you're topside. The problem of stuffing you in there is that we have to wait the full re-press cycle to get you out. Plus, we can't leave the plunger in there. Proprietary tech and all."

"Roger that. That was some impressive work with the shields, sir. Thanks to you and the kid for saving my skin," Mack said.

"Well, I had to because we're throwing it right into the fire. TC has a rescue order from fleet. The *Reliant* is spinning up for a close jump in-system, and we were specifically requested. Seems nobody wants to wait for the new boat smell to wear off before making some moves. If we pry you out of that can, do you think you're up for round two?"

"Depends. Got me a better offer than a Drusic marriage proposal?"

Raptor laughed. "Sure thing, little spoon."

Mack stood beside the tables with a holoprojector in the center. He was surrounded by members of both the Alpha Section agents and the legionnaires comprising Bravo, everyone relaxed like this was just another office get-together. A dusky, leather jacket-clad leej, call sign Rocco, greeted him like a long-lost buddy, ready to pop a beer. As is often the case in small, exclusive units, the top stripes, or what a laymen might call senior level NCOs, had a way of drifting into each other's orbits by way of their reputation. In the REC-Teams, there was always the story of this guy, on that team, who pulled an impossible rescue over the goofy named death planet of death. When two guys like Mack and Rocco met in real life, it was often a chance to get together and compare notes. Especially when one was taking over driving the team from the other.

Unfortunately, Mack's whiskey induced orientation at the hands of the outgoing team sergeant would have to wait until their next snatch and dash was mission complete. The easy camaraderie switched to attentiveness as the TC took over the meeting.

"Settle down. Before we get rolling, who had Cherry getting eaten on his first roll?" Nathan asked, lofting a credit chit so everyone could see it.

Murmurs went around the room. Chief Cantrell stepped up and slapped a chit into his waiting palm. "Yeah, yeah. No reason to brag, TC. You've gotta admit, I'm usually right about this sort of stuff."

The Team Commander took the chit and collected two more from the assembled leejes. "Oh yeah, Chief. You sure are, but for once, I'm glad you're wrong. We have the first confirmed interaction with a kython in over a century and the Republic nerds are going haywire over it. Hope you three are ready for a ton of publicity, because you're going to be on all the holo-docs going over the story for years. Ah! We can say we knew them when."

Thresher shook his head, grinning wickedly. "No can do, sir. IG said I'm not allowed to be anywhere near fame, money, or women. Part of my parole."

"Excuse me, Cherry?" Chief said, feigning outrage.

"Actually, it's call sign Thresher, chief, but no offense intended," Thresher said. "But you're an XO first and a woman second, according to military regs."

Chief Cantrell huffed. "Clearly the Military Diplomatic Corpsman who gave you that line never had babies. It's like I gotta pee every time I even *hear* water, so don't go telling me I gotta put my femininity on the back side of my rank, Corporal."

"Yes, ma'am," Thresher said in as apologetically he could while the team laughed.

Someone in the back of the room played the sound of the ocean through their smart watch. The Chief whirled about, one hand pressing on her lower abdomen, the other aiming her finger-gun. "Stringer! I know that's you!"

Laughter peppered through the briefing, with even the techs taking a break from their stations to join in the revelry.

"Hey, you pack of kelhorn-faced knuckle-dusters, simmer down so I can get through this," TC said, taking control again.

The legionnaires at the back of the room shooshed one another, then knuckled dusted each other's shoulders to another round of laughter. When they finally settled down, the assembled leejes gawked with their eyes wide, feigning rapt attention. The clowning came to an immediate stop when Rocco knocked twice on the desk he was using for a seat.

TC pointed to the NCO. "Thank you, Sergeant. Now that I can get a word in edgewise, we got a recovery order straight from DOS. This is your VIP. Doctor Lasana Kavir."

The woman that appeared in the image floating above the table was elegant, although her icy stare foreboded a no-nonsense intensity that was sure to play itself out during the course of the briefing. Most academics and aid workers on the wrong side of local militants could usually be bargained out of most scrapes. If REC-Team Pelican was getting the green light, things had gone very badly for this woman, despite her intense expression.

"Human?" Lahm asked.

"Lorisam," TC said. "They're an edge species that could pass for human in a pinch but, on closer inspection, are anything but. You rarely see them outside of their world because of specific dietary needs."

Lahm adjusted himself in his seat as if the action would let him see more of the image. "What's so different?"

"Lots of redundant features," TC answered. "Double heart. Multi-chambered lungs. They appear human but are twice as strong. The food thing is a pain, though, because most of the stuff we think of edible is poisonous to them. Of course, they act a bunch like humans, which means they're constantly at war with someone. That aside, Doctor Kavir is an expert in cybernetics whose expertise has crossed over to micro bionics and cellular-based nanotechnology. The Republic wants her found and returned, pronto."

"Do we have a last known?" Raptor asked.

TC pointed to Martin, then spun his finger in a circle to let the electronic engagement operator know he wanted whatever the man was looking at. A lush, blue-green planet replaced the doctor's image in the floating holodisplay. "This is Nuzon. Just inside the zone of what most civilized places would call the galaxy's edge, on the fringe of Sinasian space. There was a Legion garrison on the northern hemisphere of the planet, but they abandoned it after a nearby research facility had a contamination event."

The Alpha Section commander pulled his hands apart, stretching the hard light image between them until it zoomed into the depiction of a small city. "Centigo Corporation, at the behest of the Republic, built a facility here, capable of housing over a thousand workers and their families. Two years ago, REC-Team Archangel, along with massive support from the Navy, evacuated the facility and put the entire area under quarantine after the contagion was released. No one knows where the vector came from or why it was so focused on this particular area. It definitely didn't come from the research station as its primary focus was in developing new skinpack technology."

Mack scratched his chin and asked, "This have something to do with Kavir going there? Do the skinpacks have applications for her research?"

"That's a possibility," TC offered. "Legion and Repub intel are being tight-lipped on why she was there, so we can only assume. Twelve hours ago, Doctor Kavir was flying into the Serrabi Falls facility in a Repub assault shuttle loaded up with Marine Raiders from the One-Three. The shuttle was shot down over the nearby city of Kerhott."

Mack flagged TC. "Why hullbusters? If she's so important, why didn't she rate a Legion escort?"

Nissa, the blind Endurian from the shop's entrance, was in the room's corner, sitting next to Martin. Mack watched her run her fingers over the strangest data slate he'd ever seen. Instead of projecting images to the surface of the glass, it reacted more like sand, pushing shaped images into her palms and fingertips the way a child would shape castles in a sandbox. She tilted a smile in his direction before she spoke, as if to acknowledge that she'd just caught him staring. "I'm blind, but I have all the cybernetic replacements you would expect, Master Sergeant. I just prefer reading this way."

Mack gave a quick nod, feeling too much like the odd man out and hyper aware of the impression he was making in meeting the team for the first time.

Nissa's smile remained warm as she continued. "It would seem our Lorisam doctor didn't trust the legionnaires. She was offered a Legion security detail and specifically asked for this particular group of marines instead."

TC nudged Nissa's shoulder. "Nissa, work with Martin and figure out who would've okayed such a strange request. Back on point, Republic Intel received the following message from Dosa Keem, a local warlord."

A man with a manicured beard and a sharply tailored suit replaced the ghostly map of the Serrabi Falls facility. Before he spoke, the ghost fixed both sleeves, securing actual cuff links before pulling on the fabric to have it sit at just the right spots above his wrists. He remained still when he spoke, his hands held at mid-chest in such a way that the operators in the room recognized as a ready posture. He could punch or draw a weapon easily from that stance. "To the esteemed members of the Republic Security Council and the House of Reason. My name is Dosa Keem. Two hours ago, we shot down a shuttle bearing the markings of your house, over the abandoned city of Kerhott. This vehicle was in clear violation of the no-fly zone put in place by your own government. All remaining passengers will be treated fairly, as long as you comply with our demands. First—"

Mack crossed the room to the image, not bothering to care that the leejes of the new team were staring. "Roll back thirty seconds. Enhance quadrant one-twenty-four-fourteen."

The AI running the projection reacted at once. The floating spectral image flickered to a closer aspect, taking a moment to render the pixilated projection in amazing detail. Individual pores on his face came into stark clarity as the terrorist's face scowled at a government too distant to do anything about what he was saying.

"Lahm, you see it?" Mack asked.

"I didn't before, but now I do," Lahm said. "His face above his left eye twitched when he said he'd shot them down, and again when he started that garbage about prisoner treatment."

TC motioned in the air for Martin to play it again until everyone in the room noticed what Mack had pointed out. The twitch was there, timed with the statements so that they couldn't be just random tics. They were tells. "Good catch, Sergeant Banes. So it would seem our petty little warlord is trading on someone else's work and is willing to get the gold for it."

"Do we have PDT on our principles?" Raptor asked in between swigs from his bottle.

The twitchy hologram minimized, supplanted by a massive map of Kerhott City. A ping on the eastern edge flashed from the ghostly display. "The ship crashed just inside the city limits in the housing district. There's the doctor in green and the marines in blue. There was a squad-sized element, the pilots and crew, plus the doc. Only six PDTs left the bird."

Raptor's expression was blank despite obvious concern. "Damn. TC, what's the order of retrieval?"

"Repub intel says the shuttle AI was cloned to the black box and removed from the craft. They only do that with asset deniability protocols."

Rocco swung his head from shoulder to shoulder. "So they torched the ship, most likely with their dead inside. That makes order of retrieval a no-contest thing, sir. We fly in, confirm the ship is karked, scoop the living blips, and fly out. Winner, winner, Raptor's dinner."

Raptor didn't seem convinced. "What's the warlord want in exchange for the prisoners he doesn't have?"

"Let's find out," TC said and then nodded for Martin to continue the holorecording. Maps and ghostly faces switched places in order of priority over the briefing table. The newly enlarged warlord continued his speech.

"—we want the following members of the Khindo Khabar released—"

Martin paused the holo. "Khindo Khabar is one of the larger political organizations on the planet. They demand local laws be merged with religious doctrine bordering on the barbaric. Officially, the House of Reason's had limited contact with them. Unofficially, the Legion's branded them a terrorist threat. In keeping with Sergeant Mack's assessment of Keem's facial issues, there's no way that his organization has the tech to knock a Republic stealth shuttle out of the sky."

The holo resumed.

"—and if our demands have not been met in the next thirty-six standard hours, we will kill one person every rotation until we have nothing to bargain with. I sincerely hope you won't allow that to happen."

The holo winked out of existence, leaving the room in the pale light of the overheads.

Raptor shook his empty water bottle, grimacing. "Time on the clock, TC?"

"We're four hours deep. No time to waste."

Chief Cantrell jumped to her feet from under her bouncing locks. "You heard the brass. Info-com being pushed to your devices on the move. Wheels up in thirty. Mack, come give me some one-on-one over here for a sec, please."

As the crowd dispersed, Mack drifted to a corner of the room. The techs slapping gear into hard cases was more than ample to mask his conversation with the Alpha Section second in command. "What's doing, Chief?"

"We took the liberty of setting up a rig with the specs you used on your old team. Anything I need to gear different?" Cantrell offered.

Mack grinned. "Much obliged for that, Chief. I should be good."

Cantrell raised an appraising eyebrow. "In the last few months, you've had some tough runs. First with your old team, then you come here and almost get eaten. You sure you're good?"

"No offense, Chief, but why are you asking me this and not Raptor or Rocco?"

"They saw a legionnaire take on something twenty times his size so that the mission went off. That's what leejes do, so as far as they're concerned, you're straight. I've been at this a long time, Sergeant Banes. I saw a man taking unnecessary risks to prove that everything's cool and he's back in the game. Which put your team at risk when they had to pull you out."

Mack nodded to each point she made, silent until she had her say. "I can see your assessment, ma'am. I had a couple of seconds to form a plan and make a decision. It might not have been the best one or even the right one, but I had to do something. I didn't know how it was going to turn out, but those two leejes and the twenty-some-odd Drusic put their trust in me. That's a sacred thing to a Wrecker, ma'am. The trust that we'll get them home, no matter what. Now, am I still messed up at the loss of my other team? Sure. But every life we save from this moment forward brings honor to their sacrifice. Every rescue buys back a bit more of my soul. So, in answer to your question, am I good? You tell me."

Her bouncy mane wagged as she shook her head. "Damn, Sergeant. I was expecting some Rocco-level of profanity or something, not a well-thought-out answer with actual syllables and adult-style sentences. Most of the time, you Legion boys can only grunt."

They both broke into laughter, watching the last of the techs drag a case in a fashion that was clearly an indicator of why they were strapped to a desk. When the laughter died away, Chief took the momentum again. "Hey Mack, what say we go rescue some marines and their creepy secret squirrel doc?"

"Sounds good, Chief," Mack chuckled. He mockingly checked his chrono, counting the hours since he'd returned from the deep. "It's been so long since the last rescue I went on, I hope I'm not rusty. I should do okay as long as I remember how to grunt."

5

THE PLANET NUZON
GALAXY'S EDGE

The heat mirages rising off the street in the capital city of Terum danced across the intersection like fetid ghosts. All make and manner of humanity mingled with a smattering of aliens along the sweltering metropolitan streets. Calling Terum a metropolis was like calling a Utopion closet a luxury apartment. Although investors from the core had seen to building up the city to its current state in the hopes of a grand return on their investment, the people that had flocked to it had done little to make improvements on the original design. Here in Calamity Square Market, the buildings did little else but amplify heat.

Skyscrapers dominated the skyline at the city center, providing secure habitats for the wealthy. Weather protection systems kept the towers free from the electrical storms dominating much of the city's weather as engineering marvels built into the structures kept them erect despite rampant typhoons. In stark contrast to the few gleaming towers, the hovels in Calamity Square were damaged, patched with off-color fixeter sheets made of corrugated nano-fiber so as not to attract stray bolts of lightning. The resilient sheets managed to hold buildings together despite the poundings they took from errant weather, and everyone seemed content to cover the holes and cracks without ever returning to repair things with actual duracrete.

Sabine pulled the face mask of her burka snug across her face, hurrying past a herd of people who had just gotten the light to cross the street. Walking into an avenue meant for grav-cars and the crazy amount of little motor bikes the locals favored was a good way to get pasted across the street. Most places on Nuzon cared little for traffic laws, relying on the reflexes of the population to make driving less complicated, which resulted in a chaotic dance whose steps only locals knew.

A rampant gust from a shop blasted her exposed eyes, giving her a moment of cool relief. It was gone as quickly as it had come, but it was a welcomed distraction, nonetheless. As the light signaled the herd to cross the intersection, Sabine followed the crowd, venturing into the deathtrap that was the street. When she got halfway through the cross walk, she reversed direction to go back the way she came, seamlessly blending in with a flock of women similarly clad in black robes that hid everything from view except the eyes.

Walking into the icy cool tea house, she noted the signs advertising an air-conditioned space, most likely as the major draw for patrons used to better conditions and better tea. The fragrant aroma of brewing beverages mixed with sweet-smelling smoke drifting in from hookahs outside. On her last trip to a zhee world, she'd insisted on a rebreather under the burka to avoid the smell of a female zhee birthing house. With stinky hashish in the shop tinging the hookah smoke, she wished she had it now.

Sabine set her purse down on a shelf, waiting for the devices she'd hidden inside to scan the room. With a complete read of the space, an AI-driven holo generated a decoy that could avoid patrons, view items on a shelf, or simply leave the shop altogether. She stepped from the burka holoprojection, wearing the coveralls of a local cannery worker along with her hijab. No one in the tea shop gave her a second glance as she walked from behind the "woman" perusing the shelves displaying an assortment of wrought iron tea pots.

Sabine glanced at her watch while patrons jostled for position beside her trying to gain the attention of anyone behind the counter. A twenty-something with a mop of black hair above a gang tattoo stepped to Sabine's part of the counter. "Good morning. Looks like storms are coming, eh?"

"Storms are always coming. The trick is to know when to venture outside," Sabine said

The tattooed attendant blinked several times before wordlessly retreating toward the back of the shop. Sabine's heart raced. In countersurveillance craft, the trick was to occupy a space no different than anyone else. Don't stand out. Don't make a scene unless it's what the situation calls for. But the longer you were out in the open, the greater the potential for all your tricks and tactics to fail. It was only a matter of time before someone bumped into the hologram or took notice of her holding up the line. The man behind her huffed twice in exasperation from the delay.

From the back room, a scarred, older man limped up to the counter. Noticing him, the patrons quieted down. It wasn't often the shop owner emerged from his office, much less came to the counter. He held a steaming to-go cup, another in a string of odd behaviors for the man whose usual appearance from the back was to throw someone out. He handed her the tea and a pastry box. "My apologies for the wait, madame."

Sabine nodded her thanks. She'd hoped the kid would have fetched the package, not Omar himself. Other patrons were already eyeing her for this special treatment, meaning it was time for her and the holo to be anywhere else. All it would take is some annoyed patron to take a social media post about the woman holding up the line and she'd have to start all over. New identity, new problems.

"*Mirimang salamat*," she said, hurriedly.

The other patrons gave her a wide berth as she turned to leave. Evidently here was someone who had the respect of the owner. Excusing herself from the huff-and-puff man behind her, Sabine made her way back into the oppressive heat, and the purse she'd set down materialized in her hand. Meanwhile, the burka-clad holo she'd separated from followed her out the door and headed in the opposite direction. The matronly illusion mingled with the denizens of the street and faded from sight.

Sabine reached into her purse, then rushed through a cross street and dodged around a speeder truck loaded to overflowing with sacks of rice. The vehicle ambled by on a bed of repulsor force, revealing a male dock worker standing in her place, holding the steaming to-go cup. Wearing the gender swapped holo, she pried the lid off the cup and removed something from inside. Wiping her fingers dry on her coveralls, she handed what was left of the tea to an old man sitting on a nearby curb and holding a holochit that projected the words, *Oba provides. Anything helps.*

TC's voice came over the tea-soaked earwig communicator in Sabine's ear. "It's dangerous to do business with Omar at that tea house. We're not sure of his loyalty."

Sabine's voice was silk-wrapped daggers. "Omar likes me. Everyone likes me. I'm not worried about it."

"If it were anyone else, I would have suggested a different drop," TC griped in her ear. "The head of the local crime family supplying guns to Dosa Keem and the Khindo Khabar is really not someone we can trust."

"Like I said, boss, I'm not worried about it. He thinks I'm working for the local lieutenant. He gets me anything I ask him to."

"And what did that cost?"

"Medicine to save the life of his granddaughter from a case of Naguri flu that came through here a few months ago. Apparently, the local pharmacies were suffering a shortage and were only dispensing to those with Republic citizenry. They denied anyone who wasn't registered."

"Fair enough," TC agreed.

Sabine walked through a construction gantry covering the walkway on a back street. She ducked past several cranes and lifts, darted through a broken fence, and mingled into another flock of shrouded women. Holographically abandoning her construction worker persona, Sabine assumed the same attire as the other women. She walked several paces away so as not to alarm them, but still close enough to seem part of their group.

"What have you got for me?" TC asked.

"Several of Keem's men have been making regular visits to Omar's as well as to his lieutenant, Haloska. Omar is probably outfitting them with guns, but Haloska is a different quantity." Sabine hailed a cab. The hoverbike driven coach split off from the road-choking traffic pattern to sidle up to the curb. She stepped in and, in perfect Kybari, asked to be taken to the suburbs.

"Ma'am. Can I have an address?" asked the emaciated driver.

"Go north. I'll tell you where to turn," said Sabine.

The cab sped away, easily merging back into traffic with a practiced method of honking and profanity.

Sabine returned to the call. "Haloska is a trusted soldier for Keem. They're prepping for something, but I haven't been able to get close enough to tell what. However, I don't think they have the package."

Noise on TC's end, boxes or crates tumbling, nearly drowned out his question. "Why do you think that?"

Sabine watched the flow of traffic outside the cab. Threats could come from anywhere in a city like Terum. "If they had a bead on it, Keem would have mobilized Haloska's men, because this cell is closer to Kerhott than where he operates from."

"Makes sense," TC grunted.

Her eyes darted, analyzing the traffic, looking for repeat glances, trailing vehicles, or watchers in the dilapidated high-rises around her. Paranoia was a requisite personality trait in Sabine's line of work. "How soon until you're on station?"

"Boots are on the ground," TC confirmed. "Wings are on the way. Keep me in the loop."

"Turn east, here," she said, tapping the driver's shoulder. She removed the micro-comm, flicking it into the street to be crushed by screeching tires and repulsor fields. Alpha Section was already here, probably arrived by civilian transport. The Legion element would insert much the same way so as not to draw attention, unless things got complicated, in which case they'd do what the Legion always does. Smash into something until it breaks. They drove another few streets before Sabine guided them toward an alley. She tipped the driver, well, then moved into the recess of the hidden cross street.

"What took you so long?" asked a bald man wearing a scowl to go with his outfit. A polo shirt over a set of fatigue pants and sneakers barely covered the hulking thug leaning against the repulsor van.

"I don't work for you," Sabine snarled. "If you prefer, I can drive myself and do away with all this cloak-and-dagger nonsense."

The brute's affectation changed. "Sorry, Sabine. I didn't realize it was you. Do you have it?"

"I do. Take me to the shop."

Brute took out a mini-slate, holding the polymer plate up to his ear. "Hey, boss, it's Nino. I have Sabine with me. Is it clear to come in? … No, she slithered into the alley like she always does. I don't think she was followed… Straightaway." He put away the slate. "Boss says we're good to go in."

"Thank you, Nino. Tell that girl to vacate my seat. I don't ride in the back," Sabine growled, as if Nino had insulted her again.

"Yes, ma'am," the enforcer said.

Nino strode into the storm shelter like a returning champion fresh from his latest win. At a table surrounded by holographic workstations, a taller, slender man moved to greet him. Dressed in a shiny, veer-shark skin suit at odds with the dilapidated building, Haloska, held his hands to the side in greeting for his comrade. The two clasped wrists, pulling themselves into a familial embrace, ending in hard slaps to the back.

"Have a good day at the market?" Haloska asked between pats.

Nino smiled. "We did! Our girls skimmed the identity data from two hundred unique accounts, getting banking and life-web data. Remember when we were kids and we used to have to steal things the old-fashioned way?"

The taller man clapped him on the shoulder. "Progress. We have wireless holoweb now."

Sabine, still in her burka, trailed behind Nino into the improvised office. She came to a stop just inside the glow of the hyper-incandescent drop lights. A flick of the wrist and the garment vanished, replaced by an athletic woman in military fatigues and a hijab.

"Sabine, what have you brought for me today?" Haloska purred. While his mannerisms were feline, Sabine thought that if the Almighty were to hand out totems, Haloska would have been a snake.

"I had tea from Omar's," she said, "but I gave it to a beggar in the street. He needed it more than you do."

Haloska laughed just like a snake would. He hissed out the beats like a snake flicking its tongue. "My father always said, if a man falls and fails to get up, help him until he can stand on his own. If a man falls and refuses to get up, leave him there, because he expects to be carried. You didn't do that man any favors, Sabine."

"I did it for me, not for him. Do you have my money?" Sabine asked bluntly.

Haloska tsk-tsked, wagging his finger. "You should know better than to ask for money up front. We're good for it."

Sabine leaned on one of the tables, causing distress to a worker whose holo frizzed out on her, interrupting the projection. "That's what you said when I got you the code slicer mods to break into the Republic shipyard. That was a good haul for which I have yet to be fully paid."

Haloska slithered up to her, his eyes locking onto hers. "I said we're good for it. Now listen here, woman. You said you could get what I need to help Keem run this mission. I know Omar got it and that he'd only give it to you. I want it, now."

In a blur of violence, Sabine pounced. Jumping over the table, she grappled the tech at the station, holding him by the throat. Nino produced a pistol from somewhere in his fatigue pants, placing two blaster bolts into Sabine's human shield, depriving the agent of her cover. With the tech's purpose fulfilled, Sabine thrust the dead man against Nino, who stumbled backwards under the corpse's weight.

The enforcer struggled to regain his balance, but she was already there. She caught him by the arm, snapping it in several places before ramming his head through another table. Picking up the desk fragment as a shield, she recovered Nino's pistol.

Sabine remained in a crouch on the ground, covered by her makeshift bulwark, aiming the blaster pistol at Haloska. "I always try to be polite, but I'm not one of your effeminate wenches who bow and scrape to you because you've convinced them it's God's will. If you don't pay me what you owe me for this job and the last, I'll kill everyone here and deliver it to Dosa myself."

Haloska was a man on the wrong side of a blaster barrel and he looked it. He stared at his friend Nino, bleeding on the floor, and then swayed before going to a datapad on the main table at the center of the room. A few taps on the slate took longer than normal in the shifting light of the flickering broken holoprojectors. A moment later, the datapad in her pocket chimed.

Sabine disassembled the pistol and tossed the parts around the room. She crossed the epileptic light show of the broken displays to stand face-to-face with Haloska. Then, she reached past him, setting the pastry box on the center table. "That wasn't so hard, was it?"

"Is he dead?" Haloska asked, nodding at Nino.

Sabine orbited him, moving to his nondominant side. "No, but he won't be playing piano anytime soon. The next time you treat me like one of those cows you call women, I'm going to cut your head off and feed it to those lizards Keem keeps as pets. Are we clear?"

"Yes, ma'am. My apologies for the late payment," Haloska said like a chastened child.

"Apologies accepted, Mr. Haloska. And just to show I'm a good sport, here is the access code for the treat in the box."

"Thank you. Will this activate the device?" he asked as if recovering a bit of the business thug he fancied himself when she walked in.

Sabine walked over to one of the terrified techs. She took a tissue from a box on the desk, wiping specks of blood from her cheeks. "It will get you into the root command system. From there, you'll have to get the tracking string to locate your target."

"Thank you, Sabine. I'll be sure to tell Dosa Keem our business is settled," Haloska hissed.

"No need, I'll tell him myself." She sauntered out of the storm shelter office, walking onto the bustling factory floor. The fish cannery stank of sour guts and metal rust as the machines thrummed, packing their gray-goop contents into thousands of containers destined for kitchen cabinets. Sabine placed a set of protective ear baffles over her head and swiped a stray clipboard from a foreman's station.

No one stopped her to ask her why she was there or where she'd come from. In another place, another life, she had been a soldier herself. Walking through the plant without being accosted had proven a universal truth she'd seen while in uniform. No one ever bothers the person who carries a datapad, looking busy and official.

Exiting the bustling cannery, she trekked through several industrial parkways before coming out to the main road back to Calamity Square. A truck full of hard-eyed militia men drove by, hanging off the back of a repulsor-powered pickup. Some sneered. Some ignored. While they weren't the Royal Marines of the legitimate government, the militia often served beside them, which meant a woman in a hijab was a clear sign of trouble, fit to be mocked, scorned, or avoided.

Once they passed, Sabine waded into the street around ground and repulsor driven vehicles acting as Terum's lifeblood. She ventured into one of the many shops about Calamity Square, ducking under a forest of rugs providing shade to hagglers making deals with merchants. Thumbing the side of a particularly gorgeous carpet, she marveled at its craftsmanship. Everything here was handmade. A strange thing in a galaxy where the press of a button could fabricate almost anything. But that was for other, richer worlds. Planets in the Core and Mid Core.

Another shopper with his back to her spoke to her in Standard. "Amazing that they thread all of these by hand, right?"

Sabine smiled. Being undercover and embedded was the only job she was right for. She couldn't imagine a time before it and the thought of coming in out of the sun scared her. In this one moment, there was finally someone here who understood her because he was just like her. It felt good to be around her own. "Your accent is terrible. You'll never pass for a local."

"I've been practicing for a month!" Lahm said.

"Your Tagolan is terrible, too."

Lahm shook his head, dislodging several errant drops of sweat. He was careful not to launch them at the rugs. Something about that seemed wrong to him. "Are we set?"

"Yeah. Package was delivered and they bought the performance. Sign-on codes are legit, but the tracking algorithms are crap. It'll take them a while to notice it and recalibrate. I knew it was only a matter of time before Keem got his hands on a personal data tracker. By passing the device through me rather than someone else, we bought ourselves some time."

"Where the hell did you find a Republic Special Missions PDT system?" Lahm murmured, keeping their conversation low and between themselves.

Sabine ran her hand along another rug, taking in the dense, silken fiber between her fingers. This one wasn't local, but it was glorious. And gloriously priced. The merchant was selling it at a markup for the trouble it must have taken to get it here.

She shrugged. "If you know the right people, you can make anything happen."

"Well, I happen to know we have your back, kid."

Sabine ran her hand across the luxurious rug. "Grateful for that. I don't want to end up like this poor guy. A trophy on someone's floor or wall."

Lahm ran his hand over the rug. "What is it?"

"Wobanki fur."

Lahm pulled his hand back in horror. "Oba, no! Why would someone want that?"

"Same reason someone wants our package. There'll always be someone looking to make a profit off of something perverse, even if it didn't start out that way."

The team Knife wiped his hands off on his jacket in disgust over touching the wobanki skin rug. "Top Cat wants a cold read at twenty-two thirty local."

Sabine handed him a receiver module. "I'll be there in spirit."

"Good to see you again, little sister."

Sabine chuckled. "You could be so lucky to be related to me."

6

"The city of Terum welcomes you, sir. Will your stay be business or pleasure?" came the digital call from inside the cramped armored vestibule.

Nathan Gallagher, Task Unit Pelican's Alpha Section Top Cat, set his passport on the counter so the woman curtly smiling at him could take it through the crysteel glass dividing them. He'd been standing for nearly fifteen minutes in the grotesque lines at the Terum Star Port, and he hadn't even gotten his luggage yet. His suit jacket rode over his shoulder, exposing sweat stains rather than the clean, laundered shirt he'd started the trip wearing. The oppressive heat and humidity circulated in the holding area, waiting to drive visitors and returning locals into local Nuzon fashion versus the extravagance of Republic dress.

Absently, TC replied, "A little of both. I came here looking for kasha worm vendors, and once that's done, I've heard the bathhouses are amazing. Pulled my back out not too long ago, and a trip out here to the baths on the company dime will get me a lot farther than trying to tap my health insurance."

The woman had placed his card on a scanning bed and was patiently nodding to his nervous rambling. Scanning from the screen to his face and then back again, her countenance took on a sour expression. "One moment please, sir."

A sense of dread dropped into the pit of TC's stomach as the customs enforcement agent keyed through a selection of options on the data board in front of her. Behind him, the Alpha Team commander listened to the huffing and shuffling of passengers looking to get their turn at the counter so they could escape into some section of Terum where the heat wasn't cooking them to a temperature of medium rare.

While all the holos and the goofy airport novels depicted teams of special operators diving from an orbital shuttle directly into a combat recovery, the realities of a Wrecker Unit were slightly less glamorous. Within an hour of lifting out of the compound on Drusar, Bravo Team's Valkyrie leejes boarded the *Reliant* and jumped out of the system while TC's Alpha Section went on to the target planet directly via their means of covertly entering the space. In this instance, "covert" meant hiding in plain sight, as any sort of military aircraft landing in the heart of Terum would set off alarms that were best left undisturbed.

"My apologies, sir," the attendant behind the glass offered. "Computers have been misbehaving all day. It should clear in a second."

"Of course. No problem at all."

Behind him, a man fanning himself with a disposable holo-sheet leaned in bad-breath close. "You only say no problem, pal, because you're at the counter. The rest of us would like a turn."

"Out of my control," TC growled over his shoulder. The man behind him had been on the commercial star liner flight he'd hopped at Kamolar Station in the Maskasar

Nebula. The station was home to a massive mining operation, which harvested precious gasses from the nebula for transport to businesses across the Republic. It was also one of the few places businesses ran their ride share programs from that stopped at Nuzon.

This was the part of his job TC hated. As team commander, he was responsible for working directly with both standard Repub and Legion agencies, which had a tendency to land him last when the operation jumped off. Rescue and Recovery ops were tricky affairs as many times they involved more than just the military arm to execute. While the DOS, the Republic Department of Security, was the initiating agency for this operation, TC had to interface with a whole scope of departments to get his team on the ground. The A-SEC commander carved out many of those meetings via hyper secure comm channels broadcast from secure facilities rated for top secret affairs at the highest levels of government as even a whiff of the info passed back and forth could spark a war.

Sweltering with his fellow passengers while the customs agents in their blaster-proof, environmentally controlled booths lumbered to process their passports, TC was beginning to think he should adopt a different strategy. Have the Bravos drop in, blow everything to kingdom come, and then pull out the principle, at which point, he could give the House of Reason—and their protocols, red tape, and sweaty lines like this—the one-finger salute.

"Sorry for the wait, sir," the agent said, handing him his passport. "Enjoy your stay in Terum."

"Thank you." TC headed for the luggage tram, where his verified passport would identify him to the porter AI and have his luggage brought forward. The side of the hyper LED light attached to the scuffed-up ID kiosk was a clear sign the machine, and the star port in general, had seen better days. The dinged-up display shimmered his picture along the cracked screen, changing the blue light to green as he removed his passport card from the system. How many years had it been that he'd worn this face? Mission after mission rolled along and each time, the promise he'd made to himself to put his face back to the way he'd had it before Operation Bird Call fell to the wayside as another mission came through. Another mission he had to lead, because how much longer could he do this? How many more did he have left?

TC walked to the conveyor, nodding to a state police officer standing at one corner of the room and almost bumped into a woman moving for the luggage.

"Mind if I keep you company while we wait for our bags?" the woman asked, taking up a piece of the nearly threadbare carpet next to him.

"It's a free Republic," TC said with a grin. "It would be my pleasure."

Nothing in the woman's posture gave off alarm bells other than the use of an actual paper fan that she pulled from her belt, unfurled, and fluttered. She was a local, as evidenced by her accented Galactic Standard and her chestnut complexion set against rounded cheekbones and a thin set of lips that pouted just so beneath her nose. But while her basic appearance painted her as a Kybari native, her posture and her clothing spoke of money and power.

He'd scanned the space when he'd entered, looking for lines of attack, ways in and out, and anything out of place in this rundown, third world airport masquerading as metropolitan. The pearl-colored walls had periodic art and decorations that celebrated local Nuzon culture without making it look cluttered and gaudy. Someone had taken time to make it aesthetically pleasing, to give the waiting patrons something to focus on as they waited for their stuff. And that's when he realized security should be on the lines in passport control, where the heat, waiting, and inconvenience of the whole affair tended to push tempers too far.

The standard security guard employed by the station was here, standing just inside the exit to the tram that would take passengers to any number of exits to the city. But to have state police here, in any capacity, was unusual. As was the woman. Her clothes were designer, not something that you would get off a rack anywhere near the airport, or possibly not even anywhere in the city. She was wearing the latest fashion from the core worlds, and she was doing it better than most of them did. She fanned herself, and he caught a whiff of her perfume. Something that pungent would go for hundreds of credits per gram—not something the average citizen could afford.

Flawless hair, flawless makeup. No sweat rings. And the trooper giving her scant glances. This woman wasn't here to pick up luggage.

"So what brings you to Terum?" he asked her.

A side door popped open, and a man in a suit came out, heading for the waiting trooper. The gentleman carried a case—TC's case—and handed it to the state trooper and the two parted ways to go about their own businesses.

"I'm here for you. The officer will put your case in my car, Mr. Sandoval," the woman said to him while he followed the trooper's path out of the area. "It's quite safe. If you don't mind, I would love for you to accompany me, so we may have a chat."

TC made sure to look at the woman directly when she used the alias on his passport. "I would be more than happy to, especially if it has air conditioning."

She lightly placed her arm around his, leading him from the concourse to a waiting armored grav-car just outside the sliding doors. The security guard waiting there was quick to snap to attention upon them reaching his station, which should have set off alarm bells with TC but didn't. Instead of walking onto the magna-railcar waiting outside, she led him to an elevator that brought them beneath the station to an underground garage that the rank and file pouring through this star port were likely unaware of. This was an exit for those with means, a convenience for picking up a favored asset required to go through customs screening before getting this far. Someone who had to be vetted before being allowed onto the planet proper.

The trooper stood at attention beside the open door to a black town car waiting on a bed of near silent force. The woman released TC's arm, sliding across real leather seating that probably cost more than the collective salaries of those above still waiting for their luggage. She beckoned to the man, a silent invitation for him to join her on the seat facing her.

With a whispering whir of gears, the door shut of its own accord, leaving the state trooper to take up the wheel and get the repulsors working the car out of the facility. As TC struggled to position his jacket around his sweaty shirt so as not to dampen the pristine leather seat, the woman waved him off.

"Not necessary. If that material can't stand to weather a bit of a manly sweat, then it's not the best. Water?"

TC took the offered bottle, taking a generous sip before asking, "Do you always go trolling baggage claims for single men, to lure them away with promises of cool water and AC, or is this a business meeting?"

Reaching across TC to get her own bottle, she matched him, sip for sip. "Business first. Then we see what happens next. Do you know who I am?"

"If my people are as good as I think they are, you're Lilibeth Dela Cruz. Which would make you the advisor general to the Governor Prime of Nuzon."

"Very good, Mr. Sandoval," Dela Cruz cooed. "Very good indeed. And do you know why I scooped you at the airport?"

"I would expect someone at the House of Reason or the Senate told you I was coming, gave you a holo, and told you to expect me so we could have this chat."

Hopefully they didn't spill my real name, TC thought.

Dela Cruz took another sip. "Right you are again, my friend. I find your presence here provides me with an opportunity I couldn't quite ignore, while making my acquaintance provides you with certain advantages as you complete your mission."

"And what is it you think I can do for you?"

"Mr. Sandoval. We very much wanted our own Royal Marines to be the ones to rescue this downed Republic asset, especially during an election year when we have two delegates seeking a position on the House of Reason. While we don't have the prestige of a core world, or even the mid-core, Nuzon has the potential to become a major force for industry and tourism for the Republic, especially if we have a delegate in the House funneling contracts our way."

TC was seeing what this ride might cost him, from where the advisor general was leading the conversation. "And that appointment, to the House of Reason's delegate chair, would be all the easier if those Royal Marines worked hand in hand with the group to rescue Repub citizens."

Dela Cruz set her water into the holder beside the armrest. "We don't know why the House of Reason sent a survey team over Kerhott, but when the DOS started losing their collective minds over the crash, well, let's just say someone who owed me a favor suggested that I pay attention. Those delegates in the House must have something pretty shady going on if they waved away an offered battalion of our best troops when your people are lost so close to Dosa Keem's territory. And then my people tell me I need to talk to you. So, whatever is going on here, Mr. Sandoval, I would appreciate it if you could get the DOS to reconsider our offer."

TC watched the city appear outside the confines of the car. What should have looked like glorious skyscrapers in the distance instead reflected the backwater nature of the planet and its fickle environment. Instead of gleaming windows and smooth duracrete, the fixeter panels on the exteriors became a declaration to everyone who lived there, as well as potential investors, that someone in the Republic wanted Nuzon relegated to galaxy's edge. Like the rest of Nuzon, this woman was angling for more. More for her community, and thereby more for herself. It wasn't bad as far as ambitions went, but he wasn't in the ambition department.

Dozonaxel Unlimited made the best in commercial grav-sled and repulsor tech, and TC felt like he was riding on a cushion of air as the trooper guided them away from the star port into Terum. But not even the lux-sled generators were enough to arrest the momentum from a sudden stop. The Alpha Section commander turned to the scene outside the vehicle.

A mammoth of impervisteel and high-quality repulsors in its own right, a city sanitation truck, complete with two people in jump suits hanging on the back, came to a halt in front of the luxury vehicle. The duo hopped off the truck, walking to either side of the vehicle. Dela Cruz's chauffeur threw the car in reverse until a company monogrammed refrigerated speeder truck pulled up behind them to arrest their escape.

"Madam Advisor General, I would advise your trooper not to fire on these people," TC said. "They are very good at their job and will not hesitate to leave you both very dead for interfering with a state sanctioned rescue operation. That being said, I think some of your ideas have merit and the ride in this car was beyond anything they would have picked me up in. Let's part ways with my thanks and a promise that I'll keep in touch."

Dela Cruz narrowed her eyes. Wearing an expression of forced cordiality, she said, "Thank you very much for your time, Mr. Sandoval. I look forward to our next meeting."

"Me too. And just so's my people don't have to shoot your people, can you have your guy pop the trunk?"

His door opened to a garbage tech in overalls and a cloth mask over his face. Swirling patterns on the mask constantly shifted, like the roiling smoke coming off a fire, to obscure any hope of description as the swirls focused the eyes on the effect. TC exited the car, taking care to recover his suitcase, and then walked into the adjoining alley. When he was midway across, the two blocking vehicles and all their personnel disappeared.

TC cut left out of the alley, noting a grav-cab's roof marquis going from green, signaling that it was available, to the red of an occupied livery. He stepped inside, closing the door behind him.

Lahm was sitting behind the wheel. He waited until TC was in and they were driving to say, "What? My cab wasn't good enough for you so you hopped a ride with the advisor general? I mean, I know I shouldn't be lecturing you here, boss, but could you have announced any louder that the Repub sent Valkyries planetside?"

"Something tells me we weren't breached, at least not to the government at large. This stinks to Oba's armpits that someone in the big house is looking to score points with the locals," TC responded. He took the offered comm bead from the Alpha Section infiltrator and slipped it in his ear. "Chief, it's TC. Can you read me?"

"Lima Charlie," Chief Cantrell shot back. "What's this I hear about you getting kidnapped? Is someone playing a prank on you, 'cause normally, the kidnapping thing is your job."

TC grunted, in no mood for even this innocuous level of banter. "Get Geiger on the line. I want to know who blew our shade getting in and whether this roll is even still viable."

"Putting it up on the board, now, sir. You want me to get on the horn and wave off Raptor until we know more?"

"Negative. We stay on mission until we can't. Did we file the ops plan with Republic Intelligence or Legion Command?" TC asked.

The display board in the back of the cab lit up with the chief's screens so TC could follow along.

"Sure did," she said. "Took a snap of Martin's cereal box and hot shot it to both groups instead of the real thing.

But in all seriousness, we file like any other REC-Team using codes and call signs over encrypted channels. Plus, you think everyone is out to get you, so there's that."

"Did I or did I not get kidnapped by the highest-ranking government advisor on the planet?" TC countered.

"He's got a point, there, Chief," Lahm said.

7

Mack leaned his back against the gear cage aboard the *Reliant*, trading documents on holo-sheets with Rocco, the Valkyrie Team leej whose place he was taking. If there was anywhere Mack felt totally at ease on a Republic carrier, it was in the gear cages assigned to the Legion. Years of smelling drying PT uniforms, gun lubricants, and thin metal cages, painted over and over as a vanity check for each unit's specific taste, had baked the scents into his nose. The aromatic intersection where the leejes could just get to work.

The two NCOs were going over mission prep and weapon loadouts when Mack caught sight of Captain Dawson at the hatch. The former flight officer turned warship captain slithered into the team room without announcing herself. Giving herself a moment to observe the leejes in their natural habitat, it didn't take long for Mack to take notice and call it off.

"Captain on deck!" Mack shouted.

The leejes in various states of dress while they worked over their gear, snapped to the position of attention at the arrival of the starship's commanding officer. The woman examined the legionnaires hitching a ride on her starship and then grabbed Snowball by the shoulder. She leveled a flat-palmed slap into his fourth point of contact. The resounding smack on a single butt-cheek echoed through the cages, threatening to break the Legion-imposed discipline.

"Now that is impressive, Snowball," Dawson said, nodding her approval. "As you were."

The leejes busted a gut laughing while Snowball did his level best not to hop around from the seismic slap that had tested the mettle of his gluteus maximus. "Oba's beard. That woman hits like a seamball bat. What do you have in that palm, ma'am, and do I need to call a Legion rep to keep me out of the brig when I ask for your hand in marriage?"

"You couldn't handle me, leej," Dawson pointed out. "The man who starts talking about walking me down the aisle has got to be drunk, blind, or both. Besides, you marrying types are too possessive. I'm hoping to make admiral before long so I can run my boat into Utopion and punch some House of Unreasonable delegates in their pearly whites. Can't do that with you clingy types holding me back."

Another round of laughter pitched through the cages as Mack sifted through the men to greet the CO.

"Officer's mess getting too cozy for you, ma'am?" Mack asked. "We asked the spoons to give us a steak we were just about to carve up if you're interested."

"I would love to, Mack, but work comes first," Captain Dawson said. "Just got an intel dump from TC down on Nuzon. Seems we have a bit of an issue with going quiet on this one. Your old man around?"

Rocco held his hand out for the data crypt. He looked it over and then flipped it to Mack. "Raptor went to medical, ma'am. Boss man's got to sign for our meds load before we hop out."

Dawson crossed her arms. "I was more hoping he was finally taking me up on my offer. I told him I could pull some strings, but the damn man doesn't want help pouring out from anywhere near Utopion's butthole, as he calls it. A net-call and an afternoon in a pod and that guy would have another forty years to drink himself to death once he's done with the Legion."

"Those rare cases of leejes who get the treatments are shipped off to school duty or staff. They never get near a trigger again," Rocco said. "Plus, Raptor knows the hock that would put you in, ma'am. He won't do it."

"I guess it's up to Mack to convince him otherwise, now that it's not your job anymore," Dawson said, punching his shoulder.

Rocco flicked the case in Mack's hands. "Yep. Now I get to go to the sergeant major's academy so I can learn to annoy even more leejes than I do now. Still, wasn't my job to tell the crazy bastard how to live his life, and it won't be Mack's."

"Damn straight," Raptor said as he entered the cages. "Good morning, ma'am. Am I interrupting something?"

Dawson waved off his concern. "Negative, Captain. Just brought you an intel packet from Nuzon. Your boys are set, but there are complications. Everything's in the box."

"And of course there was no talk about favors or cancer treatments?" Raptor asked.

"My ship," Dawson declared. "I'll say whatever I please. On the other hand, your boys have some issues. That one in the skivvies just proposed. I'd say that'll be some corrective counseling from you at least. Isn't that right, Captain?"

"Nutcase like that most definitely needs therapy. He couldn't handle you, ma'am."

Eyebrow raised, Dawson said, "Precisely right, Raptor. You let me know if you change your mind on that other thing and I'll escort you there myself."

Raptor held up a finger to indicate message received, before barking his own call to the troop, bringing them to attention. "Atten-HUT!"

"Carry on," Carmilla "War Dog" Dawson said as she left the cages to stalk the alleys of her ship.

Turning away from a blushing Snowball, Raptor found his team sergeants snickering. "You got something for me?" He took the case, setting it down on the workbench that doubled as the team's intel table.

"Seems that TC got kidnapped by the advisor general on the ground for a little meet and greet. Tell me about the AG, Thresh," Rocco asked their resident cherry.

As the newest addition to the team, Thresher was bound to receive the lion's share of the prep-work, be expected to know the who's and what's of each mission, and be asked, on occasion, to recite the Legion creed backwards. "The advisor general is the top advisor to the governor prime, who is the head of state on Nuzon. The AG briefs the GP about the governing of the planet while also keeping an ear to the ground so she can suggest the best possible courses of action. Most AGs are selected from either the military or the secret police, but this one, Lilibeth Dela Cruz, used to be a high-priced lawyer for the Centigo Corporation. She won tons of litigation on behalf of her previous employers and became the first nonmilitary appointee to the position in the last thirty years."

Raptor scanned the holo-sheet he'd pulled from the data crypt, swiping through several pages. The sheets had the consistency of real old-world paper, but had min-iaturized circuitry embedded within that made it cut- and tear-proof while also allowing it to display information on its surface as though it were printed. One sheet could contain an entire library of books, and the pages had mul-tiple settings to allow "flipping" from one page to anoth-er. Raptor seemed to prefer the swipe method. Words flashed across the surface of the paper as he got to the desired pages.

"TC suspects that while this Dela Cruz is all about what's going to benefit her people, she may have ties to this Centigo Corporation still and be looking out for their interests on the side," Raptor said.

Mack took the sheet from his commander, scanning over the pages where Raptor had highlighted several ar-eas of interest. "We only have a hot minute before we in-sert. Is there time to dig into what actually happened at the Serrabi Falls facility?"

"TC's Electronic Engagement Operator is probably digging into that right now. But you can bet wherever there's a big corporate cover up, some government tool isn't far behind," Raptor said. He swept up his silvene bottle to take a swig, instead hovering while caught in thought. "With our A-SEC on station, we're going to have all the geek support we can handle. Martin's a digital blood-hound. If there's anything to find, he'll sniff it out. Case in point, our guy just confirmed that this Doctor Kavir was consulting with gene therapists for her research. That right, Creep?"

Raptor's acknowledgment tracked the team's heads to the other side of the cages. The senior field medic for the team, Staff Sergeant **César** Lauro, call sign Creeper, scanned across his battle board. "That confirms with what I'm seeing here, Rap. Martin hooked me up with the deets on those new skinpacks, and man, this is some next generation stuff. Makes the skinpacks we use now look like Band-Aids. Once the bean counters green lights 'em, Kavir's new trauma tech is going Legion-wide."

Raptor aimed his bottle back at the senior medic. "Normally, some lab coat loses their sled fob on a hostile planet, the gub'mint sends whatever they feel might get the job done to get it back. This ain't that, boys. They specifically let this lady dictate a ride in and out. No Legion."

"Sounds black bag," Rocco said. "Shy?"

Sergeant Shiloh Abesina set down the bolt for the weapon he'd been cleaning. When he spoke, his voice was deep and powerful, the kind of voice you wanted to narrate your life to make you sound more interesting than you actually were. "Not taking a Legion escort means she didn't want Legion command to take notice of anything she was doing. Even if she had a point on station, real leejes would be obligated to report any incident of mass casualty, or bio-chem weapons they found. Taking a MARSOG team means she also didn't want the other side of the house to see what she was doing."

"Pardon me, Sarn't," Thresher said. "A little help for the new boots? Who's the other side of the house?"

"Oh, now you're the new boots?" Raptor said, snapping his attention to the newest member of the team. "On mission, you were cool to dole out your own call sign. Hey Rocco, who gives call signs?"

"Fate, destiny, karma, or any other stripper-sounding name for your lot in life, sir," the outgoing team sergeant said.

"Just checking," Raptor responded. "Please, Shy, drop some knowledge on the new boots."

"Black bag units, new guy. The stuff we hear about but never see. Repub Special Activity, Tactics, and Operations. Units like that. Some even darker. If I had to guess, they had the doc developing something for them and it got out of hand, which is how this Serrabi Falls facility got axed. She decided to go back to either gather or gat all the stuff still there and somewhere along the line she got shot down." Shy held up both index fingers. He swung them from his periphery to line them up, just as any drill instructor would do to line up iron sights on a rifle, back when Basics had to contend with such things.

Thresher nodded, as though he were now certified in all matters *other side of the house*. "I get it. All the secret slither stuff. Just like in the holo-vids. License to kill, and all that."

"You have other things to worry about, Cherry," Shy said. "Like getting your overly inquisitive backside over here and helping me rig this rifle for loadout."

The two team sergeants collapsed on Raptor, sipping from his silvene bottle while the rest of Task Unit Pelican finished locking down their kit. The team commander rolled up his holo-sheet, waving it at the two senior NCOs. "This is a hornet's nest. We have an insurgency population looking to destabilize the local government claiming responsibility, the local government looking to get in on the game, and our slicer jock ripping stuff on the principle from the net that we aren't even being given by Sector Command. This is a hot pile and I don't like it. We're a rescue team. We're not here to shape current events, so we should have access to everything on the table, and not be forced to sneak cookies from under the tablecloth. You picked a helluva time to leave, Rock."

Rocco shrugged. "You want me to push off the academy? Cite some mission critical something or other?"

"No," Raptor said flatly. His resolute answer left no doubt that he was good with Rocco's choice, even though he would have it otherwise. "If you sign off on your replacement, that's good enough for me. Mack, face-to-face with Stringer over there. He's our robo-wrangler. Have him load heavy for this. I have a bad feeling, and I'd rather be wrong and take the chewing for ordering heavy rather than being in the wind wishing we had something we needed. I'll be back. I'm going to run some of this intel by a third party. Tommy! You're with me."

Mack and Rocco watched their team leader attract Tommy Lau, call sign Shredder, into his orbit as he left. Of course, looking more like a Tommy than a Shredder, the leej constantly wore the former and not the latter. The two team sergeants went to work putting the next piece of the plan in motion.

Resting against one of the worktables, Stringer spun his tablet to the approaching senior NCOs. "That's a lot of stripes heading my way. Might make a guy nervous."

"Did you catch Raptor's last on a heavy bot loadout for this one?" Rocco asked.

Stringer stepped aside, showing his tablet resting on the table. "So far, got a whole pack of peepers, creepers, icers and dets. Everything has kinetic batteries, so they'll charge while they move. That doubles the runtime on those bad Larrys. Got a spider too, but you know how the docs love those, so I'm keeping that in my pack until we need it."

"Stringer, you said you got creepers. Is that how the senior doc on the team got his name? He good with those bots too?" Mack asked.

"Nah, Sarn't. Creep got his name because he hovers," Stringer explained. "One minute he's nowhere to be found, and the next, he's behind you. Just poof, ya know? Creeper doesn't do it because he wants to be a kelhorn or nothing. He just wants to learn everything and doesn't like to interrupt. He's behind me right now, ain't he?"

Creeper waved behind the drone wrangler's head. "Hi. Sorry to interrupt, but these boys are probably going to ask for a big 'un. If that's the case, can you make sure it has litter capability? Saves time in the field when we don't have to synth-cord litters to the outside."

"Got ya, Creep. No worries," Stringer confirmed. "See what I mean? So, do we really need a heavy?"

"It sounds like we're dropping into a complicated mess," Mack said, taking the role of senior NCO from Rocco before he could answer. The man was still on deck with them to fill in any gaps. While Mack liked having him on deck to navigate any weird team dynamics, it was time for the incoming team sergeant to take the lead. The sooner they'd confirmed zero gaps, the sooner he could get to the business of making this team *his* business. "Why not order an ISM? The K-15s have the kangaroo-rat pouches on the side for wounded. Plus, they just did a massive overhaul of the Infantry Support Mech's AI, so they run a lot smoother."

Rocco and Stringer looked at each other in surprise.

The drone wrangler's grin nearly split his face. "Alright. Alright. New Top knows his stuff. Not gonna lie, New Top, but we all thought you and the War Dog had a thing going to get you in here after that last Valkyrie hop."

"Hey," Rocco barked, stern enough to let Stringer know he'd crossed a line, but quiet enough not to invoke a team meeting.

"It's cool, Rock," Mack assured the outgoing NCO. He turned over his palms to show Stringer the deep scars gouged there. "Every time I close my hands, I have these scars to remind me of the cost of this job. We did everything right that day. That's the kind of crew we ran. And the universe still spit in our eye. There wasn't a day out there we didn't pay rent on these wings. That's what it takes to be a Valkyrie leej, ya know. Now, War Dog Dawson? She's another story. I hear a couple of her ex-husbands are still in traction and that is not a difficulty setting I can handle right now."

The Team Pelican boys laughed, and Rocco nodded his approval, even as he chin-checked the other members of the team to get back to work instead of directing their forward sight picture into his business.

"Welcome to the team, Big Dog. Hey, I know you and Shiloh know each other from back in the day, but if there's anything I can do to help, hit me up," Stringer said as he went back to his board.

Mack pointed to the leej, then tapped the table. "K-15. Improved AI architecture. Two, if you can get 'em."

"On it, Sarn't," Stringer said.

The two senior leejes returned to the team sergeant's gear cage. Rocco slid out his name panel from its slot, taking a moment to hover over it as the two stood there. "This is your home now, Mack." Rocco reached into the breast pocket of his flight suit and produced a new nameplate with Mack's name on it for the empty space.

"Thanks for that," Mack said.

"Got to tell you, bro. I don't know a lot of leejes that would have jumped back into this after what you went through out there. When I first heard you were taking my place, I was worried for my boys, but judging by the looks of it, they got this and you handled. Now I'm worried about you, because you could have owned that dude back there. You could have forced your play as top stripe in this outfit, and no one would have faulted you for it.

"But you addressed the issue and then brought yourself to that leej's level so you two could meet in the middle. That's leadership gold right there, bro. Smooth as a Tennar's tail. My concern here is that your style is smooth because it's porcelain and something's going to crack it. I'm not trying to punk you, Mack. But damn, I know I would have been straight-up busted after what you went through. Still, every time it looks like the cracks are coming, you go all impervisteel and just shrug it off."

"I have my bad days like anyone else."

That truth was something all aboard the *Reliant* had experienced firsthand.

8

REPUBLIC DESTROYER *RELIANT*
TWO WEEKS EARLIER...

Sweat and blood. When you boil down all life in the galaxy, that's what's left. What was it that Rescue Instructor Hanson used to say to the leejes that trained under him? Sweat in training so you won't bleed in combat.

Going to find that old leej and talk to him about that one day, Mack thought, tasting the copper of his own blood on his tongue. Sweat droplets rappelled down his scalp into his eyes, the salt stinging eyelids rubbed raw from sparring with his fellow legionnaires. Mack squeezed his eyes shut. He'd go by touch now.

On the side of the mat, Sergeant First Class William Deckard, the senior NCO for the *Reliant's* Legion QRF, slapped his hand on the deck repeatedly to get the attention of Mack's grappling partner. The seasoned legionnaire shouted a litany of instructions to the corporal caught in Mack's Guard position. Curses, directions, and promises of extra duty for the kid shouted from Deckard's mouth as Mack swept into the kid's neckline for a cross collar choke.

His muscles strained as he clutched thick, cord-like fabric of his sparring partner's gi. Only it wasn't fabric; it was impervisteel cable. He pressed his eyelids shut, as if to shunt power from one bodily system into his grip. Isn't that how it's done? Close your eyes, grunt, and make it happen. Sweat in training so you don't bleed in combat. All around him, the sound of men and women grunting, heaving, forcing, fighting vanished. In their place was the shooting, screaming, grunting, and dying of combat.

Unbidden, his mind went back. Returning to... then. The time. The disaster.

It always started with the crew chief's screams rising frantically up over the sound of the heavy SLIC engine roaring at the back of the craft. "The line snapped! It snapped. Holy mother truckin' Oba, it snapped! Hold it one sec, big Sarge, I got you!"

Mack was holding the line. He could feel the weight of his boys on the line. All that heave was taxing him past anything he'd ever had to hold, lift, or pull. Sonic amplification in Mack's bucket isolated and magnified the clatter of the chief scrambling for the cable splice to connect it to another line. If he hadn't been grunting, he could use the tongue toggle in his bucket to knock down some of the noise so the speakers didn't force him to hear all the screaming, death, or the rapid pounding of his own heart.

Mack's vision was blurring from the strain. It took another effort to snarl, "Hurry up, Sivo! Need that splice yesterday! The line's cutting my gloves!"

"I got—" The sound amplification made it all too clear that a blaster bolt from the ground just punched through the crew chief's helmet. The way the man's head bounced off the decking when he fell confirmed it.

In Sivo's lifeless hand was a cable with a clip that would save the legionnaires dangling beneath the SLIC as it roared high above the ground. The lifeline was only centimeters away, but to risk removing a hand to reach it was to almost surely release those boys to their doom.

"Dagoy!" Mack roared, calling on another reserve of strength to shout the words and maintain his grip. "I need you to put down so I can get my guys inside! Dagoy! Captain, please!"

If the pilot heard, he didn't answer. Instead, the SLIC climbed.

Mack could feel the line painfully slipping from his grasp. The cable tore through his gloves, shredding his hand down to tendon and bone. Blood and sweat poured over the deck. Wait. How could sweat be pouring on the deck with his bucket on? He cried out to any deity in the universe who would bargain, pleading for another moment of strength, for impervisteel hands, for anything that would let him hold the line.

Ragged, blaster burned wire slithered through his grip, darkening with the blood and gore it ripped away from Mack's hand as it slowly let out of his grip. The cord went from slightly tacky to outright slippery where his blood oozed into the cable threads.

Beyond the deck, the rest of his Valkyrie team below Mack dangled from a SPIES cable and had to be aware that they were slipping away into the abyss. One of those men was Captain Reese Wood. The captain screamed a litany of orders through the L-comm, pain and fear vying for control over his voice

Mack, the lone leej aboard the shuttle began wrapping his arm into the cable, its heft crushed his armored forearm guards. Another blaster bolt sailed into the SLIC's open cabin.

The bolt bounced from the fuselage, rebounding off the plate shielding until it struck the embattled legionnaire in the back and threw him forward. Mack fell onto his belly from the impact and watched helplessly as the crimson slathered line flew from his grip, its tail end whipping a scar into his helmet as a final insult to his failure. The men tumbled from the cable, disappearing through the treetop canopy's burning branches and ash-laden timber.

Over the L-comm, Mack could hear their screams all the way down.

They fell to their deaths in fire and pain, surrounded by an uncaring enemy who would use them as war propaganda or trophies, or worse. What could be worse than any of that?

For Mack the answer was simply living. Facing another day with the guilt. Right there, the moment after it happened, he became aware that he could never carry the weight of what had just happened. He pushed forward to the sweet release of gravity, wanting only to join his brothers in death. The wind rushed in his ears. Was his bucket still on? He could jump after them. He could be on the ground with his brothers.

Dimly, he became aware of hands gripping his shoulders. They wouldn't let go. He was being restrained. They wouldn't let him die with his brothers.

"Mack!" The voice was distant, as though someone was calling him in a crowded room. "Master Sergeant Banes!"

It hadn't been one of the voices from that day. It was someone else. Some*where* else.

Mack was back in the pit. That's what the leejes called this place. Some folks took to calling it a dojo after all the spaces in Sinasia where off duty leejes often went to learn the next big thing in close up violence. He was in the pit on the Republic carrier, *Reliant.* Lying on a training mat surrounded by Republic legionnaires. The top one percent of the one percent the military had to offer. His brothers. The room was thick with the smell of sweat and effort. If you multiply the scent of used gym socks by the stink of a slaughterhouse, and mix in the occasional twinge of antiseptic, you might come close to the nasal assault from the room.

Four legionnaires held him down. His breath came in heaving gasps; his eyes started to focus. Across the room, Doc Onoue was working Corporal Imeda like he was tenderizing a steak.

Mack whispered, "What happened?" The voice came out louder and drier than he had expected it to sound.

Sergeant Deckard was behind him with his legs wrapped around Mack's waist, his arms around his head and chest in a seat belt hold. When he spoke, his voice was soft and firm. "You and Imeda were down for some serious rolling, brother. You got him in a rear mounted choke and kept yanking past his blackout. We had to pull you off."

"Oba, no. I'm sorry. Please, I mean... I'm sorry," Mack croaked.

Everyone always mentions the sweat and blood. No one ever talks about the tears. The deep lamentation for brothers lost. Screaming into the dark for not being able to take another step or fire another bolt. The other leejes released his arms, giving him free rein to kneel forward toward his unconscious friend. It was rare for a leej to break down in public. They were a tough breed. There were mandated therapies for this sort of thing. Tonal messaging to help the mind disassociate and rest at ease. Other, more invasive methods as well. Anything to keep a solider ready to fight.

This wasn't something most of the leejes had seen before. The odds were higher that one would find a narwhal swimming in space rather than a legionnaire throwing a boo-hoo to the universe. If the unicorn moment did happen, it was rarer still to get the sobbing type. When a leej broke down into a blubbering mess, his brothers quickly carted the trooper off to an undefined location to scream away the hate. But it happens where it happens.

Deckard whispered in that way that brothers connected through blood and violence sometimes did for each other. Threading his grip into Mack's judogi, he said, "It is what it is. Own it."

Mack watched as Doc pounded on Imeda's back in sweeping motions with his palms. The hard slaps brought the younger leej around. He shook himself awake.

"Did I win?" the newly conscious leej groggily asked.

"By DQ," the Doc said, relieved.

The room broke out into laughter. Leejes swarmed the man, rubbing his back, arms, and legs to get blood flowing to his extremities. They clapped him on the shoulder, calling him things like "Sand-Lion" and "Tyrannasquid."

Deckard broke the reverie. "Guys."

The senior sergeant had let Mack go, but still had his fist tangled in the thick fabric of Mack's jacket. For his part, Mack was laughing, clapping with the other leejes and wiping away tears. Imeda led the charge, heading over to the man who'd choked him out. The assembled class responded in kind, each kneeling or sitting by their brother with a hand on him. The gym went quiet as non-legionnaires watched the spectacle.

But what had happened, happened, and it wasn't long before Mack excused himself and left for the showers.

Imeda watched the legionnaire go, knowing how rare breakdowns like that were in the Legion. "What's going to happen to Mack?"

"He's carrying that weight because he wants to," Deckard said softly, knowing that the other leejes around him were listening. This wasn't something any of them had seen. It didn't happen.

"Regs say," Imeda began, second guessing himself for a moment before he went ahead and said it. "Regs say we're supposed to report that."

Deckard nodded. "Mandatory psych eval so the Republic can do what they'll do for all of you some day, leej. Someone'll put him back together and send him back out until he runs out of juice. Sergeant Banes knows that same as I do. Same as you do. Way I see it, he figures he can make 'em pay better by rememberin' than forgettin'."

A silence fell over the mats. None of the legionnaires would go to one of the psych-bots and make a confidential report. Deckard was fine with it, and Deckard was the voice of Oba himself.

Sensing this, Deckard nodded. "That said, you all better protect ya neck the next time any of you roll around with Mack."

After the incident on Kabillon, Mack's fitness to be in the Legion was in doubt. Psych evals held by probing, specially programmed bots, incident reviews, and his OICs hovering over him, all looked for the tiniest misstep to yank him from the line and put him out of the unit pending a full psychological reconstruction and all that came with it. It wasn't that they thought he couldn't recover on his own; it was more about the rent.

Every day, a legionnaire proves he has the physical and mental toughness required to wear a Legion crest.

Doesn't mean that the constant micromanaging doesn't bother you. But you get used to it. Can't let the Legion crest sword get rusted. If Mack were honest with himself, this new team was doing the same thing, especially after the incident in the pit. And while Mack understood where they were all coming from, it bothered him just as it would bother anyone who had put in the time, proven their worth, and still got questioned on whether they could or should.

The only ones Mack really had to prove himself to was himself and the old man, and Raptor. Both had given their approval by the simple fact that they hadn't left him on Drusar. And right now, there were more important things to worry about. The mission that TC and the others were developing needed to take up his attention. Still, as Mack jocked up in the team room, he felt the need to defend himself from a question that Rocco hadn't asked.

He didn't need to.

"I have my bad days like anyone else," Mack said. "The best thing for me is to surround myself with rock solid leejes. Ain't no cracks when you have all that armor."

"Damn straight," Rocco said. He slid his hand across Mack's name plate above the locker's door, striking it with his fist loud enough to rattle the cage. "Take care of my boys, Top."

Mack chuckled and offered up an ancient adage for a team NCOIC's responsibility to take care of his men. "Blasters and beans. A platoon sergeant's privilege. It's like being a mom. You ain't got time to hurt with all these brats you need to take care of."

He knuckled Rocco's offered fist as a last goodbye to the outgoing leader.

A sudden commotion brought both men's heads whipping around in the direction of the noise. Rocco shook his head in disbelief as two Valkyrie leejes started wrestling just outside of the squad cages. "Sheesh. Hey! Shy, Creeper. Don't you kelhorns have something better to do? Because my boots are still on this boat and ain't nothing in the rules says I can't put you over my knee one last time."

9

Mack handed another case to Creeper, who passed it along the human chain into the stealth shuttle preparing for departure on the staging deck of the *Reliant*. The senior medic passed it to his guys to be listed, locked down, and tested with a firm boot to make sure it would survive the rigors of space flight. The human conveyor had been at this over the last ten minutes as they secured the ferried equipment to their ride.

"Oh hells, yeah!" said Snowball, as the hulking K-15 mech moved through the staging deck.

"Couldn't get two?" Mack asked Stringer, who guided the mech toward them.

"They're unpacking the second one now, Top," Stringer said, guiding the machine onto a pallet. Unlike the later version, the K-19, which had treads instead of legs, the K-15 was in essence a driverless tank with two methods of locomotion. For fast-moving duties against enemy armor, the machine could float around on repulsors and attain speeds close to one hundred kilometers-per-hour. While assisting dismounted operations, the Infantry Support Mech's primary purpose, the machine could unfurl six armored crab-legs to negotiate varied terrain or settle in as a fire support platform and mobile cover.

"Good job, dude!" Mack said, pointing to the self-satisfied drone jockey. "Wait a minute! Why is it hauling a port-o-fresher behind it?"

Laughter from the ramp clued the master sergeant into what the answer might entail. Halting any explanation with an upturned hand, Mack stalked around the K-15 mech to find the door to the hyperplastic outhouse had been gorilla-taped shut.

"So not cool, guys!" Thresher shouted from inside the port-o-fresher.

Mack stripped the tape enough to rip the door open and got an eyeful more than he bargained for. Thresher sat sideways on the fresher seat lid with his limbs splayed about the portable potty for support so he didn't fall over and lose control of the lid in the fresher's bouncy slide across the deck.

Stringer approached the new team sergeant with his hands held in supplication. "I can explain, Top."

Mack adjusted his stance to include folding his arms over his chest and looking like a Drusic who just lost a bet.

"I needed something that rhymed with Thresher," Stringer explained.

Mack's stance and stern expression didn't change. "Stringer, that's about the best prank I've ever seen. In fact, it's so good, I'm officially placing you in charge of all incoming personnel. How's that?"

"Understood, Top," Stringer said while stifling guffaws. "C'mere, Fresher! Help me get this bot rigged!"

"Fresher!" came the stereo cry from the assembled leejes at the back of the shuttle.

"Boys already talkin'," Creeper quietly said. "They dig your style. Get it done and I'm your boy. Fail it and I'm your bastard. Good deal."

"I do what I can," Mack said, at the sudden appearance of the senior medic. "Can you keep this train on the rail? Time to be a bastard."

From across the hangar deck, a senior naval NCO walked with the speed and precision of a ship-to-ship missile. His rapid pace and hard stare locked onto Mack like the best of guidance systems while busy spacers jumped to clear a path for the hard-charging petty officer. Catching Mack, he motioned for the Wrecker Team sergeant to follow him toward a set of lancers parked close by. "Need you with me, Master Sergeant."

Arriving between the two ships, Mack snapped to parade rest to show respect to his fellow NCO, Command Master Chief Petty Officer Davidson despite being from two different services. "What's the word, Command Master Chief?"

"Dawson sent me. She wants you off her ship five minutes ago, Mack. She said the original plan was to jump in system, drop you guys off, and then you'd board a commercial boat down to the planet. Instead, she has us dumping FTL, kicking you out the door in your own bird, and jumping right back out. The only ones who would catch us jumping in-system would be any spooks on the ground. But something weird is going on. The XO's a point. The second she got wind of a FRAGO, she started rounding up MAs on the double."

"That's not good." Mack's stomach turned at the mention of the XO. Then he saw Raptor running across the flight deck.

The team commander returned the twin salutes from the NCOs emerging from beside the locked down fighters. "No time to play nice. Command Master Chief, did the XO send you?"

"I don't work for that leaf, sir," the Master Chief corrected, noting the rank insignia of a leaf identifying the commander serving as the XO.

"Good deal. You know what's doing?" Raptor asked.

Davidson shook his head. "Just that War Dog wants you off the ship quick, sir."

Raptor clenched his jaw. "The DOS was the one to push this rescue order through Legion Command and Fleet, but now the House of Reason is contesting it on multiple levels."

"How does the XO play into this?" Mack asked.

Raptor whistled to his team, still loading the assault shuttle. When he had their attention, he held up his arm and laid it on top of his other in a chopping motion. Whatever the signal meant, REC-Team Pelican went into overdrive. Buckets locked into place, completing armor systems and controlling all the flow of their conversations through the L-comm. Grav-carts containing the rest of their gear loaded as fast as the leejes could move them.

Raptor voice was practically a growl. "Me and Tommy were doing a quick dip into the net for mission stuff when we came across a pull order from Legion command. They're yanking me off mission and replacing me with a point. The *Reliant*'s XO is the House of Reason mouthpiece they're going to use to do it. I asked Dawson to play along for now."

"Can't happen. They specifically barred points from the REC-Teams," Mack said. "It would be like giving some kid a shuttle full of leejes and shouting 'take us in,' because he played Shuttle Simulator Five."

"Some delegate got the Legion commander to let women into selection. You think they're going to listen to our very good reason for no points flying Valkyrie wings?" Raptor shot back.

Another leej in full armor ran up with a squad hot on his heels. Removing his bucket, his hard eyes and a fresh discoloration at the jaw line—most likely from a rejuvenation treatment settling an injury—stared down the scene like a sand lion come to claim his pride. He slammed his wrist into Raptor's. "Rap. We came as fast as we could."

Beside the freshly arrived Legion officer, platoon sergeant Deckard dropped his bucket from his skull, gracing the hangar with his smirking face. "What's doing, Captain Rashad? You got us here. Put us to work."

"Saber. Deckard. Nick of time, boys. Nick of time," Raptor said, returning a hard slap on the leejes' armor. "Points and Unreasonables are about to pour out a bucket of stupid on deck so we can't do our jobs. Need you to run interference."

Saber threw his arms out. "So I get to mess with that tightwad XO and the House of Reason at the same time? It's not even my birthday."

Mack returned a signed datapad to a deck officer as the final check mark to get the stealth shuttle ready to deploy. Across the deck, the landing signal controller crossed the light bars he held into an X, then put one in front of the other, a signal for the pilot to hold his spooling aircraft. Mack held onto the ramp's hydraulic arm as the executive officer strode toward him with a leej he didn't recognize.

Flanking them were four of the ship's masters-at-arms, kitted out in armor and weapons ready to do their duty.

"Master Sergeant Malcolm Banes, I'm Commander Juliet Norris-Foster."

Mack saluted her, not bothering to put the extra strain into getting his arm past the armor to do it justice, like he often did with officers he respected. "What can I do you for, ma'am?"

The XO's lip pulled back into a sneer at the question's phrasing, then haughtily said, "I am here to present Major Robert Tyler of the Second Legion to assume command of Rescue Team Pelican. In addition, you are to produce Captain Rashad immediately, as he will not be going on this mission."

"By whose authority, ma'am? With all due respect, I have an operation's order here that says—"

"That will be more than enough, Master Sergeant," Tyler said, raising his voice to be heard over the engines and nearly dropping the bucket at his side for the effort.

Mack walked down the ramp to tower over Major Tyler, who took a step back. The master sergeant held the man's stare before turning to address the senior naval officer. "Ma'am, I need to see your orders from Legion Command."

Raptor emerged from the ship, stopping by Mack with his hands resting on his hips. Raptor held his place instead of saluting Norris-Foster, who nearly turned red at the insult. "What's going on here, Mack?"

"They claim to have orders saying you're being pulled, sir."

Major Tyler walked around Mack to hold up a datapad to the hovering leej. "Captain Emilio Rashad, as per medical records obtained by Legion Command and in accordance with the standards set forth by the same, you are hereby relieved of command until such time that you are restored to full health and pending a medical review board as to your fitness to rejoin our ranks."

Raptor didn't even glance at the presented data pad. "I have orders saying that I am fit for duty and assigned to this mission, Major. It seems we are at an impasse, and since I have minutes before the *Reliant* jumps out of FTL and we're out the door, this will have to wait."

The executive officer simmered during the exchange. No longer able to keep her composure, she shouted, "Captain! Remove your helmet, now!"

Mack waved off her command. "Sorry, Commander Norris-Foster, but according to naval regulations, being on any hangar deck of a Republic carrier requires head protection and safety markings. You have neither. Technically, you shouldn't be here, and the major is also in violation with his helmet off. Are you really asking Captain Rashad to perform an unsafe act by removing his bucket?"

Before the XO could respond, the major put on his own bucket and tapped the datapad in front of Raptor. "Captain, these orders come straight from Legion Command. I don't want to pull you from your men. But I must."

"That still doesn't rate you to take my place," Raptor said, not bothering to take the offered datapad.

"I have been a Legion officer for almost ten years now, Captain. I'm sure I can fill the role as required."

"Captain Rashad, if you do not surrender your position, I will be forced to arrest you and remove you myself," Norris-Foster said, her nose climbing ever higher into the air.

Raptor closed the distance so the woman, not wearing any comms gear, or any other gear save her uniform, could hear him clearly. He casually disregarded the masters-at-arms, moving their hands to their side arms, as the common serviceman in the Republic had a healthy respect, and in some cases fear, of being on the wrong side of a legionnaire's attention. "Ma'am, as a legionnaire, I surrender nothing."

The diminutive appointed naval office stepped back, right into the path of an oncoming motor cart hauling gear. *BEEEEEEP*—Raptor snatched her forward before she got clipped. Shock, fear, and embarrassment washed across her face.

"Thank you, Captain," Norris-Foster whispered begrudgingly.

Raptor ignored her proffered thanks. "Master Sergeant Banes, I'm not about to let the people down there get slogged because I can't step away. You run the team. Major Tyler can go as an observer. He can make suggestions and liaise with the *Reliant*, but yours is the final word since he's not Valkyrie-rated."

"You can't make that call," Norris-Foster sputtered, enraged on behalf of her fellow-appointed officer, despite the Legion point not seeming to share the outrage.

Raptor walked past her and through the MAs. "That's how it plays until this gets handled, ma'am. Unless you want to be on the SNN telling people how your little dog syndrome cost us the lives of a famed researcher and a handful of marines."

Mack snapped to attention, saluting Raptor as the man walked away. He laughed at the little commander storming after the Valkyrie CO, screaming at him with every step. Stomping back up the ramp, he shouted to Creeper, "Tag and lock this leej, Creep!"

"On it," Creeper yelled back over the whining hydraulics. He motioned for the major to ascend the ramp and join him at a spot near the back of the deck.

"Um, we're not strapped in," Major Tyler said as the ship, rising on its repulsors, nearly tipped him over.

"You get used to it, sir," Creeper offered. He went through the man's gear, ripping and clipping things on and off the unblemished matte-gray armor as he settled things according to Pelican's kit SOP. After a last look to see that seals and buckles were how they were supposed to be, he asked, "You HAHO rated?"

"No. Low-atmosphere jump qual'd. Why?" Tyler shouted, though there was no need as Tommy rigged him into the team net.

"Oh. You're really not going to like this next part—um, 'next part, sir,'" Creeper said, as he noted the man's rank.

Major Tyler snapped his fingers toward Mack, hoping the motion would get the man's attention over the engines' roar. When it didn't, he said over the L-comm, "Master Sergeant Banes, I read the mission's brief. This was supposed to be an insertion aboard civilian transpo."

"Well, that's what happens when House of Reason delegates leak sensitive info to people outside the chain of command. We must adapt, sir," Mack shot back. "And if you're not rated for orbital insertion via High Atmospheric, High Opening, you got two options. One, you stay here on board with the pilot when we go out. Two, I strap you to the mech. You choose, but either way, we're going orbital. The shuttle and our boy Snowball insert somewhere out of the way where he gets to kick it and wait to pick us up."

"Secure me to the mech then," Tyler said in a tone that was as committed as it was defeated.

Another leej joined the scene at the back. "Major Tyler, is it? My name is Stringer, and may I say, that's a bold choice. But no worries. I'll be your in-flight stewardess today. Happy to have you on mission and ready to ride the friendly skies with us. I'm going to take your long arm and lock that to the gear housing on our mech. If you would please step over here. Thank you."

Mack remained standing until he felt the vehicle's sway come to a bobbing halt. He dropped into his seat and directed the comms to Snowball. "We need to be off the deck in a hot minute, Snow."

"I'm right there with you, Mack. It'll be just like dropping you guys over the Hassica Ocean on Drusar."

"Except if we aren't out the door the second those star lines go flat, that point XO is going to lock us in," Mack noted.

"You worry about your point, I'll worry about mine," Snowball chuckled.

With half an eye on the mission clock, Mack watched the appointed major get stuffed into a compartment on the side of the K-15. The aid and litter compartment snapped shut, sealing the officer in with inflatable impact baffles to keep him from experiencing shock after the twelve-ton machine stepped out the door from orbit.

Creeper dropped into his own seat, locking his restraining bars with a thumbs-up, his shoulders shuddering with laughter.

"Pelican out the door!" Snowball announced.

The vehicle shot into the void. Instantly, the weight of the *Reliant*'s artificial gravity disappeared. In the void, they were weightless. With leejes strapped in, locked down, and in place, Snowball kicked the engines into full burn to drive it along its course. A few seconds of thrust later, and the stealth assault shuttle blasted into the expanse.

"Mack, we're on the burn. Sticking my nose into the track. Time on target for ditch is two mikes. Clock is running. Snowball, out."

Mack unlocked his harness, giving his arm freedom enough to signal they had two minutes before the door opened and they were vacuum-bound. The men had already conducted parachute rigging and pre-jump procedures before taking their seats. Everything had been set... until a Point XO and her shiny point-leej boy-toy shoved their nose into an operation already in play. Poor form. But poor form didn't have any position on the deck, as the Valkyries of REC-Team Pelican removed themselves from the crash harnesses and floated around the cargo bay.

Snaps and clacks felt through the deck plating, coming as magnetic grapples rigged to the outsides of their boots locked them to the ship. Two of the Valkyries ripped cargo boxes free from their rigging and made last-minute checks that their parachutes were primed and ready to do the job of delivering their load to the rock.

"One minute," Mack told his team, holding up a finger. He turned away from the heavy magnetic grapple the K-15 had on the deck as it took its place as the lead element in the chalk. Tapping the tongue toggle, he flipped to the bio signs screen for the emergency-inserted Legion officer. Based on the man's vitals, Mack decided the major was probably having the time of his life.

Twin racetracks ahead of the ramp were treated to a tremendous view of the planet awash in golden fire as the sun warmed the horizon to their front, leaving the globe blanketed in darkness toward the nose of the aircraft.

Light filters slammed in place at the detection of solar radiation unfiltered by the atmosphere to protect the legionnaire's vision against the spectacular glow. A beacon appeared in their HUD below an overlay that showed their flight track once they jumped.

Mack held his hand in a C, showing thirty seconds counting down the ramp as it completed its movement and locked itself open. Creeper, their jumpmaster, made final checks at the ramp, looking for obstructions, the *Reliant*'s positioning, and any impending ships moving toward them that could make the jump dangerous. An anonymous leej piped in Techno-Synth workout music through the L-comm to accompany Creeper's performance. Dancing himself to the center of the ramp, the team's senior medic flashed two thumbs-up and motioned for everyone to mind the mech as it replaced him at the head of the jumpers.

Slapping the machine on the back of its armored plating, Mack caused it to disconnect its feet from the deck. Minor spurts from its thrusters pushed the machine from the ship, taking it out over the planet sprawling below. Gravity demanded the robot take an immediate trip straight down, clearing it from the leej's field of view.

The chalk raced from the ramp, timing their positions out of the spacecraft to give themselves enough room to maneuver along their flight tracks in order to aim toward the beacon on the ground. Inside the shuttle, Snowball watched the exterior cameras as the Valkyries and their treasure trove of kit dove from the vehicle in the sweet embrace of gravity. With the jump complete, he buttoned up the hatch and primed the shuttle for silent running and a smooth trip toward the ground.

Throughout the L-comm, communication algos filtered out the heavy sounds of leejes working their breathing into stable rhythms amid groans and grunts to stabilize their exit from the aircraft. The glorious blue marble that was Nuzon lay beneath them, appearing as a fixed object they were never destined to meet. The leej team vented microbursts from attitude thrusters locked to their kit, setting them into the correct posture for the fall.

"All Pelican elements, this is Creeper. Make your spread point two and make room for Kilo. Mack on signal?"

"Passenger is good for signal," Mack said into the comms. "Pulse is strong and stupid."

"Copy. All Pelican elements, I have the clock. Turn and burn for course track, Creeper out," the senior medic said.

The team adjusted their courses via thrusters, spitting bursts of smoke from the freefall insertion rig to turn them toward their necessary bearing. They moved away from each other according to Creeper's course track in their HUD, making corrections to position and attitude. Highlighted overlays showed in brilliant colors so as to show up against the gorgeous panorama bathed in sunlight below them.

The first bits of dense atmosphere buffeted against their armor, shaking the leejes inside like a rattled soft drink can. Mack huffed as he tried to dial in the counter vibration software in his bucket. It was supposed to tack eye movement against combat conditions to give the wearer a clean view of the display. All it was doing at the moment was shaking his HUD out of focus like a funhouse holo. Mack shouted a series of commands at the bucket's operating system and was treated to a clean read of the team falling at speeds bordering on hypersonic.

Warning indicators flickered in Mack's vision a second before a buffet of air shook him against the rapidly fading sound of thunder. Just another day in the Legion doing things like breaking the sound barrier.

Passing into an altitude low enough to be hidden from the sun over the horizon, the team raced toward the darkness of a nighttime sky. Night vision systems auto-activated, giving the members of Rec-Team Pelican a clear view on their way down to the cloud cover. Known for its storms, the AO they were jumping into was blanketed in dark, obscuring nimbus clouds they would have to fly through.

"Lots of chop up ahead, Top!" Creeper called into the net.

"I see it," Mack replied. "Dispersion kit in the jump rigs will handle any sparks that hit us on the way through. We should be good."

"What about the point?" Creeper asked.

"The mech is rated for things like ion hits. We'll find out if it's rated for lightning when we pour that guy into the dirt," Mack confirmed.

Within moments, the members of Rec-Team Pelican disappeared into clouds swollen with vapor and the violence storms bring.

10

Mack reached the ground and then slapped the riser release on the parachute harness with armored knuckles. He pulled the buckle cover open to expose the retention wire, then used his thumb to pull the release to deflate the chute, which happened when the suspension lines were free of their anchor. After snapping the rest of the releases, Mack freed himself from the parachute rig and placed his weapon into operation. The NK-4 blaster rifle was a shorter, more compact version of the N-4, making it a great jumping partner. While it didn't have the "reach out and touch someone" range of the regular model, it offered a compact package handy for close quarters battle in the confines of a city, orbital station, jungle compound— wherever they found themselves.

"Snow, it's Mack. We are one hundred percent on the ground. Rigging for motion and mayhem on the quick. Zero casualties. All equipment AOT. Over." The master sergeant hauled in his chute, scrunching it inside of a kit bag for an easy carry to their assembly point. He snapped his ruck onto his back, not bothering to extend the arm straps and instead choosing to rig it for magnetic attachment. As his bucket's HUD signaled the pack locking to his armor, the display died away in favor of an overlay showing all the leejes doing the same. Weapon, kit, KTF. Perfect form for a crew to get after it, following a jump.

In the early hours just prior to midnight local time, Mack jogged across the grassy terrain until he met up with the mech. The K-15 had perfectly angled into a depression and landed with its legs extended, allowing it to position itself in the wadi without worrying about the odd angle. He strode up to the machine, patting it on the outside. "K-15, identify and declare status."

A prompt floated into his HUD.

Text or voice internal to bucket?

The question amused the legionnaire, as they typically got their kit straight from the packing peanuts and had to program them for rescue operations more than once. This one was already referring to the helmet as a bucket, meaning Stringer had done his job the second he brushed his gloves against the armor.

"Internal voice, please," Mack said awkwardly as he toggled the tongue switch in his bucket.

"I am LCD-2388, call sign Maggie. I am activating to enact recovery order 7732041, in accordance with the rescue and recovery mandate put forth by Legion Command seven-point-one-four hours ago. We have landed at twenty-three, twenty-one Local Standard Time in a temperature of twenty-one degrees Celsius. Winds are at twelve knots, coming from the north by northeast."

"Roger that, Maggie. My knees confirm the wind speed on that landing. Are you at one hundred percent?" Mack asked.

"Negative, Master Sergeant Malcolm Banes. I am not. There is currently a fidgeting Legion officer struggling for a release switch in the number one aid and litter compartment. Since there is no release switch from inside the compartment, his frantic maneuverings will do nothing other than potentially cavitate this unit, which has the potential to misalign any defensive measures I might take."

Mack liked this bot already. Stringer was already giving it a personality. "You might want to release him then, Maggie. Wouldn't want him to mess with your groove."

Maggie's smooth and husky voice returned to the L-comm, sounding like a career military woman. "Thank you, Master Sergeant Malcolm Banes. Releasing compartment number one."

"It's just Mack," he said, letting the bot know she could use his familiar call sign to cut down on the time of repeating his name and rank every time she spoke. He stepped away from the mech as the compartment opened, spilling the major into the soft sand at the bottom of the depression.

Major Tyler landed in a flurry of limbs, scrambling to remove his bucket. The rapid-fire deployment of his stomach contents vented into the sand, and he panted, dry heaving, as the rest of the team caught up to the mech.

"You ever ride down like that?" Mack asked Creeper, who was first on the scene.

"Sure. Special Operations Medical Course," Creeper confirmed.

"You lose it, too?"

The senior medic checked the major's status through a link to his armor. Other than an intense sense of nausea and a heart rate like a Digi-Death Metal drummer in full swing, the man was in perfect shape. "No. Going through puberty keeps that kind of thing from happening to most men."

"Keep an eye on him and let me know if he suddenly sprouts whiskers or his voice cracks," Mack said. He gathered the rest of his team, collecting each man's parachute kit bag and depositing them under the mech. He tapped Maggie on the side of the armor and the infantry support mech understood and executed what the NCO was asking of her. With one leg, she scooped out a divot of sand nearly three feet deep. With another, she shoved all the kit bags from the arriving legionnaires into the hole.

"Um, Rooster, is it?" Mack asked, pointing to one of the approaching leejes.

"Why yes, Master Sergeant, I am Rooster. How may I be of service to you?" The man's armor was harshly scratched, insignia abraded, rather like the leej had been in a wrestling with a sandblaster.

"Looks like you had a rough landing back there. If you're not too roughed up and you got a gear popper, I'd appreciate it if you dropped it over there." Mack pointed to where he wanted it.

Rooster moved to the underside of the hulking machine, acting as the rally point for the team. He placed a grenade into the dirt, turning rings on the outside of the weapon in time with whatever display in his HUD matched the gestures. "Pardon me, Major. You might want to move away. The grenade is going to eat the chutes. You don't want to be anywhere near it when it does."

"Thank you," Tyler said, nodding weakly as he collected his bucket.

Rooster pulled the pin, releasing the arming lever on the grenade. The lever shot to the top, springing a small vent on the underside. Maggie crawled laterally across the depression, scuttling like a crab, to avoid the quiet yet devastating weapon. If the leejes weren't in the middle of a security halt, prepping gear, and readying themselves to move on the objective, they would have seen the chutes and spent equipment boxes dissolving as trillions of nanites ate away at their structures. Devouring the target materials, the equipment denial nanites used their meal as the building blocks to replicate, further speeding up the process. Within moments, the chutes and the grenade body dissolved into sand.

Plasma grenades issued to legionnaires in the line units to destroy equipment or obliterate evidence of their passing through a combat environment was standard practice. But this mission had a sensitivity clause attached. They'd nixed the very loud, very visible burner grenade in favor of the more modern and more expensive one to handle any sign of them dropping into Nuzon for a visit.

And of course, there were chutes which would eat themselves up without the need for such grenades. But every operator had heard the horror stories of those chutes erasing themselves while in mid-fall. Better to come in the old-fashioned way and eliminate the evidence once both feet were safely on the ground.

In the operation order, Raptor had detailed their Alpha Section on the ground had uncovered multiple factions looking to be involved in this particular rescue once the Department of Security had issued the recovery request. It seems everyone either wanted to lend a hand to help, because of the optics, or one to cover up whatever was going on. Optics too, Mack supposed.

Creeper sidled over, showing Mack a display in his augmented reality HUD. "Our tack is on station and waiting for us at the western edge of the Kerhott City. They advise moving in from this heading so we don't get slagged by our new best friends."

"What new best friends?" Mack asked.

"Apparently we're working hand in hand with the locals on this one," Creeper remarked in his typically dry tone.

"The hell we are. We'll go over that with the tack once we're in place."

"Excuse me, gentlemen. I really should be informed of what's going on here," Tyler said, recovering his bucket.

"And you will be, sir," Mack said, his tone neither condescending nor placating. "Normally, Raptor would have remained on the shuttle with the pilot and run the ship like a C2 vehicle. But you insisted on coming along, so you'll have to ride right seat with one of our wreckers at all times."

"Right seat?" Tyler asked.

Creeper tapped him on the shoulder. "It's where all the student drivers sit. Coach sits on the left. For the first part of the mission, we're going to put you with Shiloh. He's our ERDM."

Shiloh was the team sniper and had just finished snapping a long case to his assault pack before waving to the command group.

"You've had time with a spotter scope?" Creeper asked the point.

Tyler nodded. "I served two tours with Marine Reconnaissance before going through Legion selection."

Creeper's bucket almost fell off in surprise. "You're not an appointed officer?"

"I was appointed to the Marine Corps, but I went through selection for the Legion."

Mack snapped his fingers. "As fascinating as this is, Major, I have better uses for my legionnaires hearing your personal life story. Creeper, Rooster, and Tommy with me. Major Tyler with Shy running the long way. String, finish rigging the gear to Maggie and then hop in with Thresher and Lobster on point. Ducky and the rest on trail."

The leejes went to work securing the last of their gear and getting with their assigned teams. The major hesitantly approached several members of the squad who pointed him to other legionnaires until Shiloh pulled the slowly recovering officer to his side.

Mack knife-handed the terrain in front of them, a grassy plain leading to a dead city beyond the berm they were hiding in. Thresher ran over the berm, taking another leej with him. With a hearty slap to Maggie's backplate, Stringer followed, riding the machine bounding off on its repulsors like a spider scampering over its web.

"Shy, it's Mack. Let me know if the point is giving you any trouble," Mack said through a private comms channel.

"Got you, Top," Shiloh responded.

The team ran in the darkness, letting their enhanced vision modes sight for them when their normal vision would have failed. The buckets drank in the cloudy moonlight and extrapolated any terrain they couldn't actually see through, as mapping software projected the most likely give and take on the terrain. Coming free of the tall, fluffy grasses after their five-kilometer run, the team came to an abandoned road, its duracrete cracked and creased. Dead highway streetlamps leading to the blacked-out city had crysteel coverings over hyper-LED bulbs—normally able to last decades of use and abuse—stood lifeless.

"Mack, it's Thresher. Approaching first buildings. Going low."

"Roger out," Mack acknowledged. The leejes on point ran to the outside of the derelict street barriers, long since rendered useless by the city's evacuation. The team made way from the lower section of neighborhood streets onto an overpass rising above the cityscape. A rusted construction rig, likely positioned to cover workers replacing guard rails on the side of the bridge, remained abandoned on the highway, its tarp fluttering in the light evening breeze.

"Shy. Marking high point for entrance into city," Mack said.

"Roger that. Moving to you now. Shy out."

Mack and his leej team jogged back down the street to the ones below, following beacons left by the point team entering the buildings. A shift of his tongue on the control toggle, and Mack had an overlay showing the position of REC-Team Pelican and their associated assets.

"Mack, it's Thresher. We're tagging our LOC on the building thirty-five meters at your fifty degrees. We have two incoming to you along the back alley, approaching you at three, four zero."

"Roger, *Fresher*," Mack said, emphasizing the junior leej's new tag. "Two incoming at three, four zero. Mack out."

Toggling the bucket control again, Mack shifted to the functions command menu and tapped the IR laser in his bucket. Only visible to those wearing a certain spectrum of night vision or a Legion bucket, the laser flared across the avenue, striking the lead runner in the chest. The person flashed a thumbs-up and traced the laser's path into the building taken as a home base for the newly arrived leejes.

A man and woman, their faces wrapped in scarves, entered the Legion sanctuary.

"Alright. New plan. Tomorrow, I am *so* starting a new cardio routine," the woman said as she untangled the scarf covering her face. She slung the pack from her shoulders, dropping it to the dusty floor. "You must be Mack."

"And how would you know that?" Mack said in the gritty digital echo coming from his bucket speakers.

"I may have mentioned you to her, Mack," Lahm said, stripping off his own scarf. "But don't worry—I talked you up real good, brah. Ya know, had to with this one. She's always on the lookout for the double cross, so she just wanted to make sure you weren't some House of Reason plant looking to strip the *shrip*, ya know?" Lahm said as he unwrapped his own scarf from his face.

"I just saw you on Drusar like five minutes ago. How did you get here ahead of us?" Mack asked.

"He's like a rash, he gets into everything," the female operative said, pushing past the Alpha Section infiltrator. "I'm Sabine. I've heard good things, Master Sergeant."

Mack shook her hand. "Thanks for the endorsement. I've read your write up on the Khindo Khabar. You got a set of brass ones on you, working arms deals to shadow that crew."

"Bigger than his," Sabine said, tilting her head toward the A-SEC knife man.

Lahm began to protest, but Mack simply patted him on the back before spinning him around to face the tablet Sabine drew from her pack.

"As of thirty minutes ago, this has officially turned into a *styggy* rope," Sabine said over an image of Kerhott on her tablet. "We're here. The Nuzon Royal Marines have deployed to the trailing edge of the city and are establishing an outer cordon, despite TC trying to keep them out of the way. Apparently, they see a rescue of your missing principle as a steppingstone for Nuzon to get onto the big stage. Khindo Khabar moved into the city some time ago using a Special Forces PDT locator to go after your girl. Unfortunately for them, the tracker wasn't calibrated for use on Nuzon, so they'll have to re-code it."

In Mack's bucket, a fresh voice entered the comms. It was Major Tyler. "So what I'm hearing is, if we guide the Nuzon Marines to the Khindo Khabar insurgents looking to capture our doctor, we could eliminate them as a threat and recover our asset with little danger to us."

Sabine glanced at Mack as though she'd just watched someone drink an entire bucket of stupid. "New guy?"

Mack kept his face hard and professional. "Sabine, Major Tyler was appointed to the team after the Legion discovered a medical anomaly in Raptor's file."

"A medical anomaly. Right." Sabine suppressed a growl and then said into the comms, "Major Tyler, is it?"

"Yes. And with whom am I speaking?" Tyler asked.

Sabine huffed, shaking her head in annoyance. "Since I don't see a bucket bobbing up and down in time with your mouth, Major, I assume you're with the sniper or the pilot. That being the case, the grownups are talking, sweetie. Best to concentrate on whatever busy work they gave you versus trying to guess on something that will get everyone killed. And before you open your mouth to protest, or whatever it is you artificial officers do, be advised you're not on the ship you came from. There's no Repub delegate holding your hand out here. You're in the grass with the snakes and we all bite, strangle, and kill."

Mack waited for a rebuke that didn't come. He switched to a private channel between himself, Creeper, and the newcomers. "Now that's something I didn't expect. A point picking his battles."

"Want us to take care of him?" Sabine asked.

Mack stared at the woman, trying to read her. "I don't know if you're kidding or not, but we have things in motion to keep him handled while we bleed him for intel on what's going on. Our sniper used to run with hide-and-seek organizations, if you take my meaning. If anyone can get him to talk, it's him. But, back to the Khindo Khabar."

"Right," Sabine agreed. "They entered the city on the opposite side, figuring that the doctor was heading to Serrabi Falls and if they still go that route, the fighters will catch her. But according to our own very calibrated trackers, Doctor Kavir and the remaining marines with her are hold up here. This was going to be the site of a new Centigo Corporation office building. Plenty of equipment, access points, and potential places to hide for someone who has the keys to the place."

"Okay, first things first," Mack said. "We have orders to black box and black rock the shuttle they came in. Then we move from there to secure the principle. How likely are the Royal Marines to wait for us to do our thing?"

Sabine gave a slight shrug. "The Nuzon and the Khindo Khabar have no love lost on each other. If they get a chance to shoot it out, things could get ugly with you trapped in the middle."

"Is Kerhott the only thing stopping them?" Creeper asked.

"You know it, brah," Lahm said. "The government at large has been enforcing the no-go zone in Kerhott, but Dosa Keem and his people have been using the outskirts as their own private playground since it happened. Both sides suspect the fallout story is a cover-up, but neither has been deep into the city to verify until now."

"Really?" Sabine asked. "I told you that an hour ago and now you're like an intel monkey. Anyway, it's only a matter of time before the locals send in their Recon Marines to drive the Khindos into the street. They know Keem's people are in here, and they are very motivated to make this rescue, especially if they can get to Keem himself."

A private message window flagged Mack's HUD, prompting him to hold up a finger to the Alpha Section newcomers.

What do you think? came the direct message from a scrubbed ID tag.

Mack folded the battle board from the top of his armor, tapping out a quick message of his own to the private net secured away from the rest of the L-comm. *Move to plane. Secure and blow. Move onto Kavir.* Not bothering to wait for the response, he looped his comms back into the rest of the team.

Creeper snapped his fingers a few times, getting the Bravo Section leejes in high gear for their next move. "Time to hit the ship, nab the scientist, and make like a shepherd."

"A shepherd?" Lahm asked.

"Yeah, we're getting the flock out of here," Mack said, finishing his medic's joke. He switched his L-comm over to the sniper playing babysitter for their new acquisition. "Shy, we're making our way to the crash site. We have Nuzon Royal Marine Corps on outer cordon. Make sure you move on the quiet and explain to the major why we aren't going to flash-ident ourselves to the locals."

The unit slithered from the building behind Tommy, launching a slew of miniature observation bots into the early morning sky. Once their gyros sensed the frenetic motion from the seamball like toss, they extended activated repulsors and soared off to survey the area.

In keeping with their positions as Alpha Section operators, both Sabine and Lahm kept tight to their Legion counterparts without an issue. While Mack had no doubt the Alpha technicians would have probably made it a quarter mile before needing an AED, these two seemed like they spent a considerable amount of time looking meek while training to be as dangerous as possible. Lahm looked like one of the locals who spent his days burning his meager wages on the VR cafe's due to his lighter skin and stringy physique, while Sabine looked like a Khabar woman, easily dismissed and overlooked until it was too late. The terrorists masquerading as a religious organization had spent decades strapping bombs to their women; it was only fair the Republic turned one of theirs into a weapon against them.

A light jog for the team transitioned into a security halt just outside of the Passida Metro Mall. Abandoned cars and rickshaws littered the streets leading up to the multi-level shopping center at the end of the four-lane road feeding what would have been a busy intersection. Reeds and grasses savaged the duracrete from between the cracks leading into the open air as the native plant life worked its way toward the sun, despite man's best efforts to tamp it down. Ahead of them, a murocah, a type of predatory lizard, undulated through the intersection, darting between the forgotten vehicles and plunging into the river leading away from Kerhott and into the sea.

The leejes became shadows, finding hides and perches amid the crumbling architecture. Mack flowed into the shadows of a tractor trailer, tucking in behind the back skids of the now silent repulsor truck. "Tommy, what do you got?"

"Looks like the marines, one floor down from the top of the mall. If I had to guess, they're looking to stalk and chalk a bunch of Khabar," Tommy confirmed, pushing the drone feed into everyone's HUD.

Mack flipped through several channels before settling on his sniper. "Shy, you got anything moving?"

"Just my opinion of the point. He's actually done this before and is pretty good at it," the sniper quietly said. "He's got a bead on a small detachment of Khindo Khabar moving around to the structure's loading dock. If I had to guess, the unit inside the mall are acting the part of bait for the marines. The real hitters come in from behind and catch them in a crossfire, Top. The marines are about to get slagged."

Mack leaned against the repulsor truck's landing strut to face Sabine and Lahm. "If we steer these boys, will they take the hint or will they just start shooting?"

Sabine with quick with an answer. "If this is a Royal Recon element looking to capture Khindo Khabar for intel, they're not going to risk a firefight against an unknown. They were trained by Republic MARSOG. They won't just go off half-baked."

"Roger that. Shy, it's Mack. Feed a round ahead of them and see if they get the message," Mack said.

A tense few heartbeats went by without no sound reporting from the rifle or the glass breaking on the mall across the street.

Shiloh called over the L-comm, "Major Tyler is very insistent about contacting the marine element instead of your directive, Mack."

"I swear, I'm going to break my boot off in that point's backside when this is done," Mack muttered. He rubbed his fingers across his gloved palm, pressing deep enough to feel the scars written into his flesh. A flip of his tongue against the helmet control toggle and Mack was broadcasting over a private channel with his new officer. "Major Tyler, is there a problem?"

"I was quiet before when our contact suggested I wasn't old enough to hang out with the grownups. New guy on the team. I get it. But I'm not wrong about this. We shouldn't be guiding the recon marines by fire. We should contact them and loop them into the operation."

"I see. And would this be a line protocol you're suggesting for the operation, Major?"

"To a degree, Master Sergeant. You see, in the line—"

Mack was starting to think he should have thrown the major out of the shuttle without a chute. "In the line, you have time to link up with indigenous forces and vet them for their allegiances before coordinating units. You also have a company of leejes behind you, so if things go pear-shaped, you have those maniacs ready to lay the hate on any local that ain't loyal. We have twelve, not counting you, and no way to accurately vet who's who.

"And since you couldn't have had time to read the intel packet before joining us, allow me to inform you, sir, that the local marine corps has Khindo Khabar loyalists in their ranks. When their enlistment is up, they go back to their little shop of terrors and teach all their buddies how to kill it like a marine. So, if you would be so kind as to confirm the marines over there have your seal of approval at being terror-free, I'll be more than happy to call them."

"Master Sergeant, while I can appreciate the tough position you're in as a result of Captain Rashad being pulled from the mission, I will no longer tolerate the blatant insubordination from this team," Tyler said with a mouthful of quiet menace.

"I see, sir," Mack said. "Then we should immediately yoke your many missions of battlefield recovery and extraction experience. By all means, sir, call them."

"Since I don't have the freq, I'll leave that to you, Master Sergeant," Tyler said triumphantly, ignoring the petty insults coming from the master sergeant and going straight for his command authority.

"Right away, sir," Mack said. He looped Shiloh into the call. "Shy, it's Mack. Pursuant to Major Tyler's request, we are to make immediate contact with the recon unit to our front and warn them of the danger they face. Direct two shots at them so they know to look for threats. Mack out."

Somewhere in the night, a round punched through the crysteel window just ahead of the marines. Their training kicked in along a mad scramble for a safe bit of cover that would withstand whatever had just punched through a reinforced window to play havoc with the nearby wall. Another round savaged the window behind them, shattering the pane into tinkling glass and falling debris.

"Mack, it's Shy. That Khindo unit is making a run for the roof and the one moving in behind our potential friends just pulled deeper into the floor they're on. Looks like they're coordinating with the unit on top."

Mack brought another member of the team into the mix. "Tommy, what's your bird's-eye view saying about our marine force?"

Tommy pushed several windows into the overlay, allowing the leejes in the comms chain to manipulate the drone feeds as they saw fit. "Got a technical coming to pick up that lower batch of bad guys. Looks like they're leaving their buddies to get rolled up by the marines. Also, Marine QRF is rolling in at them right now. Got a Reiner and Royce Twenty-One Eleven combat sled coming in at them full of angry, gun-toting recon guys. This place is going to be busy."

"Master Sergeant?" Rooster called into the net. "If I may make a suggestion? I would use the confusion of the ensuing firefight to take this route directly to the downed shuttle. These buildings would provide excellent cover and allow us to slip through in all the crazy."

"Why yes, Rooster. What an excellent idea," Mack said, mimicking the man's academic tone. He switched his L-comm to address the rest of the squad. "We're moving along the following track. Front and back side security on a swivel watching out for additional units rolling in from either faction. Shy, pick up and get a bite on the crash site."

Sabine shimmied across the dirt that collected under the landing struts for the mammoth transport vehicle they were hiding beneath. The sound of her faded fatigue pants grinding along the grit made Mack reflexively close his hands to feel the scars again.

"We have people securing the crash site, but with all this attention, we won't have it locked up for long," Sabine said, urging less antagonism in the team and more movement toward the objective.

"Solid copy. You think they're in the market for a slightly used point?" Mack responded.

Sabine chuckled as she tucked her scarf around her face. "Couldn't hurt to ask."

"And speaking of asking," Mack started, "I have this nagging question that's been bothering me since we got here. Khindos, your *people*, you. All of you are pretty keen to step into an active quarantine zone without so much as a hazmat suit. What gives?"

Sabine shrugged. "People started paying big money to Omar's people to get into the city. People left in a hurry and that meant leaving things behind. Some were willing to drop big credits to get those items back. It didn't take long before a bio-suit got ripped and nothing happened to the guy in it. After that, word spread pretty quick."

"So if there's nothing here getting people sick, why is the government still enforcing the no-go zone?" Mack asked.

Sabine touched her finger to her nose to let the master sergeant know he was on point with his question. "If I figure that out, you'll be the first person I tell. Well, maybe one of the first ten."

11

If Mack had been regular army, his job as a platoon sergeant would position his people to have all the snacks and charge packs they could handle to make it through the mission. Keeping everyone fed, fit, and ferocious was expected of every Army and Marine NCO running a platoon on mission. As a Valkyrie, Mack's job contained all of that along with the added responsibility of commanding the team in the field. The officers handed out the mission; the team sergeants executed.

He didn't need to dole out jobs to his people as they set up shop in a building overlooking the crash site. Except for Major Tyler, legionnaires knew their role backwards and forwards unless they were caught unawares. In those rare times, leejes would perform the act most unholy and unthinkable to any officer. They would improvise. If the old saying among the Legion officer corps was to be believed, the best way to minimize destruction was to keep a leej according to plan.

But while Mack was new to the Pelicans, he knew the associated personalities, and that made them easy to wrangle. The guys on mission with him had spent years honing their craft, so that each operation was just another day at the casino, and they already knew where to sit when the cards got dealt. Mack looked up from the surveillance in his bucket to see Shy moving through the blacked-out building.

"You got my guy?" Mack asked.

"Tag in, tag out," the sniper responded. He took the black case carrying the spotting optics with the tripod from the major and shook the man's hand. "If you want to legit try out for the teams, Major, I'll put in a good word about what you did on the scope today."

"Thank you, Sergeant Abesina," Tyler said. The major withdrew as Shiloh threw the case to Rooster, who stepped up to take the officer's place.

"Haven't been here five minutes and Top's trading me out. Was it something I said?" Rooster asked the group.

Mack flicked his hand toward the sniper. "Don't care. I only care that you're dive-rated."

Rooster's shoulders bobbed, a sign he was laughing in the armor. He trotted off with Shy to disappear into the darkness of the hallway outside the building.

"Why does he need to be dive-rated to act as a spotter?" Tyler asked.

"He doesn't, sir," Mack responded. "Just a personal joke between us."

Sabine stepped up to them, unwrapping her face from her scarf and leveling a smoldering look directly at Major Tyler. Her hard stare spoke volumes about what she thought of Tyler being there, and the Master Sergeant yielded to her with his hands at his sides in surrender. She was going to have her say, and he knew better than to be the go-between.

"Major Tyler, I'm Sabine. I'm an Alpha Section Special Warfare Agent assigned as a deep cover operative on Nuzon. Sabine is not my real name, and this is not my real face, so I have zero fear of what I'm about to say coming back to bite me.

"We have a group of militant criminals guarding the wreckage of the ship for us. They're acting like they're stripping it of anything useful, when in reality, they're keeping the Khindo Khabar away from it. I have spent nearly two years of my life developing these assets and on the best of days, I describe our relationship like walking a razor-sharp tightrope. With that in mind, if you do anything to kark this up for us, I will knife you in the spine. Do we have an understanding, Major?"

Major Tyler broke away from the woman's intense gaze and looked at Mack. "Are you just going to let her threaten a Legion officer like that?"

Mack shook his head while keeping his eyes locked onto the major's. "Unlike your line units, we've gotta work near the scary things in the dark out here. Sabine just dropped a bucket of brutal in front of you and you didn't even flinch because you didn't bother to see what was in it."

Tyler snorted. "None of what you just said even makes sense."

Sabine re-wrapped her face in the scarf as she pushed her way between the two men. "It means exactly what I said the first time: if you screw this up for us, I make you pay for it in pain."

Lahm held his hands up as he shimmied between the two leejes, joining them as they watched Sabine angrily depart. "Sorry, guys. She's wound kinda tight. I'm sure she means nothing by it. I'm pretty sure those four people she killed by hand in front of their commander had it coming. You're probably good, though, sir."

Lahm took off after Sabine before Tyler could answer, leaving the officer staring, horrified, as the pair descended the stairs.

"Catch," Mack said, breaking Tyler out of his disbelief by throwing another spotter scope. "I need you to watch the far alley while Sabine and Lahm go down there to negotiate for us."

"Master Sergeant, I am not going to assist that woman in doing anything," Tyler hissed to keep his voice down. "We should take our forces down there and liberate the craft from the four guards before calling in the local marines to secure it."

"Major, things are not what they appear. I thought you were with Marine Reconnaissance?"

"I was. Platoon commander with Bravo Company, Second Reconnaissance Battalion, before being moved up to staff." Tyler's chest nearly inflated in a practiced show of where to pin the medals.

"How long did you spend as the PC?" Mack asked.

Tyler continued his resume while Mack looked out the window. "Not that it matters, but I was on the guidon for six months during a training rotation before getting moved to staff. I served a year as the liaison for Second REC before qualifying for a slot in Legion selection."

"I see," Mack said flatly. "Well, sir, all that time with recon qualifies you to turn on that very pricey piece of Legion kit you have in your hands. Can you look toward the alley at your nine o'clock and tell me what you see?"

Tyler followed Mack's request, drawing in a sharp breath as he did so. The spotting scope transitioned through several low-light vision modes when the high-gain thermal read temperature variations from the side of the buildings framing the alley. It flashed an alien with flat ears in the corner of the display, a designation for anomaly detected, and then switched to another vision mode. Low-yield microwaves burst from the transmitter on top of the scope, passing easily through the structure while being read by the device's receptor. The magnetic imaging took in surface vibrations, structural anomalies, and density patterns before the scope rendered an image of no less than nine men in one building and seven in another, waiting. The weapons lying around the empty apartments were a glaring red flag that they probably weren't here to see about better accommodations.

Rather than reminding the surprised officer there was a better-than-average chance many of the men down there were marine-trained, he said, "Let me know if those guys hit the street."

Mack took stock of his men and their reports on scene, detailing the positions they were in, the targets they were covering, and routes of escape. Beyond the lifeless high-rises and skeletal shops, the K-15 tank bot ticked along the grassy terrain, ready to level quick, indirect fire before rocketing into the square. The unknown in all of this was the Khindo Khabar.

Sabine walked casually past the barricades that once separated the very metropolitan building behind her from the lush grass, now grown wild in the park. The lush landscape bowed under her weight with a spongy give until she crested over the first part of the crater marring the luscious terrain. As though a cultivation bot had gone off script and torn up the park, the long impact crater had plowed through the grass, ripped past the once glorious pond, and ended by crashing into a playground. The cause of this scar in the land was the crashed shuttle, and the ship was now embedded into an igloo of playground climbing bars, turning it into a giant crushed spider.

A burly man wearing drab olive army fatigues, a plate carrier, and a balaclava over his face waited for Sabine. She shook the man's hand, punched him playfully in the plate, said something too quiet for the others around the fallen ship to hear, and the two shared a hearty laugh. While the men surrounding the downed shuttle seemed at ease, their hands holding their rifle's pistol grips was a clear indicator that they were still alert and ready for things to go south.

Sabine activated her earwig communicator. Everything spoken from that point onward would be in Mack's ears as well.

"So, no Omar today, Yon?" Sabine asked.

The burly criminal held his hands out in surrender. "He heard about your dustup at Haloska's place." The man wagged a finger in Sabine's face without menace. "He loves you like a little sister, but wasn't keen to be in your way, just in case things were still hot."

"Me, hot?" Sabine asked. "I'm as cool as they come, Yon."

"Tell that to Haloska's boy. You broke his arm."

"They broke their word, Yon. I didn't come back to this mud hut of a planet just to be treated like some *putangina*, thrown into a burka, and plopped in a corner. I brought serious tech and connections with me from the Repub, and I have as much to gain or lose as the rest of you. I don't care that Nino works for Haloska or that Haloska works for Keem. And I would have done the same to *him* if he'd tried me like that."

Yon offered Sabine a cigarette. When she declined, he leaned down to draw out a burning stick from the tiny fire to light it. "I would've paid to see that. Keem talks very strong, but sometimes he doesn't always pay. Always the gods or the prophets or whatever. Funny how the prophets only want us to go without pay and never tell *them* to pay double, eh? But you, you always pay. You always deliver, Sabine."

"Speaking of which, this is for Omar." She handed over a credit chit and followed it up with a waxed pastry box. "And here's a little something for you and the boys to keep you warm while we work."

"You're good people, little sister." Yon raised his hand above his head, spinning the cigarette around so that his people could read the signal from the adjacent buildings. "Try to make it quick, huh? Keem's people are still hunting for that lady that came from the shuttle."

"We'll be here and gone before you know it."

"That's our cue," Mack said through the team link. "Throw on the ponchos and keep your weapons out of your hands. Shy and Rooster are on overwatch."

"Excuse me, Sergeant?" Major Tyler said as the legionnaires filed around him down the stairs. "Why are we—"

Mack toggled the private channel and cut him off. "Major, as per our actual commander's orders, you are here as an observer. Hands off a weapon until we're away from the ship. Nonnegotiable."

Another tongue touch in his bucket and Mack had a direct line to Tommy.

"Yeah, boss?"

"Tommy, I need you to monitor the major's comms. As the team electronic engagement operator, do you have command override for our gear?" Mack asked.

"I got what you're laying down, Top. I'll put him on an eight-second delay and monitor for anything hinky."

"Thanks, Tommy," Mack said as he followed Tyler down the stairs and into the playground just outside of their building. Clad in their camouflage cloaks, the legionnaires fanned out around the crash site like a hungry vuline pack. Mack and Tyler neared Sabine and Lahm with their hands visible, folded at their waist.

"Top, it's Creep. Pilot is dead. But I have two marines alive. Going to need you in here."

Mack transitioned his hands from his waist to holding them upwards to show he had nothing in them. "Sabine, I got two injured inside and Creeper needs another set of hands."

"What?" Sabine barked. "Yon, there are survivors inside?"

The Khabar fighter flicked ashes from his cigarette and gave an unconcerned shrug. "Sure. We checked everything over before we called you and found them alive. My sister's a paramedic in the city. We convinced her and a coworker to come out. Figured we'd get a bonus if we did what we could to save them."

Sabine gave a wry smile. "You crafty son of a... Good job, Yon. You tell Omar he just scored big."

"Meh. We do what we can." Yon flicked the cigarette toward a broken swing set.

Mack and Tyler jogged over to the downed ship. The side was split apart as though it were a present some giant three-year-old had ripped open. Mack ducked the sharp impervisteel and used a bent support strut to swing himself in. A woman with a head covering and a colorful medic flight suit looked up at the approaching legionnaires. She gave a small smile and then returned to going over the man's injuries with Creeper's two medics. Another man knelt beside her, his sleeves twisted up past his elbows—the coworker Yon had mentioned. Long-dried blood dotted his forearms as he handed Creeper an IV bag.

Creeper gave introductions. "Mack, this is Doctor Alvarez. He's got this guy patched, but we got some serious injuries and he's already operated on him twice to keep him alive."

"This man needs to be taken to a hospital," the doctor insisted.

Mack nodded. "Soon as we can. What do we got?"

Creeper moved the blanket keeping the hullbuster warm after the doctor cut away his armor and top. A large metal strut protruded out of the man's abdomen. A standard skinpack, cut into a disc and caked with blood, covered the man's wound. Creeper's notes slid into Mack's HUD, showing that the doctor had arrived on scene, found the man alive, and performed significant field surgery to close off any bleeding while protecting still functioning blood flow.

"Doctor, my name is Mack. This is good work."

The doctor nodded in respect. "Thank you. But we couldn't move him, or I'd have taken him to a hospital myself. The metal is too strong for us to cut with what we have on hand."

"What you've done saved his life," Mack said, looking about the shuttle's interior.

Omar's people had proven why Sabine worked with them. They knew a good opportunity when they saw it and were not afraid of the hard work it took to make it happen. The cargo compartment, although compressed, was littered with medical equipment. Beeping alarms and flashing lights displayed the patient's status and transformed the otherwise dark space into a strange flickering disco. Sabine must have paid heavily in bribes and favors to keep the marine alive, and the Khabar were happy to provide the service.

Mack noted the man's vitals were good enough to get him out of there, but the piece of the shuttle in his gut would have to remain until they could get him to an actual hospital. Scanning the shuttle-compartment-turned-ICU, the master sergeant didn't see any extraction gear. Good thing they hadn't try to pull the pinned man free using equipment not up to the task.

"We'll handle this part," Mack said, shaking the doctor's hand. He brushed aside the clutter of spent medical packaging, sponges, and bandages, eventually moving on to move the tray someone had set up for instruments the doctor had used to save the marine's life. "Lobster, I need you in here on the quick. Just make sure not to spook our friends keeping watch outside."

"On it, Top," the man said through the L-comm in his nasal voice.

Mack waved the point over while continuing to push instructions into the net. "String, put Maggie on standby and get in here with an icer." Mack spun on his knee to bucket to bucket with Major Tyler. "Sir, I need you to wrap your mitts around the piece of impervisteel sticking out of this man's stomach."

"I... uh... I'm not trained for that."

"Shy said that you were good on that scope earlier. I watched you too. Steady hands. That's what I need now, Major. I need a steady set of hands. This doctor did a bang-up job of keeping our marine alive, and we want to reward that effort by making sure we're not the cause of any harm. You feel me? You hold onto this and don't let it move, not even a hair. This is your patient now, Major. His life is literally in your hands."

The major continued to stare at the metal protruding from the man's side. "But what if I..."

Mack pulled a rod from his equipment belt. He pressed the instrument to the man's skin and passed the data from it into Tyler's bucket. "Right here we have his small intestine, the cecum, and appendix. The metal nicked the intestine, but the doc sealed that off for now. The rest of it looks good, and if lucky, a quick trip to a med bay and this guy can go on to bust hulls for a bit longer. But not if that piece of steel shifts and shreds him like grated cheese. Your job, Major, is to hold this steady."

"Behind you, Top," came the nasally voice of the Legion breacher. Lobster climbed into the hull, nearly hanging upside down in order to get a better look at what he was dealing with. "Oh yeah, man. This doc is like Finestro. Ya know, that kid a few years back who did all those hand paintings all the net jocks turned into anti-government memes? The memes were crap, but that art? I tell ya. Anyway, the doc has foam body supports to keep the guy angled just perfect for working on. I can reach the pipe. String?"

Sitting between the two patients, Stringer messed with a bot that looked like a metal crab with a bottle on its back. "Set. Bot has enough gas for a two-minute hard burn. After that, we need the last of its three-minute gas time to cool the steel enough so we can change out the bottle."

"Done," Lobster said.

"Tyler, are you ready?" Mack asked.

"Yes, Master Sergeant."

"It's just Mack." Mack looked too the Doctor and then tapped the visor of his bucket. "Doctor, this is gonna be bright. You might want to look away. Alright, kids. Hit it."

Stringer let the crab legs unfurl, setting the mini-version of the Maggie-mech beside the padding holding up the marine. Lobster produced a cutting torch and gripped it at an angle above the shard. One slip with the torch, and the marine's less than formidable flesh would blister and sizzle away. Not good.

A pulsing countdown timer flashed in everyone's HUD. First three red lights. Then three yellow. After the third green dancing light dot disappeared, Lobster's torch flared to life. The miniature crab bot sprayed a nitrogen blast just beyond where the torch was cutting, keeping the metal surface cold past where it was going molten. While gobs of liquid impervisteel hit the floor, the bot had the spray perfectly angled to account for the cutting torch's heat against the metal shard.

"Thirty seconds," Stringer called into the clock.

Major Tyler gripped the metal shaft, his hands as steady as when he held the spotting scope. Mack approved. Hopefully, that would keep the officer out of their way while they worked the scene.

Stringer pushed another update into the team over-lay. "One minute."

"Three quarters of the way through," Lobster croaked as he hung upside down in a bulkhead, his plasma torch blazing.

"Two simple little tools and we can free this man," Doctor Alvarez commented. "How much further good could we do if we had such things?"

"You wouldn't be worried about what the people around you could do with kit like this?" Mack asked. He was careful to keep any hint of mocking out of his voice, being more concerned with the man's answer than he was about making a statement about the people on Nuzon.

"No. If I use it to save one life, I be saving the world for that person. Who knows what they could accomplish with a second lease on life?" the doctor said and injected something into the marine's IV bag.

"Fate is funny that way," Mack admitted. He tapped Tyler on the shoulder and directed his gaze to the marine's discarded helmet. It had a vinyl patch with a smiling skull holding an anchor in its teeth, declaring, *Marine Raider*.

Under his own bucket, Tyler gave the tiniest nod, concentrating on his task. Mack could read it on him—*Keep it still. Hold it down. Do no harm. Hold it down. Do no harm.*

"Minute thirty," Stringer interrupted, snapping his finger to get Lobster's attention.

"Ten seconds, Captain Pushy," Lobster responded.

A metallic snap sounded through the bay, transferring some of the marine's weight onto Mack, Tyler, and the doctor.

"We got him. Tyler, keep that spike steady, sir," Mack called out. "String?"

"Maggie is prepped and ready for evac," the Legion bot handler said.

"Good deal," Mack acknowledged. "Ducky, it's Mack. I need a MEDEVAC to meet Maggie at the edge of the city. Set that up for me, will ya?"

"Wilco," called the Pelican's tactical air controller. One word and the operator was already in the net arranging transport for the wounded while working with the rest of the team to establish a landing zone for pick up.

"Prepping two skids," Creeper said over L-comm.

Ahead of them, Tommy scoured the pilot's compartment. He worked around the cockpit like an H8 junky who'd lost his fix between the couch, slipping through the dangling mess of wires, crushed struts, and ravaged view port. A push here and a pull there, Tommy dug until he signaled he had what they came for.

"Bird's on station, Top," Ducky said into the L-comm. "Got some back flash for you too, once we're clear."

"Got it," Mack replied.

Creeper removed a piece of rolled plastic from his pack, spreading it out behind him in the only part of the troop bay large enough to do so. He slid back a compartment in his gauntlet and tapped a button. The plastic's micro-cell surface reacted to a current burst from the armor, which caused the sheet to go from flexible to solid with a hard snap.

Using all available hands, the crew inside the downed shuttle transplanted the impaled marine onto the litter, using elasti-bands to secure him in place. Creeper and Fresher hoisted the marine from the deck, and through a combination of crashed-ship-obstacle-course gymnastics, they ferried the stretcher from the downed craft. Moments later, they were back to recover the second Raider.

"This guy has the three C's, Mack." Creeper indicated toward the last marine. "Definitely not ambulatory, but nowhere near as karked as the other guy."

Major Tyler looked up from his gloves soaked with the marine's blood. "Three C's?"

"Concussed, contused, and confused. Bulkhead hit him pretty good when it buckled during the crash. Separated right shoulder and broken humerus. Three ribs broken from the bulkhead, hitting his side plate like a seamball bat," Creeper said.

The aid and litter crew removed the second marine as Mack made room for them to move past. "Doctor, ma'am, you're probably going to want to get out of here. It's not going to be safe to be in here."

"Understood," the doctor said. "What about all of our medical equipment?"

Mack pointed to the emergency medical monitor near his boot. "We'll help you pull out the big gear. Small stuff is going to take too long. Let's just say this ship is about to lose all its value."

The doctor waved to show he understood. "Ah. You're going to blow it back to Utopion. Good. It was stinking up the place, anyway."

Laughing, Mack held out his hand. Alvarez took hold of the monitor and Mack's glove, giving both a firm grip as he picked his way along the twisted insides of the shuttle. Yon's sister likewise picked up the heavier of the instruments, an anesthesia infuser that would probably cost someone their career if it wasn't returned.

Motioning to the remaining gear, Mack said, "On our way out, everyone picks up something to help these people. I don't know if they're being compensated for all of this or not, but the least we can do is to help move the kit they'd probably have a hard time replacing."

Tommy reached for a surgical box on his way out of the ship. He stopped just long enough to stare at Mack when the team sergeant thumbed toward the hole in the shuttle to get his team moving in the desired direction.

"What was that about?" Tyler asked.

Mack tapped the side of his bucket. "Status update. Tommy cloned and crushed the secondary black box for the shuttle. Key logs, security codes, maintenance records. Stuff like that. We only had to worry about slagging the secondary because the primary isn't here."

"Why would your tech keep that from me?" Tyler growled.

"He didn't. He reported it to me, and I'm reporting it to you, sir," Mack said. With the explanation given and the major's hunt for rank validation in check, the team sergeant gestured to the gaping tear in the shuttle's hull. "Shall we?"

Tyler gave an enthusiastic nod. "About time, Master Sergeant. Let's go out there and get our box back."

Mack dropped his glove onto the man's shoulder plate and halted the officer's heroic charge out of the ship. "Sir, the recovery and transfer protocol was entered prior to the black box being yanked. All of that was in the mission brief. Neither the Khindo Khabar nor the criminals pulled it. The marines onboard did."

"Oh," Tyler whispered. He shrugged off Mack's grip, staring at a fixed point through the hull for a moment. "You should have led with that, Master Sergeant."

12

When Mack exited the shuttle, Sabine and her allies were waiting.

"Big Mack!" Sabine said. "Yon has people on the roof. They're telling me Dosa Keem has a crew running towards us."

"We blown?" Mack asked.

Sabine shook her head. "If we are, it's not my people. Either way, you need to be somewhere else."

"Don't have to tell me twice." Mack cut his bucket's external speakers and brought his next round of barking into the L-comm. "All Pelican Elements, this is Mack. Change of mission. I need two sets of hands on the litter to make the LZ. The rest of us, go for roost."

Creeper pointed to his medics. In response, a duo of Valkyrie leejes flowed around the major to reach the litters. Fresher and Blanks produced a pyramid-shaped device from their packs, which they attached to the corner of the electro-formed stretcher. With a snap and a hum, the devices sparked to life when they locked onto the plastic. The litters bearing the marines floated to roughly waist height, making for an easy push by the legionnaires.

Fresher guided the two skids together until the micro-repulsors latched onto one another. He pointed to the city outskirts and began his run into the shadows while the other medical leej, Blanks, sprinted ahead with his rifle at the patrol ready.

"Shy, it's Mack. Status on incoming?"

"They weren't wrong, Top. Got two technicals full of angry dudes heading our way, north of your position. Most likely entrance will be the access road to the park leading southwest into the playground. I can see rifles and they have some sort of heavy gun locked to the center of the bed."

"Good copy. Pelican is on the roost," Mack responded. He turned to Sabine, shaking her hand, then Lahm's. "Thanks, you both. Always a good day to bring another heartbeat home."

While the team said their goodbyes, Yon lit another cigarette, passing it back and forth over his head instead of running it in a circle. At seeing the signal, the members of the gang poured out from the buildings along the parkside edge. Dressed in mostly jeans and T-shirts, the men were also armed with PK-9 blaster rifles and an assortment of various styles of body armor. They fanned out into the playground to surround the wounded shuttle with Sabine and Lahm disappearing among their number.

"Tommy. Set it off," Mack said into the L-comm.

A brilliant flash lit the interior of the shuttle, slowly phasing to a blueish flicker as apocalyptic heat and flames consumed the inside of the craft. The wood chips covering the playground caught fire, bathing the area in an eerie kaleidoscope of color as blue and orange flames flickered in the dark.

With each floor they climbed, Mack stopped to take note of the Khindo Khabar soldiers standing around the flame like some forge lit bonfire. The shadows played off their faces as though darkness and fire had transformed them to the terracotta warriors Mack had seen on Kabillon during his last time out. Seven rescues during that campaign, and the one with the statues haunted him the most.

His team had to sift between the sculpted rows representing some lost tribe of soldiers from a past that no one really remembered. Rumor had it they depicted Savages from the days when they raided the galaxy. Some conspiracy theorists even suggested that within those stone effigies lay real Savage marines, dormant and waiting for some code to wake them to their dread purpose.

Mack didn't believe any of it. All those statues, and now the men in the park acting like them, reminded him of his team. His boys. He dug his fingers into his palm again, feeling the scars there.

How do you forgive yourself when you're reminded of your failure whenever you close your hands or eyelids? Mack wondered, wondering further if he ought to go ahead and get those scars repaired. It was an easy procedure.

He put the thought on the other side of the *Not Now* wall in his mind and finished the climb into one of the many buildings surrounding the park.

After checking on Major Tyler, Mack had to agree with Shy that the man had the physical ability and the skills to do the job, which was much more than he could say for other points he'd met. The man seemed to be that rarest of appointed officers. Officers like Tyler became dead set on proving everyone wrong, proving they were capable of doing the job, so they went through the training necessary to become a legionnaire and crushed it like it was a mission from the high heavens. If only the best would do, then they would become the best.

As Mack recalled, the House of Reason started the appointed officer program to give civilians in positions of authority access to certain military resources during times of crisis. The secretaries of Health and Life-Form Services, the Surgeon General, and certain members of the Centers for Disease Research and Control all had appointed military rank bestowed by the House. During the conflict on Psydon, the government had insisted the appointed officer program was a perfect fit for a military struggling to find qualified leaders in the wake of the Savage Wars and the slew of brushfire conflicts ravaging galaxy's edge. That was when a program that had been reserved only for the Army, Marines, and Navy was finally forced into the Legion.

Mack wondered why some enterprising leej didn't saunter up to the podium in the House of Reason and just punch the delegate in the mouth for even bringing the motion to the floor. Well, it was all ancient history now.

As he filed into the room with the rest of his leejes, Mack caught a side window in his HUD, calling for his attention. "You having as much fun as I am, TC?"

"Loads," the Alpha Section commander admitted. "I love digging into all the government stupid and then being forced to dance around it so I don't get it on my shoes."

"Same," Mack agreed. He grunted his response more than he'd wanted to, out of a sense of awkwardness in dealing directly with the Alpha Section. With Raptor hemmed up in whatever this point business was, it fell to him to work with the A-Sec commander. "TC, I got a short SITREP for you. We're done with SSE. All sensitive items were either taken or torched. No sign of the principle so we're moving onto alternate target site to pick up the trail.

"Good Copy. I'm hot dropping a file to you while you seem to be stationary for the next few. Lahm says you're waiting for the Khindo Khabar to pass you by," TC said.

Mack found Tyler being attended to by Creeper. The senior team medic had the man's gloves off and seemed to be checking him for cuts and abrasions after holding the steel bar in the marine's stomach. It would give him enough time to finish this conversation with TC.

"As soon as they roll through, we'll take a run on the doc," Mack said. "What's up?"

"Take a look at that file. Something is off here, and you seem to have a good eye for when something's off. My team went to great lengths to keep Raptor off the MED-DET's radar. So either I have a leak in my team, which is next to impossible, as I know what the back of everyone's teeth looks like, or..."

Mack laughed at the joke, hoping it wasn't too obvious to the major. The man seemed to have his own personal tic detector to decipher everyone's little tells for when they might be talking about him behind his back. Probably a skill necessary when you got appointed to a position you didn't deserve. Still, the joke was funny. TC knew what everyone's back teeth looked like because, as the A-SEC Commander, he'd practically scoped them from back end to back teeth, just to make sure every team member was on the level.

"... the House of Reason has a heavy interest in this doctor and needed the Legion officer out of the way. What that says about her, I don't know."

"I'll run it over when I'm not running down the doc herself. SSE collection and destruction complete on target site one. Thanks for this, TC. Any word on our boy?" Mack asked.

"Raptor went from the dock to locked in his quarters, from what I understand," TC said as though he were coughing. "Outta here."

After TC cut the call, Mack approached his most senior leej, Creeper, working on their blood-stained officer. "How's the patient, doc?"

"I'm fine, Master Sergeant," Tyler quickly responded. "The sergeant was just helping me to sterilize my gloves from all the blood I got on them, in the event I must dirty them up again."

"We tend to get muddy and bloody in this job, Major. If Creeper's done with you and you don't mind, I'm going to want you by me while this thing goes down." Mack pointed to a pile of stacked desks and assorted furniture at one end of the otherwise empty floor.

The duo moved to the stockpile, positioning chairs and laying long faded curtains about so they could rig buckets and scopes to watch the scene play out below them. Handing over the spotter scope again, Mack put the major in the most advantageous position by which he could spot for the team. At least he was good at this.

"Got multiple mics set up on this," Creeper said. "We'll hear everything going on down there."

Mack's bucket nodded in time with Creeper's assessment. "Just got an intel drop from A-SEC. I have a Royal Marines freq for you. Wait on Rooster's call, but let's see what Sabine and her guys can do before we risk spoiling their plans by rolling in the marines."

"Roger, out," Creeper said, cutting the comms.

Mack worked his battle board until he noticed Tyler periodically looking at him. "You got something for me, Major?"

"I hate to be the guy constantly asking questions, Master Sergeant, but yes."

Mack let the conversation hang for a moment as he co-opted the feed from Stringer's drones flying overhead. They had a good field of view for the engagement about to happen and would spot anything the Khindo Khabar would try to field in the event things in the park got heated. Taking a drone snapshot, he fired the image into the mapping software loaded into his bucket to make a range card for the area. As he flicked images around the virtual tabletop, Mack went back to his conversation with the appointed major, "Actually, sir, we like questions. Old saying in the teams is, when working with sister forces, the only stupid question is the one you don't ask."

The major grunted. "My OIC used to say that. Old recon leej."

"Where'd you two serve, sir?" Mack asked.

"Aboard a destroyer with a complement of leejes. I was the L-comm control officer assigned to a Legion S2 aboard the ship, there for the Legion platoon on board," Tyler said, almost as if he were reading it off a data sheet.

"The question, sir?" Mack said, steering Tyler back to the original point.

"All this... cloak and dagger. We have Gungnir Platoon waiting on deck aboard the *Reliant*. Why not just employ a light infantry raid to blow through the Khindo Khabar and recover the doctor? I was under the impression *that* was the Legion way. KTF."

"Politics, sir. It's all politics. The Khindo Khabar has been gaining ground in certain parts of the planetary government by claiming that the Republic is fleecing them. And they would be right. On the other side, the legitimate government was installed by us, aka, the Republic.

They want more pull on the House floor, so they need this rescue for the optics. And right now is where we give it to them."

"We will?" Tyler asked.

"Yes, sir. You ever do Legion combatives?" Mack asked, returning the question with one of his own.

"Not since selection, truth be told."

Mack arranged more of the virtual sand table as he talked, using augmented reality overlays in their HUDs to detail what they needed for this next bit. "I love doing combatives because it's like playing chess without being given any time to think about your next move. You do or you get the three. And to answer your next question, sir, that's a *nap, tap, or snap*, ending the fight. Combatives applies to this thing we do by showing us that victory is about timing, and at my age, a little deception thrown in for flavor. Check your HUD, sir."

The major's bucket tilted slightly away from center, causing the drapes to fall over his bucket's screen. Not that he noticed, as his primary view was piped into the bucket from the spotting scope and the side window in his display was now showing a news broadcast. "Is this live?"

"No sir. Prerecorded by the locals back at the Royal Marine Air Base. It's going to say how they found two marines alive in the crash and their Royal Marines are continuing the search for the doctor and her security team. Blah, blah, blah," Mack said, finishing his VR sand table and pushing it to the team. "We drop our marines to their marines for pickup. They get our guys to a real hospital, they get the win, and we were never here. Everyone's happy."

"Except the Khindo Khabar," Tyler said.

"Now you get it, sir." Mack said. Guys like Tyler weren't all that hard to get dialed in. They wanted what all appointed officers wanted. Validation. The hard part was teaching them validation comes on the job and not from it.

Below them, the technicals pulled into the still burning crash site. Men rushed from the beds of the trucks, which were brand new by the looks of them, to square off with Yon and the rest of the cartel. Sabine and Lahm remained among them, although their position in the back against the flickering shadows cast by the fires kept them hidden from view.

The door on the lead truck opened, spilling Haloska from the side of the cab. "Yon? No Omar?"

"Busy. Family stuff," the cartel head man responded. "Same for you? No Keem?"

"Busy. Family stuff," Haloska parroted. "The reason I'm here is we're having a tough time with a piece of equipment Omar sold us. Tracking algos aren't lining up. Come to find out the system isn't calibrated for work on Nuzon. You know anything about that?"

"I'm not a merchant. I work security," Yon said.

Something in the man's tone appeared to aggravate the Khindo Khabar enforcer, prompting him to come from behind the vehicle to stand a few paces away from Yon and his men. "And I'm not in the habit of having to deal with middlemen selling us defective junk."

Mack felt the tension rise. Long seconds passed as the commanders stared each other down. Haloska stood defiant while Yon leaned casually against the ruins of a swing set. As the men behind them shifted uncomfortably, a lone cowled fighter burst from the back of the *sicarios* to stand in between the two.

Haloska laughed, clapping slowly to show he was more amused than insulted. His lieutenant shifted uncomfortably at the newcomer as he adjusted a sling holding his right arm.

"Sabine. You show up in the damnedest places," Haloska barked. "To what do I owe the pleasure?"

"Give me the device and I'll program it for you," she said.

"And have you send me on another wild bullitar chase? No thank you," Haloska wore a humorless scowl as he spoke. "I came here to use the downed shuttle to recalibrate the scanner, and here you are with the ship in flames. Is that so I have to see you and pay you for the fix?"

"Marines rigged the shuttle to burn in the event anyone messed with it," Sabine lied. "I didn't touch the device. I got it from Omar and gave it to you. As promised. I can get it to work for you, though. I won't even charge you for the service, seeing you were so prompt in paying me the last time."

Nino reached for his pistol with his good arm, looking to end the insolent woman once and for all. Haloska stopped him with a grip on his shoulder.

"No. I deserved that," Haloska said. He turned to Sabine and snapped, "You rig it and we'll be on our way."

Sitting in rapt attention, Tyler messaged Mack, "Is this where we do it?"

"Not yet," the senior leej responded. He watched the A-SEC agent program the device and hand it back.

Haloska studied the device and smiled. "The Centigo building. I should have known that. Sabine, you're okay. I don't care what Nino says about you."

The groups kept weapons at the ready until the trucks pulled away from the park.

Mack started handing out orders. "Creeper, get us moving. Shy, we're out to the next position. Keep us on the scope."

"Roger, out," the sniper confirmed.

Mack handed Tyler the case for the optic so he wouldn't have to keep handing over the device. The major packed it away and magnetically locked it to the back of his armor as though he'd done it a hundred times before. Before the final snap secured it to its new home, REC-Team Pelican was already rushing from the structure.

"I don't get it. You didn't call anything in," Tyler questioned Mack through the comms.

"Didn't have to. Rooster confirmed an active signal the second Sabine programmed the PDT. She passed the freq to the Royal Marines who are probably tracking them right now," Mack said, stuffing his poncho back into his pack. "Come on, sir."

The major absently followed the master sergeant, listening as Mack continued his explanation. "The PDT tracker has its own mission sig. If the Royal Marines have that ID string, they can track the bad guys."

"That's... well done, Master Sergeant."

"Follow me for more cool recipes, sir. Next up is a Melocidon Twist with a splash of Pthalan rum. Pretty tasty." Mack pointed to where he wanted the major to go.

REC-Team Pelican flowed from the building just as the sounds of blaster fire echoed through the streets. The sharp cracks bounced off the abandoned cars and litter in the streets in a cacophony of violence funneled to the team through the avenues. Evidently the Marines had caught up to Haloska.

Reesh cats bounded away and sought whatever cover they could find as the team passed them by. Silently moving while drinking in mountains of tactical data from drones feeding their buckets, the Legion rescue team worked their way through the blocks on their way to the next objective.

While ducking into the open door of a forgotten pastry shop, a regular broadcast squelched into Mack's bucket over one of the standard freqs he was monitoring.

"Mack, it's Sabine. We're clear of the wreck. The power cells are out, so if you Legion boys want to do that thing you do, go for it. Hey, apologize to that point for me. Tell him I'm happy I didn't have to gut him."

Shaking his head, Mack motioned for the team to slide from the empty shelves covered in dust and mold over old wrappers on forgotten plates. Sabine was some-one who liked to poke. She knew full well that Major Tyler heard everything she just said. It didn't matter if the pok-ing was warranted or not, she just wanted to see the reac-tion the poke would get. In this case, doing it to this partic-ular point might not end in career suicide.

"You just did."

"And Lahm said you were cool," Sabine said through the comms. "Be safe, new guy."

"You too, old lady. Mack out."

A series of buildings and twisting streets through the dead city brought the leejes to a side alley just outside of a mass transit stop. A powered down kiosk, labeled as the ticketing agent, sat in eternal slumber beside a cov-ered tram stop with several glass partitions separated by duracrete outer walls. The team entered the cover with the enthusiasm of a haffa snail sliding into a new shell. The perimeter of the enclosure was cluttered with wind-tossed street trash caught against the walls, where rain and weather turned them to an ever-lurking crust against the base of the structure.

"Mack. It's Shy. Fresher and Blanks are coming back in," the sniper chirped over the L-comm.

"Have him approach from the pastry shop behind us," Mack instructed.

"Hey, Top. I didn't have time for anything on our way through. Can you have the kids pick up some snacks on their way back?" Lobster requested in his nasal droll. "Tell him I'm totally good for it."

"I'll get right on that, Lobster," Mack said drily. He'd had precious little time to spend with the team prior to jumping out, but it seemed a nod from Rocco had put him in a good spot. Normally, teams like this had a feeling out period, where everyone waited for the senior leej to crack a joke or drop some snark, just to see where the boundary lines were. As the team had watched, and cheered Mack's first hop with REC-Team Pelican, and roared at jokes made while the hulking leej was trapped in a tiny tube with the massively aggressive Drusics after the rescue, they felt comfortable enough with the man to drop in some humor here and there.

Major Tyler had another question. "Shy and Lobster are obvious enough callsigns. What's the story behind Blanks?""

Creeper was close by, covering a side of the tram stop with his rifle leaning against a protrusion in the stone. "Word is, it's all he shoots. The Skiadopoulos line dies with him, sir."

The L-comm erupted with laughter.

"Two things," Blanks said. "First, kark you, Creeper. Second, how do you explain your little brother if that's true?"

Again the comm blew up with laughter.

"You ever get a nickname, sir?" Stringer asked once the chuckled died down as he piloted his drones overhead.

"Just from my family," Tyler said. "I was the third son in line for the family business. My brothers didn't want to split things three ways, so Dad pulled some strings to get me an appointment to the marines. Screw them, I thought. I'll make my own way. Shrugged off my approval with the delegate that appointed me and went for the Legion at the first opportunity. Couple of nicknames there, but nothing that stuck, because once a point, always a point, right? No one cares enough to tag you if they think you didn't pay the ticket to ride."

"Damn, that's hard, sir," Stringer said. "You passed selection, though, right?"

"I did. But like I said, once a point... And it's nowhere else as true than in the Legion."

Shy put an end to the sharing. "Guys, I hate to interrupt when we're all finding love in the Legion, but we have a problem up ahead."

Ahead of them, the unfinished Centigo building remained locked behind a fence covered in green canvas to keep trash from finding its way through the chain-link. Cautiously slithering from between an alley, a blacked-out technical shot full of blaster holes and pocked with blast damage chugged to a stop outside the fence. Haloska dropped from the cab, holding a tricked-out PK-9 slung around his neck. The fighter, who was clean the last time the team had seen him, had his polo shirt and khaki pants stained from a combination of blood, dust, and what looked like grease. Nino, his lieutenant, dropped from the opposite side of the cab and leaned against the covered chain-link as he wiped blood from a scalp wound.

The encounter with the Royal Marines had proved less than fatal for Haloska. The accompaniment by several Khindo Khabar fighters explained why.

Two more fighters rolled from the extended cab, holding their own rifles at the ready as they scanned their surroundings. They walked away from the vehicle, shining ultrabeams into shops, down alleys, and across the street to where an entire REC-Team had camouflaged themselves to watch the building.

"Well, that's going to be inconvenient," Stringer said.

"They don't look like they have a reservation," Lobster agreed.

Mack rolled his neck. "They either dusted or got away from our royal marine friends. Time for them to find out there's no escaping the Legion."

13

It took almost no time for the REC-team legionnaires to position themselves for a hasty ambush before Haloska's slow-moving technical truck. Best guess was that Haloska knew he'd been double-crossed by Sabine and was now looking for her in all the dark places, hoping that his Khindo Khabar friends would finish what he and Nino could not.

Light from the Khindo Khabar ultrabeams swept into the transit lounge, illuminating the structure and the camouflaged leejes lying in wait. Beneath their obscuring ponchos and piles of trash, the spread-out operators worked into a killing posture for the newly arrived thugs. The essential part of any good ambush was the shooters, but security for the striker element had to be given an even amount of detail. Rampant tales of Repub Army and Marine units being counter ambushed by the Duros during the Psydon conflict a generation previous had served as an example of what not to do.

Blanks, Fresher, and Creeper retreated into recessed alleys and doorways to provide rear security for the hit.

Mack worked through sonic amplification and detection algos in his bucket, filtering out the ambient noise in the kill box to detect any other vehicles making their way in. When he was confident they would have some quality time with their targets, the master sergeant keyed a ready prompt into everyone's HUD.

On the green light, Mack and Major Tyler squeezed off mirrored blaster bolts, drilling the two flashlight-carrying insurgents between the eyes. As if the dead fighters falling to kiss duracrete were its own trigger, a silent, high-density shot fired from a much higher vantage tore through the skull of the third man. Ultrabeams tumbled from lifeless hands to cast the scene in an eerie flashing display as brain and bone matter, once belonging to Haloska's lieutenant, Nino, splattered across his face.

Standing beside his truck, Haloska gasped in shock at being covered in pieces of his friend, barely comprehending it all when legionnaires materialized out of the darkness to approach him like wraiths come to haunt the living. Their digital barks came grating from buckets, demanding that Haloska drops his weapons and raise his hands. The man quickly went from shocked to compliant.

Fresher slapped a set of ener-chains on him, the power settings ratcheted to max. The increased shock through the compliance device ratcheted up Haloska's arm when he tried to struggle against the manacle. The gangster was fully in the grip of his flight or fight response and tried a bit of both to wrench himself away.

"Got a fighter," Fresher called into the link.

Mack bagged Haloska's head with an isolation hood, completing cutting off the man's auditory, visual, and olfactory senses from the outside world. The legionnaire pulled the prisoner backward, forcing him off-balance and into a stumbling walk toward the gate.

Mack helped Fresher push Haloska against the wall beside the exterior gate, making plenty of room for Lobster to trot up and work the lock.

"Let's see if he's feeling talkative," Mack said to Fresher. He raised the Haloska's isolation hood and grabbed a handful of the gangster's hair, roughly guiding the man's face into a very up-close view of a Legion helmet. "How did you know to come here?"

"I will not talk to you," Haloska spat.

"Pulse for one," Mack said to Fresher through the L-Comm.

Fresher punched a compliance pulse through the ener-chains, shocking the prisoner rigid until the charge gave way, nearly dropping the man to his knees. Haloska panted furiously from the charge. Great gobs of drool dripped from his mouth, a sure sign that the zap had the correct effect.

"I'm raising the voltage. The next time I shock you, it'll trigger a stroke," Mack informed him. "How did you know to come here?"

"We had a tracker," Haloska admitted. "They're rechipped."

"Republic PDT trackers are high ticket. Where did you get it?" Mack asked, pressing the man's face harder against the wall.

"One of the survivors wandered outside the city!" Haloska lied. "We got it from him."

Mack released the criminal's head. "I guess a stroke isn't on the menu for you today." The Valkyrie team sergeant returned Haloska to Fresher, who dropped the isolation hood in place.

The Centigo corporate headquarters loomed above them, its unfinished building top rising out of the structure like a skeletal crown. In contrast to the rest of the city, the development appeared modern and refined, more in keeping with the Inner Core. Had the corporation completed construction, the tower would have become a beacon for other industries considering Nuzon as a commerce friendly community.

Lobster plied his skills into the gate, easily cracking the locking mechanism. Centigo security erected the chain link fence to keep people from entering the construction zone, rather than for actual security. While no one planned to stay anywhere near the city after the outbreak, some enterprising employee had the presence of mind to lock the gate on the way out. A simple clip and a snip, and the team pressed onto the main courtyard and into the overhanging architecture framing the lobby entrance.

"Tommy," Mack said into the L-Comm, calling the electronic engagement operator forward.

The operator jogged through the now open chain-link gate, past the rest of the leejes securing the expansive courtyard. By the time Tommy made the outer security door for the building, biometric sensors and security algos were thoroughly beaten into submission, granting the digital wizard access to the building's core operating systems. Arched display windows set into the blackened walls on the building's ground floor exterior granted the leejes an unobstructed view of the lobby. Brilliant marble architecture inside amplified statues of planetary heroes long past that framed the stairs and speedlifts leading higher in the building. Or at least, they would have if the building had been finished.

"Outer door is open, and I have their security under my thumb, Top," Tommy said. "Tags are in your HUD. We're getting proximity tags from the PDTs. It's a good bet the principle is inside. The A-Sec egg heads were on the money guessing they might head here."

As the rest of the team made for the door and the leejes shut the gate, a brilliant light shone from the buildings several blocks away. As the light dissipated, a rising cloud of dust and debris in the early morning sky could be seen. The blast's echo finally caught up to the visuals, rocking the duracrete beneath their feet and rattling windows throughout the block.

"That would be the local marines dropping something heavy on that shuttle, courtesy of TC," Mack said, solely for the major's benefit.

"What about the fallen marines?" Tyler asked.

Tommy answered as he motioned the rest of the REC-Team into the entrance hall. "Sabine's crew made sure they were pulled. The local forces will find them in a hot minute and broadcast another glorious victory for the people in returning their bodies to the loved ones."

The legionnaires flowed across the slick marble floor like ghosts. Between them stumbled Haloska, bent at the waist with his hands behind his back, clomping along in a frog march.

"Why did we even capture this man, Master Sergeant?" Tyler asked through the L-comm. "It makes no sense. We knew about the transmitter and the biotags. Why keep him alive at all?"

"Remember our little chat about appearances, sir?" Mack countered. "Well, when his people eventually find him, he's going to rattle off about our time together, which should throw suspicion off of Sabine, seeing he just lied to protect her."

As the team slid around the expansive welcome desk, Mack pointed to the prisoner. Fresher guided the man down to the floor, depositing him in Mack's waiting grip. Thrusting his knee into the center of Haloska's back so that it rested on the ener-chains to drag the prisoner's arms down, the team sergeant wrapped one arm around the man's shoulder and chest in a seat belt hold while his free hand tugged back on his head.

"What exactly..." Tyler exclaimed into the L-comm.

"Dead man's loop, sir," Fresher explained. "He holds his upper half and I loop this synth-cord around his ankles so I can tie it to that side of the desk. Then we lay him flat and run another around his neck. If he stays still, he's cool. But struggles bring strangles."

"Struggles bring strangles," Mack shook his head and chuckled at the phrase. "Let me know when you're good, kid."

The major knelt down next to the team sergeant, switching from the team net to their private channel. "Sergeant Mack, this is inhumane treatment for a prisoner of war. You wanted to take him, you need to take care of him."

"You're welcome to stay here and keep an eye on him, sir, or put a bolt in him to make sure he's no longer an issue. Otherwise, Creep is going to tranq him long enough for the Royal Marines to find him, and for us to disappear," Mack said.

"Set," Fresher called into the net to confirm the prisoner's ankles were locked down.

Mack slid the man across the marble until he felt the weight of the desk through corded legs. He looped his own line around Haloska's neck and ran the free running edge to the other side. A quick tug and the line went taught. The captive moved one way and then another before relaxing to the center, where strangulation wasn't an issue. The team sergeant took a hand from the younger leej and was yanked back to his feet.

"Tommy. Lead us in," Mack said through the L-comm. He tapped Major Tyler on the shoulder to pry his concern from the prisoner to their line of march.

The assault line of legionnaires stacked outside the stairwell off of the main foyer. System checks displayed in augmented reality over their HUDs, showing the shooters in the stack the security system was in their control and ready to obey, including blinding anyone to their presence.

Fresher was first in the stack. He palmed the door open, revealing an empty stairwell as quiet as the grave. The leejes were on their way to the next floor once the junior operator completed a sensor sweep for wires, multi-spectrum lasers, or anything that might give them away.

"The building had security protocols in place after somebody tripped the power five hours ago," Tommy said. "Everything on this floor was magnetically locked. Looks like they're holed up on the second."

Creeper butted into the comms traffic to put his experience through the line. "Quick reminder, the guys we pulled out the wreck were MARSOG marines. Cherry needs to double-check any hatch he crashes so we don't wear a door full of explosives."

"Roger that," Fresher responded. "I bet you look terrible in boom."

The line of leejes moving up the stairwell each took an angle to control as they stepped in time with each other.

Fresher made the landing, continuing to check for obstacles in their path that would hem them up. The leej knelt down on the landing, halting further progress on the objective. "Door is open a crack, Top. I also have what looks like a thin wire running across the last step before the landing."

Fourth in line, Stringer placed a hexagonal plate the size of a Legion challenge coin on a step. The tiny object sprouted six needle-thin strands of metal that extended nearly half a foot from it. Bends in the strands formed into spider legs, and the machine skittered its way up the railing and onto the landing, where Fresher halted.

On the team's HUD, a window popped up. The video tracked the ticking bob of the spider bot as it negotiated the steps toward their concern. It tiptoed over the wire and over to the door leading into the second floor. The bot veered around to look up at the stairs, checking for any security measures, before making its final approach. Thousands of calculations in a millisecond had the bot reasonably sure—to within a fractional percentage point—that the stairwell was free from any other low- or high-tech security alerts that would give them away.

The bot slid a viewing line through a crack in the door. Someone had rigged the wire to a series of fizz-pop cans resting on a chair beside the exit from the stairs. Tripping the wire would pull the assortment of trash onto the floor, warning anyone within earshot that they had a problem.

"Good sign," Creeper said.

Mack scanned through his SOI roster of radio procedures and frequencies for the operation. The MARSOG emergency freq highlighted in his bucket before descending along an algorithm strand into his radio for broadcast. "Any station this net, any station this net, this is Pelican Zero Seven, over."

High-gain microphones in their buckets picked up the scramble made when someone farther down the hall dropped to their feet and sifted through gear. The frantic sounds of weapons being pulled from their resting places were not lost on the team.

"Pelican Zero Seven, this is Angler One Bravo. I do not recognize your call sign. Please authenticate, sour."

Mack smiled. Good. These guys still had their faculties, which means they could probably aid in their own rescue. There was nothing better than sending a bunch of heartbeats home. "Angler One Bravo, this is Pelican Zero Seven. I authenticate tulip."

Silence followed his answer to the age-old security measure of sign and countersign. Established as part of their Operations Order, the code words would be an easy way to tell a friend from someone who just looked that way. The radio squelch finally crackled, returning the marine's voice to the comms. "Status and LOC, Zero Seven."

"LOC is a cracked doorway on a set of stairs, your POS, break. We are REC-T and waiting on your go, over," Mack said. He used the standard call sign for a Republic forces rescue team in play, hoping the man would not only know the term but accept it.

Almost on cue, two marines in plate carrier armor and helmets sporting N-6s poured into the hall. One split from the other and halted in the passage, while the other continued to advance along the wall toward the hinges of the door.

Mack put a command through his bucket to the team, walking back the stack to the base of the stairs and leaving Fresher just below the landing. Rifles remained in their assigned sector with the REC-Team leejes not giving up their triggers until the meet and greet was over.

The door slid open with only the arm of the marine visible as she pushed. The marine down the hallway kept his face through his rifle sights on what looked like an empty set of stairs. As the door swung perpendicular to the doorway, the radio broke squelch again. "Zero Seven, this is One Bravo. Face to a name, over."

Fresher stood, his arms held to his sides. He activated the speakers in his bucket so the man holding the door open could hear him. "Republic legionnaires. Six in the stairwell. Others on station."

"Oba," sighed the marine on the floor as she took sight of Fresher. "You damn near scared me out of my silkies, leej. Bring your boys in."

One by one, the leejes advanced through the doorway to meet their marine counterparts. As the second man in the stack, Mack walked past Fresher and the now kneeling doorman marine to meet the one in the middle. "I'm Master Sergeant Malcolm Banes. I'm here with a REC-Team to pull you out, Staff Sergeant."

The shooter stood from his spot in the hall, extending his hand and locking wrists with Mack. "Real good to meet you, Mack. Staff Sergeant Wrigley. If I'd known you were coming, I would've made us some kaff."

Mack patted the man on his shoulder armor. Both marines looked tired and dirty, as though the last twelve hours had been less than the trip brochure had advertised. But while they were dirty and a bit dinged up, they seemed to wear their game faces.

"Heard the kaff here sucks," Mack joked. "Better stuff with us. How's about we pull you out so I can prove it?"

The hullbusters led the recovery team through a break room and down another hallway before coming to a set of double doors. With Fresher and Stringer remaining on security at the stairs, the marines were okay with abandoning their position in the break room to bring the leejes to their charges. They entered some kind of business office. Rows of cubicles covered in plasteen protected furniture normally adorned in holo projected screens and keyboards. Each desk sported the latest in hyper-core data crypt technology—a considerable investment this far from the galactic core—except the marines had strung the costly furnishings together at the center to form a barrier for the crash survivors. A woman in jeans and a turtleneck stood at the sight of the returning marines.

Wrigley brought Mack directly to the VIP. "Ma'am, this is Master Sergeant Banes of the Republic Legion. He says his recovery team has a ride for us and I'm inclined to take him up on it."

"Master Sergeant. I'm Doctor Lasana Kavir. Has Staff Sergeant Wrigley filled you in on our situation?" the woman asked.

"Nice to meet you, ma'am," Mack said, withdrawing his hand when she didn't shake it. "The only thing he's told us is that somewhere in this escape plan, there's kaff."

Unlike most people in her position, the woman was all business. There was no excitement at being rescued, not even a hint of gratitude. Even her crystalline blue eyes were appraising much more than they were pleading. Not what Mack was used to. With his previous rescues, the eyes always pleaded. In contrast to the doctor, Staff Sergeant Wrigley's eyes went from predatory to *please get us outta here*, once Mack and his leejes convinced him they were who they said they were. Not the doctor. Her eyes were sizing him up. *Will this big oaf get in my way?* she seemed to be thinking.

"Well then. He did you a disservice, Master Sergeant. We were about to leave this location until you showed up. Our plan was to move to the Serrabi Falls facility and raze it to the ground," Kavir said, as though it were already a done deal.

Mack scanned the room. Creeper and Fresher were already assessing injuries to the marines that hadn't risen to greet them. There were three hullbusters who looked mobile, hostile, and capable of doing whatever was asked of them. One had a series of head lacerations and a covering over his nondominant eye. Despite the bandages, he seemed to be ready for a fight or a ride out, whichever came first. The last two were resting on a bed of poncho liners and bundled plastic as they slept through more serious injuries.

"Well then. If you don't need us, we can just be on our way," Mack said, thumbing back the way they came.

Kavir pursed her lips. "I don't appreciate the snark, Master Sergeant. Is there an officer among you that I can deal with? Because you're not going anywhere until I say so."

Mack looked to Wrigley, who shrugged. Before he could level his best weapon's grade argument at the woman, Major Tyler stepped ahead of him.

"Major Robert Tyler, ma'am. Republic Legion. I would be happy to discuss whatever you feel is keeping you from leaving with us."

Every leej in the room focused hard on their work. It took all of their willpower not to pitch the man out a window. They'd all heard the field reports from REC leejes who'd descended to rescue some government asset, only to be told they couldn't leave because of X reason. While the reason might well be important and well worth hearing out, the responsibility of the REC-Teams was to recover the asset. Period. Hard stop.

A Valkyrie leej was welcome, even encouraged, to listen to whatever the asset thought was important and needed to be relayed, as long as they were moving one foot, tentacle, or tail in front of the other to get them on the shuttle and back under Republic protection. Having the major come set up a tea party with the doc to talk about what she thought was important was antithetical to what they were doing here.

But the major wasn't finished, and what he said next was much more to the team's liking.

"If you would just follow us, we can talk about it on the way to the aircraft, ma'am. And if you decide to, say, fight us on this, our very capable legionnaires have enough tranquilizers with them to knock out someone twice your size."

The woman's angry stare could've melted Parminth of all its glaciers, and Mack could see her wheels turning as she looked for some way to reassert her control. Tyler held her gaze, his expression one of discipline, not arrogance. If Mack didn't know any better, he'd have pegged the man as a hard-nosed, fire-forged legionnaire.

"Top, it's Shy. We got two technicals approaching on blackout drive. Looks like twelve or more men looking to get some trigger time for the evening," the sniper said into the comms.

"Creep, how long until we can exfil?" Mack asked.

"As long as we don't have to box or burn this office of anything, we can be out of here in a deuce. These marines are ambulatory, although the two over here aren't in fighting shape. What's up?"

"Do what you can so we can make a hasty exit. We have company," Mack said before diving back into the

L-comm. "Shy, it's Mack. Is it just boots and blasters or do they have heavy gear?"

"No armored vehicles or bots. Looks like repulsor trucks and guns, Top," the sniper observed.

Mack calculated the odds of his force getting into a firefight with Khindo Khabar regulars and what that would mean for them extracting the doctor on a rocket ride out of the AO.

Meanwhile, the doctor was in the middle of berating Tyler over the Khindo Khabar's unscheduled visit.

"—because the only way they could have found us was if *you* led them here, Major," she spat.

"You had a personal tracker implanted for the trip, ma'am," Mack interrupted her. "The insurgents used a night market scanner to find you. That being said, you get your wish, because you're staying right here until we put out the *do not disturb* sign."

The team bot-jockey pushed a series of overhead feeds to the leejes, showing the incoming Khindo Khabar dismounting from the vehicle. Orders flashed through the L-comm, echoing back to confirm their receipt. The team inside the abandoned office space vanished except for Fresher and the major who remained in place to secure Doctor Kavir and care for the wounded.

Mack flowed into the hallway at the base of the stairs, with Creeper following close behind. The moment their boots contacted the marble floor, another legionnaire slipped from the shadows and took the lead. They trekked toward the welcome desk where they'd hidden their Khindo Khabar prisoner, Haloska. Farther down the hall behind them, another Legion fire team faded into a darkness full of hanging plasteen sheeting and scaffolding abandoned by workers fleeing the unfinished structure when the planet's woes began.

"Mack, it's Shy. Rooster is directing team two through the back entrance. They're going to deal with Khindos trying to sniff our butt."

"Roger, out," Mack said and went to the far side of the desk their prisoner was tied to. From there, it would be an easy hop backwards into a hallway that would grant him cover from the entrance should the need arise.

Creeper did the same on his side of the desk. The legionnaire noted that Haloska was still in place and seemed to be causing no trouble. If half the file on this kelhorn were true, it wouldn't bother Creeper in the least to put a bolt through the man. He'd just have to remember to pull the isolation hood from his head first. Those things were expensive, and he didn't want to do the paperwork to explain the loss.

Stringer sent a direct message indicating that he was in place behind a vaunted statue at the back of the foyer. The monument depicted a long-ago hero, some legendary warrior prince from Nuzon's pre-colonial era. Far and wide across Terum, architects solemnly depicted this subject with very little artistic variance. This particular sculpture's base was nearly as tall as the front desk and supported the towering visage in tribal garb holding a box kite style shield and a sword whose end resembled a chisel. Cast in bronze and standing on a marble floor, the statue must have been breathtaking in full daylight. While Stringer could appreciate the craftsmanship that must have gone into such a monument, he admired it more for its position as an observation point and its ability to act as cover.

A relentless tapping serenade against the structure as a rainstorm began to open up overhead. The dusky space outside the windows, landscaped with stone walkways and littered with empty plots that never received the trees reserved for them, became a blur behind a curtain of rain obscuring everything a few feet from the glass.

The Khindo Khabar fighters outside were quickly soaked and ran to the overhang preceding the entryway doors. There they shook and wiped away excess water from their weapons and clothing. The sudden downpour had not only soaked their clothes, but it also sapped their discipline to move as a more coherent fighting force. The fighters stood haphazardly as they wrung out their gear and lit whatever passed for cigarettes that managed to survive the sudden deluge. Almost no heed was paid to the fact that they were right on the doorstep of their targeted building, as if the pending raid for potential kidnap victims was simply another day on the job and they were just taking a smoke break.

A man in mismatched military fatigues and a plate carrier missing the back plate moved to the door and gingerly tested it to see if it was locked.

The L-comm snapped back to life with Shiloh updating the team sergeant. "Mack, it's Shy. You have seven at the door and five moving to the back. A driver is staying with each of the two vehicles they came in. You have men moving to the door with blasters, but more than a few have old-school slug throwers."

"Can you hit both drivers?" Mack asked.

"Not from this spot. Moving," Shiloh countered.

The Khindo Khabar man waved his hand, bringing up a rail-thin fighter to the security plate set into the wall. Moments ticked by as the man kept scratching his head, adjusting his stance, and fidgeting his annoyance at being unable to break the building's security. The man, who must have been the team leader, began to fidget as well. He hooked the back of the man's web gear and pulled him out of the way before pointing to the security screen.

They couldn't slice their way in, so they'd try to shoot the doors down.

The seven-man team formed themselves into a firing line across the crysteel window and opened fire. Punishing blaster strikes and chemically fired slugs slammed against the glass, each hit thudding on impact as spider-web cracks tinkled across the surface. The mad minute ended in empty charge packs and rifle mags, and the team leader called a halt to the attack.

While the shooters' side of the window was dusted with surface spanning cracks, impact craters and blaster scoring, the interior of the security window was completely intact. Mack would have taken the time to be impressed if he wasn't planning out how to best kill this team for ruining the view.

"Tommy, let 'em in," Mack huffed.

The door leading to the foyer clinked as the magnetic locking system opened. At the front of the stack, the team leader took a cursory look at the security plate near the door. With the gross amount of gunfire that had scored the surface, he didn't question his luck and pulled his way into the building.

Now the legionnaires could hear her voice, which hadn't come through the thick security glass from the outside before. "You, get over to the desk and see what else is running. Maybe we can find out what floor they're on. The rest of you, stack on either side to cover that hallway."

The skinny technician who'd tried to hack the door walked hurriedly over to the massive front desk, still dripping water from his chest rig and the messenger bag slung to his back.

Mack was hiding under the desk, which spanned near the entire wall, flanked by a hallway to each side. He aimed his pistol to just where the man's waistline ended and the underside of the desk began. He could tell by the tech's body language that the kid was trying to wake up a holographic interface with the building's system, but wasn't having any luck. Nor would he. The Legion team, hiding all around them like zombies in a graveyard, hadn't turned on the power.

The tech soon was able to troubleshoot the problem. "The power must be off."

"Get it going, then!" the team leader shouted.

The technician hurried to do whatever he could. He slapped his wet bag onto the desk and bent down, gripping the counter while his eyes adjusted to the dark underside. Water dripped from his clothes and shemagh, tapping the floor in strange patterns as he noticed an oversized bundle under the desk—Haloska. The tech grunted with curiosity and reached for the prisoner. His hand hovered millimeters above the strange fabric of an isolation hood when a metallic rattle skidding across the marble floor distracted him.

The tech's mouth dropped in horror when he saw Mack's darkened helmet move for him in a blur.

The legionnaire's pistol barked a supercharged particle into the tech's eye, snapping his head back and dropping him to the floor. Before Mack could holster his pistol, Creeper tossed twin bangers thrown to opposite sides of the foyer that exploded with a fury of light, noise, and pressure. Out from behind the desk, Creeper engaged the fighters, moving into the hallway toward the stairs. Blaster fire then erupted from the gargantuan statue, catching insurgents in the chest as Stringer punched them into the afterlife promised them for fighting against the Republic.

With bodies dropping onto the floor, a clear sign his team had handled the other shooters, Creeper dumped twin shots into the men on his side of the fight. His blaster bolts tore through the flimsy armor they wore, dropping each with precision before any of them could recover from the staggering effects of the grenades.

At the opposite end of the long desk, Mack transitioned to his rifle. He slammed bolts into each man's upper torso where the heat and impact of the shots would ruin both pumps and pipes. The impact of a blaster bolt at such short range made quick work of the men, driving them into the marble with wet slaps. Mack held his weapon toward the end of his hallway in case anyone had slipped past him, and could hear ancillary shots across the foyer, most likely from Creeper finishing off any targets on his side.

Mack checked the HUD for team position and barked into the net. "Tommy, sitrep."

"Eleven E-KIA, including their commander. Zero boom-boom for our side. Drones in the air detected movement coming at us. I think we've worn out our welcome."

14

Geiger Sinclair waited for his valet to return beneath the Solaria Terum Resort and Casino's covered roof. He patted some stray water droplets from his usual attire, a comfortable business suit, whose cut and finish were far beyond the skill of any tailor in Terum. The luxury sled he waited to be retrieved was equally unobtainable for most on this world.

The Team Commander had chosen Geiger specifically because the man could blend in anywhere. Clean shaven and with his hair pulled back, the wealthy elites staying in the resort saw him as one of their own and would often cast longing glances. More than once on this mission, he'd been offered keys to a suite and a promise of private fun and entertainment. But let the agent drop his hair over his eyes and add a hint of mud to his face and he was a man who fit in perfectly in the favelas and hovels on any number of worlds. The TC had once called him a "living skeleton key," and those who had seen Geiger in action agreed.

A moment later, a Severyn Kabal convertible grav car pulled beneath the porte-cochere. Outside the lush accommodations of the resort, the planet had mercifully decided to shed some humidity by dumping rain in the pre-dawn hours, which made Geiger's wait outside the climate-controlled resort that much more enjoyable as he ended a long night of gambling and high society entertainment.

A valet stepped from the sleek speeder and made his way around to the man waiting for the vehicle. The harried-looking young man bowed slightly to the waiting patron. He gestured to the idling vehicle, its engine thrumming like a massive predator just waiting to pounce.

Geiger slipped a loaded credit chip into the attendant's hand and pointed toward the sled. "Never let these people have the satisfaction of staring you down, friend. There's twenty thousand credits on that chit for you *if* you do two things for me. Switch jackets and then take this car for a ride that you'll remember."

The confused attendant looked at the chit in his palm, then back at Geiger, as if waiting for more permission. This had to be some kind of test.

"Jacket. Joy ride. Unless you'd rather I give this little quest to one of your friends?" Geiger asked.

"N-no. No, sir!"

Geiger brushed an errant strand of shoulder length, dark brown hair behind his ears and handed his tailored suit jacket to his new friend. "That's the spirit, lad. Now make sure you give her the business before the turbo kicks in. She's a bit dodgy right up to the point where that hits, but when it does, it's like jumping into hyperspace."

"This isn't... you're not with the resort, are you?" the valet asked. Already doubts were overcrowding the youth's mind.

Geiger tapped the speeder. "I am not. Let's just say there are certain people who want to have a go at me. I'd rather they follow you. Since they don't really want you, you're in the clear, mate."

With a grin that hadn't fully weighed out all the impli-
cations of that statement, the valet donned the offered
jacket and dropped into the seat. A quick rev of the engine
and the Severyn Kabal lit out from under the overhang as
though the devil himself was chasing it.

"That's a good boy. Drive it till the repulsors go cold,
kid," Geiger murmured and then tied back his hair. He
snapped the valet's jacket to drive out the wrinkles and
then shrugged himself into the red garment. He was patting down the sleeves when a man walked out the casino,
a beautiful woman on either arm. A smiling, blonde beau-
ty held out a ticket, not bothering to take her gaze from
her date to so much as look at where she was waving it.

Geiger reached out and took the ticket between his
fingers. "Right away, ma'am."

The agent's accent and his finely cut slacks taper-
ing down to leather shoes might have been missed by
the girl, but they caught the wealthy gambler's attention.
"Now, who woulda expected a Sudlow accent all the way
out here? And those shoes. Who you trying to fool by pla-
yin' the part of car fetcher, sir?"

Geiger flared his hands in surrender. "Guilty as
charged, sir. Name's Miles Obiri. Sudlow, indeed, since
you called it. But I scored me a little piece of work in the
upcoming holofilm, *Night Moves on High Power*, currently
in development. This here is a bit 'a method acting in between doing some stunt fighting in the barrios, down city.
I'll be right back with your car, sir."

Geiger winked.

As the patron praised himself at having a good ear and
better eyes, especially when selecting his current batch
of arm candy, Geiger sprinted away to the parking garage
where the hotel parked the man's grav-car. His nose crin-

kled as he came from the stairs and was assaulted by the smells painted in the corner outside the landing.

While he was no stranger to people's rudeness, he found it particularly crass when a person just whipped out their private bits and relieved themselves right where others had to walk. But then, most parking garages were operated by bots. Only the ritziest of resorts paid for actual, living help. Perhaps the bum didn't know any better.

Geiger shrugged off the yearning to punch someone on general principle and located the car, a Duravo extended cab truck with a stretch kit that extended the repulsors nearly a foot outside the frame, making the truck look larger and more formidable than it otherwise would be.

Geiger gave a cursory inspection of the truck bed and *tsked*. The gambler with an armload of women half his age had never put anything heavy into the bed of this vehicle. "Not even a scratch," he mumbled.

The agent hopped up into the driver's seat and strapped a slicer module under the dashboard to disable the security settings intended to work against him after he stole the man's truck. A nearly inaudible beep from the device told him he was free to work magic or mayhem in the repulsor vehicle now that he had full control.

"Poor bloke is gonna be nickered when he gets the bill on this rag," the agent muttered. He primed the power cell and started the vehicle with a rumbling roar. As the AI adjusted the seat, it presented Geiger with a litany of other features that he might enjoy. He told the comfort and control system to bugger off, then tapped the micro-comm in his ear. "'Sup love? A bit busy here, yeah?"

Nissa, the Endurian psyops agent for the Alpha Section, purred in his ear through his earpiece. "That was slick, dropping a smoke bomb into the room service. The delegate's aide yanked the lid, expecting a roasted honch flank, and got a lung full of smoke instead."

Geiger gave way to a wide grin. "Bought a batch of stinkers from some kids in the market selling fireworks. Best five cred I've ever spent. Especially if you have a holo to go along with that account, pretty lady. One rarely gets to see the fruits of such labor."

"You'll be much more interested in your car. They dispatched a catch team to go after it. Four guys in a government sled. Not subtle at all. That valet is quite the driver."

Geiger pull out of his parking space. "How's about the delegate? They yanking her and the aide?"

"Delegate Ramsada is being packaged as we speak. Underground garage. No chances taken when someone manages to sneak a smoke bomb past security and into their luxury suite. The aide was brought to the room with the remaining security team. Kindly proceed to the overflow lot."

Geiger casually drove through the lot, taking light turns and easy starts and stops to move through the lanes. He bypassed the ramp leading to the exit and followed the looping garage to an overflow lot away from the main. Once the truck was on a straightaway, he tapped the throttle and pushed the vehicle towards a speed that was explicitly forbidden by Republic law on any world when driving through this kind of structure. Warning holos blared and cited fines with possible jail time for the ever-increasing speed as the work truck that had never seen a day of work rocketed across the parking lanes unfettered by the system's security and safety features.

"You sure this van is the one?" Geiger asked as he buckled the restraining harness. In the distance was a work van labeled with a *Geek Fleet* logo on its side.

"Martin said he would bet his favorite cancer-causing cup on the guess. And what tech worker would park his van a block away instead of using the hotel's loading dock? This is hardly the sort of casino a blue-collar worker would be welcomed to."

"You've convinced me, Nissa. And as much as Martin loves that thing, I'd not wager against him anyway." The security agent pushed the accelerator like a schoolyard bully, just as the parking structure flashed a warning alarm and a series of spinning yellow and red overhead lights to warn potential pedestrians and motorists on that level that there was a speeder out of control.

Out of their control is more like it, Geiger thought.

He aimed the brush guard on the very expensive all-terrain hauler for the target van that Martin had identified in the overflow lot. The truck slammed into the van, crumpling its metal hull and nearly folding it in half. The stolen grav hauler's weight times its speed also shattered the duracrete retention barrier at the back of the parking space, pushing the van over the embankment to the next floor down, where it landed on two parked cars.

In the quiet, Geiger looked down approvingly at the truck's interior. The crash ballast had deployed during the strike, and the AI was in the process of hauling the inflatable bags back into the steering column, side boards, and doorjamb. Geiger was thankful the vehicle was equipped with the anti-impact KwikFoam, which, while safer, was a mess to claw out of. "Looks like they're not going any-where on the quick. How's our delegate looking?"

Nissa was quick with an update, taking that the agent was talking as proof that he could still go following the crash. "Just got into the car. Gov-Sec is mounting up be-side her. You have a minute, Geiger. Not minutes."

Geiger took the report as a challenge and reversed the throttle. He pulled the long-bodied truck into a tight loop that caused the vehicle to slip and slam its bed into a parked grav sled on the other side. Ten or so paces away, a woman in dark slacks and a T-shirt stood dumbstruck as she clutched onto the maid service uniform folded over her arm.

"Sorry about that. Charge the damage to Delegate Ramsada, care of the House of Reason," Geiger said as he sent the thrusters the other way and jostled the truck on its new course.

Security warnings flitted across the windshield and played their continual reprimands over the cabin speak-ers. He happened to think he was driving pretty well, al-though the constant flutter of holographic men, women, and alien life wearing local and federal uniforms was an-noying. "Nissa, if you have a line to Martin, can you get him to slag the various no-no displays I seem to be collecting at the moment?"

The Endurian cooed into his ear as the holos died away. "Another stink bomb would have gotten those out of your sight..."

A tight, descending turn brought the truck back in line with the main stretch of road leading out of the parking structure. Overhead LEDs and floodlights, along with the signs showing direction of travel, brightened up the latest obstacles in his path. All along the run, pieces of the floor rotated up, becoming duracrete barriers that would keep the truck from making the exit.

"Nissa?" Geiger asked like a lover expecting a surprise.

"Martin says to drive. He'll have it rigged by the time you reach it."

"Bloody hell." Geiger slammed the throttle down to the console, pushing the truck at full speed toward the outside. He scrunched his face against a probable impact as the heavy Duravo engine roared across the floor.

The first of the parking security barriers rapidly dropped into its housing in the floor, just like Nissa said it would. The action repeated itself along the remaining barricades until the last of them seemed to flutter. Revisiting his previous curse, Geiger hit the elevation control for the repulsors, driving the vehicle high enough to slam the top of the cab into the parking structure's roof. He managed to sail over what was left of the remaining barrier, sheering off part of the repulsor on his way through.

The truck careened into the street, bounced several times, and hit a row of parked cars. Grinding metal shrieked and the repulsors shuddering as they tried to keep several tons of vehicle suspended above the duracrete. In a barely controlled slide, Geiger made the entrance to the underground structure and poured on the thrust for a drive-ending stop. He fishtailed the truck bed block the entire lane leading out of the hotel and then dropped from the cab, pausing long enough to flash the slicer mod with the command for it to cycle up the power battery in a way that would most definitely void any warranties the owner had on the truck.

Patrons and staff had by now exited the front of the hotel as Geiger walked from the doomed vehicle. He slung his red valet jacket in a wide arc before dropping it over his shoulder so that, when later questioned, it would be the only thing most people would remember. The truck exploded in an arcing blast of fire and electricity, billowing black smoke, flying truck parts, duracrete shards, and debris. Any lookie-loos dropped for cover, and when they got back up, no one noticed a long-haired Geiger, quietly watching in his white shirt and tailored pants.

"Are you okay? Were you hurt?" Geiger asked the woman standing beside him. He'd changed his accent to match that of the truck's original owner. Another tidbit thrown on the trail to scrub his scent. In response to his question, all the stunned woman could manage was to point at the red jacket lying across the lawn.

When she managed the sense to nod that she was fine, he turned to walk from the crowd, holding another slicer module up to his ear as though it were a commlink. He threaded through the curious and concerned, making for the elevators beside the main lobby. A quick turn here, a sensor tap there, and Geiger was in the speedlift and moving for the top floor. "Status?"

Nissa reappeared on the comms. "They're pulling Ramsada through the lobby. Local police are forming up outside to run a motorcade. The aide and the rest of the security team are running surveillance from their room."

"Am I clean?" Geiger asked.

"Martin scrubbed you from the feeds. Replaced your face with the actor you name-dropped earlier," Nissa giggled.

"Savage."

He stepped from the lift to make a mummy-bee line for a room a few short steps away. Outside the anonymous door, Geiger slid in behind the room service cart left outside. Geiger pulled a towel from the cart and threw it over his shoulder to take eyes off his meticulously white buttoned-up shirt. He wanted people to notice something from the hotel. He nodded to several people moving about the hall, who, despite a smile full of teeth that were custom ordered to be the envy of anyone who saw them, he was largely ignored.

No one ever notices the help, he thought.

An Endurian woman in a hijab exited her room, holding the door open just enough to warrant an invite. "Sir."

"Ma'am," Geiger said to Nissa as he dropped the cart beside her room.

She shut the door behind them, placing a *do not disturb* sign on the handle. A pull of a garment bag hanging in the spacious hotel room closet and she joined him at the bed, where she laid out the contents.

"Better than last time," Geiger said. He tossed a set of light body armor around his shoulders and cinched it tight to his frame. After removing a shoe box from the bottom of the bag, he disassembled it to reveal a blaster set into a hidden compartment. He magnetically locked the holdout weapon to the armor and pulled a balaclava over his head. The mask shifted from gray to black, and a fanged mouth appeared over his normal one.

"You look stunning, dear," Nissa said.

"Thanks, love. Meet you downstairs in a tick?"

She quietly withdrew from the room, pulling on a hotel serving jacket as she left.

Geiger slid open the balcony door, taking in the scene below. Drones flitted in the air all around the courtyard as the police and rescue vehicle lights painted the street outside the hotel in shifting colors. As the affair continued to play out, Geiger threw his leg over the balcony. He hung from the side of the enclosure where people were less likely to look and slowly lowered himself to his arms' full extension. The duracrete building exterior was a nice change to the slums and favellas he often had to climb through, where sharp corrugated metal and dilapidated stone cut his hands and gave Repub medbots more excuses to pump him full of exotic inoculations.

Now for the fun part, he thought.

He released his grip on the balcony, dropping nearly ten feet to the one below as nimbly as a wobanki. A kip-assisted pull-up later, and Geiger was legs over the new balcony and staring at the occupants inside exactly one floor below where he'd fallen from.

A man and woman stood over a second lady who was typing, tapping, and waving through various displays. Periodically they argued, tapped what was probably their own comm beads, and worked the system they thought they had under control. In truth, Nissa had tagged their CPUs earlier in the day when she came in as a hotel employee to change the sheets. It often roused suspicion to restrict housekeeping from doing their job, so they'd let her in. A micro-transmitter conveniently placed, and Nissa gave Martin full access to any system the security team had in the room.

Geiger cautiously opened the screen door leading to the group by activating its outside display. When the door swished open, the trio looked up, saw the man on their balcony who wasn't supposed to be there, and scrambled for various implements to use on people just like him.

The Alpha Section agent acted first, shooting a stun bolt at the computer tech as she reached for something below the table. A shimmering pulse wave locked the woman's muscles in place until the strain sapped her consciousness and deposited her from the chair to the floor. In the time it took her to slump from her seat, the other security agent reached behind to his waistband and produced a heavy blaster pistol.

That thing would provide a much more permanent state of unconsciousness.

Geiger dove fully into the room and slid behind a luxurious couch. He popped up and dumped a stun bolt into his adversary before he could decide whether to try and blast through the furniture or go around and flank the intruder.

The last woman made no attempt to fight and instead broke for the door at a sprint. She bobbed and juked through the hotel room as though this was a common occurrence or she had been trained. Geiger tried to get a shot off but didn't have an angle on the woman as she took flight from the suite.

The door to the room flung open with her at a dead run when she came face-to-forearm with a clothesline strike that sent her sprawling. Nissa put both hands to her mouth and gasped in surprise. "Oh dear. I am so sorry, madame. Let me get you sorted out."

Geiger was already on the job of restraining the unconscious security agents when Nissa pulled the woman back into the room by her ankle and shut the door. "Not a bad hit for a blind gal."

"I do what I can." Nissa winked. She took a handful of the woman's hair and guided her through a stumbling course to the couch. She produced a cloth liberated from the bathroom and dabbed with water and thrust it into the prisoner's hands to clean the blood trickling from her nose and mouth. "Ms. Alina Hathcoovery, aide to House of Reason Delegate Ramsada. We have a few questions about your boss."

15

Mack really hated missions that went this long, and the tongue toggle was definitely a big check mark in the Suck column when it did. After a while, all the saliva and grit from pulling the bucket on and off built up, making it really unpleasant to work through. Of course, as a legionnaire, he ignored a lot to accomplish the mission, but that didn't mean he liked it.

His team were on the creepy side of things with the doctor, who insisted every few minutes they had a more important job to do here other than the one the REC-Team came for. For his part of the mission, Major Tyler reiterated that they had plenty of time to discuss what the doctor was so dead set on blowing up when they were out of here. He had even said they could enlist the local marines to do an air strike on the facility. She'd shot him down, insisting that there were things in there that had to be handled first, by her and her alone.

"Master Sergeant?" Tyler asked as he strode up to the lead blasted-up technical that had once belonged to Haloska.

"You're with me, Creep, and Fresher, sir," Mack said, thumbing toward the cab of the truck that dwarfed the newly arrived technicals everyone else was riding in. While Haloska was obviously a terrible person, he had good taste in grav trucks. Mack was also glad the other Khindo Khabar were nice enough to leave all these vehicles behind when they died.

"Copy. But we need to talk about her concern." Tyler grimaced even as he said the words, as though he didn't want to, either.

"We'll do that once we're away from the mob coming after us," Mack said, tracing a circle in the air. The leejes poured out of the building, in some cases assisting wounded marines on their way to the trucks.

Creeper threw his pack into the second truck's cab. "Just got some analysis back from our algos. Bots picked up a comm burst from that team before we dusted them. The big boss, Keem, wants this science chick in the worst way, Top. We got more people about to show up."

In under a minute, the three trucks sped off through the graveyard cityscape on their way to the outskirts. Mack drove the last vehicle in the stack, mixing the rest of the crew with the rescued marines and their charge, Doctor Kavir. "Fresher, list it off for me," Mack ordered as the convoy took a deep turn, bringing them away from the city center.

"One hully has a broken arm and ribs. The other guy's shoulder dislocated when the ship came down. Feels like hamburger in there, too. Now if you're talking about the doc, she had words with the major. He may have been a point in the marines, but he handled her like a genuine leader, Top. Still, best I can tell, she has some sort of project that was left running when things went off the rails, and she came to shut it down so they could destroy the base."

"Why not just drop orbitals?"

"The major asked the same thing," Fresher replied. "Seems there's something there that only she can shut down, and there's the possibility that it could survive an orbital strike."

"Oba," Mack said, more to himself than the kid. He switched to a private channel with the major to see if he'd gotten more than Fresher had. "Sir, did you get anything pertinent out of the doctor?"

The trucks sped onto a highway that took them on an elongated loop out of the city. Beneath them, long-dead neighborhoods flashed by as the vehicles careened past dark apartment buildings, shops, and homes. All abandoned by order of the Republic. Rushing by buildings that once promised a fertile future for the natives of Nuzon, Mack thought back to the intel report detailing how something murdered an entire city overnight.

After several workers at the Serrabi Falls facility came down with a bacterial infection that killed in a matter of days, the local government ordered a city-wide lockdown, including those at the research station. Repeated attempts to quarantine the facility workers failed with cases springing up in Kerhott, this time killing people in as little as a few hours. When the government extracted residents from both locations, fresh cases died away almost immediately. The city's carcass and the attached research station were quarantined as a monument to the dead and to an incident the locals wanted out of their memory and their sight.

Like Mack, Major Tyler's thoughts on the last few hours distracted him. When he noticed the master sergeant waiting on his answer, he shook himself back to the here and now enough to respond. "She said that someone attempted to use her research in bio-based nano-technology, but it got away from them."

"That explanation ain't gonna cut it once we deal with this tail," Mack said of the Khindo Khabar vehicles they'd so far narrowly avoided. While other forces had a tendency to downplay organizations like these, relegate them to a status as backwards cavemen who got their jollies by playing with farm animals, the Legion and, by extension, the Legion Recovery Teams, had no such illusions. These were dangerous men who'd received training at some of the nastiest hot spots kicking up dust and blaster bolts out on galaxy's edge. They could field drones and sometimes, their own aircraft to track the rescue unit. It was only a matter of time before REC-Team Pelican had to go to ground to avoid a very motivated force.

Almost on cue, the roadway ahead of them lit with a small orange explosion, showering the freeway in duracrete and impervisteel.

"Top! Got two in that building on our two o'clock, two-fifty meters. Accuracy ain't for crap, but with an RPG like that, it's more a matter of getting angry at the grid square!" Shiloh said from the back of the first truck.

"Can you change their mind about shooting at us?" Mack asked.

"I got this one, Top," Stringer said.

The convoy came to an abrupt halt. Repulsors flared and whined as the three trucks kicked into reverse and trotted backwards down the highway. Stringer reached into his pack for a small rectangular box, which he threw over the guardrail. The quad repulsor rails unfolded as it fell, its gyroscopic sensors detecting the erratic change in momentum to push it to flight. It soared on its buzzing ascent toward the building where a series of smashed out windows allowed the rocket team to set up with a clear view for the takedown.

"They're reloading!" Shy shouted into the comms.

The three trucks raced backwards on a swerving track to get to the last off ramp they passed. Driven by Lobster, the lead truck clipped the side of the guardrail more than once as he strained to keep the rickety machine traveling where the steering control told him it was supposed to go.

"Man! Going to take a hit for that during the AAR!" he joked.

Mack could almost imagine the *shoomp* of the new rocket being loaded into the front of the enemy's launcher right ahead of the securing pin locking it into place. They were on the downslope of the freeway, going back the way they came. If they could stay a hard target for a few more seconds, they'd be behind the crest and out of the line of fire.

A heavy blaster bolt sizzled across their windshields like a shooting star in a dark sky, arcing from the city outskirts right into the target. The side of the building detonated with explosive force, shunting their two attackers out of the structure to fall several stories to the duracrete below. Flaming debris and ruined facade rained onto the bodies, making the spot where they hit intensely visible through the Legion buckets.

"What the hell was in that drone?" Creeper called into the net.

"Targeting software," Stringer called back. The team could almost hear his smile over the comms. "That's a good hit, Maggie. Bad guys splattered. Thank you for the assist!"

Now Mack was smiling too. Somewhere out there, a miniature, AI-driven tank was playing the part of guardian angel.

"Target down," the K-15 bot responded, her voice husky yet feminine. "Remaining on station to cover your move. Maggie out."

The trucks trundled past the off ramp, allowing the legionnaires to reverse the repulsors and drive in the way the manufacturer intended. Lobster kicked the stubborn donk of a grav truck into gear and recovered his spot as the lead vic, running the convoy into the city to circumnavigate the gigantic hole the Khindo Khabar had blasted into the freeway.

"Mack, it's Stringer. We have a large force in technicals that just broke through the royal marine cordon and are moving deeper into the city. We're going to be a sand bear bashing a *skreehive* if we try driving the main roads."

"Roger that," Mack acknowledged. "Lobster, it's Mack. Find me a place to lie low for a minute to reorient."

"Roger, out," Lobster said, turning his truck through a back alley that was going to be a squeeze for Mack's larger vehicle.

As the two trucks ahead of him threaded the needle, Mack switched into another private channel over the L-comm. "Rooster, you got something for me?"

"Sure do, Mack," Rooster said. "I just did some light reading while we were on the roll. TC and War Dog sent me packets on the QT. Oh, and I'm probably facing court-martial when I get back."

"They opened your bunk back on the *Reliant*?" Mack asked.

"Couldn't keep it quiet forever," Rooster said sourly. "But we've got bigger problems than my career ending. We got kids with dirty mitts trying to stick their fingers in our pie."

16

Mack's torch cut through the last of the lock on the overhead door, turning it into dripping metal and rapidly cooling globs on the dusty street. He observed Lobster cutting into another lock, REC-Team Pelican's master breacher making the rest of them look like rank amateurs at the task. As Major Tyler cut the last of his lock—a job given to him so more experienced legionnaires could stand security—Mack gave the other two a nod.

They thrust the overhead doors of Sedeño's Fix-It Shop into their housings, making spaces for the three technicals to roll into the service bays. Fresher ran inside to survey the interior, pushing aside various things that were left behind during the hurried evacuation. Vehicle creepers, tools, hoses, and engine parts lay discarded, mid-task. Thousand-credit tools left to rust.

Based on the vehicles in the lot, Sedeño's must have done some serious business before the quarantine. Mack nodded at a Duravo Falcatta, a sports car he often fantasized about for his retirement from the Legion. The thing was coated in a hearty layer of dust streaks after the rain, but looked like if there was any power left in the old muscle car, she would purr to life and rule the streets. A car like that here, so far away from the core, meant that someone in the city had been a player, and they came to this shop to fix their broken toys.

Just like Mack was about to do. He slipped inside just as the last of the technicals backed into the bays, leaving Creeper to shut the overhead doors. Once his truck was in place, he swung his camouflage cape over the windshield to block any ultrabeams from seeing them steal premier parking spots. He leaned over the open window to address the major. "We have a giant Khindo Khabar parade about to pass us. Once they're gone, we get back on the highway and make like a shepherd."

"And get the flock out of here," Tyler said, as if he'd learned the secret to the universe.

"Roger that, sir. Keep the seat warm. I'll be right back." Mack dropped from the step bar onto the duracrete floor with a clatter. A wrench skidded away from his boot and disappeared under a technical, right down into the technician bay cut in the floor. It rattled on every piece of metal until it came to a clanging stop.

"Not that they'll probably hear you in there, Top, but you might want to warn folks to watch the loud music," Shiloh said from his position on the roof.

"Roger, out," Mack said. He waded through the clutter that marred what looked to be a well-maintained slate floor with technician bays cut into it. When the Republic ordered the evacuation, it must have been a drop-and-go scenario in the otherwise orderly shop. Parts hung in neatly arranged, secure stations along the walls, and rolling toolboxes had all their drawers secured, saved for the tool chest top, which were all open. The floor told a different story. Sedeño and the crew left parts, hoses, and tools behind when they left the shop. Mack tracked through the clutter on the way to the other technical.

He slid into the seat next to Doctor Kavir, pausing long enough to remove his bucket. Ducky and Blanks made a move to leave, but Mack motioned for them to stay.

Doctor Kavir picked up on the vibe. "I take it you want information?"

Mack shrugged and handed her a protein bar packed with enough calories to sustain three people for up to a week. The top of the package bore markings with a unique poison warning for anyone who wasn't from Doctor Kavir's family tree. "Lorisam. Unique dietary restrictions. You need to eat this and tell me why I just got a re-tasking to drop off these marines and then help you." Mack winked to Blanks, hoping he would take the hint to broadcast the exchange over the L-comm.

"I can't say much," Kavir said, heartily chewing on the bar.

Mack nodded as he reached for his own bucket. "That's fine. Then I'll stick to the spirit of your mission rather than the details you won't give me. We'll board our shuttle and drop some ordinance on the facility once we're in the air. Problem solved."

"No. You can't, Master Sergeant," she said around a mouthful of nutrient bar puffing out her cheeks.

"Yes, I can," Mack said, reaching into the front seat for Blank's battle board. "You see, Doctor, here's the thing about getting a Valkyrie team. On mission, we're supported by a section of special agents and technicians who are some of the best in the galaxy. They're also Dark Ops scary on a level that oughta keep you up at night if you're planning on misbehaving. So here's what we know...

"Before we could even leave the ship, not only was our involvement in the rescue leaked to the advisor general here on Nuzon, but our CO was yanked through some shady back channels. His replacement being less proficient than him, and who had circumnavigated the required Valkyrie courses, leads us to believe he was placed here for something. So, this holo is for you, ma'am."

Mack handed off the battle board with a holo ready to play on the screen and patted his guys on the armor as he exited the truck. Engines sounded in the avenue outside, echoing against the garage bay as multiple grav trucks laden with Khindo Khabar fighters raced by. The hum of their repulsors faded, to be replaced by the pinging noise of someone trading blaster fire.

"Shy and Stringer are climbing down the roof, now," Creeper said.

Mack clambered inside the cab, then signaled for the major to trade places with him. Abandoning all pretense, Tyler climbed into the back like an enthusiastic kid ready for a ride with his parents. Mack took in the display across the instrument panel, telling him the truck was still more than operational. They had plenty of charge in the fuel cell to get them out of the city. He reached for the windscreen to recover his cape in time to see another convoy of trucks racing by. Instead of head-wrapped fighters struggling for purchase in a technical adapted for a fight, the trailing line of vehicles were repulsor-floated combat sleds full of Royal Marines who looked more than capable of punishing the insurgents for their interference.

"What was that thing with the doc all about?" Tyler asked. "And shouldn't we fall in behind the marines?"

"First answer," Mack began, "is that I shared your conversation with Commander Norris-Foster from the CIC just prior to you replacing our boss. Valkyries do work with legit scary people. They're the kind of folks who know that everything in a CIC is recorded. And while the commander rightly surmised the system couldn't render your convo over the noise, you didn't take that chance. You used your bucket to record the interaction. Smart."

The major froze. Mack gave him a minute, watching the rearview for the sniper team to hop into the truck beds. He pointed outside the window to Fresher, who opened each overhead door in succession to let out the vehicles. When all the trucks were free of their hiding places, Fresher threw himself over the side rail into the vehicle bed. A slap on the roof was all Lobster needed to throw the throttle forward.

"As for your second answer, Major, you'll have to wait and see," Mack finished.

Pulling into the street, the three vehicles formed a column as they retraced their route back to the highway. Creeper pointed to a map their buckets were superimposing over their view. "If we go three blocks over, we can bypass that big hole we put in the last road."

Mack nodded, and turned his attention back on the major and his reaction to being outed. Tyler sat still, focused straight ahead, as if that would keep him from being noticed. Then maybe he wouldn't have to respond to the unspoken accusation Mack had just leveled.

The team drove from under the overpass, sliding back onto the highway as fast as the technicals would carry them. All-out speed was a marine tactic when on a main supply route like this, but Mack wasn't going to let the Khindo Khabar running this show continue to dictate actions on the objective. The team had been boots on the ground for too long in an operation like this, and it was time to get the assets out. Streaking past holo signs on the MSR, the lead vehicle used their bucket overlays to plot their way out.

This time, they wouldn't be taking a straight shot out of the city. A little IMT was the best course of action here, even though they were mounted. The basic army, and in some cases the marines, still used the age-old tactic of individual movement tactics training to get fire teams across danger areas when cover was in short supply. An abrupt sprint for only a few seconds, followed by a sudden drop, could make the difference between gaining the objective or a blaster hole. Mack's plan was to maximize the speed of the highway system leading toward the outskirts while taking advantage of the chaotic city layout and avenues below for better cover.

Driving up a hill in the suburban section of the city, the trucks had transitioned from businesses dotting neighborhoods crammed with apartment buildings to small homes breaking up the forest that mankind's presence was intruding upon. The slate gray and flaccid browns of the city gave way to suburbia's hearty greens and deep browns.

Mack slid his truck beside a dormant water fountain with a stone woman holding out her hand to release a bird. The neighborhood seemed asleep, waiting for someone to wake it up to life again, unlike the city proper, where the atmosphere felt cold, still, dead. Movement caught Mack's attention. An animal with a teddy bear's body and a long tail jumped from a nearby tree onto the roof of the house across from the fountain.

The small cul-de-sac centered on the fountain with three squat, two-story homes positioned on the hill like spokes radiating from the center of a wheel. The first two buildings had roofs that slanted away from each other, as if the two buildings might have started as a single structure at one point, though Mack figured that probably wasn't the case. It was strange to him that there were only three homes here, and the third angled roof made it seem like there was something missing. Perhaps a fourth home in the middle had been washed away in one of Nuzon's relentless storms?

Yet in villages like this, there was rarely rhyme or reason for the aesthetics that went into building the houses. The aesthetics usually came later—a wrought iron fences here, a specialty carving there, a wind chime collection across the yard. The fountain was a nice touch, Mack thought. A shame for it to get all shot up.

Mack and the rest of REC-Team Pelican worked the task of dumping wounded marines against the fountain when the front door on the odd house opened toward the street. Snowball ran out with his kit bag ready to assist with the injured.

"Nice spot, sir," Mack said.

"Ya know, while you cats were running all over the joint, I've been forced to wait here and camp stove a cup of noodles, drink kaff, and break out my battle board for some alone time. It was awful," the Legion pilot said, full of false lamentation.

"Maggie here with you, too?" Mack asked.

Snowball pointed to the hill below them. "She's in the next block down. Something about better lines on target along your route."

Mack pointed to the bucket thrusting up from the top of the kitbag, which should have been on the pilot's face. "You get our change of mission?"

"I hid the shuttle out back. Re-stock and re-load your kit," Snowball started before getting to Mack's question. "Yeah, I got it. Did you show the doc our point-not-a-point made a drug deal to get on mission?"

"Sure did," Mack said, glancing toward the truck still containing the sulking Major Tyler. "But that's not my focus right now, sir. A-SEC got word we gotta make this run, but we don't dare do it by air. We took the highway and nearly got dusted by Khindo Khabar shooting at us from buildings in the city. I'm not going to risk you or the ride out trying to reach the objective."

"Mighty kind of you." Snowball quirked a smile.

The leejes turned at the sound of a ruckus behind them. Doctor Kavir, not one to wait for anyone to give her permission, took the anger she'd bottled up during the ride to the neighborhood out on the technical door. Strength borne from the augmented genetics of her species flared as she angrily tore the truck door off its hinges. The popping shriek preceded a crash as the hatch slammed against the cobblestone street and bounced several times before coming to a rest against the fountain.

"Get out here, now, you sycophantic halfwit!" Kavir yelled.

Tyler removed his bucket and stepped to the woman, not refusing to back down but keeping his expression blank.

"You think trading my work for a shot at being one of them is going to make it true?" Kavir barked. "You bring back a sample of my work and turn it in to that House of Reason lackey on the *Reliant*, and then what? You get appointed to be on their team? Just like that?"

"I would have already knocked her into the fountain," Snowball muttered.

Despite being in the hot seat, Tyler kept his calm. "The House of Reason has determined that calling them Valkyries is offensive to some—"

Kavir turned to the severed truck door at her feet and kicked it. It bounced several times along in a noisy clatter before landing on the grass.

"On second thought," Snowball remarked.

The doctor continued her tirade at the major when no one stepped forward to stop her. "You think I care about the heavy petting politics from the people you work for? Those people took my work and turned it into a weapon, and I won't let that stand. And neither will I let you bring a sample back to that twit, so she gets her spot sucking a senator's toes under the desk."

"Doctor," Mack said, quietly and firmly.

"What!" she roared at him.

"We need you to take this into the house," Mack said, gesturing to the door Snowball came from. "We have company inbound."

"I thought we lost them," she said.

"We did, but then we had one of our operators rescue that guy we had tied under the desk. She sold our location to him."

Furious, Kavir stalked up to him, her clenched, knuckles white. Mack had read the file, and the door was proof that members of her species were definitely not ones to scrap with. Although nearly a foot shorter than him, her considerable biology made her seem much taller. "Why would you allow that?"

"Optics, Doctor," Mack sighed. "Now please, get in the house so we can see this through and get you where you need to go."

The technical rolled up the street, cautiously approaching the three stolen trucks that had ferried the marines and the doctor away from their grasp. Haloska scowled at the sight of his truck. Blaster holes and explosive scoring trailed along the side of the panels. While he knew Keem would reward him handsomely for capturing the Repubs, the sight of that gorgeous enameling being marred by a gunfight irked him.

He climbed out of the cab, signaling the rest of the men to do the same. Four trucks' worth of Khindo fighters scrambled from the cabins or jumped from the beds to fan out in the square around the fountain.

"Got blood here," one fighter said.

"Not enough for me to worry. Let's get this finished," Haloska barked. He gestured for his men to fan out and take positions around the buildings, forming a net in case his prize tried to run. "Remember, they have legionnaires with them. Charge packs at maximum and you should be able to punch through that armor. Their government has been skimping on their protection and it ain't what it used to be."

The rumble of military grade engines approached. He left the fountain and waited in the middle of the road. A combat sled floated into the cul-de-sac, the electric hum of its engines drowning out the jungle. A Royal Marine officer appeared from the back hatch, a sneer painted on his face, his hands fixed to his blaster on one side, and his radio on the other marked his authority as he stared down the Khindo Khabar enforcer.

"My men are reporting a search of the neighborhood to our commanders. That should keep the other marines away to give you the time you need," the officer said, as though choosing his words carefully.

"And we will see they are handsomely rewarded for it," Haloska said back before returning to his men. He sat on the fountain's border, waiting for the signal that his people had their hands around the doctor's throat. She was worth a lot to the Republic, and if they had her in custody, they could take a load of Republic credits in ransom right before they cut her head off into a bucket.

Keem was clear on this. They hadn't been the ones to shoot her down, but his contact in the government was becoming more and more insistent that Doctor Kavir had to die. They had to kill her before she could finish what she came here for. The contact had promised big money for the cause. They had ensured that Kerhott would belong to the Khindo Khabar. Doctor Kavir's head rolling around the floor would be proof enough the job had been done.

"What's taking so long?" The enforcer sighed. He wrested himself from his less than comfortable spot on the fountain's border and climbed past the technicals ringing the fountain. He unclipped his radio from his belt, turning it several times to get the push-to-talk button under his thumb. "Sayeem. Sayeem! What are you doing in there?"

Another voice broke the radio's squelch instead. "Haloska, it's Raoul. I'm behind the building and I can't see them in there."

"Have they moved to the next house?" Haloska asked.

"No, boss. The others are in there, but now they're not answering either."

"Get to cover, now," the enforcer snarled. He motioned for the two fighters with him to duck behind the trucks, with the fountain against their backs as cover. "Raoul, what do you see? Raoul. Damn it!"

Two blaster bolts punched brain matter belonging to Haloska's men across the side panels of the technicals. They slapped into the vehicle's side with a dull thud and slid down with a wet squeak, painted in blood and gray matter.

The enforcer waited for the eventual bolt to send him to the throne of heaven for his reward, and when it didn't come, he thanked Oba and turned to face his attacker. Two Royal Marines were in a kneeling, unsupported firing crouch, their blaster rifles in a motionless demand that if he so much as breathed too fast, they would fire off his invitation with Oba himself.

"What is this?" Haloska growled.

The Royal Marine LT's answer was his rampant walk forward, blaster pistol raised. He thumbed off the safety, making an audible click as the jungle around them went quiet.

"Wait! Wait! Wait!" Haloska barked. "I can pay you more!"

"What makes you think this is about money?" the lieutenant asked. The single bolt punched through Haloska's head, dropping him in a heap beside his men. "Legionnaires. You can come out now!"

Mack walked from the side of the building, making his way to the Royal Marines now standing casually beside the fountain. When their officer extended his hand, Mack took it and gave it a solid shake. "Thank you."

"Sabine sends her regard," the officer said in thickly accented Galactic Standard. "We can take your wounded in my sled. My two others will get you out of the city to Serrabi Falls since Sabine said that's where you're going. If you have a shuttle, don't launch it yet. Dosa Keem has many people breaking the cordon and coming for you. They have missile packs."

"Understood. Thank you for the help," Mack said.

"We help you and you help us. All the Khindo Khabar are dead. Yes?" the lieutenant asked.

"They are," Mack confirmed, gesturing to the houses. "Dosa Keem is risking a lot to send all these men in here after us. Especially with the city being quarantined."

The lieutenant ordered his men back to the combat sled. "You've seen this place. No sickness here. Tell everyone."

17

"I need to see this through, Master Sergeant," Staff Sergeant Wrigley said flatly. He finished loading his last marine into the combat sled and completed the task with a handshake to the local lieutenant.

"He ain't the only one," Sergeant Laora Kines agreed.

Mack remembered her from the hallway where the Valkyries first encountered the marines. She'd opened the stairway door and exposed the leejes to Wrigley's scope at the Centigo building. Both marines looked fit, albeit also wearing that look a trooper got when they'd been in the field longer than expected. Still, they were MARSOG marines, and if the mission wasn't done, they weren't either.

"A Legion support element is here to relieve you and you just want to dive back in and get muddy with us?" Mack asked. He watched for their reaction while he pressed his thumb into the scars under his gloves. He knew what they were thinking and why they wanted to see it done.

"Our orders were to get Kavir to target. We're done when that's done, Master Sergeant," Wrigley said.

A message from Creeper slid into Mack's HUD.

Raptor wouldn't turn down the triggers.

Creeper was right. Raptor seemed hell-bent on giving people their moment. That's what made him an outstanding officer. Raptor watched his leejes do a job up until they took it to the edge with no hesitation, at which point he'd push them out of the nest. And now look. The man wasn't even here, but his influence on the team was palpable.

"Kines, you're with Doctor Kavir in the second vic. Wrigley, hop in with me." Mack hitched his thumb toward the waiting vehicle. It was a simple choice to take the marines, seeing as he'd trusted the senior medical leej this far. Mack didn't have time to worry about what else Raptor would do if he were here. The situation was rapidly turning into a repulsor-powered dumpster dive, and he didn't have the time or assets he needed to get it done right.

He yanked Haloska's corpse free of the truck frame and pulled the other two away so they wouldn't get pulverized when the trucks moved out. He wasn't sorry the insurgents were dead, but he didn't have to be crass about it either.

"I'll hold the shuttle here until you make more noise. When the Khindos start throwing blaster bolts your way, I'll get this girl in orbit and hang tight for the call," Snowball said. He smoothed down his wiry hair in preparation for dropping his bucket back over it. "Any reason we're not letting the marines, or better yet, a leej platoon handle this?"

Mack shrugged as he got behind the wheel. "We're already here and the boss wants to know why he got jacked for this."

"Fair enough," Snow agreed. "See you on the other side, Master Sergeant."

"Be safe, Chief," Mack said. The team sergeant pushed his movement order through the L-comm and the truck convoy sped from the cul-de-sac, leaving Snowball to his own devices. Mack adjusted the rear display to see

Maggie, the K-15 infantry support mech, jump from behind a garage and pull up its legs in favor of its repulsors. The armored machine raced behind them until the hill gave way to a street intersection where it veered on its own course to keep from immediately identifying the group as Repub adjacent.

Power cores belonging to Reiner and Royce Twenty-One Eleven combat sled screeched their high whine into the avenues ahead of them. The Royal Marine lieutenant had promised combat sleds, and they kept his word by taking the lead in the convoy. The twin R-n-R sleds twisted their singular N-50 turrets back and forth while cruising from the heavily forested suburban homes set into the hillside neighborhood. Animals unaccustomed to the presence of man or his machines darted away to seek cover in vacant houses and the jungle canopy above. Driving twenty tons of armor, the Marine escort ignored the darting animals and eventually broke away to whatever unit had spawned them.

Roads once kept meticulously free of vegetation were barely visible through the jungle floor, angrily reclaiming its territory by growing over both street and highway barriers alike. Lush green, moss encrusted vines stretched across lamp posts like some bizarre jade spiderweb, creating a tunnel effect along the highway.

As the convoy wound through avenues, reclaimed by the jungle and leading to the research station, the L-comm broke the silence.

"Mack, it's Chief Cantrell. You got a minute for me?"

"Always, Chief. What's shakin'?"

"TC and the geeks are busy trying to make sure your presence there isn't causing a political dust storm, so I volunteered to drop some knowledge your way."

"One second, Chief," Mack said.

The vehicles slowed to a crawl, negotiating downed trees one of the bigger storms had knocked into a logjam. Switching into the lead vehicle position, Mack used the brush bar on the heavier truck to plow their way through the tangled timber along the highway. Revving the engine against the dug-in trees, Mack used the repulsor truck's brush guard to force a hole big enough for the two technicals to pass through.

"What in Oba's eyeball is that?" Creeper said, pointing out the window.

A part of the terrain dislodged itself and then shook violently, shrugging off vast swaths of grass and vines. The tremendous animal climbed from the mire it was napping in, using one of its wickedly jutting tusks to ram a tree back into the front bumper. If there was anyone not paying attention, several hundred kilos of fallen tree against an impervisteel bumper was sure to grab their focus real quick. It shook itself free from the lumber and clinging vines to reveal a hairy beast covered in armored plates with dark, earth-colored fur jutting out between them.

"Is that a piggasaur?" Tyler asked over the L-comm.

"Anger-back," Rooster answered. "It's a wild boar native to the planet. What is it with you and the wild-life, Mack?"

"Why is the local swine as big as a combat sled?" Creeper asked through the net. "I'm not one to judge, but you do seem to have a type, Master Sergeant."

"Oh, you know me, I like a challenge. Chief, you're going to have to give me a minute!" Mack threw the truck in reverse with a flash of the warning indicators for the benefit of the twin vehicles behind him. Nearly in unison, the drivers slapped the accelerators hard in a winding retreat away from the animal before it figured the fastest route around the tangled trees. Its squeal ended in a barking growl right before it crashed through the underbrush to avoid the road.

"I think he wants to give us a piece of his mind for messing up his living room," Fresher said into the comm. "Here he comes."

The anger-back rammed into the side of the second technical, nearly buckling the quarter panel and bending the bed. The impact threw Sergeant Kines into a tumbling mess of limbs and body armor. While the leejes in the cab positioned themselves for close combat with a weapon-ized ham sandwich, the animal shook the entire vehicle, trying to pry its tusk free from the metal.

"Rooster, Ducky, and Wrigley. Get out of the truck and see to Kines," Mack ordered. "Lobster, reverse throttle, hard right!"

The leej driving the technical pushed the repulsors as hard as they'd go, spinning the vehicle in a half cir-cle with several hundred kilos of angry swine attached. The weight of the truck was enough to drag the pig with it in a stumbling path that put it right in line with Mack's bumper. He slammed on the accelerator, ramming the animal with the brush guard and sending it on a frenet-ic tumble through the jungle. Vines and fronds whipped into a tornado of green as the huge animal tore through the foliage.

"Is it dead?" Tyler asked.

The animal definitely was not dead, judging by the rattling and rustling of the young trees farther down the road. From the way it had charged them without hesita-tion, the anger-back acted like it was usually the winner in most fights. In this case, it had never been treated like a seamball knocked into quadrant three, and was taking a minute to recover its wits.

"Mack," Rooster called out. "We got Kines. Let's get this train moving!"

The team sergeant reoriented the heavier grav-truck, once again throttling the hefty log out of the way to clear a path. The convoy slid through the opening and continued to meander up the road toward the facility. Mack opened a root command window and piped in a feed from Rooster's bucket.

The man was using slip knotted synth-cord to tie Sergeant Kines's broken body into her poncho. Rooster's field of vision slipped over to the cab where Ducky was crawling through the back window to the cockpit. Another twist of the lens, and Mack was now staring at Staff Sergeant Wrigley, who sat with his back pressed up against the bent sidewall of the truck bed.

"Rooster, what happened?" Mack asked.

"She was already dead when we got there, Mack. Killed on impact when that thing knocked her out of the truck," Rooster said, accepting his duty to deliver the bad news. His voice held finality, remorse at another trooper lost. "I'll keep an eye on the staff sergeant."

"Thanks, Roost," Mack said. While there was a part of him that hurt at the loss of a marine to something so random as an animal attack, he was also glad that his leejes didn't fire a weapon, potentially giving away their position. The sounds of a street fight between the Khindo Khabar and the Royal Marines could be heard in the distance, but there was nothing shooting on this side of the city and definitely not out in the jungle. Anything they could do to minimize their signature and keep a fanatical pack of religious zealots off their trail was worth it in the long run.

And when Mack thought about the word anything, he pressed his hands on the top of the controls so he could feel the scars under his gloves again. That woman shouldn't have died. None of them should have.

"Chief, talk to me," Mack said, recovering the call from Cantrell.

"Sorry for the loss, Top. I hate to drop in behind that, but got some news from the guys pertinent to this hop. We ran an op on Delegate Ramsada's aide. We just got done squeezing her for the good stuff."

"Why not squeeze the delegate herself?" Mack asked.

Cantrell huffed, as though that was what she wanted to do, but was denied. "Those take time to break. And they get all complain-y afterward. As if they could even ID us for violating their civil rights, and all that junk. Like they're not doing it to the whole galaxy. Still, aides break pretty easy when you threaten them with jail time or leaking their sex holos or whatever."

Mack smirked at her remark, although the situation was less than funny.

"Listen, your girl Kavir was in bed with Dela Cruz," the chief stated.

"The advisor general?" Mack blurted.

"One and the same. Seems the AG lured Centigo and the good doctor with promises of tax breaks and being treated like royalty. But when the doctor's work got featured in med journals, it caught SATO's attention."

"Our friends over at Special Activity, Tactics, and Operations, right? Black bag within a black bag?" Mack asked. "Let me guess, the guys with the dark indoor sunglasses show up on Kavir's doorstep and she does something crazy?"

"Got it in one. That's what the Delegate told her aide. They believed Kavir intentionally released the virus. So everyone's forced to abandon ship because it's on fire. If the delegate's suspicions are correct, Kavir bought herself time to work out a recovery with Dela Cruz."

Mack turned the truck onto an access road, leaving the jungle for a raised trail with a clearance from the vegetation. Crushed stone lined the sides of the elevated trail surface, with only the barest of weeds and plant life coming through. "Where does the delegate come into this?"

"Good question! Dela Cruz used her political connections to rate a Valkyrie team to rescue her investment in the doctor. But Delegate Ramsada was part of the House of Reason committee that dug into Kavir's research. That woman hedged her bets to get what she wanted and pulled a whole lot of strings to get it."

"So they can shift it from one black bag to another." Mack's head was spinning from Cantrell's revelations by the time he drove up to a set of double security gates barring their path. It was as though the facility had made a bargain with the jungle to keep the road passable and the gate untouched. A bot exited the duracrete wall. Roughly the size of a seamball, the diminutive little bot trilled out its message in Signica, a bot language common to those used by the big corporations and the military. Mack was about to rig his bucket to translate when he saw Doctor Kavir walking toward his truck.

The bot turned and narrowed its bulbous lens at the woman. Behind the duracrete walls separating the jungle from the station, two pylons rose from the surface, folding back and forward until heavy blasters unfurled themselves from the structure. Weapons snapped to the doctor, who held her place. The bot's hovering eye flicked and tilted, hawk-like, as if considering the best way to take down its prey. The cannons moved in time with the bot, while thousands of targeting calculations flashed between the two in less time than it took than for a heart to beat.

The bot's Signica chirped, and both security guns and the sentry disappeared back into the wall.

"We're clear to enter now," Kavir said. "It just had to see me to mark the entry."

"Good to know," Mack said, motioning for the woman to get back in her vehicle.

Instead, she crossed her arms and leaned back, nose lofted in the air. "He can't go in."

"You really want to have this argument about the major now, while the Khindo Khabar is breathing down our neck?" Mack countered.

She turned on her heel, stomping down the roadway. Mack watched her until she finished her temper-laden trek by remounting the vehicle.

Cantrell was in his ear again while the doctor mounted her ride. "Mack, according to dirt that Martin and TC were able to dig up, it seems Kavir was extracted by a SATO team, only they couldn't hold on to her because of her connection to Dela Cruz. Too high profile. And take a wild guess what those cats looked like when they showed up?"

A grainy image from a security cam dropped into Mack's HUD, just as his bucket's AI slid in a warning that he hadn't hydrated enough today. He deleted the bucket's insistent message from the House of Reason's combat statistics group, allegedly sent to "help" keep the very expensive legionnaires alive. Deleting it made space for the grainy image, but the poor-quality picture looked worse enlarged. Mack continued to stare at it as algorithms in his bucket read his eye straining for clarity and extrapolated based on general size, shape, and nature of the screenshot.

"Legionnaires?" Mack asked.

"We don't know if they're real leejes, but I can tell you these SATO or whatever they are will probably come sniffing around the litter box if Kavir is getting ready to do her business," Cantrell said.

"Great. Now I have that image stuck in my head. Thanks for the info, Chief. Can you push this to everyone except the major?"

"Shoot. You ain't killed that ankle-biter yet?"

"Nice one, Chief. Mack, out."

The master sergeant led the convoy through the gate, taking note of them swinging closed behind them. "Creeper, Shy, you catch the gates?"

"Sure did," Shiloh said. "The place has power, unlike the rest of Kerhott. They got a jenny, somewhere."

The vehicles crested a hill to see the facility formerly hidden from them by the terrain. Cut into the side of a depression, the two-story building overlooked a river feeding a waterfall only a hundred meters away. Mack scoffed at the sight, as the name of the station implied a grand vista with a tremendous flow of water cascading into a lush pool below. While the river was wide, the drop of the falls was only about two or three meters at the most. The water churned at the basin of the pool before rushing on to a much smaller river that wound itself into the jungle. It was more like white water rapids than it was a waterfall.

Mack's rearview display showed the vehicle behind him pulling off to the side of the raised road before making its way down the hill. He stopped just ahead of it and kicked up the L-comm to see what had happened. "Lobster, this is Mack. What gives?"

"Mack, I got you on speaker with the doctor. She says we have to wait at the top of the hill so she can go down first."

Kavir weighed in to give her side of things. "Master Sergeant, I know I've been tough to deal with and I don't deserve any consideration from you, but you should know that I need to go down there and reset the security system. Anyone down below will have to enter a security key to get by, but anyone wearing Legion kit will be shot on sight."

"You want to explain this, lady?" Lobster barked through the speakers.

"Let it go, Sergeant," Mack said. "You were driving so you probably haven't heard it yet, but Chief Cantrell just sent an audio file of her giving me the lowdown." Mack waited for whatever number of heartbeats he guessed was the proper length of time when Lobster would have shot her before he continued. "Cross-load everyone into our trucks and give her the wheel."

"Sure thing, Top," the team breacher said with a mouth dripping with malice.

"Thank you, Master Sergeant," the doctor said.

Kavir took the dented technical on a rumbling course down to the front of the Centigo research center. She brought the vehicle close to the entrance, beneath a display of flags paying homage to the worlds on which the corporation had built its legacy. Cautiously, she exited the repulsor truck, moving with her hands at her side as though she expected some shooter to drill her full of holes if she'd hidden her hands. Each step toward the entrance was halting and calculated.

Two porticoes circled open on the walls beside the doors, unveiling a slender bot in each station. The things looked like protocol bots, complete with their wiry and gangly frames that set off the uncanny valley alarm in anyone who saw them. In some bots, that was by design. No one wanted to be around something twice as smart, fast, and durable as a real person without some identifying factor it wasn't one.

Mack stood with the rest of his men by the trucks, watching the affair play out through their bucket's optics, zeroed for the distance in case they needed to dump searing blaster bolts toward the entrance. He wasn't worried about his leejes hitting the doctor. Legionnaires were the one percent of the one percent the military had to offer, and his Valkyries were roughly the three percent of that. If you had Valkyrie wings on your uniform, it meant you could rain hell as well as heal.

The Vals spent almost as much time shooting as they did in their SAS, their section assigned specialty. Whether medicine, mechanics, or mayhem, each REC-Team legionnaire spent untold time with their finger against a trigger, so when the time came, they could dump bolts on the body with savage accuracy. A Valkyrie leej didn't get near a REC-Team, much less a rescue order, unless their blaster was as sharp as their scalpel.

The machines came free of their stations. The affair was deliberate and programmed, the bots moving as if on rails.

They stopped a few paces from the doctor to address her. Mack nudged the major. "Sir, need you to rip out that scope and get a listen on them."

Without comment, Tyler followed the master sergeant's directive and placed the spotter scope on the trio. While he'd been silent throughout the trip after his leaked drug deal video at the garage, each time the team needed him, he dove into the task like a ferocious anger-back. "She's giving them override codes to re-task them. She's pulling the mandate they fire on personnel in Legion armor as priority targets."

Moments passed and twin machines stepped out of her way and waited for whatever she directed them to do next. She waved over her head, beckoning the team to make the trek down the access road to the facility. Kavir signaled for probably a moment longer than she needed to before returning to the cab of her own truck to wait.

Way overloaded and well past retirement age, the ramshackle yet sturdy trucks meandered down to the front of the Serrabi Falls Research Station. Mack pulled up the driveway to another grand foyer, a staple of Centigo Corp's architecture if ever there was one. The absence of anyone moving about, juxtaposed with the thunderous white water close by, made the place feel like the eye of a storm. Quickly, the legionnaires dismounted and formed a defensive perimeter, using the trucks as cover.

Doctor Kavir's expression softened as she stepped by Mack to face the master breacher. "Lobster, I apologize if it seemed like I put security in place to shoot at only legionnaires. The people who started this like to dress the part. I was being cautious."

"Is that why you didn't roll with a Legion protection detail?" Lobster asked.

"A Marine Corps Special Operations Group from galaxy's edge on a deep float was probably not on anyone's short list for my security. Little chance of being infiltrated. I'm sorry, Staff Sergeant Wrigley."

Standing tall, Wrigley kept his posture erect, but his shoulders shuddered. Holding back the tears, as he said,

"We knew the risks, ma'am. My marines have done good work here."

"Superior work, Staff Sergeant," Kavir corrected.

"You keep talkin' like that, Doc, we might decide we can't live without ya. Make ya a permanent part of the team," Lobster said sarcastically.

Mack snapped twice. As a team sergeant, it was always a good policy to note when to step into the jokes or when to let them ride. It was an easy get on his last team, because he was the long dog, the guy who'd been there all along. Here, he was the new boss stepping in. But the clock was ticking down and it was already half past get-after-it-o-clock. "Alright, you guys. Hug fest isn't in the brochure. Shiloh, someplace high. Stringer, with him on scope and drone this place six ways to Sunday. Doctor, we assume you're here for a data download."

Kavir flinched at the statement, although she kept her bearing as she pulled her own pack from the truck. She handed Mack a data stick. "You would be correct. I need your team to rig the facility to detonate, but only after I purge my archive from the system. The primary power cells are fed by hydrodynamic power harnessed from the river. While the capacitors aren't enough to blow the structure, the backup generator is more than capable."

"Is it nuclear, ma'am?" Lobster croaked.

"It is, Sergeant."

"Fresher, Rooster, Creeper, and Tyler with me. We're going with the doctor," Mack said. "Everyone else on the boom."

As the team dispersed, Doctor Kavir beckoned Mack to the side. "Major Tyler can't be allowed near my work."

Mack kept his speaker volume low so only she could hear him over the sounds of the rushing water nearby. "I understand your frustration, Doctor Kavir, but my people are clued into what he is possibly planning and, as I was so recently reminded, I shouldn't turn down an available trigger finger."

18

"Two minutes until the download is complete," Kavir said.

Mack twisted back toward the observation deck, looking out onto the falls. Stunning. While Executive Board Room Number Two featured command interface controllers that gave them access to the facility servers, the view outside was something else.

You could see it every day, Mack thought, *and it'd never get old.*

Several floors below, his legionnaires were hard at work planning to destroy that view. Nuclear backup generators were a cheap way of keeping power flowing to unstable energy grids on planets far removed from the galactic core. And while such facilities were away from the core's amenities, they were still slaved to the politics. The House of Reason demanded that any reactor, even the micro types in the Serrabi Falls building, come equipped with an FFD device.

A Factor Fail Detonator detected the radiation levels on the reactor, and if such levels ever spiked to a consistent radiation dose without input from the staff, it would destroy everything within a certain distance to eliminate a caustic reactor leak. Mack had read the specs on the FFD when they'd gotten into the building. That particle wave explosive would turn everything within a half klick into a very uniform glass parking lot, but the larger region would still remain habitable. Of course, there were other ways to prevent a caustic leak that didn't involve an explosion, but those increased costs by orders of magnitude. A core world would have those safety features. Out here... not so much. The FFD it was.

"Tommy, two minutes until the Doc says we can light out of here," Mack said.

"Roger that, Top. Lobster says he'll have the system in our hip pocket just ahead of us running for the door. We'll have a command option on the FFD and can blow it at will. I'm also watching the doc. I have a mirror on everything she's pulling. But... there's something in the system she's not tracking."

"I'm sensing a running theme. Hit me."

Tommy pushed a schematic for a bit of net architecture into Mack's HUD. "Someone rigged multiple points of failure into the data stores. We knew flipping the switch for the FFD would trigger a comm burst, but there's more here. Try to shut down the power to the system? Broadcast. Confirm a delete for over thirty percent of the data? Broadcast. We're going to have to come up with something clever to keep this info to ourselves."

"Sounds like something those SATO clowns would rig. My guess is, since no one sticks around when they hear 'virus,' they bugged out before they could send the info," Mack surmised. "Can we blow the comms relay?"

"Lobster's going up there next, but I bet they have a fail-safe for that, too."

"How about disabling the code?" Mack suggested.

Tommy huffed at the idea. "I could, but it's going to take me a lot longer than two minutes, boss."

Time to bring the doc up to speed, Mack thought as he leaned over the station where Doctor Kavir was working. Part of her pack's contents spilled over a clam shell compu-deck she was hammering on with the intensity of a Legionnaire given to a 24-hour leave. Mountains of data played across the holoscreen, passing from the system into Kavir's deck, and then into a wired box resembling a thick battle board. Mack tapped on the case, calling her attention to it. "That's why they shot you down, isn't it? They didn't need you if your part of this research is on a reinforced computer built to survive a crash."

Kavir pursed her lips. "Those Legion agents, or whatever they were, knew it too. The ones dressed like legionnaires."

More misdirection. More of other teams having more information than his.

"Doctor, until you hear from me, do not delete any data from the system."

Her fingers hovered over the inputs as she stared at him questioningly. "Why not?"

"My system expert just found more trip wires in your network. Copying is okay, but don't hit the delete button," Mack explained. "We're trying for a work-around, but it's going to take a few minutes."

Kavir's expression soured. "I thought you said we were running on borrowed time, Master Sergeant?"

"Still are, ma'am. But we only get one shot at this, and if your whole deal is to keep this information from getting out, then this is the way we got to do it."

The doctor slammed her hands onto her hips, about to make another trademark tantrum when—*CRACK*—she flinched. Behind her, holographic system screens flickered; the duracrete wall splintered. Doctor Kavir slumped to her knees, her hands fluttering over a smoking hole in her turtlenecked shirt.

"Creeper!" Mack called out.

"I got her, Top. Make the call!" the medical sergeant shouted back.

Mack slid his back against one of the many workstations in the room. "Shiloh, this is Mack. I got a shooter past the ridge on the opposite side of the river. Do you have a lock?"

"Drone's caught the flash, Top," Shiloh said through his calm narrator's voice. "Sending a peeper to track and stack. The shooter was outside our perimeter. That's a pro-level trigger."

Across from them, Creeper and Fresher were on the floor with the doctor. They'd cut open her shirt to expose the wound. And while such a shot would have permanently ended any of them, she was moaning and struggling against the leejes to get back to her feet.

"How is this even possible?" Tyler croaked, laying prone like the others, his eyes wide from the sudden violent spectacle.

"Not human, sir," Creeper called out. He injected enough pain meds to prove his point, it much more than what was needed to put any of the legionnaires to sleep forever. "Mack, she's holding on, but she's losing juice quick. We can't move her until I finish sealing this."

Suddenly, Mack's palms ached with the ghosts of Kabillon. He slowed his breathing and watched the bio-sensors in his bucket read his heart rate settling. According to some of the best and brightest he'd ever served with, the only time a plan went according to plan was during the planning of the plan. This wasn't that, and he wasn't on a SLIC over Kabillon. His ghosts could go to hell. "Shy, this is Mack. I want to know the second you put that shooter down."

"Roger, out."

Mack rolled over to see what kind of cover they had to the door. "Creeper, Fresher, and the major, stay with the doc. Me and Rooster are going to snoop through the medicine cabinet."

The two leejes crawled on their bellies, moving from furniture, to workstation, to shelving unit, until they made their way to the door. Once they were free from the portal, they bounded in an all-out run toward the lift.

"You thinking what I'm thinking?" Rooster asked.

"Sure am," Mack replied. "Put the doctor's toy box to good use."

Rooster punched Mack's shoulder as they got to the lift. "Hey, you're going to blow my cover."

Knife-handing a desired direction to his fellow leej, Mack gave an order. "Tommy, get me a layout and keys to wherever the doctor was keeping her magic miracle patches."

The leejes raced from the speedlift once they were on their desired floor, running in the hallway with dull thuds along a lush carpet. Mack wondered if the rest of the private sector had it good enough to cover their floors in pillow-topped fabric or if the military was just that cheap. A map sprang up in his bucket, pointing out their course to one of the station's many labs.

That Tommy needs a raise.

Several footfalls later and Mack was at doors marked Lab 6, while Rooster knelt in the hall, covering the T-intersection beyond them. The door vented a heavy body of steam along the hatch seams while a warning spouted in several languages through the hallway's PA system.

"*Attention. You are now entering a controlled environment. Enter DECON and remain motionless with your arms and legs spread wide.*"

Mack jumped inside and picked up the L-comm. "Tommy, get me in here yesterday."

"Bypassing DECON, now," Tommy said.

The opposite door opened into a sterile-looking white environment full of equipment racks radiating like spokes in a wheel around a series of several tables at their center. Lighting sparked to life once the sensors detected Mack in motion, bringing the room into full view. At the end of the racks along each wall, a chamber bubbling with a syrupy fluid occasionally moved as though the liquid inside were following the master sergeant.

"Mack, you want rack four. Starting from the top, shelves one through four should have lunch boxes full of what you're looking for," Tommy instructed.

Mack dodged through spray hoses attached to lugs in the ceiling and around medical carts full of equipment he'd never seen before. As a Valkyrie leej, he'd seen most medical equipment across the breadth of the Republic. Their training required them to serve in trauma rotations through MASH units and in the nastiest parts of the Republic where gang violence was not only commonplace, it was expected. Yet some of the tech surrounding him was still alien on levels he couldn't even describe.

Mack tried for the required case, and instead of the door hinging open, the light inside turned red. A loud buzzer sounded.

"*Warning, unauthorized access attempt. You have two attempts remaining.*"

"Are you kidding me?" Mack shouted. "Tommy, what's faster—cutting or slicing?"

The L-comm buzzed as his electronic engagement operator worked digital warfare from his side of the call. "I'm sorry, Mack. I didn't see the cases were locked. The AI running the biometrics are internal to the case and not on the system. I can't slice it from here."

"Cutting it is." Mack ripped a plasma torch from his belt and snapped it against the cabinet frame. A flat locking bar that slid out and away from the frame secured the door even as it allowed the hinges to swing. A secondary magnetic lock kept the hatch secured in the event the lock was cut. For a bunch of science geeks, the cabinet designer had done a pretty good job in securing the thing using impervisteel and blast-resistant view ports. However, the sides of the thing seemed to be a single layer of metal, and Mack didn't need the contents of the entire case. A couple containers would do.

He pushed to cut through a thicker part of the plate, careful not to force it and end up with his hand covered in slag. "What happens if I get locked out?"

"You'll have to report to a supervisor," Tommy mocked.

"Good luck with that." Mack nearly fumbled the torch as the first globs of metal liquefied hit the floor around his boots. A ping, followed by the sudden appearance of Shiloh's blindingly bright icon appearing in his HUD, spooked the master sergeant. Another fiddly feature on the bucket courtesy of some purchasing agent who'd never had to wear one while suffering a two-way shooting range. The lens dimmed to obscure the cutting torch, but left the rest of the display at the same brightness. Mack smashed his tongue against the gritty toggle to answer the comm.

"Mack, it's Shy. The drones are picking up movement in the jungle around the access road. We ID'd at least three groups of fighters headed our way. One of the teams is running with some guys in light body armor with enclosed buckets. They don't look amateur."

Gripping his torch for the next series of cuts, Mack scowled. "SATO teams, probably. Maybe even the one that extracted the doctor the first time. Something tells me they took a play out of Sabine's book and contracted the Khindos."

Shy came over the L-comm with another report. "We punched the ticket on the sniper, but his buddies are sticking to the canopy, so we don't get freaky. Drones are picking up some gear that we didn't see in their toy box during the last brief. They caught a glimpse of man-portable surface-to-air, Mack. If I had a guess, they don't want us making off with all the fun in here."

Mack finished his cut, extinguished the torch and dropped it to the floor. He knocked on the scorched plate, dropping it into the space beyond with a tap as it struck the boxes on the other side. His combat glove, made to resist impact and extreme temperature, took hold of the matte-black, grooved container marked with a metal tracking label.

"Shy, wasn't the doc worried about the crazy security in this place smoking anything in a Legion bucket? Where's those guns at?" Mack asked. While he waited for Shiloh's reply, he strung a synth-cord through the cases, sliding the free running end through the pop out handles on each.   "Tommy says it has an assigned engagement area. They haven't crossed it yet."

"But it's there. Good. Hopefully, this stuff is made to better specs than their security," Mack said, more to himself than his sniper. He tied off the bundle, sliding the bandoleer of military-looking lunch boxes into the hall. "Run 'em up!"

"You're not the boss of me!" Rooster exclaimed. He caught the package on the run, slinging the bandoleer over his neck and sprinting for all his worth.

Mack punched through the storage racking, trusting his Legion-issued armored gloves to protect his hand. He removed the pulverized sections of the shelf, making room so he could grasp millions of credits' worth of Centigo Corporation's R&D. Sticking his arm into the storage locker, he twisted and turned to get at the right angle, like an agro-bear jamming its paw into a viper-wasp hive for honey. The awkward position put him in line with the rotund cylinders at the end of each row.

"Tommy! I'm looking at a tube on the wall. What is it?" Mack asked.

The answer came in an instant with not only the tube's identity but also a litany of facts that would make a college professor roll her eyes. "Those would be cellular suspension units for the nanites used in Kavir's special fix-it packs. The nano-bots utilize a hybrid of mechanized biotech, so not only does the—"

"Highlights, Tommy. Thanks. But I'm looking at one that has no AR-Code and just has a number. Seventeen-Oh-Eleven," Mack said, sending his screenshot to his Legion tech specialist.

"Ah. Based on the files I just shredded open, that would belong to one of our SATO kids. The group is labeled as SPERLOC. Stands for Special Research and Logistics Command. I ran it through Shy. He says it's a front."

Mack repeated the procedure for creating a bandoleer out of the rugged boxes containing what Tommy had tagged as the king of all skinpacks. And while Kavir had come to rescue her research and burn all the physical copies of her work, Mack decided this much of the stuff was more apt to save her life. As he threw the bundle over his shoulder, he drew his attention back to Seventeen-Oh-Eleven. "Any news on what it is?"

"Glad you asked," said Tommy. "Our black bag guys brought in a super brain to take the cellular-based nanites the doc cooked up to create a battlefield stim on stim."

Mack had seen mass dose infusers like the cylinders on the wall when he was stationed on Engador. They'd secured medicine runs to some of the nearby systems, and Valkyrie O-J-T covered batch loaders like this one as a matter of recourse. He traipsed to the strangely marked housing, stopping to search the trays and carts around the storage partitions until he found what he was looking for.

"Give me the specs, Tommy," Mack barked.

"It has to be used with a biocomputer worn by the user. If you're going to do what I think you're going to do, they should be in the racks close by. They sync to it when they're injected and go to work on the user. If you're human, the nanite cycled performance enhancer has the potential to make someone as strong and fast as a combat bot."

"Oh, is that all. Got it. Thanks, Tommy." Mack found the crysteel tubes for carrying the work en masse and inserted one into the filling chamber at the bottom of the tube. Liquid whooshed into the tube until a chime announced that it was topped off. Unfurling a rolled pouch on his utility belt, Mack tucked the tube away, then continued his search for the control system.

Something bumped his thigh, and with a flinch, the master sergeant turned into a waiting tray ejected from the bottom of the cylinder. A small digital device, not un-like a wristwatch or wearable GPS like they gave out in the basic army's recon course, was mated with an au-to-injector.

"Mine," Mack said, swiping the objects from the tray. "Creeper. It's Mack. Coming back to you. Sitrep."

"Kavir is almost ready to move," Creeper said, sound-ing surprised. "That being said, we have three pla-toon-sized elements trying to hem us in. Shy spotted some shuttle swatters in the mix and those fake leejes the doc was jaw-jacking about."

The senior leej dropped his purloined items into his dump pouch beside the tube as he sprinted back to the lift. "If you can push the doc to another room, pick one that gets you away from the windows. Something deeper into the building. I'm coming to you now."

Mack rolled through the hatch into the waiting stares of his legionnaires. The pristine dining facility on the oth-er side of the kitchen transom lay arranged in neat rows of tables, littered with spoiled food stains and wrappers. Evidently fleeing people were just as desperate here as in Sedeño's Fix-It Shop. The researchers must have rushed out in a hurry.

In the time it took for Mack to grab the vial and get back to his people, REC-Team Pelican had rearranged some of the chaos into an impromptu fighting position. Heavy dining facility style tables were overturned and stacked two deep interlaced with covered food-serving stations, creating a firing line in the event they needed to address unwanted visitors shooting through the windows or deal with anyone working through the building to the corporate chow hall.

The team had spread through the kitchen, working hard to slip from the noose rapidly closing about their necks. Lobster had Major Tyler and Staff Sergeant Wrigley low-crawling in and out of spaces within the dining room, setting up demo in the event the Khindos breached the building. With their battle boards perched on the stainless-steel serving counter, the trio worked through their brand of digital voodoo to push the team closer to the objective.

Make like a shepherd.

A T4X medical bot worked behind the cover of a serving station, leaning like an evil crypt keeper over its sleeping victim. The victim, of course, being Doctor Kavir.

But where Mack's imagined monster was the villain, T4X was very much there to help. Its eyes projected high intensity lights, shining with a radiance that would be the equal of any surgery suite in the building. Shuffling through discarded medical wrappers and dropped surgical expendables, the robot worked the scene with the efficiency of two expert nurses. Its four arms, like the radiating tentacles on certain species of Tennar, flashed back and forth between the legionnaires, asking for implements in the macabre medical scene, and the KDK printer mech standing behind them.

Like a chunky brick standing on its side, KDK had its own telescoping, rotating support that allowed it to change elevation based on the height of the surgeon. It rolled through the facility on twin outboard treads, its tinny speakers radiating a *bromm* sound as it moved, alerting passersby it was needed elsewhere. Having the bot on station was a boon for the legionnaires, as it could print anything, from surgical tools to living tissues for skin grafts, and in some cases, cloned organs. Although having a KDK was the ambition of any surgical suite on a host of worlds, they were prohibitively expensive, and almost impossible to acquire for any world not near the core.

"Hey, Mack," Creeper said with his arms up to his elbows covered in blood. "We found a block bot. Can you believe it?"

"Astounding. How long until we can move?" Mack asked.

"Soon-ish?" Creeper shrugged. "We've done all we can with her at this point. Her primary heart and the top lobe of her lung is cooked. She'd be dead if she were human. But we have all this gear and the medical twins rocking the robot thing, so there's that. With her physiology, she could be ambulatory if we got her stimmed up, but we're only going to have a hot minute to get her into the shuttle. She won't make it if we have to hump out."

Above their heads, the building shook with the rattle of heavy blaster cannons coughing death at them. A half second later, the walls thundered and shook.

Tommy snapped his fingers to call attention to him at the back. "Roof turrets just went active on the river side. Strike that. They just went active on all sides. Looks like our Khindo friends just made the engagement area. Drones have them ready to use those SAMs. Yep, now I got lasers painting the targets to take out our defenses."

"I thought the doctor said this place was a fortress?" Creeper said as he tore open another of Kavir's special trauma patches from the recovered lunch boxes. He applied the adhesive to the woman's chest, rubbing it with the blade of his hand to ensure a solid bond.

"Oh, it is," Mack assured him. "Take a look out that window. Remember the butler bots outside that greeted our good doctor? They answered the doorbell and brought friends."

19

The first thing a trooper ever learns in basic training is that no plan survives first contact with the enemy. Instructors hammer this idea home through relentless OST, or occupational specialty training, and then over and over when they get to their unit. Nowhere in all the military branches spread across the Galactic Republic is this pounded home harder than in the Legion. And if epic doses of suck were required to teach rudimentary units in the military about this, the levels outside the dining hall of the Centigo Corp's Research Facility at Serrabi Falls were enough to teach a master class.

Blaster fire launched from the jungle by the Khindo Khabar, using the terrain as natural fighting positions at the edge of the engagement area set for the building security. The fighters swarmed in, leveled shots of small arms fire, then retreated to a safe distance to see how long it would take for the guns and bots to go back to standby once the attacking force retreated, or at least made it seem that way.

With no security element running the system, the bots were on a sort of autopilot. They were left to their own devices and the parameters hard-coded into their AI by the security team before they left the facility almost two years ago. The night that the people of Serrabi Falls found several men dying of a strange contagion that swept through the facility. The night Doctor Kavir had escaped.

But during the third rush of the Khindo Khabar, the bots didn't disengage and move back to their sentry positions. Something had kept them out and waiting, standing outside like silent sentinels guarding their tomb of a building. During the third rush, Tommy had taken control of the bots and changed their mission objectives and putting them to work to get the Valkyries and their charges away from the gunfire and off the ground.

The original bots that came from recessed porticoes to speak to the doctor, shed their concierge persona in favor of going pure war machine. Hidden blasters apertures hidden in the palms of their hands projected dizzying blaster fire into the jungle ahead of the service road. This decimated a Khindo assault team attempting to use a tarp covered in leaves to confuse the bots. They discovered all too painfully that it didn't work.

The first bot leveled a hurricane of blaster bolts from its palm, punching into the advancing squad and catching the tarp on fire. To finish off the intruders, the second machine kicked the anger-back dented truck. Flipping end-on-end, the truck crashed onto the squad, killing more of the men who had survived the hellacious blaster barrage.

The intricate sensors on the twin machines picked up the first traces of whistling as incoming mortars threatened to pepper the building. Outgoing waves of fire from the structure's roof dealt with the descending mortars, decimating them in flight while the bots watched with their dispassionate face plates scanning the terrain for further threats. The threats came from the jungle to the side, where a heavy weapons team launched a barrage of rockets at the bots.

The rocket salvo moved too fast and too close to the ground for the facility's counterfire system to train accurately enough to stop them. In a detonation of tremendous, smoke encrusted explosions, the two mechs disappeared within the foggy destruction covering the target area. When the smoke cleared, the bot closest to the jungle was destroyed, and its twin was pulling itself along the fractured duracrete with the only arm that had remained on its torso after the destruction.

A single blaster bolt, not unlike the one that had threaded Doctor Kavir, lanced out from the jungle and into the bot's power cell housing. Another explosion racked the structure, raining bits of duracrete and broken bot.

A rush of fighters ran from the jungle opposite the main entrance. They managed to get halfway between the canopy and the start of the access road when the security guns fixed to the roof opened fire. The fusillade of blaster fire coughed from the top of the building, raining iridescent hell on the advancing forces. They stumbled in the wake of the targeted counterattack, with several of their number splattering into the manicured lawn, while others escaped the wholesale slaughter to the security of the jungle. Only this time, the guerrilla fighters were off in their calculations, marking where they were safe and where they weren't.

Two titanic robots, covered in armor and bristling with weapons, came from the sides of the building to take up positions at the corners. With the twins shattered into scrap, the heavy security mechs plodded from their housings on a platform rigged with spider legs under a torso wrapped in impervisteel plate armor and brimming with weapons.

One bot remained as a defensive measure while the other ran at the jungle, skittering across the blasted street, over the broken truck, and past Khindo corpses to the halfway point in the no-man's lawn where it had solid target locks on the runners. Its first shot from its shoulder-mounted rail gun lacerated a thicket and turned the escapees into fertilizer for a jungle that definitely didn't need the help.

Palm-vented blaster bolts flared out to kill the rest before they could disappear into the tree line. As high-gain multi-spectrum detection systems tore through the jungle to identify the next of its targets, a recoilless rifle round struck the ground nearby. The hyper velocity round tore through a patch of land like a meteor. The bot whirled on its attacker—a gunner near the riverbank, who, startled, fumbled his weapon and scrambled away.

The spider-legged machine rotated on its platform, bringing it in line with this latest attacker. It raised its arms to level equal blasts in the man's direction when a bolt flying across its front interrupted the shot. It waited for a series of seconds and then the heavy security mech's seismic and waveform analyzers registered its partner destroying a different Khindo rocket team, freeing the hesitating bot to launch its own salvo at the fleeing target.

Explosive bolts caught the escaping gunner, blowing him and several of his friends into the river. Their bodies swept away into the rushing current, a soon to be convenient meal for some river beast.

The mech sentinel rushed back to its side of the building, taking control of its corner and signaling back to the leejes inside that the initial defense had been successful. The loss of the twin bots, a ruined truck, and decimated landscape notwithstanding.

"What do the scans say?" Mack barked. He ticked off the feed, returning his gaze to his fellow legionnaires.

"Drone recon has a significant force of Khindo Khabar breaking away from marines in Kerhott and making their way here," Tommy said, marking the display for team access. "Rough estimate is at least one thousand fighters heading this way."

"Our boy Dosa Keem isn't going to let us get away with slapping him on the ass and then running for it," Mack commented. "But that isn't my biggest concern. That fake leej team could be out there plotting some nefarious stuff to trip us up."

"You just wanted to say nefarious," Rooster said.

As the last of the echo from the explosions outside died away, a flutter washed over the system. Tommy tapped at his battle board to isolate the issue and keep it from slagging their gear. "Looks like we got a tick on the dog. They got an interface module past us during the explosions."

"That's leej-level tactics right there," Creeper said as he rolled the last of some bandaging across the trauma pack on Doctor Kavir. "The security system would have detected something like that if it wasn't for the big bot battle gunfight outside."

"How long until they break us?" Mack asked.

"That's where it gets weird. The mod isn't going for the guns," Tommy said. "It's going for the system. They're trying to set off the FFD."

"No," Doctor Kavir interrupted from her spot on a food-prep-table-turned-surgery-suite. Her eyelids were flying at half-mast and she had that groggy voice that followed a person out of anesthesia. She slurred out, "They're trying to trigger the upload. That's why I caused the outbreak. So this wouldn't happen."

"Why would you do something like that?" Wrigley asked. Apparently, the marine staff sergeant hadn't been party to all the doctor's plans before he'd signed on.

The doctor coughed, struggling to find enough breath to answer the marine NCO. "Weaponized strain of Naguri flu. Short life span. Most of the population was immunized. Only way to get people away from my work."

"But all those people still died," Wrigley protested.

"Foreigners who never got the shot," Kavir said amid a flurry of coughs.

Mack waved the staff sergeant down, preferring to deal with problems they could work right now. "Welcome back, Doctor Kavir. We thought we'd lost you, there, for a minute. We're close to getting you out of here, ma'am, as soon as we kill that drone and find a way around the locals. Tommy, do you know where it is?"

"It slipped right by our heavy security bots and climbed to the interface station for the dead mechs," Tommy grumbled. "Bots are trying to handle it, but I can't lock down the system at the same time I'm trying to keep some half-a-hacker from blowing the FFD."

"So don't lock it down. Let it loose," Major Tyler said, from his position surveying the battlefield with the spotter scope.

"Come again, sir?" Rooster accused more than asked.

Tyler ignored the man's tone, even though his rank demanded he put the younger leej in his place. "Not that I have to answer you, Corporal, but in my time as a Legion—"

"We know your background, Major," Rooster interrupted. "Currently serving fleet as an L-comm control officer, heaps of praise from former commanders and glowing OERs, yadda, yadda, yadda. We don't need the resume. We need the specifics of your idea."

Tyler whirled on the junior legionnaire only to have Rooster remove his bucket and slam it on the metal countertop between them. The scoured and worn helmet had no rank or insignia. His ID Tag in the HUD and his scuffed-up gear was how everyone on the team knew who he was. But with the scratched bucket between them, Major Tyler was now face-to-face with Captain Rashad.

"How are you here?" Tyler croaked.

"Better question. Why are you here?" Raptor countered. "Because it's not to steal anything like that video suggested. That twit on the *Reliant*, Norris-Foster, was willing to use her connections to get you a spot in Valkyrie selection if you brought back some tech. But the tech she wanted was in that jar Mack had. You haven't even moved for it, which means you're a solid leej. So, what. Is. Your. Idea, sir?"

Tyler's shoulders deflated as he locked eyes with the leej commander. "Stop fighting the code. It's probably deeply embedded in the system. So instead of trying to prevent the throw, just change who catches it."

"That's good juju, sir," Tommy offered. "Sir, as in Raptor, not the other guy, Major, sir."

"Can you do it, leej?" Raptor asked, lofting his bucket. The captain's face was haggard, as though deception and worry had worn him down. "Can you get the upload to transmit to Snowball in the shuttle versus where they want it to go?"

"If you trust me," Tyler said.

Boom, boom, boom—thunder from above. They'd run out of time.

Mack got the team's attention. "That, gents, is the sound of the guns on the roof going hot as the Khindos try for another run at us. Major Tyler, work with Tommy and get a new address for that upload, sir. Creep, need you to finish bagging the patient. Blanks and Staff Sergeant Wrigley can stay to give you a hand. The rest of us need to punch this lady on outta here and get her to a hospital, fast."

"You got a plan?" Raptor, formerly Rooster, and now Raptor again, asked.

"Not end up in a decomp chamber at the wrong end of a Drusic marriage proposal?" Mack said as he kitted up.

Raptor set his hands on the table, giving him the only rest he was about to get as he laughed at Mack's joke. "And can you be more specific in the tasks, conditions, and standards thereof, Master Sergeant?"

"Oh yes, sir." Mack broadcast wide into the L-comm, alerting everyone on their net to the plan. "Snowball, this is Mack. I need you in the sky and ready for a hypercomm burst transmission. All ADA should be focused on us, so there's less chance of them worrying about your tail. Download the data to the black box on the shuttle."

"Oscar Mike," Snowball called back, using the ancient colloquialism for being on the move.

"Boys, Stringer's drones have air defense and anti-armor on the hill road we came through. We're going out there with security bot support to take it back. We need to hold it long enough to pull in Maggie. She rides out with the doc and the staff sergeant to the waiting Royal Marines. Ducky, I need you to affect that linkup with Sabine."

"What's a Maggie?" Doctor Kavir asked through the haze of drugs and bandages.

"Will do, Top," Ducky said, chuckling at the doctor's question.

Mack slanted his comms for a direct line to Tommy. "I need you to pack up the doctor's compu-deck and that black box from her first shuttle. She was using it like a portable drive."

"Pack it up or am I SSE?" Tommy asked.

"What's your job, leej?"

They both knew the answer to that one. A legionnaire assigned to a recovery team had three missions when on the ground. Recovering mission critical assets lost in the field, asset deniability, and sensitive site exploitation. Or "find and rescue the pilot, destroy his craft so nothing is left for the bad guys, and learn what you can about them so it won't happen again."

"On it, Top," Tommy said.

A tap on Mack's armor got his attention. He spun around.

Creeper.

"Top, no time to sand-table this out, but new guy, Fresher, rigged a MAPO in AR. When this is all done, if no one comes for him, can we keep him? Huh? Can we?"

Creeper might have been the second-highest NCO on the team, but he joked like the class clown who constantly needed attention.

Mack tagged the waiting icon for the mission objective overlay in his HUD. It wiped over his screen, showing waypoints and mission critical map markers scrawled with Valkyrie leej jargon. "This is good. He do this by himself or did someone help him?"

Creeper shrugged. "Oh, you know—team sport, team credit. Listen, Top, the doc has been looking at your butt while all this was going on, and although I tried to tell her you really only go for Drusic males during life-or-death situations, she still wants to give it the old college try."

"Master Sergeant," the doctor began as she pulled aside a face mask filtering in nanite-infused oxygen from a small box lying beside her. "I see you got a bottle of the black batch nanites in that pouch. That's why we came here. That's why we have to destroy this place and keep the data from getting out."

"They're not here for the skin packs?" Creeper asked.

Kavir rocked her head from side to side. "It was never about the skin packs. Those were already set to go Legion-wide this year, and then military-wide once we had the stock. The nanites—they came with a PDT and an injector, yes?"

Mack produced the items, which she arranged for use. She locked the GPS-looking reader to her wrist, clipping it to the back of her smart watch. The system grafted itself to her skin, where it drank in bioelectricity to power the device. A swipe across her smart watch, and the little device hummed to life with a small display that went dark after a few seconds. She filled the auto-injector, then plunged it into her thigh.

"Whoa!" Creeper called out as he struggled to reach the woman before she emptied the entire contents of the injector into her leg. "We just did some pretty ugly surgery on you, and we don't know what is in that or how it will react to your new med patches."

"But I do," the doctor said as color flushed into her cheeks. Her eyes fought against the light with her pupils dilating to the size of credit chits. Creeper shared the vitals monitor he'd been running on the doc. The Lorisam's unique physiology displayed in the stats, showing a powerful heartbeat and respiration returning to normal as a second, weaker heartbeat appeared in the display.

"I thought you said the second heart was cooked?" Mack asked his medical sergeant.

"I should be good for a few hours now," Doctor Kavir said. "Make no mistake, I'm nowhere near capable as a legionnaire, but at least now I can shoot, move, communicate, and possibly aid in my own extraction. Isn't that what the Valkyrie movie said was your thing?"

"That holo was terrible," Creeper said. "No tech advisor on scene, and that dialogue! Dreadful."

As if in punishment for the joke, rampant blaster fire shattered the observation window overlooking the dining area. Furious bolts and chemically projected slugs smashed into the improvised barriers. Smoke and ozone filled the air outside. The doctor crinkled her nose.

"Would that stuff help us?" Mack asked.

"You'd need a signature on file. Without one, you could stroke out," the doctor yelled over the gunfire coming from outside the kitchen. With each passing moment, she seemed more herself.

"Mack! We're moving," Raptor called out.

"Take it!" Mack shouted back. He slid the AR map over his view, seeing that his leejes were already in motion. "We're taking the street. Doctor, stay here with Creeper until Maggie shows up."

"Who in the Nine Hells is Maggie?" the doctor shouted.

Mack ran through the back of the kitchen in a half crouch and luckily avoided being domed by a stray blaster bolt that winged off something outside. The bolt struck a series of hanging pots knocking them into a clanging mess on the rubberized kitchen floor. Mack slammed into the double doors, dumping himself into the hallway with several leejes already moving to the loading dock.

"So there I was, my first day on the job, and I encounter a sea monster that could have made me famous. Now I'm covered in kitchen grease and blaster bolts," Fresher said through the L-comm.

"Joke less, move more, Cherry," Raptor called from his position as second man in the stack.

Mack drank in the data coming into his helmet. He should have stayed in the kitchen with the doctor to call out instructions for the hit. But someone had to be out here keeping Raptor out of trouble, and with the amount of incoming fire they were receiving, the CO was going to need all the trigger-tappers he could get. The fire team wound through the hall, ending their rush at the overhead door from the loading dock.

"Three, two, one," Stringer called over the L-comm.

Fresher slammed the control for the white overhead door, which slapped into the ceiling with a resounding *whoosh*! Outside, a hulking, heavy mech on a spider's chassis took up the entire width of the opening.

"Unit One-Four-Alpha waiting for advance on objective," it called through its speakers.

"Advance," Fresher confirmed.

A launcher unfurled from its back to lock into its waiting hand. As the machine tapped its way on the impact suppression support struts it called legs, it angled the back end of the launcher away from the legionnaires.

"Back blast area clear. Firing."

The magnetic accelerator powering the rail gun fired a canister full of flechettes at nearly nine kilometers-per-second across the space next to the building. The shock wave of the munition going kinetic dislodged dust, dirt, and plant matter in the loading dock surrounding the bot as it continued to move toward its newly acquired objectives, courtesy of Tommy taking control. Whatever impact strikes had hit the bot before it launched the rail gun were quickly silenced in the weapon's wake as it crashed through the jungle.

The leejes poured out of the dock with Mack trailing. To him, the clack of boots across the duracrete seemed at odds with the rapid fire, light electric thumps coming from the hulking security mech as it moved toward the road. Under Tommy's control, the war machine crept toward the Khindo Khabar who controlled the road at the top of the hill.

Running behind the clattering spider war-mech, Mack noted several ravaged craters in the jungle. Evidently, the bot had fired the rail gun more than once in defense of the facility. Smoking holes in the vegetation were littered with the broken dead of Khindo Khabar fighters who'd gotten too close to the war machine and the station's many guns. At least twenty fighters had died in this one spot. If there were this many in each of the blast craters caused by the security system, it pegged the Khindo Khabar leader, Dosa Keem, as a man that spent his people's lives easily and without regard.

Whoomps sounded behind them as the auto cannons on the roof barked out a serenade of destruction into the trees, capped by the slower and more distinctive fire of Shiloh's N-18 sniper rifle. With the road in sight, the bot continued its methodical path toward their enemy while the legionnaires took a hard turn into the jungle.

Vines and smoke choked the space as soon as they entered the dense tree line. The leejes spread out, breaking into two fire team wedges that allowed them more mobility and greater cover as they moved. They ducked and crawled, jumped and slithered their way through the tangle of brush on a furious rush to make the next waypoint before the Khindos could fully wreck their new armored pal.

Ahead, Fresher held up his fist, signing for the entire team to sink to their knees and evaporate into the jungle. A line of Khindo fighters walked as security just ahead of a four-man team lugging what looked like an old-timey machine gun. The Khindo weapon's team aimed the girthy metal barrel menacingly toward the legionnaires, promising high-cycled, metal-slugger death.

"Mine," Raptor said through the L-comm.

As if working by hive mind, the leejes slowly turned in their hides, moving enough of their camouflage ponchos to put them in line with this new batch of targets. The members of REC-Team Pelican considered it a bonus that their victims just so happened to be bringing them new toys to play with.

Signal indicators barked along their HUDs and the leejes each fired a shot. Mack's rifle bolt slammed into the skull of the man holding the barrel for the deus ex machine blaster. He'd waited a half second after everyone else pulled the trigger. With the guys on the back plate dying first, Mack's target lost his grip last, which meant the barrel wouldn't fall first and get caked with mud and vines.

Stalking from their positions, the leejes crept to the enemy team. They brought out Legion-issued knives shaped like combat meat cleavers and did the wet, sticky work of conserving ammo for the fight that was sure to come, just in case any of the shots hadn't killed their targets outright.

Mack pulled open the ammo can for the weapon and was pleasantly surprised when he didn't find charge packs.

20

The leej team crawled another few meters and came to rest where the jungle thinned out, in no small part due to the efforts of the spider-legged heavy security mech currently terrorizing the Khindo Khabar on the road. The rail gun was designed as a support weapon for the mech, and the bot only carried a back-fed reloading system of eight canisters for the gun. Of course, hardened impervisteel flechettes moving at nine klicks per second worked pretty well for throttling insurgents trying to fix gun emplacements to take out the ones on the facility.

"Two technicals on the road at the top of the hill. One behind the hill hanging back," Stringer called out from his perch beside Shiloh on the roof. "The back truck has a drone jockey with two aerial peepers overhead tethered to the movement of the vehicle. Be careful moving where the canopy gets thin."

The Khindo Khabar were most likely running civilian drones on a standard signal, unlike the Legion machines which tethered to them through the L-comm. Certain civilian models used for security came equipped with multiple vision modes, although they still wouldn't have the tech to see the legionnaires through the camouflage ponchos that now covered their advance. Ablating heat, while they changed colors to match the terrain and employed sound baffles to muffle their movements, the Legion cloaks hid them from most drones on the market. Unless the bad guys had scooped up advanced models from the night markets where other bad guys liked to shop, these drones didn't have a shot at seeing them.

From the angle they seemed to be pointed at and the patterns in the air they were tracing, Mack guessed the Khindos were focusing on what was coming down from the facility rather than what had just crawled in through the back door to kill them. Mack took in the view from the security mech, One-Four-Alpha, currently taking fire from the road at the hilltop.

The spider mech darted in and out of the jungle, careful not to drag any of the incoming shots toward the leejes crawling behind the enemy like vipers. Several rounds pinged off the mech's reinforced armor, merely scorching it, while the Khindos lobbed the occasional fragmentation grenade at its legs. Happily, the Centigo Corporation had spent a pretty chit reinforcing the narrow legs with enough hardened impervisteel wrapped in armor. The minor blast damage only scratched the paint.

Focused blaster bolts plowed through the insurgents' firing line, forcing the Khindos to dart along the sides of the road where a sluiceway for water runoff gave them some cover from the bot's onslaught. One bolt punched hard enough to sail through one fighter's flimsy plate carrier—that was minus the plates—and straight into the engine block on the lead technical. The power cell caught fire and soon the truck was spilling acrid, spark-tinged smoke across the road, further concealing the legionnaires.

"Mack, it's Stringer. If you're going to roll out the surprise, do it now. My creepers show a platoon-sized element coming up the road. They want that access point controlled, and they think spending the guys to do it is going to get it done."

"Roger, out," Mack confirmed. He pushed commands through the HUD, waiting for the flash back indicators from the leejes telling him they were on point. "Teams one and two. Pull 'em in!"

Several blasts of crisscrossing blaster fire sailed from the leejes hidden among the vegetation. Wrapped in copses of trees or behind rocks jutting up from the terrain, the Valkyries of Rescue Team Pelican assaulted the Khindo traffic control point with targeted fire, killing four in the first barrage.

"Team one, fall back; team two, cover," Mack directed.

Beside him, Fresher and Blanks halted their attack on the TCP, turning to run farther into the jungle where the canopy all but obscured them from view. Once they were in position, the team dropped to the cover of a twisted root of palm trees wrapped by ground-hugging fronds and low hanging vines.

"Firing!" Fresher called into the L-comm.

"Moving!" Ducky shouted through the net. He and Lobster sprinted through the jungle while the besieged One-Four-Alpha and the rest of the assault element continued to punish the fighters on the road.

For a mad minute, the Khindo fighters dropped into the recessed side of the street, treating it like a trench to move through without being shot. Their shooting kept the heavy mech down below the hill where it was having a difficult time acquiring targets, and their movement through the sluiceway also seemed to control the returned fire coming from the jungle. But when the platoon-sized element showed up, the fighters turned from cautious to combative now that they had friends backing them.

Renewed heavy shooting ignited from the enemy's side of the road, passing back and forth beneath the repulsor vehicles. The repulsor fields warped the shots along their trajectories, sending the bolts in wild misdirected arcs. Trees and duracrete took the brunt of attacks meant for other targets.

"Mack, it's Tommy. Upload in progress."

"Roger, out," Mack confirmed. "One more bound. Team one."

The legionnaire special teams leap-frogged deeper into the jungle, further obscuring themselves amid the canopy and shadows while still lancing the road with effective, accurate fire. For its part, One-Four-Alpha also repositioned, moving to a section of road where a column of palm trees and boulders marked the boundary between lawn and jungle.

"Wait for it," Mack said, looking to his commanding officer playing the part of machine gunner beside him.

During the second rush, the renewed strength of the fighters at the Khindo-controlled TCP ran for the road. They spread across the trucks riddled with score marks and punched full of holes, one team moving while another covered. Soon the force spread into the jungle's entrance, using the thin copses as cover as they shot into the dark. Without optics, they might as well have been firing blind.

"All Pelican elements, dozer. Dozer. Dozer," Mack said, pulling a poncho from the fully emplaced machine gun they'd stolen from their last victims. The wide-mouthed subdued barrel stuck out from a pile of vegetation while the gun pivoted on its tripod.

"Going hot," Raptor said behind the weapon. He mashed down the butterfly trigger, feeding a steady diet of linked grenades into the weapon. A four-round burst flew from the gun to race through the firing lane they'd prepped the gun for. A moment later, the rounds detonated on the truck, finally rupturing the smoking power cells. The battery packs catastrophically failed into a full detonation, bouncing the truck from the ground. It detonated midair into a tornado of molten fire and flak. Billowing white smoke, it bounced on the duracrete, falling into the roadside ditch to crushing Khindos.

Raptor coughed out another burst from the decimating machine gun then lobbed the thirty-millimeter, high explosive, dual-purpose grenades into the second vehicle. A few rounds didn't detonate, but punched melon-sized dents in the vehicle's frame. Sounds like an auto-hammer blasting an impervisteel plate echoed through the trees until the last of the five-round grenade burst remembered their purpose and exploded on impact.

The power battery on the second truck exploded, sending sparking gobs of fuel gel in all directions along with pieces of the truck turned into hyper-velocity flak. Secondary explosions sent a wave of fiery shards into the backs of the Khindo fighters facing the hidden legionnaires. The enemy on both sides of the road absorbed the shock of the twin explosions in five short seconds.

With flaming wreckage raining across the hood, the driver of the third vehicle threw it in reverse, leaving stunned and crippled soldiers in the road to absorb whatever came next without cover. The engine whined as the repulsor dragged the vehicle backwards on a fishtailing reverse course down the road.

"He's out of the lane," Raptor shouted into the comms.

"This is Call Sign Maggie. I am entering the engagement area from the eastbound access road. Target acquired, Captain Rashad. Commencing destruction of enemy victor," called Maggie's husky voice over the net.

Past the legionnaires, a heavy blaster bolt sailed into the scene and punched the technical in the center of the cab. The bolt meant for armored vehicles and knocking aircraft out of the sky turned the center of the truck into a fiery wreckage sliding along the access road as it lost power. Another bolt flashed into the truck, blowing it from the duracrete into a ditch. The bouncing, burning vehicle came to a crashing stop as its repulsors failed, turning the technical into an anchor.

Maggie the K-15 infantry assault mech raced along the road at near max speed until she came in line with the legionnaires. Seeing the approaching war machine, the leejes jumped from their positions to steal a ride from the gravity-defying bot. Mack and Raptor carried the grenade-spitting machine gun with them, trundling from the jungle last as they carried the heavy load. The leejes pulled the machine gun from their leadership, placing the weapon on its tripod along Maggie's back plate.

"Raptor and Ducky, run this back to the shop and ready for exfil," Mack said. "One-Four-Alpha, get back to your station and reload that rail gun. We're going to need it. The rest of you, with me. Let's make things difficult for our new friends."

Fresher pointed across the manicured lawns leading to the river on the other side. "What in Oba's bathtub is that?"

Rockets lashed out of the jungle, white smoke plumes trailing as they took flight. Point defense batteries on top of the facility rained burping strokes of violence across the flight path, sending torrents of blaster fire into the incoming munitions. High-explosive detonations burst in the early morning sky, leaving gouts of smoke where the rockets formerly dominated the distance between the two points.

The security AI used its counterfire radar to home in on launcher hidden in the jungle. A salvo of roof-mounted mortars thumped from the facility, whistling their way into the jungle on that side. Devastating explosions flared in the unrelenting dark of the canopy, obliterating entire squads of insurgents in waves of high-angle-delivered incineration.

During the assault on the roof, another recoilless rifle round struck the spider mech while it protected the side of the building facing the river. Although the mech had the high ground, the Khindos had spread along the riverbank to create a killing field where multiple firing points converged against the bot's armor. With his attention divided, a fighter on the jungle side shot the heavy anti-tank round into the side of the bot, who was directing fire against insurgents using the riverbed as cover. Although the weapon hadn't killed the mech outright, it crippled two of its legs, severely hampering its mobility.

Considering the Khindo fighters were focused on the remaining heavy security bot, Maggie turned on the burners and resumed her approach to the dining facility with Raptor and Ducky along for the ride. Raptor directed grenades against the riverbed as Ducky fed the belts to the ravenous weapon, since the automatic grenade launcher had a two-mile range for indirect fire.

"Well, ain't that a match made in heaven?" Mack barked, pulling his leejes' attention back to the task at hand. He motioned for them to reenter the jungle to see to the next part of the plan.

Lobster remained in place after shooting several of the Khindos who didn't have the good sense to die right away. It was bad business leaving someone alive if they were only going to wake up and try to kill you. The legionnaires crawled around the team demo expert as he went about setting charges in and around the smoking wrecks.

Mack answered an L-comm chime. "Talk to me, Shiloh."

"We're ditching the roof, Mack," Shy responded. "Getting too hot up here. That fake kill team or whatever is directing the Khindos to slag our defenses and doing a damn good job. They took out the PDC on the back side of the building, and we're down to the two heavy security mechs and one has a limp."

"Roger that," Mack replied as his team reached the corner of the jungle before the road. "Link up with Tommy and Raptor. We're prepping the stage now for our principle. In the meantime, have Stringer max out those bots for our defense. Are there any more bots in the facility other than the heavies?"

"We have two personal security bots left. Tommy has them tasked to run security through the facility. It's a big campus, Top."

"Tell Tommy to program those for M-and-M and send them out. We're not going to be here long enough to worry about this," Mack directed.

"You got it, Top. Shy, out."

"M-and-M?" Fresher asked, making himself a fighting position from the trees where he could see the road.

"Murder and mayhem, kid," Mack responded. He chose his own spot for cover, ready to lay down covering fire for Maggie to pull the doc and the marine to safety. Past the once neatly manicured grass, Maggie had slammed through the dining facility window and parked herself in the center of the room. A magnification on his bucket, and Mack could see them loading the doctor in the trauma carrier on Maggie's side. Wrigley fought his leejes on getting in the mech but gave in to Creeper, who threatened him with a good deal of violence unless he complied.

"One minute until exfil," Creeper said into the net.

A blaster bolt sounded somewhere through the trees, and Mack searched the feeds on Stringer's drones for the source of the shot.

"I'm hit," Lobster called back. "Didn't see where the shot came from, but it's somewhere near the other side of the road."

"Stay there!" Mack said. "I'm coming to you. You two stay and cover the road."

The senior NCO charged through the trees, using one of the previous tears in the jungle from One-Four-Alpha's rail gun to fast-track his way back to where he'd left the team demolitions expert. Tracking along the smoking crater in a sprint, he found Lobster where he'd fallen into the ditch on their side of the jungle, his weapon aimed up and ready for whatever came next.

"Right behind—" A burst of blaster bolts leveled at him from close range cut Mack off mid-sentence.

He dove toward a twisted, tree-covered depression between him and his attacker, using the terrain to soak up damage from the shots. Another flurry of bolts pinned him into his cover, preventing him from returning fire.

"Hold this, suck pump!" Mack tossed a fragger, and heard the scramble of the fighter on the other side jumping away. The blast went off before the enemy combatant could make the jungle floor. A thunderous boom echoed through the trees, spraying sod and vegetation. As the debris rained down around him, Mack sprinted from his hide to another copse of trees on his right. He reached the new spot with a thud, slamming himself into the dirt. Then he hit the activation lever on a banger and launched the grenade toward the same spot as the first. A high-intensity pressure wave accompanied by intense light and sound ripped into the space, leaving the jungle silent after the shock effect passed through.

"Knock that off!" came an angry voice to Mack's rear. The voice was accented and precise, like someone from the core or mid-core worlds. Definitely not a local.

Mack rolled out and away, only to be cracked violently in the head with a rifle butt from a charging soldier in armor. The bucket held and the armor did its job, but Mack felt every bit of that impact. Standing over him with the rifle ready for another swing was a man in legionnaire reconnaissance kit. It was at this moment, looking into a Legion visor with the fighter pulling back the weapon for another hit, that he knew this guy wasn't a true legionnaire. The kit was right. NK-4 shortie was right for the area of operations. But this guy wasn't a leej.

Using a rifle as an impact weapon was a last resort against unarmored opponents. A strike against a joint was ten times more efficient in rendering the opponent pliable, especially when the ligaments tore or a bone broke. Hitting an armored head doesn't have the effect the holos and entertainment vids say it does. Knocking someone out requires a tremendous hit and the head to be braced against something to take the full force of the blow. Removing the armor might help too.

With a solid hit, an attacker might get stars in their opponent's vision, a flash blackout, or possibly some intense vertigo, but a complete knock out required the kind of force this guy's weapon and posture just didn't possess.

Mack guessed that the banger must have shorted out the econo-leej's charge pack. The foe took another swipe. Mack ducked the attack, rolling across his shoulders to bring himself in line with the fighter. He dropped the flat of one foot on the man's armored ankle while the other hooked behind the knee. With a pull-push motion, he tripped the other fighter as gunfire echoed behind him. He fast-crawled over to the enemy leej, throwing his body on top of the inert weapon to pin it between them.

The impostor rained blows into the spots where the Legion armor didn't quite work. He at least knew to do that much. A hit to Mack's armpit with a follow-up elbow to the neck. Several hits created enough space for the man to pull his sidearm from a plastidex holster.

Mack savagely went for the arm, keeping the weapon aimed away from him in the process. Controlling the pistol kept his hands too busy to prevent the man from reaching up with his free hand and stabbing him under the plate. Mack roared into his bucket and then did something his opponent misinterpreted. He hiked himself farther up on the man's chest, making his opponent think he was angling away from the blade currently probing the tissue above his hip for something vital.

As the knife-wielding fighter pushed for a deeper stab, Mack rotated along the man's chest, throwing his feet out to the side until his knee landed on the bicep of the knife arm. With his hands around the other and now in a dominant position, Mack wrenched the arm backwards and swept towards the man's head. Muscles in his opponent's shoulder ripped free from their anchor points as tissue, taxed well beyond its ability to stretch, shredded like meat on a serving table. The shoulder tore from its socket in a loud pop that sounded like someone clucking their tongue through a loudspeaker.

His adversary released his grip on the knife, howling in electronic agony through the speakers of his helmet. As the man spasmed in pain, Mack swept one hand behind the ruined shoulder and fell to the side. He groped for the sling on the dead weapon, pulling it toward him tight enough for it to creak as he braced the man's head with a shin he'd dragged up for the purpose.

Somewhere in the deep parts of his mind where fear and regret lived, he could hear the faint thrumming of a SLIC engine. He could taste copper in his mouth as he pulled tighter against the sling. The synthcord under the sling's fabric pressed into his scar, bringing all the memories of when he wasn't strong or fast enough. The chorus of ghostly screams from his old team falling to their deaths rose in his memory only to fade as Lobster shouted out colorful insults mixed into threats he was directing at someone. The taste of blood and sweat returned as Mack arched his back to add his body weight into the choke. With blood rapidly closed off by the vice created by the real legionnaire in this situation, the fighter passed out.

Mack withdrew the knife from his abdomen, a slippy little punch dagger, and plunged it up under his unconscious opponent's bucket before angling it down and slamming it through the man's spine. With no time to waste, he vaulted to his feet, vertigo still swimming in his vision. He dragged his rifle back up and began a stumbling rush through the trees, straight into the path of another explosion.

The master sergeant hit the dirt as detritus and plant matter rained through the trees, taking far too long to finish falling through the heavy fronds of the canopy. "Lobster!"

"Over here, Top!" the leej called. "Still breathing."

Mack slid out from the perimeter of the trees into the depressed sluiceway where he found his man. "How bad, and what was that boom?"

"Armor took most of it, but my left arm is cooked," the nasally leej whined. "I used one of the demo charges we rigged for the drive-by. Had two wannabes on the other side of the road shooting at me. I'm not a big fan of that cosplay crap."

"I think you won the argument of who wore it better, though," Mack said. He took stock of the man's armor. One of the two shooters had overcharged a weapon to punch through the heavier Valkyrie kit. The bolt hit and skipped, tearing out some of the synthprene and punching a hole through the upper arm. "Undersuit looks like it's sealing up. And I just so happen to have some of these handy Doc Kavir patches that are guaranteed to do things no other skinpack will do."

Lobster groaned as Mack helped him up. "Oh yeah, what's that?"

"Hell if I know, I didn't read the rest of the package. C'mon," Mack said, guiding the leej out of the ditch. "You still got enough boom on the road for the drive-by?"

"Oh yeah. I just used a little to paint that side of the road," Lobster croaked. "Side note. I hate to be the bearer of bad news, but you're leaking."

"It's a slow leak. We'll patch me and you when we get to the drive-by point," Mack huffed. He didn't know how bad the stab actually was, but his armor was already in the process of applying what pressure it could and adding coagulants to retard the bleeding. Getting back to the firing point they'd set up so he could dig into his ruck for Kavir's special patches would go a long way toward keeping both of them in the fight.

Arriving at his remaining men, Mack fell into his pack and fished around for the bandoleer of lunch boxes.

"What happened to you two?" Fresher said as he came from his position to work the patches onto the errant legionnaires.

"Fake leejes hit us from across the road. Used him as bait and hit me when I came to check on him," Mack said. He took the patch from the younger leej and tore it from the packaging. Prying apart the armored plates, he applied the patch beneath the synthprene undergarment. Doctor Kavir's new miracle trauma dressing went on much easier than the lowest-bidder-produced skinpacks that were handed out through the Legion. Although Republic skinpacks were toted as the greatest thing since the repulsor was invented, they were not at this level of good.

Mack felt a tingle as something in the patch went to work. The sensation of pain faded away as a sharp bite methodically poked him in the side along the wound tract. While not intensely painful, he was aware of it, and each time it happened, a feeling of numbness over the spot replaced it. Bringing up the bio-comp in his bucket, his armor was tracking a rapidly sealing wound channel that recovered at an astonishing rate. Mack gave serious thought to raiding the rest of that lab once they got back to the facility.

"Oh, that's intense," Lobster crooned. "I mean, it's like when you go to those little places on the strip where the Sinasian ladies put your feet in the bucket and the little fish in the water eat the dead skin off 'em, ya know?"

Mack shook his head. "No, Lobster, that's definitely just you. But I'd like for the rest of us not to get shot or stabbed from here out and just take your word for it."

21

Just once, TC wanted to have his ops center somewhere nice. They didn't need a corner penthouse with a view of the ocean, but something with room service and a bed that didn't feel like they'd stuffed the mattress with rolled up socks would be a welcomed change.

In fact, having any mattress at all would've been better. Instead, they'd rented several rooms on multiple floors in one of the worst districts in Terum City. Sabine had set them up with good food, good references to the locals, and a suitable location where everything was reachable in minutes versus hours. The only thing that wasn't good was the accommodations. But they had power, and that was all they really needed.

What he didn't have were technicians who knew where the garbage cans were. No matter how hard he tried, he just couldn't convince his technicians not to litter the place up like some zhee refugee camp. Every operation they'd been on, TC had to play Mom for a bunch of supposedly grown adults.

"We know. We know," Martin protested, despite TC not actually having said anything about the mess. He flipped his bangs out of his eyes for the umpteenth time that day while he held his hands up in surrender. "We'll clean it as soon as we get through this next batch of code."

"You said that two batches ago," TC countered.

Martin took a lengthy sip from the fabled cancer cup and straw, then offered, "You know, boss, we have a process. I mean, you have a process too. And we don't bug you about your polo shirts having buttons even though you never button them up to the top. All of us just assume it's part of your process."

"You know what else is part of my process?" TC asked. "Keeping the chief busy so she doesn't go hydra-bear on you and maul you off the balcony for leaving this place a mess."

The techs all hovered their noses above the screens to spy the chief pacing back and forth in the middle of a call. The woman tapped her ear-comm, muting her mic in order to get in a word or two.

"Don't you heathens look at me for this," Cantrell barked. "I've already offered to end you nerds and sub-let our tech needs through the locals. I bet they wouldn't leave my room a mess."

Miraculously, the technicians at the makeshift work-stations suddenly found religion and plasteen bags to put their trash into.

"Boss, I got a shark on the line. You're going to want to take this," Cantrell said, pointing to the slate connected to her earpiece.

"Thanks, Chief," TC said. He looped his own earpiece on, tapping the center to connect to his battle board. Several pings in just the right rhythm and pitches later, and TC was good with the encryption level assigned to the call. He snapped twice to get Martin's attention, then made a chain link sign with his hands to indicate what he wanted for the comm. "Director Lawson. I'm kind of in the middle of something, sir, but for you, I've got some time. What can I do for you?"

The man's icon on the battle board was static for a moment until the buffered data came through the encryption. The director's rounded face snapped to the display at TC's icon going from static to active. "Damn, man. You don't look like you aged a day. And for Oba's sake, when are you going to get the treatment to put your face back to the way it was? It's been a few, hasn't it, Nate?"

TC nodded at the assertion. "Certainly has, Dave. Certainly has. So, what's up?"

"Well, I got myself a bit of an issue over here at DOS headquarters. My people are telling me you have a REC-Team stomping through Nuzon. Is it that thing with the Centigo doctor that got shot down?" Lawson loosened his tie with one hand while he stirred a white teacup with the other. He tapped the cup nervously, then produced a bottle of caramel-colored liquid to add to the beverage. The syrupy contents flowed easily through the crystalline bottle into the drink, Lawson adding just enough to flavor and not enough to slur his words.

TC grimaced. He'd had a feeling that he was going to get this call or one like it when reports from Mack and Raptor on the ground filtered in. A scant glance from Martin riding a barely perceptible nod was all TC needed to follow through with this man, who was technically his superior. "I copied the Republic Department of Security on all elements of the rescue order. You should have it right there on your system, Dave. Was there a problem?"

Unfortunately, TC already knew what the problem was. He'd received word from Captain Dawson aboard the *Reliant* and knew it would trigger the hounds barking at the gate. Raptor had asked his friend Saber, the

Gungnir platoon commander, to pose as him until they could figure things out. Without removing his bucket, Saber returned to Raptor's room and hid there until his friend could return. Someone must have wanted a visual confirmation on Raptor, bucket-free, to ensure the wily officer had gone along with the order.

"Yeah, it seems we already had an operation on the ground there, working things out. You know how it goes, Nate. One hand not knowing what the other one is doing." Lawson drew the cup to his mouth for a noisy sip. "I'm just trying to save us from the paperwork of a potential blue-on-blue here."

Blue-on-blue, a reference to the indicators on a map overlay for friendly forces shooting at each other. They were all supposed to be blue, which meant there shouldn't be people in cobbled-together Legion kit shooting at his people.

"If this team already on the ground is Legion like ours, we can save a bunch of trouble and just clip them together in the L-comm. Do you have an LS or DO number I can give my guys?" TC asked.

Lawson steepled his fingers, letting them tap in sequence as he considered the question. "C'mon, Nate, you know I can't give details like that over an open line. What I can do is ask you to call your team and back them out of the AO before things get difficult."

A second glance toward Martin got TC a thumbs-up from the technician while keeping his face firmly connected to the straw on his carcinogenic cup. "Dave, let me see if I can help you with this, especially since the line is encrypted. You have no ops plan registered in the system for this, which means it's not your play. DOS missions are Legion executed only, so we have the best in gear and training available. No L-ID number means someone is pulling a string on your back so that the right words come out."

"Now you listen here, you little punk—" Lawson fumed into the comms, flinging his arms wide and spilling his drink.

"Oh no, Dave, we're far past name-calling here," TC said as though he was about to fan out the winning hand for the card table. "My guy just shot you a removal order for Captain Emilio Rashad, the Bravo Section commander for Task Unit Pelican. This is a medical summons declaring the captain unfit for duty because of ongoing cancer treatments. Just one problem, Dave, he's never been to cancer treatments. So this doctor who drafted this, a lieutenant colonel, lied on an official Legion document about a legionnaire."

Lawson's eyes shot back and forth, reading the document as fast as he could to confirm what his counterpart was showing him. Another document popped between them, showing Raptor's complete medical record from Legion command.

TC pointed to the tech who brought an audio file into the link for him. "We also have this recording of a House of Reason delegate, Ramsada, speaking with this man, whom we can't find anything on. I found it strange that a delegate would be talking to a ghost, so I used one of my own to track the audio. It comes back to a voice print ID used as security access to the DOS. We have a record of accesses of the voice, but no identity linked to it. Funny that it was used to access your wing of the building on more than one occasion."

"How dare you?" Lawson asked, slamming his fist on the desk and rattling the teacup saucer.

"I dare quite a bit, actually. Including telling my man Rashad the name of the highest-ranking nitwit who'd ruined his career." TC pointed to the recording still hovering in the mixed display. "I really hope that anonymous guy who keeps showing up isn't on that mission to Nuzon. Because if he is, the leejes of REC-Team Pelican are going to dust him like target paper on the range. Then who's going to protect you?"

"What are you getting at?" Lawson spat, still angry but shrewd enough to hang on and see where the closing trap was headed. Men like him always looked for the way out.

TC shrugged as he turned to face the camera on the board. "Here we have a light colonel doctor, arrested by the Legion for conduct unbecoming and attempting to compromise an ongoing Legion operation. Short version, treason. Delegate Ramsada, currently being secured by local authorities to be questioned by Marine Corps Special Operations Command for enabling a terror cell to shoot down a Republic shuttle during a sanctioned operation, endangering the lives of Repub citizens. Short version, treason."

Lawson slapped his data board, attempting to end the call, but only jumbling his video feed.

"But you," TC continued, even though Lawson's screen faced the ceiling, "you tried to burn Raptor, a legionnaire. Who does that?"

Barely touching his keyboard, Martin displayed the stats for Lawson's system. The records from the cybernetic interface node implanted in Lawson's skull, the height of supposed un-hackable communications, were on display for TC to peruse. Martin working hacking miracles with one hand while drinking Adrena-Berry fizzy pop with the other might have been proof of false advertising for the node.

"My guys currently have their fingers in your cookie jar, Dave. They have your biometrics at an off-core bank where Ramsada deposited a truck ton of money, which we'll eventually link to you using DOS assets to insert a black-budget team on Nuzon. I wonder what Captain Rashad will think of that after being kicked out of the Legion."

"Someone just kicked me from their system," Martin said with a scowl. "I could have sworn he didn't have anyone on staff that good."

TC shrugged and turned to Nissa joining them in the room. Her expression hinted to TC she wasn't at all fine with the accommodations.

"Did you catch that?" TC asked her.

"I've been to the office before. David Lawson is hardly what the agency would call a fit man, seeing as he pays someone else to wear the bio monitor during his biannual PT test," Nissa said. She reached out for a water bottle, eyes locked on the screen, gingerly searching until a helpful analyst placed it in her hand. "Thank you. Ninety seconds to the lift from his office. Roughly two minutes to the secure basement. Another three to open a line in the cipher station."

A live feed appeared over a workstation depicting Delegate Ramsada being held under Marine Guard in her room in the hotel. Several marines in dress uniforms hovered over the woman when a duty uniformed trooper entered the scene. The new marine handed a folding comms device to her superiors, which caused them to exchange glances. After a quick bit of chatter, the delegate took the device and answered it.

"Delegate Ramsada, it's Dave Lawson from DOS. We have a real problem. Can you talk?"

"Of course, Dave. What's troubling you?" Ramsada asked, as though reading from a script.

"We've been made. I need protection from a legionnaire."

An earth-shaking *boom* from Maggie's main gun exploded into the jungle facing the main entrance, blowing down a copse of trees in a fiery rainfall of burning palms. Dirty smoke hung in the choking, humid air, obscuring Legion lines of sight to the enemy firing position.

"Master Sergeant, it's Maggie. I am loaded and ready for exfil," the mech said into the net.

"We're ready for you, Maggie. Bring it home!" Mack shouted.

The mech ripped itself from the structure, scattering broken struts and shattered glass across the access road leading to the loading dock. Maggie unfurled her legs and rested her armored bulk on the reinforced supports. Another bellow from its main gun fired off a bolt the size of a hool's dorsal quill. The burning, kinetic fury of the shot tore into the edge of the lawn, spraying the jungle's edge with a wave of dirt and rock.

"Mack! I got a target lock on our girl!" Stringer shouted through the L-comm.

Maggie understood the warning and bounded off the ground on a bed of repulsor force, tucking her legs beneath her She rocketed toward the back of the building, with One-Four-Alpha running after her, taking the target lock onto himself. She made for the corner, right into a scene of carnage as the twin security-bots-turned-assassins hacked and shot at the Khindo Khabar insurgents looking for a back way into the building. They stripped the fighters of their weapons and then stood guard at the base of the hill some meters away from the river.

One-Four-Bravo, the second of the heavy security mechs, limped into the targeting beam searching for Maggie. Bravo fired multiple blaster bolts from its palm, turning that side of the jungle into a shooting range backstop.

"They got that targeting beam fixed," Shiloh called. "But I can't see what kind of weapon it is."

"Can you get close?" Mack asked.

"Sending." Shiloh's shot rang out from the top of the executive boardroom on the top floor of the building. His bolt pierced the boardroom window and flitted across the lawn into a tree some two hundred meters away. The energy projectile smashed into the tree bark, shaving off a girthy section of the trunk as it caught the tree on fire. "I can see the guy ducking me. One of our mystery rent-a-leejes."

Major Tyler snapped an image through the spotter scope and sent it to the team. "That gunner is repositioning to get another shot on Maggie. Looks like some form of man-portable missile system rigged for the ground. If they have more of those, we're going to be here awhile."

Mack smirked at the insight. For a point, or whatever the hell he was, Tyler was shaping up to be a hell of a spotter. Too bad he was an officer. He'd come across plenty of men who'd exhibited the same traits in the Legion. They proved themselves as valuable combatants or an expert at some desirable skill, only to get promoted and have the unit suffer for their lack of being able to negotiate a series of command decisions. And now Tyler's quick eye on the spotter scope probably just saved the doctor riding in the drone. "Shy, if you or the major see that guy stick his brain bucket above the mud, put him back down. In fact, do us a solid and take the old girl out for a jog."

Shiloh immediately took the reference for going off leash. He shifted to the MANPADS gunner's right and drilled the first man he saw. The kinetic impact of the N-18 precision rifle platform sent a gloriously robust bolt into the man's head with such force that it broke his spine and slapped him against the shooter behind him. Tyler called out distance and direction for another shot, which Shy greedily took. The bolt sailed into another series of fighters looking to dig into the hill for a fighting position. One shot killed the first man it hit and shaved off the cheek and ear of another.

The firing line at that side of the compound stopped. The enemy fire teams frantically sought cover away from the devil legionnaire painting death at a distance. Even with the threat of a sudden end to their victory for the Khindo Khabar, not all of the men hid from the fight. A fire team slunk away below the tree line, using the hustle of their people to hopefully confuse the legion sniper.

Stringer pushed an overlay into everyone's HUD. Scores of red blips, heat signatures being read by his drones, withdrew from the crest of the hill to the jungle beyond before turning toward the access road. "They're moving the party uphill where they think we're going to make a run for it."

"Keep driving them that way," Mack said. "Reconfig the defense guns to dump a load of suck in their direction."

From his perch inside the kitchen, Tommy directed the facility defenses to renegotiate the engagement area. The original system designers calculated sectors of fire to keep the weapons from shooting constantly and melting the barrels from overuse. With Mack's directive, Tommy was about to do a little gardening the hard way.

Auto defense turrets went into overdrive, slamming bolt after bolt into jungle at the top of the ridge. Point defense batteries meant to knock out incoming rocket-propelled munitions and mortars redirected their calculations to join the turrets in turning the well-defined demarcation line between lawn and canopy and slag it into mulch. The sheer violence of the affair was so loud, those in the building could feel the vibrations through the floor on every level.

On the back corner of the facility, the M&M bots cycled their blasters against Khindos looking to gain entrance to the back door. When their confiscated blaster rifles went dry, the bots repeated the process by picking up weapons from the dead as they moved through.

"Mack! First light security drone is down," Stringer said through the net. "Khindos just got some reinforcements coming out of the river and they just chewed him up."

The master sergeant calculated the time it would take to drive the Khindos to the top of the hill near the ruined vehicle, using targeted fire. The scene played out in his mind as a countdown, even as the ghosts of his past haunted his consciousness with doubt. He'd played this game before, and his men paid the price for it. Last time he'd counted on the line holding. This time, he would count on his people instead of his kit.

Just as Mack was about to give the go order for the K-15 extraction, Tyler shouted into the net, "I got a rocket gunner moving away from the road. He's moving toward the river."

Almost as if he'd heard them, the gunner stood, defiant, lifted his rocket, and fired. Shrieking across the lawn, the missile sizzled from the jungle in a rush toward the facility, blasting through Tyler and Shy's boardroom window.

Where were the point defense cannons? Busy sweeping the jungle for Khindos. With all defenses turned to offense, there was nothing left to strike down the incoming missile.

Shattering through the glass, the projectile detonated. Shock waves of plasma and explosive pressure decimated the boardroom floor, tearing the roof from the building. Lux furniture and d'Velour carpet, pristine holo displays, and a silvene kaff station all reached critical temperature in the mass reaction explosion punishing the structure, incinerating in a fiery rainfall of smoking debris and ash.

"Shy! Tyler!" Mack cried out over the comms.

What had he done? He'd effectively baited a hook and dangled it over the water, only to have the shark jump into the boat.

Suddenly, the L-comm sparked to life. Relief flooded his system.

"Mack!" Tyler coughed into the net. Hack and heaving, he struggled for breath. "We're good. We're both banged up but can still KTF."

"Mack, I just saw the feed," Raptor shouted into the comms. "That was an AP missile!"

"If they have more of those, we need to take them out before Maggie can fly!" Mack shouted back.

"I'll pull One-Four-Bravo and hit the wood line to kill that shooter," Raptor volunteered. "Can you bring the hunt from the other side?"

"On it," Mack barked back. He turned to Lobster and knocked his bucket against the master breacher's helmet. "I'm taking the new kid to help the boss. As soon as you or Blanks see the signal, get that mech moving."

"Roger, Master Sergeant," Lobster said. With his good arm, he pulled the magnetic webbing from his armor, handing over the rifle grenades and his launcher. "KTF."

"Oh, make no mistake about it, bro. We're going to kill them first, kill them last, and kill them all," Mack said as he snatched the weapon and crawled away, leading Fresher in his wake.

22

Mack sprinted across the access road behind the hill, steering clear of the voluminous blaster fire being traded by both sides. The Khindos were taking as direct a route as possible toward the blacktop to secure it and keep Doctor Kavir from riding out in the mech. Although they didn't observe the legionnaires stuffing her inside like so much luggage, they seemed laser-focused on stopping anything from going in or out of the facility. If they stayed true to form with so many other documented attacks against the Nuzon people, they would eventually storm the place and take prisoners to make an example of, or sell back to the Republic.

That's if.

Because right now, their tactics were being directed by the faux legionnaires. And their team leader was smart. He'd judged correctly that Mack and crew were trying to secure the road for some purpose, and was in the process of denying it to them. Within the confines of his bucket, Mack berated himself for not keeping at least one gun on point defense to knock any incoming indirect or missile fire from the sky.

That was the kind of mistake that cost lives. And there he'd be, alive and looking at shredded kit as evidence he'd failed, again. Evidence his Valkyrie wings had lost their gleam.

But as he led the kid through the vine-encrusted palms and thick vegetation on their way to kill a missile gunner, he knew. That was all garbage. While he'd had his fair share of bad luck and plenty of suck, he was still a legionnaire. The wings were on his chest. And with every heartbeat run past the goal post, Mack proved to himself that he belonged.

Especially with the kid behind him sucking wind as they dashed madly across the road. They just didn't make leejes like they used to.

"Hunker down," Mack called through the L-comm.

The two-man fire team dropped into the vegetation with their ponchos pulled over them to break up their outlines and absorb the shadows. Just beyond the tangled bush full of spines and colorful flowers, a troop of Khindo Khabar traipsed through terrain, flattening vegetation and pushing their way through a devouring jungle.

"They setting up by the road?" Fresher panted.

"Probably," Mack agreed. "We own that side of the street and the heavy security mechs with us are shooting at the hill, so they're doing what we just did. They're crossing the road below the hill and circling around to sneak in the back entrance."

Fresher followed close behind Mack as he continued to slither through the brush. "Shouldn't we tell our guys they have incoming bad guys?"

"Stringer can see them. They know. Just like they know about that," Mack said, pointing.

Down the road, the Khindos had arrived in technicals and unloaded their gear and people beyond the hill in hopes the leejes in the facility couldn't see them. They'd left their trucks parked across the access road to obstruct anyone trying to drive from the facility. Luckily, the repulsors on a K-15 ISM were more than capable of driving right over the grav trucks.

"So, instead of all this traded gunfire, why don't we just slip into the jungle and disappear where the Khindos won't find us?" Fresher asked as he climbed down from a low tree onto a batch of flat stones at the bottom of a cut.

Mack slid down next to him. A survey of the area showed the cut in the landscape probably carried rainwater from the top of the hill to the bottom to some pond or similar terrain feature. It made for a great path to move around the insurgents undetected. In answer to the kid's question, Mack said, "We have three jobs, kid. Find the pilot, blow the ship, and gather intel. We've done one out of three."

"The doctor being the pilot and the facility is her ship," Fresher guessed.

"Winner, winner, Raptor's dinner. Let's move," Mack prompted.

Spastic eruptions of gunfire covered the tramp of leej boots moving through the jungle, burying every twig snap and gravel crunch under a chaos-laden soundscape. Working in fits and starts, Mack and Fresher applied an ancient method of movement used by snipers since before mankind took to the stars. *Stop, Look, Listen, and Smell* was a mantra that had saved countless lives during many a marksman insert. With buckets on, the team couldn't smell without going through some displays that could either allow outside air into the helmet, or analyze parts-per-million in search of a specific request. That took time, and the buckets more than made up for losing the aromas of war by way of enhanced vision modes, particle detection for chem attacks, and auditory sensors that would make a dog jealous.

A titanic explosion interrupted the chatter of blaster fire and reverberated throughout the jungle. For a moment, the insurgent gunfire lessened as they lay against the terrain, hoping that whatever had just touched off was on their side. The far distant chirp of blasters intensified, a sure sign the leejes hunkered into the facility were using the time to their advantage.

"Was that us?" Fresher asked.

"Yep," Mack confirmed. "Dream Team Boom-Boom. Lobster attaches a brick of high-ex to a drone and Stringer flies it to a spot where the Khindos are likely to cross. Motion trips the AI, waking up the drone, and the boys decide when to blow it. The insurgents we saw crossing the road just had a bad day."

Listening to the shots renewing in earnest, the duo climbed from their brief halt to pick up the pace. Their squeeze along the cut became more perilous when the planet dropped one of its irregularly scheduled rainstorms for the day. The deluge hit the canopy first, flitting through the leaves until thick streams of water poured down.

"Watch your footing, kid. Sprained or broken ankle is not on the menu today," Mack said. At the top of the cut, the two leejes readied themselves for a straight-out street fight.

A motley assortment of Khindo fighters positioned themselves into loose squads around a low ridge just inside the tree line. An older man in a plate carrier and no shirt wiped his brow furiously as he connected charge packs to a rapid charging station attached to an ATV. Beside him, another man with a set of tactical glasses moved his hand over a map covering the top of a weapon's crate. One hand pulled back near his cheek, a simple motion to expand an image in AR, while his other brought a radio to his ear.

The proffered radio call brought in a squad from over the hill. They loudly exchanged some manner of conversation Mack's bucket couldn't translate. It must have been some pidgin dialect the bucket wasn't slotted for as he recognized the occasional word in Galactic Standard. But it was enough. A combination of wild gestures and half understood words clued the master sergeant into the Khindos' plan.

The returning group had just come in from the road to restock on charge packs. That's what happened when your military training focused on quantity rather than quality. They were going to lead the force cloistered about the ATV to the road to create a firing line. A grizzled veteran covered in facial scars took a new bandoleer of charge packs and slung them over his shoulder. His men mimicked the hustled exchange, and with a quick whistle, Veteran Guy brought everyone to their feet. After forming into squads, the group vanished into the vine-laden palms and rain-slicked mud.

Mack motioned for the kid to slide to his right amid the low-hanging fronds marking the top of the cut. Becoming the bottom ends of a triangle with their targets positioned as the apex, their firing points gave them the angles needed to take out the remaining men. Rain slapped the jungle canopy, splashing into torrents cutting through the muddy terrain, muffling careful Legion shots.

Each bolt found a permanent address in the enemy skulls, dumping their heat and kinetics through brain and bone matter alike. The leejes jumped from their hides, racing across the muddy jungle to reach the vehicle, kicking away enemy guns and double-tapping bodies as they passed. With their enemies' blood now feeding the trees, Mack cloned the map reader's battle board while Fresher rigged the mobile charging station with his own version of boom. A thin wire attached to a plugged-in charge pack traced underneath a synth-cord keeping the charger held to the vehicle. Looking like it belonged as part of the machine, the wire connected to a grenade taped to the underside of the ATV fender. Pull the charge pack, you get the boom.

"Trap set," Fresher signaled through the L-comm.

Mack finished cloning his target's device, slotting the info for a burst-comm to Tommy so he could sort through it, looking for anything useful. He was most interested in the map. It was a satellite snap over Serrabi Falls, showing the facility, the access road, and the surrounding jungle for a kilometer. What most interested him were the tactics the Khindos used to keep the map current. Dot markers, indicating squads, moved through the spaces in the image as the battle between leej squad and insurgent fighters played out. A picture window above a dot flared to life, this one able to be read by the bucket's language filter.

"Espinosa's Squad at approach to access road. Set."

Mack hit the radio. "Tommy, I just sent you an info burst. The map is being updated in real time. Push it to the team and see if you can trace it back to source."

"Roger that, Top." Tommy replied. "Mack, how close are we to having those AP missiles knocked down? The kids are getting antsy riding in the trunk."

"Moving up now. How are the defenses holding up?" Mack asked.

"We only have the one heavy left. Both personal security bots got slagged by a group of Khindos being led by a fake leej. PDC on that side is down and the AP missile punched a hole in the roof. Took the PDC and a blaster cannon on that side with it."

"Stay frosty, legionnaire. We're almost on the other side of this," Mack said, right before he slid into a new channel. "Raptor, it's Mack."

The comms lit up with a man breathing heavily into his bucket. Wracking coughs sounded through the net, indicating that the team commander was having a bad day. "On it. Master Sergeant. Approaching enemy position. Now. One-Four-Bravo, lagging behind. But still with me. You good? Leej?"

Slipping into the team roster, Mack stole a glance at Raptor's vitals and what he saw wasn't good. Critical incident mapping software in his bucket showed the captain was having problems processing oxygen from a decreased breathing volume. The bucket increased the O2 Sat in regular intervals through his air supply, but the biosigs were less than stellar. If Mack had to guess, Raptor had been using whatever sludge was in that silvene bottle to combat the effects of his particular breed of cancer. Many were the companies and charlatans throughout the galaxy offering cancer-fighting treatments at a fraction of what the core worlds pharmacies charged, besides offering it all with full anonymity.

But further query into the captain's medical state revealed Mack had guessed wrong. Raptor had been hit multiple times in between when they'd set up the ambush for the missile team and where they were now. Three impact strikes registered along the chest plate with no penetrations shown. Aside from an increased oxygen mix being force-fed to the captain, Raptor's armor was also displaying a pain suppressant being pushed for a broken rib.

"We took some hits, sir, but we're still trucking," Mack said. "We're approaching the OP to target one. As long as we don't get washed down a hill, we will be there in two mikes. You good, sir?"

"I had a right of way argument with some of the neighbors. One-Four-Bravo handled it. He's waiting at the jungle's edge to cover our scoot back to the building and I'm in place now," Raptor huffed. "Let me know... when you're there and we'll... kick this show off."

"Roger, out." Mack picked up his pace and flicked a waiting comms window from the kid.

"He didn't sound good, Master Sergeant," Fresher said, sounding solemn.

"That's why we're pouring on the speed, kid. Let's get this over and done with so we can all get a drink." Mack slid into a dense growth of ferns infesting an area between several trees. The oblong, purplish ferns were rigid and most likely sharp enough to cut leather, never mind skin. When people wondered why so many species of jungle fauna had thick fur coats in such a hot environment, flora like this was the reason. Mack's armor got chipped camo as he shoved into the underbrush far enough to get a micro-lens through the growth.

Wirelessly linked to his bucket, the micro-monocular was just powerful enough to get the master sergeant visuals of the terrain below. For the second time, Mack was not happy with what he saw. The Khindos below them had once again used the terrain to their advantage, staging minor fighting positions close to the jungle's edge. Utilizing natural rises and depressions in the landscape, the insurgents set up two fighting positions from which they could dominate this side of the jungle against the facility's countermeasures.

From their depressed location, the fighters could run forward, lay down fire on the building, then fade back to the cover of the jungle canopy. Looking over their impromptu fire base, Mack reasoned the Khindo Khabar positioned here had weathered several counterattacks from the Serrabi Falls defenses. Expansive, deforested lanes through the jungle swept up to the fighting positions and then over them, courtesy of the heavy security mechs launching their electro-mag projectiles into the jungle. With blaster scoring marking up the trunks and heavy swaths of palms burning from incoming bolts, it wasn't a stretch to see this was where the Khindos launched most of their attacks against the station.

Some parts of the trees surrounding the target area seemed to weep tears of blood from beneath their hatch-marked trunks. For a moment, Mack wondered if it were a sap native to the area, but with it only occurring through the lanes, it was a good bet there used to be insurgents fighting from those spots. That is, until mech-launched flechettes tore through the jungle, splattering anything organic across a kilometer of forest.

Three members of the force scurrying below the master sergeant and his recruit were adorned in Legion light reconnaissance armor with the trademarked buckets that marked them as the one percent of the one percent of Republic forces. Unfortunately for them, their performance had proven them otherwise. Regardless of their inability to rise to Legion standards of combat conditioning and doctrine, they were still armed with Legion kit and weapons, which put them in a whole different category than the Khindos they were advising.

"If we move to a better position, the motion trackers in their buckets are going to tag us and we'll be karked," Fresher said.

"Won't be a thing. We let Raptor swoop in and give them a face full of talons. They'll be too busy with him to notice us splatter them back along the lawn," Mack countered.

"That's going to be a problem," Raptor interrupted. "I have a fighting position right below me and I don't see you."

Mack froze as he toggled the HUD for the map they'd taken off the Khindo leader they'd just dusted. "Damn it. We have three fighting positions in between us, Rap. The two on our side have a batch of shooters in one hole and then three of the fake leejes popping canisters for the AP launcher in another."

Raptor took several loud, gasping breaths. "I got a single wannabe-leej on my side with a long gun and that AP launcher. Looks like he's working on that map overlay you guys just pirated."

Pouring over the enemy map, Mack noted newly formed black dots with green pulses set against the facility on the opposite side of the map from where the blips showed squad leaders. "Rap, it looks like the Khindos are running drones or using old-fashioned eyeballs to mark where our fire is coming from. This kelhorn is probably going to slither into a gap to drop another missile on our guys."

"Not today," Raptor gasped through a wracking series of coughs. The Valkyrie team commander sipped on his bucket straw several times to quiet the rasp in his throat. When the itch in his chest died to a mild annoyance, he said, "The map shows shooters in the tree line, and our three fox holes. I'll dust my guy and you two dust the

Khindo QRF they got in the hole closest to you. We'll box the fakers when they try to get an angle on us and set up a shooting gallery in the event anyone else comes looking to see what happened."

"Roger that. Sixty seconds," Mack noted, trying not to let his worry about the team leader hacking over the comms sound over the net.

"Good copy. Get it done."

Mack swung his grenade launcher from his back, swinging it around to the front as he let his NK-4 to rest beneath him. He vented the breach enough to see the first of the thirty-millimeter grenades showing in the action. With one in the pipe and four loaded into the internal magazine, Mack was fairly certain he could put rounds on target. Pressing into the bucket's toggle, he worked himself into a weapons control screen, cycling the grenades for an airburst detonation.

Targeting algos were interrupted just as he was about to lock in distance and elevation for the grenade fuses. A warning screen threw a tantrum into Mack's HUD, showing that Raptor's heart rate had slowed, although his numbers were working their way to normal for a legionnaire.

"Raptor, this is Mack. Got some funky readings on your armor, sir," Mack warned.

"You know that experimental goop you brought back to the office? Let's just say I made sure to five-finger discount my own batch before we left," Raptor replied.

"The doctor said that without a scan, that stuff could send him into a stroke," Fresher said urgently.

Mack watched as Raptor's bio-sig normalized, showing readings that were in keeping with a fully functional leej. "He's a Legion officer who's got more rescues under his belt than you have pairs of socks. How's about we let the one officer we're supposed to have on this trip do his thing and when he asks for help, we come running?"

"Roger that, Master Sergeant," Fresher agreed. "Target lock sent to our guys."

"Now that's what I wanna hear." Mack watched the timer roll to zero and used his trigger as the green flag to launch the violence. Sighting on the squad of Khindos in the depression closest to them, he rocketed five grenades from the semi-automatic launcher as fast as he could pull the trigger. The rapid thump of the rounds racing from the barrel was all too clear in the near silence that followed the withering rainfall.

The Khindos turned just in time to watch the grenades lob in and detonate above them. Black plumes of concussive force mixed with burning fragmentation as the high-explosive dual-purpose grenades shredded the insurgent fighter squad. The dusty, glittering shockwave cracked tree trunks and blew vegetation away from the impact zone, littering the surrounding terrain with shredded debris. With a clear view, the twin leejes ID'd at least a dozen Khindos blasted into the mud.

Repeated, echoing gunfire over the ridge was their sign that Raptor had engaged the not-so-leej with the AP launcher. Almost on cue, one of the three bucket-wearing enemy crawled to the top of the embankment to get a better view of the attack. Shiloh rewarded the man for his effort by evaporating the top half of fighter's bucket with a shot made through a combination of Fresher's optics and his location on the map.

The last two knock-off leejes dropped to their bellies, attempting to vanish from whatever was targeting them. They crawled toward the lip of the terrain, hoping the rise would keep them covered from the terror that had just turned their teammate into little more than a bloody mannequin for all his gear.

"Good hit, Shy," Mack called into the L-comm. "Raptor, I'm still hearing blaster fire on your side. Sitrep?"

"AP launcher guy is down. I have it and am trying to circle back to the heavy mech. The big show and those karkin' fake leejes are calling back their buddies," Raptor replied.

The grinding thunder of a rocket engine sounded through the trees, its familiar whistle acknowledged by real and fake leejes alike as the aero-precision missile on a wild ride to ruin someone's day. It darted through the canopy into the path of a squad of men answering the call of their supposed Legion advisors under attack. Trees, plants, and anything crawling through the same detonated in a furious explosion that ripped the terrain into a deep crevasse, and a rolling mushroom cloud burned its way through the canopy.

As the booming echo died, renewed blaster fire sailed from tree line closest to the access road, across the lawn, and into the path of the leejes attempting to knock out their stolen missile launcher. Several shots tossed up plumes of dirt and struck wet tree trunks, leaving smoldering scorch marks. Mack and Fresher pushed themselves into the terrain to weather the onslaught being leveled against them.

Like a vibro-scythe harvesting grain, another section of the jungle disappeared as One-Four-Bravo and Alpha vented their rail guns simultaneously. The high-energy weapons tore into the jungle, cutting down bodies, scattering gear, uprooting trees, and spraying mulch.

"Mack! Run for the station. We have you covered!" Raptor shouted into the L-comm.

"We'll bound back and lay down suppressing—" Mack began.

"Run, now! Don't stop!" Raptor shouted, counter-manding his order.

The leejes bounded from their position like chas-tised leej recruits, sprinting through blaster fire. They ran. Ducking branches and through tracing blaster fire toward the high-gain booms from Maggie's rifle and the thunder leveled by the facility's remaining defenses. The site had transformed from a pristine station set among a lush jun-gle to a hotly contested war zone.

Just as their boots were about to strike duracrete, a bolt slammed into Mack's back plate, knocking the wind and his feet out from under him. Fresher slid into the grass, using his body to cover the master sergeant while he flicked his selector lever to burst and rained burps of energetic violence in the shot's direction. The purloined grenade launcher machine gun roared to life behind them, with one of the Valkyrie leejes going kinetic on the weapon to turn that part of the jungle into a murder-ous deluge.

"I'm good." Mack got to his feet, running hunched over with the rookie, covering him with his own armor. Ahead of them, Maggie flew from the building. She throttled the road ahead of her with the main gun dropping rhythmic doses of cannon fire toward the access road while her co-axial gun leveled blaster bursts into the jungle in jerking targeting sweeps.

As the mech reached the hill leading to the decimat-ed blockade of trucks, the road erupted in an apocalypse of primed explosives courtesy of one master breacher. Lobster's skills turned the escape route into a grave site for any insurgent fighter stupid enough to fire from there.

The chained explosives set off a shock wave that blew apart the first two meters of forest and shattered Khindos who, only a moment before, had been very much alive and pulling the trigger on their weapons as fast as they could.

The blast wave tumbled the ruined repulsor trucks into the waiting bevy of Khindo vehicles parked along the road. Flipping and burning, the broken grav-truck-turned-fiery-grenade struck the first of the parked speeders, crushing it under its bulk as the heat and flame ignited its power battery. It caught fire on the rain-soaked road, billowing smoke and the rank smell of burning metal and rust.

Maggie raced into the fire, increasing the max height of her repulsors to sail above the carnage wrought by the leejes. As she zipped above the first of the wrecks into the fire and dust brought about by the devastation from kilograms of high-ex turning terrain and equipment alike into flak, Maggie fired off her main gun. The bolt shattered the last vehicle in the ramshackle parking job, turning the speeder into a backstop, keeping the other vehicles from following. Her repulsors crushed the cabs on the older model sleds and technicals, turning what was once an insurgent convoy staged for pursuit into a blackened, burning scrapyard.

Fresher carried the hunched master sergeant over to the waiting hands of their team as debris from the massive explosion rained down around them.

Creeper took hold of Mack's shoulder armor to better support him. "Everyone inside for phase two!"

"Negative!" Mack shouted as he dropped to a knee, heaving with every breath after the bolt had struck him in the plate near his stab wound. "We have to get the cap!"

"Khindos just took out One-Four-Bravo!" Creeper shouted back. "One-Four-Alpha is still up and going in after him. We're covering it with the grenades we have left for the boomer machine gun. He wants us to cover his run to the river and he'll meet us on the other side."

"That was not the plan!" Mack shouted, shrugging off the hands reaching for him.

"Top! This is on him, not you. We either boogey now for phase two, or we all die trying to fish him out. He trusted you on Drusar, now you have to trust him."

Mack swore at the top of his lungs and stumbled into the building after his crew.

23

Raptor vaulted over a tangle of shattered tree trunks decimated by the rail gun acting the part of a lawn mower. That it also mowed huge batches of weeds wearing Khindo Khabar gear was a bonus. With a fresh infusion of voodoo tech bringing the Legion officer back to fighting form, Raptor bounded through what cover he could find through acres of forest level by combat.

Dosa Keem, the Khindo Khabar warlord who'd started this mess, put out the word that Oba had seen fit to trap the infidels into the poisoned facility the Republic had isolated from the rightful Sons of Nuzon. If a warlord had stated all fighters loyal to the cause should make haste to the research station, some would have sat back and watched it all play out. But in declaring that Oba had played a role, Keem inflamed the very flammable Khindo population, fanning the embers into a full-on blaze.

Even as the legionnaires backed by station defensive systems killed scores of Khindo fighters, Keem's men swarmed the jungle, whipped along by a frenzy of hate and fanaticism that was barely being funneled toward them by the Royal Marines. Raptor thought about the chance meeting with Dela Cruz reported by his Alpha Section counterpart. There were so many ways that encounter could have played against them, and TC had worked it like the puppet master he was.

A freshly cycled charge pack and Raptor was back in the game, throwing bolts along his retreat to the river. He feathered the trigger, tracing shots into the jungle to kill a Khindo fighter with every muzzle flash. Painting himself as a target meant the enemy guns trained on him were not aimed at his men, which allowed them to concentrate on their extraction versus trading shots with the locals. The Valkyrie officer skipped his next bolt off an enemy fighter's plate carrier into the man's throat.

Another mag swap and Raptor pushed farther into the untouched jungle. More trees meant more cover, and he was keen to use it on his way to the river. While in the nook of a large tree, Raptor inserted the feather chip he'd stolen from the fake leej, after he forced the man to pay the asking price for the armor. A tap on his battle board began the download from the circuit-laden piece of plastite.

The indicator in his HUD showed a loading bar displaying the progress of the hijacked information filling his device. Raptor breathed rhythmically as he tried to force down the pain from his ribs as a mounting pressure filled his sinuses. He watched the status bar progress and imagined it was showing the next generation battlefield stim he'd taken, working to fix some new problem delivered via the bad luck faerie plaguing this mission.

At least it wasn't his cancer. That seemed under control, thanks to an off-the-books doctor working in Drusar who'd given him the good stuff. It was part of the reason he'd requested the assignment working out of that particular planet. But the hits he took by the Khindo Khabar, shadowing the rocket jockey he'd dusted, had done some damage. That guy's security team worked hard to keep

him Legion-free while he launched aero-precision missiles at them. They'd watched the leejes take hits from the
wood line, and as a result, the Khindo team tuned up the
power output on their blasters to hit harder than normal.

The progress bar beeped, showing the kidnapped
data was fully installed. He connected a link to Tommy and
broadcast the intercept codes so the entire team could
share in whatever treasure he'd unlocked. A deep inhale
allowed him to test if Doctor Kavir's super goop was doing
its job, keeping him from feeling the lancing pain in his
side as he tried to move. If the government didn't disappear him for trying the nanite infusion developed as part
of a black bag program, he would have told R&D that trading the injury pain for a headache that poked like an ice
pick in his eye was definitely a design flaw.

Boots crunched through the undergrowth, waking
him from his reverie.

"We know you out here, Republic. We know you legionnaire. You no belong here. You come out and drop
you weapon and you go," the fighter called in heavily accented Galactic Standard.

High-gain sound detection in Raptor's bucket picked
up more feet maneuvering through the tangled vegetation all around them. They were taking a page from his
playbook, boxing him in for the kill.

He could really use a full Valkyrie team now. For the
moment, Raptor was responsible for his own way out of
the frying pan while dodging the fire. He tracked his bucket across the jungle for the best possible escape, and the
Legion kit, full of sensors designed to look for holes in an
enemy's plan, responded with just the right thing at just
the right time. Raptor flicked on the sighting protocol in

his weapon optic and aligned it just where his bucket told him to, around the trunk of his tree.

The bolt flew into the jungle, striking a mound of earth and tangled brush not ten meters away from the group ready to rush him. Something—large—squealed furiously, and the bucket-less Khindos looked around for its source.

Does death-by-pig invalidate the whole "heavenly rewards" thing? Raptor wondered, imagining the look on their faces as several tons of pissed-off anger-back chased them. It'd be fun to see that look with his own eyes, but instead of waiting around for it, he took the hesitation as an opportunity to run. A couple fighters shot after him—all missing—while the monstrous hog dug itself from its wallow, shrieking and flinging muck. A second anger-back appeared in Raptor's path, barking and stomping its foot in annoyance that the man-things had interrupted its nap.

The Legion officer pulled the trigger the second the new hog stepped from the jungle. The bolt struck the armored plates around its shoulder, scorching its leathery hide. It squealed and thundered after the legionnaire. For his part, Raptor reversed direction and sprinted back toward the Khindo Khabar.

"Tag!" Raptor yelled. He raced by the stunned insurgents, leaving them to their fates.

Khindos sprinted toward the lawn outside of the tree line to have better footing to escape the enraged giant boars. It probably didn't register in their minds that the hogs would also have better footing, but they ran for it, anyway. Of the fighters who'd tracked Raptor back to his hide, none of them took another shot at their escaping enemy.

Raptor veered around some vines to change direction and head deeper into the jungle. He'd sprinted nearly fifty meters, while the screaming Khindos got trampled and gored to death behind him, when a blaster bolt slammed into his shoulder pauldron and tumbled him into the muck. Warning sensors and frantic displays cited possible tissue damage.

Raptor dismissed a House of Reason–mandated suggestion to report all injuries to one's superior for follow up at the nearest TMC, then scanned a waveform in his HUD. During his run, the battle board uploaded the pirated frequencies from the feather chip into his comm system.

"Target is down. Only a glancing shot, so he's probably still alive," came the voice in Galactic Standard through the pirated comms.

"That was a nice trick with the pig, though. Did you see the size of those things?" commented voice number two.

Raptor continued to listen to their chatter through the net while he rolled to his side. The spooky nanite system controller attached to his gauntlet signaled it was working to correct the injuries and put him back on his feet. As the pain above his hip flared from the cracked rib, he wrestled against his blasted shoulder plate to free up a piece of kit on his gear. Until the nanites reset to compensate for this new level of suck, Raptor was going to have to work through this, Legion-style.

He primed the activator lever for a short fuse and tossed a banger as far as his injuries would allow. The grenade sailed toward the spot he'd just abandoned, unleashing sonic devastation and a searing light. Combined with the intense overpressure rebounding between the trees, and the weapon was sure to further annoy the two porcine juggernauts, finishing their stampede across the pulverized Khindos.

Raptor leapt to his feet and clipped his weapon to his chest plate, devoting all his strength and balance toward a sprint into the dark. Blaster bolts followed his sporadic run through the tangle as he used the distraction caused by the stomping animals to break trail in his escape of a rapidly growing net where Khindo fighters looked to knock him down for good.

"He's cutting back toward the river," Voice Number One observed through the comms.

"Have Lionel's crew come up from that direction and do the guy," Voice Number Two responded. "We can't take the chance this leej isn't alive enough to stab us in the back when we go for the station. We take this guy out and then blow what's left of the defenses. Khindos get the doctor and the leejes as prisoners while we recover the batch."

"Roger that," First Voice confirmed.

It wasn't any clearer to Raptor who these guys were, but his gut—despite being loaded with cancer and a throbbing rib—decided they had to be slowed down enough for the boys to get phase two good and set. Having a battlefield concoction driven by smart nanotechnology constantly hardening against increasing injuries sounded like a recipe for disaster. How long until some clever slicer learned how to hack the systems controller and make those combat bugs do whatever they wanted? What would happen to any force using the system if the slicer programmed them to harm rather than heal? What if the Night Market got a batch? Religious extremists like the Khindos or the zhee, hopped up on this tech, could make a nightmare out of any world they claimed as their own.

Raptor licked the coppery taste off his lips as he slid into a gulch to avoid the raging anger-backs, Khindos, and their Leej-Lite handlers. The mud crumbled under his boots, letting him drop into the water below. The tributary coming off the river wasn't as fast moving as the river itself, but it made for a good enough hiding spot from everyone currently trying to send a bolt through his neck. Resting against the bank, a massive fish as long as he was tall, bumped into him, its face-tendrils flickering to taste him. The animal bumped twice before taking the hint from Raptor, who pushed it away. It seemed everyone wanted a piece of him today.

"You still with us, boss?" Mack called into the L-comm. After opening the channel, he fired another bolt through the shattered crysteel window from their ad hoc fighting position in the foyer. In answer, bolts sailed back at them, pinning them behind the cover in a dazzling array of flash and smoke.

"I'm at the opening to the river on my side," Raptor said. "We still got those proto-leejes crawling around and directing the fight. They aim to hit you guys in the next few to go for the goo. Everything set?"

"Lobster and Tommy have the FFD rigged. We'll fail the defenses and lure them in once you're clear," Mack confirmed.

"Khindos rushing for the big house is the sign I'm clear, Master Sergeant. Status on the doctor and the marine?" Raptor asked.

Tommy poked into the net. "Delivered to the Royal Marines, Rap. They're being taken to the big hospital in Terum."

"Sir, you also have a significant force moving toward you from the south," Stringer said. "Drones have it pegged as a company-sized element of Khindos departing the access road and moving through the brush to circle the station. We're running out of time, Rap."

"Understood," Raptor said. "Priority targets are the pseudo-leejes if you see them. Do not let them get into the batches of Doctor Kavir's enhanced nanites. If these guys are who we think they are, they are playing for her research, and we can't risk them getting close."

"The whole lab is rigged in the event they get in early, Rap. Anyone so much as touches the doors outside, the whole place melts down," Lobster said.

"Good copy. Heads down, boys, and I'll see you on the other side. Raptor out."

Mack was about to go back to shooting Khindos through the glass when he noted a flashing direct message hinting at the periphery of his HUD. Remaining on a knee, he pulled open the screen from Raptor.

"Hey, just in case things go wrong, there's a file I just sent to your bucket. The password is the mythological beast we encountered on our first hop," Raptor said.

"You know something you're not telling us?" Mack asked.

"Just don't end up naked in a barrel of Drusics this time, Top. Get our boys home. Raptor, out."

Mack huffed a short laugh and instantly regretted it as the pain reminded him he'd been stabbed. As if he could forget. Rolling out from cover, Mack sighted down on several muzzle flashes in the jungle and let bolts fly to target, extinguishing them from a repeat performance.

Around him, shouts of "changing packs" and "covering" echoed through the foyer. A drone warning cycled through the team display, signaling an impending heavy attack. Seconds into the mad scramble to escape the foyer, a recoilless rifle round blasted into the entrance and detonated against the marble front of the reception desk. The two-stage munition turned the stone into radiating flak as the shock wave destroyed what remained of the shattered crysteel weather screen.

Explosive force and rubble chased the escaping leejes as they retreated away from the compromised entrance toward the more heavily protected building center. As the clatter of falling debris rained onto the once smooth stone floor, another round punched into the space. The explosive shock compromised the awning from the second floor overlooking the entrance with a creaking groan. Enormous cracks grumbled in the foyer as the terrace above the entrance floor succumbed to the destruction of its supports and toppled with an apocalyptic crash.

Miguel jumped into the tributary toward the dead man floating there. The Khindo fighter threaded his hand into the old-style plate carrier the corpse wore, most likely issued to him for this operation by his Datu, his chief. The gaping hole in the man's skull was proof that, while it was better to have armor, it wasn't everything. Of course, Miguel had scored a helmet and no armor, so with it, he could face the Repubs with little fear, as he would be more protected than the other soldiers.

"Hey! Leave him there," Raffa called from the bank. "You know, rat sharks swim through those streams just as much as the whisker fish. And all it would take is a hint of blood and those things would be on you faster than your face in a plate of food!"

Miguel gestured rudely to his squad mate. "You're not the boss of me! And he's not using his armor anymore."

"Your funeral, dummy," Raffa admonished.

Despite Raffa's insult, Miguel knew things. He knew the corpse hung up on the reeds didn't need his armor anymore. He also knew that with the man's blood flowing downstream, the rat sharks wouldn't be drawn from upstream by the scent of it in the water. Sharks swimming upstream would splash so he'd see them coming. He knew things, even if Raffa said he was stupid. If his squad mate was so smart, why didn't he fight harder for a helmet?

Another explosion echoed through the trees. The friendly legionnaires must have gotten the replacement seventy-five millimeter recoilless rifles up to the positions. He told the one guy in the full armor that they needed to make that happen sooner, but Miguel wasn't a squad leader. They didn't listen to him.

Instead, dozens of people he'd been in the camp with were now dead. He'd learned to fight and survive in the jungle beside them so they could one-up the Royal Marines. But the armored outsiders spent them like they were counting out change to a peddler at the bazaars. Sure, if the local government, and even the galaxy, was going to take them seriously, it was a smart play to take the rescue force and that doctor hostage, like Keem said.

But not at the expense of dozens of the people he grew up with dying in the process. What good was building a world for the will of the True God if there was no one left to share it with?

Miguel shucked the rest of the armor free from the near headless torso, holding it up to inspect it for damage. It wasn't painted in green, like the rest of his gear. Miguel would have to sort that out after the infidels were dead. Tan would do for now. He'd just have to get it dirty enough to blend in with the rest of the jungle. Besides, the rumor was that they were fighting enemy legionnaires who didn't have the Sons of Nuzon's best interests at heart. They had kit that allowed them to see in the deep canopy, even at night, or find a warm body by seeing its heat. Miguel had watched the docu-holos. He'd seen what they could do. So the armor could stay tan for now.

He nearly dropped the armor back into the stream when a whisker fish bumped against his leg. He thought it was the sharks Raffa had warned him about, only to see the nearly two-meter fish floating there with its probing tendrils reaching through the water for him. Miguel really wanted to kick at it, but he thought better of it. They weren't dangerous and made for good eating when roasted on the grill and served over fresh pava root and scallions. If he left it alone, maybe God would bring it back to him, away from the shooting and the infidels and his stupid squad mate, Raffa.

Miguel climbed from the stream to walk back to the trees, where Raffa was waiting for him. Another explosion sounded off in the distance, this one producing a gargantuan inky cloud from the top of the building they were supposed to be raiding. "That was some boom, eh, Raffa? Hey, I got the armor off that guy in the water. No rat sharks, but I found a whisker fish. Hey, are you listening to me?"

Raffa coughed, frantically motioning Miguel over to him.

"Yeah, I know. Lionel said we're supposed to watch this section of the jungle for the infidel, but getting that armor will make me a better fighter," Miguel said as he bounced the recovered plate carrier, hoping to dry it off faster. He rounded the tree to see Raffa attached to the trunk by a slender wire that was cutting into his neck. The garrote was tight, slicing into the flesh even as it choked him against the hatched bark of the palm. Miguel dropped the armor and ran for the back of the tree where two slender plasteen handles had the wire twisted around them as anchor points Raffa couldn't reach.

Miguel ripped his machete free from its sheath and cut the razor-thin metal. Raffa hit the ground, gasping and holding his neck. He choked several times as he padded his fingers around the flesh to see if he even had a throat after the attack.

"What happened?" Miguel whispered.

"What do you think happened? Get your gun, you imbecile!" Raffa rasped from hands and knees.

Miguel tossed the wire aside, turning to recover his weapon, when an armored legionnaire dropped from the tree above them.

He landed in front of Raffa, driving a knife resembling a gut-hooked meat cleaver into the choking man's neck. A violent rip tore out trachea, blood vessels, and neck muscles on its way out of his body before the savage gut hook took hold of the spinal column. Raffa didn't have long to ponder his lifeblood flowing into the mud as the armored nightmare used the knife's hook against the spine as an anchor and blasted the side of the Khindo fighter's head, snapping the neck. A flick of the knife threw the man to the ground like meat cast off from the butcher's block.

Miguel dropped to his knees with his hands held up. "I prayed to God for better armor, and there it is. Now I pray to him to spare me so I may fight you once I have better armor, like yours."

The Legion devil stalked around behind him, letting the sounds of his knife sliding into the scabbard announce his presence when he was out of Miguel's sight. The Khindo fighter remained motionless as he watched the machine blaster he'd left with Raffa get hefted from the ground and disappear behind him.

"If I don't go home with that, Lionel is going to kill me," Miguel said apologetically.

"Lionel's already dead. Take the armor and go," Raptor whispered into his ear.

24

Mack pulled his last leej into the back part of the hall-way, where a set of stairs would have led to the floor above them, if it wasn't blasted out of existence only mo-ments ago. "Now comes the hard part—staying alive long enough to drag all the wolves into the net."

"Snares," Lobster said as he climbed over the ruined staircase. "You catch wolves in snares."

"What part of this face says I care?" Mack asked, point-ing to his bucket. He patted the leej on his injured shoul-der, eliciting a sharp yelp from the man as he pushed him to the rest of the team. A toggle of the L-comm and he was catching a call from Stringer. "Go for Mack."

"Top, my drones are about to run out of juice. Got some last looks before they do," Stringer said.

"Send it." Mack took the first feed, watching from a high vantage where he could see most of the front and sides of the property. The savaged lawn contained the wreckage of multiple heavy security mechs, blasted from their original, very functional and dangerous, condition into piles of scrap littering the grass. Several patches of the lawn were on fire along gaping craters dug in enor-mous stretches across the landscape. Khindo fighters ran across the open area as they rightly guessed the leejes had retreated into the building. With the station defenses ruined over the course of the attack, there was nothing stopping the insurgents from fighting their way inside.

Major Tyler jogged up to Mack and Fresher as they ushered their wounded teammate into the back stairwell leading to the sub-levels below. "Mack, I need a moment."

"If I had it to give you, sir, I would. But we're about to punch the locals in the mouth for knocking us down and I don't have the time," Mack replied. "So unless you plan on staying with us to lay harassing fire, I need you below with the rest of the team for exfil."

"Raptor's pinned down," Tyler blurted. "Stringer's drones. Feed four."

Mack followed the major's suggestion to check the video stream. Just beyond the canopy, a periodic flash of blaster fire barked out from the trees, followed by return fire from the Khindos. The insurgent forces chased the shooter, only to be repulsed by a series of explosions and counterfire from deep within the jungle.

"That force approaching from the south spread out when they got close. A squad-plus traced up the river-bank by the falls. They found Raptor and hemmed him back into the jungle. That captured frequency Raptor clipped from the fake leej said they're coordinating the Khindos to pin him down. They killed the two anger-backs and are working their way to him. He's not going to make the river unless someone backs him up," Tyler insisted.

"We're running on borrowed time here, Major, and I need every leej I have. Once we shed this place, we have just long enough to swim as fast as we can with our in-jured to beat the particle wave from cooking us very dead," Mack said. "And we still have to make our defense here believable enough that they try to push us. We need this to look like we're holding out for the Royal Marines."

Tyler superimposed an AR map between them, taken from the drone shots. "Top, I can swim out from the spillway into the river. Make landfall on the bank and come at them from behind to give Raptor the opening he needs to get wet. Then I'm back in the river and outta here. I'm a former Recon Marine, Mack. I may have been appointed, but I can get him home."

"Mack! They're approaching the foyer and sweeping. Outta time," Creeper sounded off in the L-comm.

"Never will I leave a fallen comrade, Major. Fine. Your mission is to bring two sets of heartbeats home," Mack said. He extended his hand to the officer, giving it a firm shake before pushing him back the way he came with Lobster's grenade launcher and his bandoleers. With no more room for goodbyes, the master sergeant switched into the L-comm. "Stringer, first crew in the door. Let them know we appreciate their business."

Crawling from under the debris, several spider-like drones tapped their way toward the incoming Khindo fighters. Dragging fraggers in their wake, the four advancing bots danced toward the enemy, dodging a couple shots before the armed grenades detonated. The blast knocked the six-man clearing team from the entrance into bags of ruined blood and bone. They hit the street outside with a wet slap, lost amid the fading echo of the blast.

"They'll send in heavies next to try clearing us out," Mack reported.

A wave of fighters, twelve deep, advanced behind the dead clearing team littering the road outside. Careful not to set up their weapons in the gore splattered in the front lawn, the new group dropped tripods onto the street to field much bigger weapons than they've been able to field this close since the attack began. An ammo bearer strung a belt of grenades from an ammo can, untangling the linked ammunition in a way that told Mack he had little experience working with this gun.

"Kind of makes you wonder why we ever switched to blasters and such when weapons like that can still muck up your day," Fresher said as he aimed down the sights of his rifle.

"Because an energized particulate surrounded in a condenser field launched from a splatter caster can do as much damage in one shot as that machine gun can do in twenty-five," Mack said. "Plus, it ain't no joy to hump the old stuff." Finishing his lesson, the master sergeant drilled the ammo bearer through his helmet, cooking off the man's face before his dead body could hit the ground.

A gunner tried to set up a heavy repeating blaster on a tripod. Blanks, nestled into the other side of the building, drilled him. His first burst shot the man through the chest, punching a hole through his torso, knocking him and his weapon into the street. The assistant gunner attempted to jump away from the very large and unwieldy power battery, only to have a burst meant just for him evaporate most of his neck and shoulder to leave the man silently screaming into the ground until his heart stopped.

The rest of the Khindos lobbed grenades into the foyer. Most fell short. They exploded among the tangled girders and scrap littering the entrance hall, only succeeding to move piles this way or that. A few of the grenades would have landed on target past the mounds of ruined building, except they were lobbed in high arcs to clear the debris and detonated in the air.

Slithering from their cover, the leejes holding both sides of the building laid down a tidal wave of blaster fire towards the remainder of the assault team. More insurgents died under Legion-directed fire tearing them to shreds while their counterattack found no purchase against the debris where the leejes were fighting from. Striking like vipers, the leejes hit and faded back into the ruined structure to wait out whatever barrage was going to come at them next.

A Khindo who'd gotten on his belly to avoid the defending leejes fired a rifle grenade from a launcher beneath his rifle. This time, the weapon found its mark, exploding just close enough to punch Blanks into the floor behind his cover. The leej disappeared, and almost as quickly, was replaced by Ducky, who dropped a relentless stream of fire into the advancing shooters from his squad automatic blaster. Fresher responded in kind, using his SAB to create an interlocking field of fire to keep them pinned.

"I'm hit," Blanks said weakly into the L-comm.

"Fresh. Keep their heads down. Talk your gun with Ducky," Mack said as he ran to the other side of the debris they were using as cover. He pulled the wounded leej to Creeper, who was at the stairs waiting to drag away the injured man like a trapdoor spider. "The fragger ripped up his armor pretty good. His bucket is slagged, and that arm is going to need some medical juju we don't have here. He's conscious and saying cool Legion things, so get some patches on him and prep him for the water."

"On it, Top," Creeper shouted back. The senior medic for the team grabbed under the man's shoulder armor and dragged him into the stairwell. When Blanks cried out at the pain of being carried, Creeper countered with, "Oh, stop whining, ya big baby!"

Mack ran back to where Ducky was laying down suppressing fire, but barked to Fresher through the L-comm, "This is your spot until it isn't. You understand, leej?"

"Roger that, Top," Fresher snarled.

Throughout the entire operation, the kid had shown he was the epitome of Legion professionalism, even if he still had that fresh-out-of-the-box smell on him. But the sound of him confirming his role had Mack wondering if he was totally innocent in the family business of negotiations and debt collections. Fresher just watched his teammate get punched by the enemy, and now he was doling out receipts that had come due as high-cycle blaster fire. Mack was just glad the kid was on their side.

"Ducky," Mack said, slapping the leej on the shoulder while he fired in alternating bursts with his SAB. "Pull and fade."

The team TACKLE, their tactical air controller, traded weapons with Mack before running for the stairs. In a few crouched steps, he disappeared behind the rubble-strewn barricade.

Mack and Thrasher continued to lay down fire for another thirty seconds when Mack made the call. "We pull, in three-two-one—!"

Both SABs went silent as the duo scrambled away from their fighting position to vanish back the way Ducky had gone. Frenetic explosions rocked the building as the twin leejes made the top of the stairs.

"We blowing stuff up again?" Fresher asked.

Mack knife-handed in two directions as they both trotted down the stairs. "Back entrance and the gaping hole Maggie made near the dining facility. We've been laying det all over this river for the last twenty minutes. Who wouldn't think to check for wires?"

Major Tyler crawled from the rushing waters of the Serrabi River to climb onto the bank. Ahead of him, two Khindo Khabar sentries watched through the trees for any sign of the fight coming at them. They appeared relaxed as they bobbed left and right to see around the thick jungle for their quarry, the elusive legionnaire cut off from his friends and left to die out here.

Kneeling in the rushing current on the soft sand of the riverbed, Tyler placed a bolt at the base of the man's spine and punched the second bolt through his friend's ear as he turned, dropping both in just over a second. He withdrew into the river, holding onto tree roots and tangles as he submerged in his trek along the riverbank. If he was still seeing Khindos waiting for Raptor to make for the river, then he was still too far north.

He bobbed to the surface soon after going back in and came up into the jungle free from any security along the bank. He scanned the jungle for movement and noise hidden within the constant high-pitched echo of blaster fire and the churning river. Climbing from the current, Major Tyler jogged into the jungle before turning north to meet up with whatever was waiting for him. He switched to a direct message in the L-comm.

"Raptor, it's Tyler. I'm south of your position and moving along the riverbank," the major said.

"You're not supposed to be here," Raptor shot back. His voice was calm but strained.

Grinning, Tyler said, "Neither are you." He'd thought about the joke the entire time he'd spent getting here and was happy for the chance to use it. Tyler's bucket algos read the echo from the broadcast and mated it with the ambient noise coming out of the trees. A way finder application populated the bottom of the HUD, showing his direction in compass degrees as an arrow marked his desired path to target.

"Did you bring something to drink?" Raptor asked.

"You're out of water?"

"No, but I'm nowhere near a nice single malt," Raptor said. "I'm seeing your bucket just shot an azimuth to me. Adjust twenty degrees north and move along that side of the river. There's about two dozen bad guys at my back that I need you to dust."

Tyler ran like he did when he trained for his appointment to the marines. Everyone else had to enlist or go through officers training. His family connections bypassed all that and his first few weeks in the Corps had been a meat grinder. He was in good shape, but not marine shape. He could walk like he knew money, but not like he knew murder. Everything his family had given him had been a lie. Since his family's reputation was little more than bankrupt currency in the marines, he'd set out to become one. Then a legionnaire. In every case, you run hard, then harder, then run like you know murder.

Major Tyler crawled into a switchback where the Khindos were fighting in a low puddle behind lanky palms standing near the water on stilt-like trunks beside squat pumpkin-sized palms. While that area provided excellent cover from the incoming machine blaster fire slapping into the pool, it would make getting free of the place in a hurry difficult, which was perfect for Tyler.

Looking down on the Khindos scattered through the pool, Tyler watched as incoming rhythmic blaster fire snapped along the tree line, either burning bark or sending geysers splashing over the fighters. From the sound of it, Raptor had commandeered a local machine blaster, a ZKD. The utilitarian nature of the gun—often called the Zeke—and its manufacture came from a company that settled out on galaxy's edge and refused to move. It seemed to Tyler that the sentiment described a good portion of people who found their way onto its trigger. But even with its sturdy nature, the amount of fire Raptor was laying down would melt the barrel if he didn't have a way to cool it soon.

Maybe it was time he got a lull. Tyler pulled the handle and stock from the grenade launcher he'd gotten from Mack. Seemed it was going to be the MVP of the deployment. When the hand grip came free, two toothy clamps opened from the top of the weapon with a raspy click. He fixed it to the bottom of his rifle and waited for the retaining clips to lock in with a snap. Pushing his thumb into the depressed charging lever, he cycled the first grenade he loaded and added another to the internal mag.

"Raptor, this is Tyler. Going hot," Tyler said. The officer-turned-legionnaire launched the first grenade into the water near the Khindos. The weapon splashed into the water behind the first group of fighters, barely registering with any of them due to all the other kinetic slaps churning up the surrounding pool. What they did notice was the eruption of muck and plant matter mixed with a minor bit of flak. The impact of the thirty-millimeter grenade sending its drowned fire and fury into them might have been debilitating, but it was only lethal enough to bury the closest man. Still, men shouting about being hit and inspecting their wounds wouldn't be shooting at Legion officers for the time being.

The Khindos adjusted their positions in the trees, some hunkering in the muck to avoid catching the force of another grenade thrown at them. Tyler's bucket algos translated the local dialect, Tagolan, into speech he could recognize. They were all complaining to the leader of the group that they wouldn't have moved this close if they thought the target still had grenades.

The major cursed to himself for the oversight. He should have known better than to shoot a grenade that small into the water directly. Toggling for the weapon cue, Tyler cycled to his grenade launcher. He found Mack's airburst setting preloaded and selected it. With his bucket's help, he adjusted for the range to target and put another grenade out.

The weapon exploded in the air this time, sending a chalky black burst of powder into the trees along with much faster moving pressure and fragmentation, and a good deal of heat. Glittering sparks rained into the water and sizzled on the surface, and Khindo bodies followed with a plunk. Tyler had caught six men cloistered together in the blast and further wounded or outright killed some he'd previously wounded. With another HEDP grenade already in the tube, he sent one just ahead of the first. This one blew precariously close to the palms, adding the timber into the conflagration of high velocity, heated metal shards burning everything in their blast radius. The shock wave blasted men into the river, geysering the water around their graves.

Terrified, the Khindo fighters scattered, trying to avoid grouping together. The tactic was more to skirt a targeted group than to make the grenadier's target selection more difficult. High-stepping to get more traction in the knee-deep pool stymied them as they tried to hustle in the clinging muck.

Tyler sent bolts from his position, picking off Khindos one at a time as the enemy scurried. A cagey insurgent got wise to there being two shooters instead of one and chose to use his last remaining moments to vent rounds at the enemy, shredding his friends. The bolts skipped off the dirt around the tree Tyler was using as cover until one punched him in the chest armor, knocking him from his perch.

The wet slap of the blaster bolt slamming home left a ringing in Tyler's ears. Even with his bucket on, he could swear he smelled burning polymer. Screaming injury indicators showed the armor had done its job, but the burning projectile had dumped its full velocity into the plate. He wouldn't be taking another hit like that.

The major recovered his perch, checking the ammo counter in his HUD that he was good for more shots before changing the pack. He swept to the other side of the tree, so as not to be caught popping up in the same place, and was rewarded by a bolt in the bucket. Alarms shouted at him he'd been hit again and the structural integrity as well as the viewing capacity of the helmet had been sorely compromised. Blistering spiderweb cracks formed along the shell, making it hard to get a solid look at anything outside without relying on external cams relaying the HUD image directly onto his retinas. Tyler checked the HUD for Raptor's position, and blindly fired the next grenade over the hill.

The wet-sounding explosion was his cue to adjust his position and continue the fight. He only hoped he'd gotten the man who'd shot him, twice. "Adjusting my POS to new location. Will send a ping to you when set."

"Covering," Raptor called back.

The sound of blaster fire filled the space between them, like a mountain scorpion striking repeatedly for its meal. Hard impacts and wet splashes echoed over the berm as Tyler stumbled into a cove of rock twenty meters from his last spot.

He fumbled blindly for his visor repair tape in his Legion utility belt, his mind going back to the mentors he'd learned from while coming up in the Legion.

"As a leej," First Sergeant Hallstrom had once said, "your bucket is your brother, father, and mother. It is your constant companion in battle, a source of wisdom and protection, and there to lecture you when you don't pick up your socks. That little bit is a dig on the House of Reason, sir. Not that I'm bitter or nothin'."

A crackling noise sounded in his armor as the tape worked to seal the cracks and clean off the scoring, returning the visor to almost pristine condition. The webbing was barely visible and shouldn't get in the way, Tyler thought. He ripped the tape free and crinkled it into his dump pouch. As he swapped the charge pack in his weapon and topped off the grenades in the tube, he remembered how Creeper had set up his gear prior to the jump. Everything was in easy reach. If he lived through this, Tyler would thank the man when he saw him next.

He lobbed the micro-drone the Vals all carried, and battlefield telemetry filled his HUD once again. Raptor was set into a hill, fending off a few Khindos in the pool below them, as well as an advancing group from the south, cutting off his path to the river. Periodic shots also came from the north, where fighters not involved in the rush toward the Serrabi building were taking up the fight to paste the legionnaire.

Tyler leaned from his cover and blasted the two remaining Khindos he could see, struggling to free themselves from the mire. Their deaths left only the sound of injured fighters below pleading with their god for help, strength, and survival. The major listened to shouting to his north, signaling the Khindos were already aware their cordon was broken, and they needed more men to close the gap.

"Raptor, I just sent a drone feed with fresh intel," Tyler said, trying not to wheeze from the burning in his shoulder and upper chest.

"Got it. You hit?" Raptor responded.

"Yeah. Took two. Still can KTF. You?"

"More but same. Any chance you got some boom left and can clear me a path along the azimuth I just pointed?"

A new directional appeared in Tyler's bucket, showing four advancing Khindos spreading out and lancing fire in Raptor's direction. "I got it. I think I can dust them from here. Stand by."

Lining up his reticle along with the directional, Tyler used the overlay from the drone to program another grenade for the distance needed for an airburst detonation. The rifle's report sent a wave of pain across his shoulder, but he held the weapon secure enough for a steady shot. His rifle grenade lobbed across the distance, punching through leafy fronds. The hang time on the round was maddening. Finally, a thundering blast echoed through the canopy.

"Good hit. Good hit. Sir, you officially suck as a point. I need you to make for the river while I feed the Zeke and run for south," Raptor said.

Before he could answer, a tidal wave of pain punched Tyler in the back. House of Reason—installed warnings screamed he'd been shot a third time and that he probably wasn't any good at this. He struggled to move as the bolt burned in the center of his back. Smoke drifted across his newly patched bucket. The smoldering assault pack had taken the brunt of the hit, but the impact—he felt like he'd tried a flip into a pool of water from a considerable height, only to land flat on his back. Crawling spiders of pain across his spine tingled up and down his skin from the impact against his armor's back plate, which took the remainder of the blast.

"Breaks my heart to have to shoot a real leej in the back," called the guy Raptor had print-logged as Voice Two. "Looks like today—"

Tyler squeezed the trigger on his under-slung grenade launcher. The rifled round exited the barrel with a poot, sizzling to target, and at its cockeyed angle, the round struck the fake leej in the leg plate.

The impact punched the man's leg backwards like a donkey kick, nearly flipping him in place and sending him sprawling to the mud. He scrambled as he cried out through the electronically garbled speakers in the bucket, now caked with mud and flora from his jungle floor facial.

Another bit of wisdom coming from Tyler's former handlers. It takes a certain number of rotations to arm a rifled grenade. Otherwise, it hits with the force of a shotgun slug.

The officer rolled over, gritting his teeth at the effort while the pain of being on his back seared every nerve ending. He forced himself to look towards his opponent, finding him among the vines, taking another shot.

The pistol bolt struck the armor and deflected, finding the seam in Tyler's armor and digging into the flesh on his hip. Agony dragged him down toward unconsciousness. His Legion armor administered stimulants, acting the part of medic-less medic as best it could, and Tyler fought back through the haze.

The major whipped his punished shoulder over to his chest as a support and dropped the rifle on top of it. His action put him just off the X and out of the line of fire so the fake leej's next shot didn't punch a hole in his bucket. Instead, the next few rounds hit the dirt behind him and then into the chest armor through a shoulder already crying for relief. The armor failed this time, allowing the bolt to punch through. Tyler shouted, screaming as loud as he could so as not to pass out from the impact. Bucket alarms shrieked red alerts.

He pulled the trigger, firing another grenade into his opponent. This one struck the man's bucket, snapping the fake leej backwards. Nail met hammer. Wails of agony from down the hill meant the major had just enough time to switch his grip. Propping the weapon into a stick caught on a tangle of vines, he flipped the selector switch to burst and mashed the trigger. Repeated waves of three-round bursts flew from the barrel. Some went high and were swallowed by the rushing Serrabi River. Others slapped the dirt around the man known as Voice Two. But as Tyler dumped the charge pack, some bolts that found their way to target, jackhammering the armor and punching his ticket to an afterlife reserved for pretenders and traitors.

"Raptor," Tyler wheezed. "I'm hit. Need you to hold a minute. Will cover."

Frantic gunfire and running sounded through the major's bucket. "Your little gunfight drew some attention. I'm keeping them off you."

More gunfire followed a yell and a groan through the comms. One of the Khindo's shots had found purchase on the Valkyrie team leader. Grating breaths raged through the gunfire. Time and injury were running the clock on Raptor's chances to make it out. On the side of Tyler's HUD, he watched the dot representing the captain darting from one position, where he laid down effective fire to kill several of the advancing fighters, to another where he suppressed their move forward, allowing him to gain purchase on his next fighting roost.

"Major Tyler. Phase two is now. I'm right behind you. Get into the water. Do it now," Raptor ordered.

Tyler sobbed. Anger rose in his belly. Searing agony from multiple hits ravaged his nervous system even as his armor desperately vied to return control of life and limb to the shot-up leej. He rolled onto his stomach, careful not to lose his grip on the rifle. Ammo counter said he had one grenade left in the tube and more charge packs if he could make a swap. He could still make a difference. He could still make an opening.

Raptor must have heard him screaming into the net. "Tyler. Get into the water. Do it, now!" The sound of an impact cut his last word short. The voice that returned was less than human, full of grit and rage fueling his continued will to fight. "Water! Go! Now!"

Raptor's L-comm fritzed out, even as blaster fire echoed in the distance.

Tyler slid down the embankment, past the dead fake-leej as he used his good arm and non-ruined leg to drag himself toward the river.

25

"Top, they just broke the spoof," Tommy called at the entrance to the top of the stairs.

Mack walked up to the code slicer and found Lobster standing nearby. "Sitrep on the basement?"

Tommy flipped the board to show the work versus taking the time to upload everything. "We have access to the spillway, courtesy of Lobster being semi-useful with a cutting torch. Major Tyler was good enough to test it, so there's that. Khindos are sweeping and looting the two floors above us. Motion trigger cam already has someone on the stairs."

Mack watched the cam as the footage played through. He tapped the screen, halting the progress in favor of a still image to take in his target. "Damn it. That's one of those faker leejes. Looks like he has his guys scanning the stairs for traps."

"Not sure where he has his slicer, but they already broke the spoof," Tommy said.

"That's the fake data upload you rigged for them to slice into instead of the actual info on the servers, right?" Mack asked.

Tommy swept across the screen, showing huge blocks of code in a green-on-black screen. "That's right. Once they check it, they're going to see that it's Lobster's entire collection of *Moktaar Monthly*, and they're going to try for a hard tap of the servers. We need to be phase two complete by then."

"Alright. Work with Ducky and prep our ride for when we pop the cork. This is about to set off," Mack said. He knuckled the man's offered glove and took his leave, bumping into Lobster as he made his way back through the hall.

The team positioned themselves along the floor housing the sub-level labs where Mack had gotten Doctor Kavir's skinpacks and black operations stim. The lab itself was trapped so that any intrusion not authorized by the legionnaires would cause a very messy burn of the room, melting anything and anyone inside.

"Here they come," Tommy said through the L-comm.

The first tentative fighters wearing faded jungle fatigues, shemaghs, and plate carriers made their way from the stairwell. They swept their PK-9 blasters, watching the hallway for any movement by the legionnaires they hunted. New sets of boots and blasters crawled in behind them, stacking up against the walls to minimize the possibility of them being shot or blasted all at once.

Mack adjusted the sound filter on his bucket and watched the captions scroll across his HUD as the first man in the stack called into a handheld radio. "Moving to the first lab, now. No sign of enemy force."

"Check for tripwires and beams at floor and ceiling. If these are legionnaires, they will try to use the building against you," came the reply from the false legionnaire.

Cautious steps put the stack of Khindos up against the hatch leading to the first lab. Through mounted trigger cams and an assortment of bots placed in ducts and crevices, Mack watched the lead man lean against the polished surface of a sign that read, Lab One. In the re-flection, Mack was close enough to make out the snarl on the fighter's face as he approached the hatch.

The point man in the stack opened the door, allowing a canister to fall into the passage. A blast wave of sound, light, and pressure passed through the hallway with enough punch to drop all the men to their knees. Hands struggled to decide which to cover—eyes or ears—as the shock wave from the Legion-planted flash-bang grenade rendered them into little more than blind, unbalanced targets waiting to be shot.

So as not to disappoint, a Legion fire team swept from the far side of the hall, swinging in to put bolts on the enemy. Every leej shot made demanded the Khindos pay their bill for their lack of tactical foresight that put them in their current predicament. Legion bolts raced along the passage, killing the point man and a fighter a few spots back from the enemy's front. The Khindo-turned-corpse in the middle of their stack unbalanced the retreat, as the sight of their blaster-ventilated friend caused panic to spread.

A shouting match erupted in the stairwell between the force retreating and the one descending. The two groups demanded the other give way as the clock continued its relentless march forward. Things got eerily quiet for a moment as shouting gave way to shuffling and a new team took their spot at the exit from the stairwell.

"Someone must have pulled a gun to reinforce their point," Fresher said from his spot against the wall.

"Fresher, lay down suppressing fire and have the two guys with you fall back toward the stairs on our side," Mack directed. "We'll pull you once they're set."

Frantic gunfire from the squad automatic blaster punched along the passage and ricocheted off the stairs in a synchronized drumbeat of violence. The young corporal sent repeated bursts through the hallway to cover the retreat for his teammates abandoning their positions. During the barrage, an enemy fighter skipped a grenade of his own off the last few stairs until it rumbled to a stop in the center of the hall.

"Fragger!" Fresher shouted as he abandoned his position to join his friends.

The ancient fragmentation grenade exploded, blowing out the observation glass on Labs One and Two, shattering equipment and pockmarking the walls. Lethal shrapnel careened into the passage and the stairwell. A combination of distance and Legion armor protected the withdrawing Legion assault team as they descended to the next level. The Khindos in the stairwell had no such luck or gear to protect them from the duracrete walls, which focused the blast deep into their ranks. Frag and flak killed more than a few men from the sweeper teams, dumping bodies down the ruined stairs. Overpressure from the weapon's concussion combined with sparking, hyper-velocity shards to sever and ignite an oxygen line.

A throaty, raspy whistle raced along the hall, followed by a jet of flame sputtering to life from the hose. Flickering orange light swept through the hall as the area near the stairwell exit filled with oxygen-rich fire. Screaming and mayhem filled the stairs as the remainder of both sweeper teams climbed over each other to escape being set ablaze by the seizing hose spraying fire across the area.

"That whistle is fire spreading through the line!" Lobster shouted as he waved everyone over to the stairwell. "Time to get it moving, boys!"

Fresher was the last man to the stairs when, with a hissing *BOOM*, the pressure in the line built to such a point that the feeder pipes in the walls exploded. One side of the passageway detonated in fire and duracrete, spewing a whirlwind of flying debris. Stone and impervisteel blasted everywhere in a fiery eruption that soaked the entire floor in rich earthy dust and ash.

"Well," Fresher coughed. "That sucked." He lay on the next landing to the stairs leading down. "Would it be too featherhead of me to say that I'm done for today, what with my leg hanging off and all?"

Mack was at the landing, looking over his man's injury. Fresher's self-assessment wasn't far of the mark. Bright red blood pulsed from the back of his knee where the armor didn't cover so the joint could bend. He called Fresher's bio-sig into his HUD. The man's knee was shredded. The most likely cause being a six-inch sliver of metal protruding from the space behind the knee. Mack ran his hands in the spaces between the armor, running a blood sweep to check for other injuries. Judging by the pocked appearance on his back armor, the shrapnel hit him at just the right time as he sprinted down the hall.

"Creeper!" Mack shouted.

"Why are you calling me, Top? You have a medic right there," Creeper said as he pointed to Fresher before dropping beside him.

"Funny. Clip that steel and shrink-wrap him so we can get into the water," Mack said from the top of the stairs. He lay across the steps to set his rifle across the debris-strewn floor. In the event the Khindos got their second wind and came traipsing down the hallway, Mack would have a stable shooting position to fire from.

Where most leejes had their combat knife, Creeper reserved space for a pair of auto-sheers meant for these sorts of occasions. With power-assisted, carbon-forged blades, the power-sheers could cut thin metal, rock, and even the hardened straps on Legion armor if the need called for it. For a shard of metal thin enough, it was the perfect tool for the job. "Not going to lie, kid. This is going to hurt worse than when the Legion doc checks your chute during enlistment processing."

"They don't do that anymore," Fresher said.

"I hate you, kid," Creeper said offhanded as he clipped the metal. A sharp clink from the piece hitting the stone landing was all the medic needed to move onto the next step. "I'm locking old peg leg's armor into place and going for wrap. Thirty seconds until move."

"That's good, because it's time to go," Mack instructed. A flick of the trigger and bolts from his NK-4 tracked along the wrecked hallway and into the Khindos, picking their way through the mess. Return fire was almost immediate and heavy as the two dead men in the front were replaced by fighters venting a fusillade of bolts from Zekes fired from the hip. Mack ducked back into the stairwell right before a blanket of automatic fire covered the stairs in scorch marks.

He bounded down the stairs, making it to the next level, where his team was waiting for him. "Last man. Move it."

Those who weren't wounded helped those that were as they slithered through the bottom level of the facility. A room on their route had its doors blown to the other side of the hall, where they rested on a bed of debris.

"This was probably the feeder room for things like O2 and other gasses. There must have been some fire retardant or inert gasses in there or something that put the fire out when it blew out the door."

"Not how that works, genius," Lobster nasally joked.

"Can we just leave him here?" Creeper responded.

Mack and Shiloh passed the wounded across to those that still had all their parts functioning. During the process, the team marksman noticed blood trickling from Mack's armor.

"That new?" Shy asked.

"Looks like I didn't give the Kavir patches time to fully adhere. Must have come off during the fight upstairs," Mack said. "Seal me up, real quick."

Shiloh unlocked the plate from Mack's armor, pushing aside the synthprene to get to the wound beneath. He took a steri-scrub from the team sergeant's trauma kit to clean the wound and dry the site for a clean stick. With a new ultra skinpack in hand, he applied it to the wound and pressed hard enough to make the master sergeant wince. "Looks like someone wanted to unzip you from your skin, Top. But you can call me Fresher's daddy if it doesn't look like it's been stitched for a few days and you just popped one."

"We'll let the doc know with a good marketplace review."

They hustled through the rest of the level to reach the spillway. With a facility built in jungle terrain that entertains constant rainfall and the occasional typhoon, being able to vent water runoff down into the river was a must for Serrabi Falls. As such, water grates were installed along the roads and throughout the facility grounds.

The leejes crawled into the spillway control station to find Tommy and Stringer working the wheel-handled door leading to the whirlpool room. The central large compartment dissipated the force of rapidly moving water through the pipes by allowing it to filter into the room and guide around the circular chamber until it passed out from the luge lower in the structure or collided with more water pouring in from the other chutes. Constructing the whirlpool in this fashion kept the stone walls in the spillway from cracking during the torrential rainstorms common on this side of the planet.

Three metallic bars keeping anyone from entering the facility through the spillway were already cut away. This was earlier handiwork by the team during the assault set the stage for phase two of asset denial on Serrabi Station. The legionnaires tumbled through the hatch and onto the ladder leading to the whirlpool below them. Now empty of water, the glistening surface of the stone covered in a light moss appeared slick in the overhead lighting in the chamber.

"Watch your step," Mack called from the top of the ladder. "When you reach the bottom, drop onto your fourth point of contact and slide through the chute. Straight leejes, grab your injured buddies and take the ride."

"Boss, I have a ping for Major Tyler moving through the river. His armor reports he's banged up something fierce, but should be good until Snow pulls him out of the drink. No lock on Raptor," Tommy said sourly.

"Hopefully it's a gear issue. Lowest bidder and all that. We straight on FFD?" Mack asked his slicer.

Tommy locked his battle board to his armor after a final check of his calculations. "Roger that, Top. The clock starts when I hit the water. Security cams show the fake leej and his boys checking Lab Six for booby traps, and they just escorted a geek like me into the server room. Time for the hard part, Top. That others may live."

"True enough, Staff Sergeant Lau," Mack said. "I'm last man. Let's get wet."

The team sergeant held his rifle at the hatch until all of REC-Team Pelican slid down the slimy sluiceway, spilling into the watery rush below. With tethers finally attached to his injured man, Tommy took hold of Blanks and the two of them disappeared into the current.

Mack logged into Tommy's tracking algo one last time to see if the slicer leej was just in a hurry when he couldn't find their team lead. Nothing was there. Either Raptor's tracker had been destroyed or he'd turned it off. Either way wouldn't matter in about five minutes. He sat on the chamber floor and pushed off into the ramp.

The thunder of white water rushing over the riverbed just beyond the runoff turned the sluiceway into a stone box filled with white noise. At the chamber's exit, Mack aimed his feet for the slide out of the facility and into the rampant maelstrom below him. Sliding against the stone, he rapidly picked up speed until he made the exit, falling the half meter into the river. The tumultuous current slammed him about like a ragdoll, slapping him off rocks and tree roots hidden below the angry tide of water racing along the riverbed.

Hitting the water in a tumble isn't the most dangerous thing to happen when a person has to navigate a white-water swim. The various schoolhouses gave entire classes on it during the Legion's mountain, rescue, and survival courses. Leej candidates had to read, absorb, and process books analyzing dangerous conditions as they make their way through Legion selection. The Rescue and Recovery Qualification course all Valkyries needed to pass in order to get their wings covered water-survival of all types and traumas. And while the instructor at the course always chose the most dangerous rivers they could find to test the candidates, there were safety protocols in place to keep the very expensive legionnaires from dying. Usually.

Mack had negotiated whitewater during real world rescues. Both times, he was injured from the op. There's a first time for everything, he thought as his helmet struck a rock while he negotiated for the surface. Ballast systems flared in his armor, increasing his buoyancy by offsetting the weight of his kit. Rampant splashes washed over his bucket, making it difficult to see until the helmet's limited AI activated optical algos using spatial mapping software to increase visibility.

Pushing his attention past the very real danger the water posed, Mack forced himself to remember the fundamentals. The little tricks that kept a leej alive when the water threatened to crush, strangle, and kill. In that moment, he felt the wire from his failed mission in his hands again. He felt the weight on the line and the helplessness of the moment. But, as quickly as it had come, it was gone.

Memories of the many leejes whose instruction had made him who he was came to replace the ghosts.

He couldn't remember the old leej's name, but he could remember the advice. *"The best way to negotiate rocky, turbulent water is to float to the surface, face up, and keep yer feet angled high and out of the water if possible. Keeping those little piggies aimed at the sky will keep you from getting yer foot caught in a tangle of sunken roots or in a pile of rocks below the surface. Want to come out of the water the same way you went in? Be a leaf and not an anchor."*

Mack thrust his feet ahead of him as the current pulled in a thrashing tumble along the river's path. He bobbed and submerged until the armor's buoyancy eventually returned him to the surface. Thrusting his arms to his sides, he waved and presented them like rudders to steer himself away from the larger rocks jutting through the spray and foam. Right when Mack felt he had the river's tumultuous pulse figured out, an undercurrent dragged him from the surface and held him down. Before his head could rise out of the wash, his toes struck something firm, followed by his heels gaining purchase.

A round, fat boulder dominated this part of the river, almost splitting the rapids into two streams. Several meters off from the front of the rock were the falls Serrabi was named for. The cascading drop was more of a staircase that Mack hoped to negotiate rather than tumble over so he could finally claim he'd hit the water one time without concussion, contusion, or worse. Mack pushed off from the rock and let the current take him.

He splashed in the current three times along the drops until the water racing around him dragged him for the highest part of the fall. A sloppy tumble down dropped him into the pool below where a jump from any falls was its most dangerous. Waterfalls of any height can create a rotational wash, casting currents that make it difficult for nonaquatic species to determine which way is up should they land safely. Many vacationers lose their way in the water and drown when they could easily stand if they only knew to try.

Finding his way to the surface, he let the current take him to a much less excited part of the river. Roughly four minutes into their improvised escape, Mack's HUD sprang to life.

"Last man, boss?" Snowball called into the L-comm.

"'Fraid so, sir. Where you at?" Mack responded.

A stone skipped off of Mack's chest, cluing him into their location. At the edge of the river, Stringer and Tommy were waist deep in the water, waiting for him to float by. Tommy waved a D-link carabiner and tossed it.

Snatching the thing out of the air, Mack clipped the tied-off link to his armor's drag handle and let the pair pull him to the bank. "That was fun. How much left?"

Tommy tapped the nonexistent chrono on his wrist. "Outta time, Top. Get in or get gone."

"I'll get in," Mack replied. He gained his feet closer to the shore, and the trio ran for the stealth shuttle tucked into a copse of trees close by. Living by the NCO mantra that he'd be the first off the shuttle and the last to board, he hit the plunger to seal the shuttle's bay doors. "Where's Raptor?"

The only answer his team gave him were the empty stares of their faceless buckets and the clicks of four-point harnesses clasping shut. The silence in the bay conveyed more pain and loss as the seconds counted down than a handful of explanations ever could.

Mack buckled himself into his jump seat and allowed himself to settle in so he could feel the shuttle's engines powering up. He pressed his palm against the harness to feel the rattle of the ship through his gloves. He squeezed so he could feel the scars.

"Detonation," Snowball called into the L-comm. "Shock wave... now."

Mack was glad to have a pilot like Snowball. The Legion shuttle jockey had primed the ship to full power in order to rig the shields for the brunt of the shock wave. Snow barely got the words out of his mouth when a tremendous turbulence buffeted the ship. Massive slams sounded outside the craft, most likely trees, huge chunks of landscape, and boulders. The nearly rocket-propelled debris slammed all around them as the explosive force of the weapon played out. Shields took the beating like champs, but did nothing for the legionnaires' nerves as the ship rocked and bounced on its landing gear.

Republic R&D originally designed the particle wave as a site denial weapon for high-valued facilities that absolutely could not fall into enemy hands. When its destructive potential was fully realized, the Republic's Energy Safety Commission had attached them to anything with intense fallout due to systems failure. Blow the source of the radiation and save whatever was nearby. Before the weapon created a massive energy wave that cooked everything to a temperature of several thousand degrees, the detonator triggered a time-release energy shield strong enough to contain the reaction.

The weapon fried anything that needed destruction to a cinder and the shield would fail, releasing the rest of the particle field to dissipate any residual radiation. Of course, the Republic considered the released shock wave as a feature rather than a bug, but then, that was how they pitched everything they sold that worked half as well as expected.

With the force of the FFD dying outside the ship, Mack scrolled through his messages to find the one had Raptor sent. Typing the word *Kython* into the security field, Mack scowled when the password didn't work. He tried several spellings and even added numbers to the front and back of the elusive password, coming up empty.

That's when he remembered Raptor didn't say Kython was the password. He'd said the password was the mythical creature they'd met on their first hop together. And

Mack could think of nothing more mythical than a Cherry who gives himself his own call sign.

"Thresher," Mack typed into the field.

The message opened into an audio file, plagued with the sounds of rattling gear and Raptor huffing into the comms. "Hey Mack, this message is for if I didn't make it out. If I'm sitting across from you in the shuttle, just go ahead and delete it. Anyways, I needed someone to know how this went wrong, and since we both know what it means to fail, you're the guy.

"Somehow, Special Activities found out about my cancer. They approached me and said they had a way to get me treated so I wouldn't lose my spot on the team. All I had to do was get a sample of the nano-stim Doctor Kavir worked up. Bring back a sample and I'd be in the clear. The House of Reason was going to get it, anyway, so who cares which rich firm developed it?"

Listening to the haunted message of a dead man, Mack absently rubbed his scars through the gloves. This wasn't some list for how he wanted the team to run after he was gone. It was a confession. Mack flinched when the audio clearly marked the captain as being struck by a blaster bolt.

Several return shots later, and Raptor continued amid coughs into the comms. He sounded like a man slowly catching his breath after being punched in the gut. "Man! This stim injection is incredible. Anyway, someone must have found out what I was doing and tried to burn me. All I can do now is try to make this right for the team. Tyler's out here with me. He's hit. I'm going after him. Look, there's no excuse for what I did, I just—I just didn't want to go out on a lie, Mack. I didn't want my last act as a leej to be for the wrong reasons. Ya know. In case I don't make it back."

Raptor's message cut off with the sound of more blaster fire filling the space. Mack sat in the jump seat for a long minute, barely registering the aftereffects of the FFD buffeting the drop ship's shields outside. A new message flashed in his bucket, returning his focus to his leejes.

"Go for Mack."

"Master Sergeant Banes," Snowball started. All the joking he was known for was gone. "With Major Tyler unconscious in the back of my ship, you're the ranking member of the team. I have roughly two minutes to fly out through all this lingering energy in the air. Targeting won't work. Tracking won't do squat. I can do a flyover if you want me to, and no one would be the wiser."

Mack felt the team watching him while he stared into his bucket. He'd initially had it close to his face for the L-comm but now the dirt-scuffed, muddy visor stared back, accusing him of the one thing he held himself guilty for, even if everyone else saw it wasn't true.

That's when Tommy's words, before their big soak, hit him again. The Valkyrie motto.

That others may live.

Throughout the mission, this was it—the niggling reminder Raptor, and even his ghosts, had haunted him about. It's what Raptor paid the Legion price for.

One by one, the legionnaires who weren't narked to the nines by painkillers removed their buckets, nodding to Mack with faces primed for acceptance. Blanks, Lobster, and Fresher were injured and needed a MED-DET sooner than later. Tyler had been shot to pieces and needed medical attention, now. The leejes who weren't shot were battered, soaked, and tired. There was also the matter of the slight tinge in his own side reminding him he wasn't one hundred percent.

"String. Do you have comms with Maggie?" Mack asked.

Tommy looked up hopefully. "Yes, Top."

Mack unbuckled the harness and crossed the space in the shuttle to the equipment rack. He dumped his empty charge packs in the bin and replaced them with fresh ones. He kept his face aimed at the rack lest the leejes who could still fight take it as a sign to join him.

Everyone except for the three injured leejes unbuckled from their harnesses and hurried to join their team sergeant. Lobster stood as well, but Mack motioned for the injured man to stay. The breacher ignored him, slapping the new, specialized trauma packs on each side of his wounded arm before sliding back into his armor.

Mack dropped the bucket over his head as he reached for Major Tyler's Frankensteined NK-4. "Snow, put us on a quick burn over by the gate where we entered the facility. The three of us will hop out and link up with Maggie. If he's out there, we'll find him."

Excitedly, Snowball called into the comms, "Oscar Mike, Master Sergeant."

"You know they'll probably bust us down to Fresher's rank for going back, right?" Creeper hinted.

Mack shrugged. "Can't bust us if we have a legit reason for going. We do. Third Valkyrie mission. Asset denial. Those FFDs are unreliable. Especially after two years and no maintenance. C'mon. What kind of leejes would we be if we didn't confirm the facility was destroyed?"

"That's a good point," Creeper agreed as the shuttle lifted off. The leejes grabbed the guide wire above their heads for balance.

For the first time in a long time, the ghosts were quiet as Mack felt the scars beneath his glove.

26

Tyler woke with a start, glancing around the pristine bay in confusion when the last thing he remembered was water and trees. And there were rocks. Big rocks. But here, multiple beds along a brightly lit bay with suspension beds periodically slid from the wall. The blankets over his legs tucked into the bed gave the memory foam surface a square appearance. Suspension bed for sure.

He stretched his hand to the side of the bed for purchase, a handhold to prop himself up, when holos appeared over his arm. Heart rate, respiration, blood pressure. Beyond the holo, a hospital corpsman wearing medical scrubs pulled some gloves from his hands to toss them into a bio-bin. Suspension beds and corpsman. He was on a ship. That much was clear. Water and trees, and the rocks of course. But how did he get on a ship? Tyler attempted to call the man over before he walked from the med bay, but found his mouth bone dry and all that he managed was a croak.

A flash in the holo redirected his attention to the board, describing an amputation of the leg below the knee. Tyler's face slowly tracked back to his feet, or rather, his foot. One. Only one. Beyond the single set of digits, he noticed a curtain and wondered if they'd drawn the veil closed to give some other soldier privacy to deal with their own personal hell. A world where they woke up and a part of them was gone.

Tyler slowed his breathing while he rapidly swallowed, trying to generate enough saliva to wet his mouth. The holo hovering just off to the side with a clear animation of the removal, prompted him to smack his mouth, trying to gather more spit to clear the dry, raspy sensation that would allow him to call for help. With no one else in the bay, he cast a glance at where his missing limb should be and tried for a wiggle of the toes. There was nothing.

Pressing his jaw tight, Major Robert Tyler gripped the side of the blanket and pulled. His leg was indeed gone. Replaced with a rubbery stump wrapped in a bandage. Another focusing breath and his breathing slowed again.

Don't panic. Don't freak out. Don't be the man they think you are; be the man you know you are, Tyler thought.

He tried to raise his ruined limb above the mimeo-cellular bedding pressed into the suspension bed frame. There was nothing.

He reached through the johnny, feeling the back of his spine for any sort of surgical scar or bandage, and his sweep came up empty. The motion sent a sharp lance through his upper torso as he finally looked down to see a medical tac-wrap circling that part of his torso. The fake leej. He'd been shot by the fake leej. In the end, Tyler had planted that guy in the mud, but not before he got his own shots on target. On him. The last thing he remembered was crawling into the river and activating his rescue beacon. Why couldn't he remember a leg injury? Why couldn't he move? What was left of the leg?

Nearly jumping from his skin, Tyler finally noticed a spacer lieutenant with a glowing face, pristine blonde hair, and curves that made the scrubs she was wearing a crime against nature for covering them. He went to apologize for the start but realized that the spit factory he'd been going for to clear his throat had failed at getting the product on the shelf. He almost lost himself in her crystalline amber eyes where there was just the hint of darkness beneath, when something in his brain, some part of an upbringing around the social elite and the society that cared about proper and polite interactions, prompted him to look away.

"I'm sorry, sir," Amber-Eyed Corpsman said. "Let's get you some water."

She handed him a cup from a suspension tray close by. Tyler took a deep sip and held off drinking more so as not to overload a dry throat. If he'd just come from surgery, they might have intubated him, so there was some caution to be had there. Keeping his eyes on where his toes used to be, he absently rested the glass on the limb he could feel. With renewed moisture lubricating the words from his mouth, he issued a weak, "Thank you."

"No worries, sir. Major Robert Tyler," the corpsman said as she read and then waved away the holo. "Vitals look good. Heart rate and BP are a bit elevated, but that could just be you coming out of anesthesia. So, are we ready for your colonoscopy?"

Tyler dropped the glass as he turned to regard the woman and croaked out a "what," in the worst puberty voice that had ever been uttered on a Republic warship.

Laughter erupted from the other side of the drawn curtain across the bay. Various devices, cups, and spent medical detachment fruit cups bounced along the floor as unintelligible comments and snort-filled giggling drifted out from the screen. Mack pulled the curtain, and while he had an amused look on his face, he wasn't hilariously incapacitated like the rest of REC-Team Pelican crammed into the tiny space the curtain covered.

Creeper extracted himself from the mob, holding a datapad and wiping tears streaming down his cheeks. "Okay. Okay. Hear me out on this one. I know it's all conduct unbecoming of an NCO or whatever but, would it be wrong of me to put 'colonoscopy face' as your contact icon in my bucket?"

"What's happening?" Tyler croaked, eliciting a renewed chorus of laughter and dropping things on the other side of the bay.

The corpsman stifled a grin while playing the role of frowning schoolmarm.

"You apes better clean up this bay," she barked. "When I come back, this floor better be spotless."

"Aye, ma'am," Lobster said as he flapped his slung, bandaged arm in her direction. "Shipshape, no problem."

"Don't make me come back here or I'll put something else in a sling," the corpsman said, as all eyes followed her out of the room.

"Fun's over. Back to work," Mack said. "Lobster, those are your fruit cups. Get to cleaning."

"Aye, ma'am," Lobster said, waving his bundled arm.

The group mob logged their talents into cleaning up their mess and returning the suspension bed into the wall, where it would be sterilized for its next round of use, whatever that may be. While practical joke cleansing protocols went into effect, Creeper pulled off the bandage on Tyler's leg, exposing a nasty-looking scar radiating out from the center of what used to be his knee. He peeled off the rubbery skin—which almost caused the officer to pass out—revealing it as a mask of some sort. He tossed it aside and pulled the major's fully intact leg from a hole in the bed.

"I'm going to give you some drugs to reverse the effect of the nerve blocker we gave you. Do not walk on this for at least five minutes. Give the meds time to do their job, sir," Creeper said. He placed the man's leg onto the cellulose bedding and covered it up, matching the hospital folds on the other side. Creeper reset the chart in the holo and offered his goodbyes to the major. "Good to see you coming around, sir. We'll see you out there."

The boys of Pelican Team passed by to shake his hand or pat a shoulder on the way out, leaving Mack as the last man in the bay. When the last of REC-Team Pelican cleared the medical bay hatch, spouting off about colonoscopy face, the door to the bay sealed and a loud beep echoed through the room. Tyler looked at Mack in confusion as the master sergeant pulled over a stool. In the background, a med bot trundled by carrying a load of autoinjectors.

"This is the part where you tell me my career is over and you wanted it to come from you," Tyler guessed.

Mack topped off the major's cup of water and handed it back to him. He reached into his pocket to produce his own fruit cup. Digging in, he said, "That depends. Do you still want to be a Legion communications officer?"

Tyler rubbed his leg, relishing the feeling coming back into the limb. "A communication officer? No, not really."

Mack nodded once. "I spoke to your Legion Advisory Officer, which took a hot minute to link up to because, technically, you were the highest-ranking Legion officer on the *Reliant*. The picture he painted of you was smart. You had a rough time in the regiments because of your past as a point. Never mind the whole 'own it' mentality you had going on. So you transitioned into L-comm security."

Tyler eased his head into his pillow. "While not on mission, it gave me plenty of time to go to schools like sniper, PSD, and Critical Trauma. When I got out of Cri-Tram, I was stoked to try out for the Vals."

"But you got tripped in the psych eval," Mack noted through a mouthful of fruit. He licked the last of the juice from the spoon and took a medical grade sani-wipe to clean it. He passed the implement and a fresh fruit cup to the major.

Tyler pried the lid from the offered snack. The action, although simple for a man in the major's shape, made him wince as the muscles moving around a recovering shoulder spelled out that he was still on the mend. "Thanks. Yeah, no-go on the psych. 'Crusader complex. Applicant is invalidated for Rescue and Recovery Selection.'"

"Crusaders make great legionnaires but terrible Wreckers-slash-Valkyries," Mack said. "So, the way I see it, since you're never going to get near a set of wings, and the points were conspiring to pull Raptor no matter what, you used them to get on a rescue order this one time. Stealing that tech for them never crossed your mind."

Tyler waved the spoon back and forth as a sign of admission. "It did. They promised me all sorts of stuff beyond the spot in RSC. But when I really thought about it, it all seemed cheap and wrong. I'd be no better than all the points stabbing everyone in the back to get to the next rung on the ladder. It would have made everything I did up to now a lie."

Mack caught himself absently rubbing the scar in his palm and folded his hands. "I get that. Sir, you have three or four rejuv treatments to go before you can return to duty. But when you do..." Mack brought the holo above the bed to enter his security code. He flashed across command screens until he found what he was looking for. "...you have three months in pre-RSC to go through to get ready for selection. Provided that narco shot Creeper gave you for the joke wears off by then."

Tyler shoved the spoon in his mouth and leaned into the holo. In bright floating imagery, orders to report to the Legion Rescue Center on Spilursa were there, brighter than the near blinding radiance of the hospital lights. "How?"

"Raptor," Mack said matter-of-factly. "He was rating you the whole time. He still had friends over in RSC, and he logged his support for you while we were on mission. If he even thought for a minute you were going to kark us, he would have thrown you to the Khindos. I mean, you tried to throw your weight that one time with the Royal Marines, but after that, you watched, listened, and worked."

"I don't know what to say. Is he around so I can thank him, maybe apologize?" Tyler asked.

The sudden lump that visibly formed in Mack's throat told Tyler that the chance to thank Raptor in person would never happen on this side of the dirt.

"The best way to say thanks is to pass RSC and make it through the Q-course," Mack said, quickly stabilizing his quavering voice. "He'll be watching while you're there." The sergeant major snatched the plasteen spoon from the major's mouth and stood to make his way out. "Any problems, call me, sir."

Tyler stretched out to grab the master sergeant's arm before he could make for the hatch. "Master Sergeant. Did we even win that one? I mean, we rescued the doctor, but for what? So some company and their pocket politicians can do this somewhere else?"

Mack stepped back to the holo displaying the order to attend the Rescue Selection Course. He waved his hand over several screens to get to the display he wanted. "This doctor and those marines are all alive because of what you did. What you risked. The city, Kerhott, is all over the news as a miracle. The Royal Marines going in pretty much verified the place is sickness-free. That's going to mean new jobs, homes, a better something to someone. You get to own that, even if you don't get to tell the corpsman to impress her."

"Thank you for saving my life, Master Sergeant Banes," Tyler said.

Mack flipped the man off on his way out. "Thanks for not being a point, sir."

"Doctor Vidoran. If there was ever a day I needed you, it would be today," suspended Delegate Ramsada said as she hung up her coat. She dropped her purse at the base of the coat rack and swirled out the latest in Utopion fashion, making sure the fabric didn't wrinkle. Dolmethian silks cost more than the average salary earned by her constituents in a year, and you paid through the nose to have them smoothed out. Certain that she now looked magnificent—but subtly so—she whirled on the doctor, only to find him not in the chair where he normally sat. "Who are you, and where is Doctor Vidoran?"

The woman across from her was definitely not human, her complexion especially so. Her glorious purplish skin had no blemish, and she was wrapped in her own gorgeous dress of Dolmethian silks showing off delicious curves the delegate would have died for in her youth, never mind now when only the latest touch-ups would do for the cameras.

"I said—" Ramsada started.

"I heard you," said the woman. Her voice drifted from under a hood accented with a shimmering inlay that made it glimmer from the barest light coming through the sensitivity curtains. "You're in too much of a hurry, my dear. Please, sit. Have some tea. My name is Doctor Yalanissa Dern. I'm handling all of Doctor Vidoran's cases today, as he had a family emergency."

"Nothing too serious, I hope," Ramsada said as she descended into the chair across from Nissa, her politeness returning as though it had never left. "Oba, this tea is amazing. Oh. I must apologize for my outburst just now. Using the name of a spiritual icon was insensitive of me, seeing that I don't know your religious preference. And before we get started, is there a preferred set of pronouns that you feel is appropriate to your galactic conditional existence, Doctor?"

"Doctor will be fine," Nissa said. She adjusted the glasses covering her eyes to keep the delegate from noticing their lack of color. "So, according to your files, I see you are struggling with some anxiety and feelings of persecution after what Doctor Vidoran calls your incident."

"The incident," Ramsada said as though it were a code word to get into an exclusive speakeasy known only to those in her circles. "Before I start with the incident, has Doctor Vidoran cleared you for that? I mean, I am a sitting delegate for the House of Reason, and they vetted my regular doctor through all the proper channels."

Nissa leaned back in her chair with her fingers steepled. She waited for Ramsada's cup to meet its saucer and continued her performance. "My dear, how would I have gotten into this chair if I wasn't cleared through all the right channels?"

"Well, there is bribery, blackmail, coercion, and those curves. My dear, even I would sleep with you." Ramsada giggled as she checked the cup to see if it was empty. The delegate leaned heavily into her chair until she noticed her vacant cup had been refilled. "How in the... how did you fill my cup? You didn't move."

Nissa lifted a holo-board from the table next to her and tapped something on the surface. "How could I have filled your cup if I didn't move? Are you feeling alright?"

"I was when I came in, other than this whole incident thing. But now, Doctor, I'm not so sure. It's like the room got all, I don't know, rubbery," Ramsada said.

"Rubbery, you say," Nissa echoed. "Was it rubbery that night when you were being held by the Royal Marines in Terum city at the Solaria Casino?"

"The incident," Ramsada whispered, as though she didn't want to share the event with anyone else but Nissa. The delegate looked away.

In Nissa's ear, Geiger called into her comm bead, "Nissa, the micro-cam in the flowers has a good shot of her face. Her eyes are as big as the saucer under that teacup."

Nissa nodded as though she were agreeing with the delegate rambling about the unfairness of her incident and how the House of Reason had placed her on administrative leave. Her sensitive ears picked up the brush of a door on the luxurious carpet in the office. Geiger came from a supply closet as he stepped over the unconscious form of Doctor Vidoran. The doctor's long face rested over his shoulder from being crammed into a sitting position. The closet had plenty of room for supplies, just not so much when it also had to hold an unconscious human and the man that drugged him.

The door closing behind Geiger alerted Delegate Ramsada, who turned to the noise and saw a man in a finely tailored suit standing behind her chair. "Oh doctor, you know what I like. This one would make me forget all about my incident. Wait. Is that what this is? Did Doctor Vidoran put you both up to this?"

"No, ma'am," Nissa whispered. "Although we're here to help you work through this. What can you tell us about your interest in Doctor Kavir?"

"And don't forget to ask about Captain Rashad," Geiger whispered.

Ramsada's drug-addled mind barely heard what the two of them were saying as her head lolled on the back of the chair to stare into the chiseled face of her newly ar-rived captor.

"One thing at a time, sir," Nissa cooed. "All the doctor's other appointments have been canceled. We have all day to spend together."

"Hey! Don't make me slap that smirk off your face, Stringer. You know I'm good for it," Chief Cantrell hollered across the firepit.

Laughter caught like dried kindling, spreading through the team as they gathered around the blazing bonfire. Hovering in the dark trees beyond them, hungry eyes surveyed the goings-on, reflecting the firelight in luminescent orbs as they worked through the best way to assault the group by the pyre. The team disregarded the local predators, as they were too small to do any damage to hardened legionnaires who'd come away from the city to celebrate a friend.

TC walked to Mack, who stood at the edge of the firelight, watching the affair play out as his leejes toasted and roasted their way through their grief. "He was more to you guys than just a team leader."

"Truth," Mack said, turning his crystalline glass so that the cigar in his hand wouldn't burn off his eyebrows as he drank. A quick sip of the caramel-colored liquid settled the bite on his tongue from the cigar, even as it warmed him going down. "Mustang officer. I didn't get the time with him like these guys had, but he was the guy you wanted to work with rather than just some guy you worked for."

"I still can't believe the team recovered his body. You boys went through hell and then... you just went back. For him. That's some impervisteel feathers you guys got on those wings. Ya know, I should probably eat something to go with this." TC finished the statement with a sip of his own glass.

"Cantrell pulled out all the stops. Chief can put out a spread, that's for sure. You don't eat something, and she might take it as a personal slight," Mack said, gesturing with his glass. He offered a cigar to TC, who readily accepted.

"Thanks," TC said. His eyes acted like those of the predators hovering in the fiery shadows when Mack lit the cigar for him. He looked at the head of ash on the end of the stogie, returning it to his mouth for a puff or two. "Are these real?"

"Only the best," Mack said.

TC pulled on the cigar enough to get the end stoked to a brilliant red and chased it with a sip from his glass. "I've never been to something like this before. Is this how all Valkyries give out awards?"

Mack stared at the bonfire as the alcohol finally started doing its job. "Nah, this is old-school. From a time when all soldiers had was metal and bone. This is how they used to remember the fallen."

"I thought the Legion would have moved for something a bit more public, seeing as how things played out," TC noted.

"Can't," Mack huffed. Willowy smoke vented from between his teeth. "Even though a point at Legion command drafted an illegal order based on illegally obtained medical information, Raptor still went on the operation, anyway. He was going to get his feathers burned for that, no matter what. It just so happens that all of this exposed the delegate and her little black bag groupies."

"There is that," TC said. He looked over the rim of his glass and took in the partygoers sampling food and drink around the fire. "Who is that?"

"Camilla 'War Dog' Dawson. Captain of the *Reliant*," Mack laughed. "You might want to go over there and rescue your boy, though. That's Geiger, right?" Mack grinned. "He seems way into her, and let me tell you, he wouldn't survive the experience."

"Nah, it's fine. If that's War Dog, then she's just the kind of heat he's into," TC said. "Hey, Mack, thanks for letting us be a part of this. He was our friend, too."

As TC disappeared, Mack had a moment to himself before he felt a presence just ahead of the predators keeping a vigil in the wood line. "You don't have to hover."

Nissa sauntered to him, wearing a gossamer gown and no shoes, as she toed her way past where the fallen leaves lay and the beach sand began. She'd covered her head in a shawl of the same material, covering the scarred tendrils marking her past ordeals. "This is some party you two put on."

"Old-school Valkyrie. They really don't do this anymore," Mack said. "Chief helped me put this together. Well, her and this crazy cab driver I met when I first got to Damyagora."

She smiled, and the firelight played across her flawless face, which stilled. "I'm curious, Mack. Why do this for someone you barely knew?"

Mack held up a feather chip to spin between his fingers. "You couldn't watch it, but I'm pretty sure someone described it to you. The video Major Tyler's drone captured of Raptor as he went out. That was the first combat action like that holo'd in, well, a long time. He deserved something special."

"I understand that, but why this old tradition?" Nissa asked.

Mack tasted from the glass before answering. "You go to combat with someone, that makes them family. Doesn't matter how well or little you know them. That experience wrote them into your soul, and with them gone, it's now your duty to carry that memory forward. This helps to cement that memory."

"I wish someone would do that for me when it's time," Nissa said.

"We will. You might not have been sending rounds down range right next to us, but what you did made our mission possible. That's family," Mack said, placing the glass into her hand.

"Oh dear spirits, no," Nissa said, rubbing her nose as she scented the concoction. "I like mine to taste of honey and cinnamon. You keep your smoke and leather."

"Well, seeing as I'm almost out, let's get the festivities done before these boys are too fat and drunk to care." Mack offered her his arm as he walked beside her to the bonfire where waiting legionnaires greeted him with yelling and the raising of glasses at his approach. He waved them down, pulling Fresher forward to serve as a guide for the sultry psyops specialist. When she was good and settled, he held up his hand to grab the attention of the group.

In the quiet of dying conversations and the bonfire's crackle, Mack gestured to his friend. "Ma'am. If you would?"

Captain Dawson drifted over to a table, glass in hand. She hesitantly set down her drink, as if doing so marred the sacred space. No food, drink, or incidental thing had been allowed near the box. That part of the table, like the hand carved box resting on it, was pristine.

She reverently lifted the box, taking it in the palm of one hand and covering it with the other. When she turned to face the group again, the woman who had survived the fires once had brilliant tears glistening in the firelight. She walked by the bonfire and settled her toes in the lake water lapping at the shore. Several paces ahead of her on the sand rested a wooden longboat and sail, its stern bobbing gently with the motion of the lake even as its prow rested in the sand. Set atop a stack of straw and kindling was Legion armor, charred, scratched. Worn.

The armor's gauntlets were folded over its chest, with an old wooden stock rifle and a hatchet resting under them. Thrust into the kindling were mementos from the mourners. Everyone had taken a turn at the boat's gunwale and put in something. Standing at the front of the ship, Dawson wiped the tears from her face to avoid dampening the little box.

"I met Raptor when he used to go by Rooster as an NCO," Dawson said. "I thought he was hitting on me. He'd walk by my bird on the flight line and tell me to light 'em up. 'We're going down to the planet, ma'am. Keep the skies angry for me till I get back,' he'd say. Always something goofy like that. One of my guys got shot up while his leejes were waiting to deploy rock-side. The plane was just burning up out there amid all the other stuff in orbit we broke that day. Spacers were taking their sweet time getting off the deck."

Dawson struggled to compose herself. The captain of the *Reliant* was normally stone-cold aboard ship. Here, she was among fellow men-at-arms. These were her people. Everyone at her back had sent rounds downrange, or at the very least, had them come from that way. Here she could be just a woman grieving for her friend. "He just ran through the atmospheric shield. No EVA gear. No rescue kit. A bird of prey, ready to kill anything out there aiming at my pilot. He gave me my pilot back, so I gave him his new tag."

Mack rested his hand on her shoulder, the action seeming to help her collect herself. These were her people. They were her tribe. Dawson turned to see tears falling from eyes that had seen too much and rested too little. She didn't envy those eyes that were forced to watch people fall, up close, over and over again. She didn't envy the master sergeant, her friend.

"Attention to orders!" Mack shouted.

The legionnaires snapped to attention. Pain and healing injuries all ignored as the training to become a statue representing the might of the Republic took hold and locked them in place. As if the universe demanded it, the military and civilian attendees alike silenced. Those who weren't military stood straight and still with their hands over their hearts.

"During the execution of Rescue Order 777481-Bravo-Six, Captain Emilio Rashad, call sign Raptor, worked with legionnaires assigned to Gungnir Platoon to secure his place on the operation despite rogue elements working to undermine the mission. Under intense enemy fire as part of Task Unit Pelican, Captain Rashad singlehandedly fought through a line of enemy fighters to secure a lane of travel for the rescue vehicle, thus completing the mission. Cut off from his men, his actions against multiple squads of enemy personnel kept heavy weapons from reaching their targets, thus increasing the efficiency and survivability of his team."

The fire crackled quietly, the lake lapped the boat, Mack missed his friend. He sniffed deep and swallowed hard to keep the regrets he harbored from coloring what he said next.

"Though gravely wounded himself, he fought enemy fighting positions on multiple fronts to clear the extraction of the very rescue element sent to retrieve him. Through his actions, Captain Emilio Rashad, call sign Raptor, brought great credit upon himself, his unit, and a grateful Legion. For his bravery and gallantry in the face of overwhelming odds, despite great personal peril, the Legion awards him the Order of the Centurion."

The legionnaires standing in witness, along with Dawson and those other members of the unit who'd worn a uniform, snapped a salute. Carmilla was first to drop her hand as she broke the seal on the carved chestnut box. Inside was a medal engraved with a Legion helmet emblazoned in front of the crest on a lush blue ribbon. She laid it around the neck of the armor, her shoulders shivering from the effort as tears dappled the black shell.

Mack moved forward and nodded to her, almost as if the action itself gave her permission to step back. The legionnaires limped over to the boat. Mack gestured to Fresher, giving him the first spot near the prow. He touched the side of the boat, followed by delivering a throttling punch into the plank. One by one, the leejes of REC-Team Pelican leveled their fists into the side of the boat with tremendous power, many of them coming away with bloody knuckles for the effort.

Mack placed his hand on the bow spirit, running his hand over the rope that connected it to the mast. He gave it a tug against the tension before placing his Legion Valkyrie wings, a set of wings set against three arrows, atop the gunwale. One hammer fist struck the pins deep into the wood and he stepped back to inspect the handiwork of his men. Nine sets of wings adorned the prow of the ship, glistening in the firelight coming off the blaze behind them.

"What happens now, Top?" Fresher asked as he wiped tears from his face.

"One for the new guy. One for the brace. One for the veteran. An arrow for each to symbolize the three missions of a Valkyrie leej," Mack said as he handed out a bow to Fresher and Creeper. His last bow he presented to Shiloh, who looked at him in confusion. "Technically, I'm a new guy, just not the new guy."

"I've never seen anything like this, Top. I mean..." Shy protested.

"The kid is the youth you need to run a REC-Team. Creeper is the veteran. You're the brace. The guy that keeps the traditions and standards alive." Mack leaned in close to the team marksman. "Plus, you're the only guy here with even a snowball's chance in hell of hitting the damn thing."

Mack turned from Shiloh and gripped the sides of the boat. With alcohol numbing the stab wound still healing in his side, he pushed the boat from the sand. It hovered for a moment close to the shore until Mack spun it for another heave out into the lake. Dripping wet, he walked from the water and took the arrow from Fresher. He lit the tip and held it away as it sparked to life as a blazing white flame. "Don't burn yourself, kid."

The three bow-bearing legionnaires set themselves onto the beach as the boat drifted out in the midnight blue lake.

Arrow nocked, Creeper turned back to the group. "Top, since I didn't serve as General Rex's personal foot masseuse in the Savage Wars, is there a time we've gotta wait before we shoot this off or, like, a safe word?"

"Man, I'll give you a safe word!" Shiloh said, slapping Creeper on the back of the head. "Light it off, son!"

The three would-be archers launched their arrows. The burning phosphorous shafts sailed through the air like three streaks of golden fire before they struck. Two sizzled into the water, but the third thunked into the boat. In a moment, the ship was in flames, dancing in the night, as the leejes and agents said their last goodbyes to their fallen commander.

When the fire consumed the mast of the ship and it fell over, Mack turned to, Captain Dawson, and gave her the kind of grizzly bear hug you only gave to those that know the deal, because they've had to trudge through it with you. Being much smaller than Mack, she leaned into the hug to get closer to his ear. "You rigged the boat with a burner, didn't you?"

"Ain't no way those drunk leejes were going to hit a boat fifty feet away with a bow and arrow," Mack said with a grin.

TC offered the man a seat next to him where his cigar and a freshened glass of scotch were waiting. "I've served with two Wrecker Teams, Rec-Teams, Valkyries, whatever you want to call 'em. I've never seen anything like that."

Mack took the glass and his resurrected cigar. "Thank you, sir. Very old tradition. Can't get any place to let you do it anymore because the Repub Environmental Protection Agency says it's too harmful to the environment. Might hurt the feelings of the local woodpeckers, you know."

TC nearly snorted his drink, giving the man a knowing smile. "Thanks for doing this for Raptor. He would have been way into this."

"You're welcome. He was a good dude. But before I forget, I have to know. Why in the nine hells do you look like a skinny Tyrus Rechs?"

TC raised his glass in toast and waited for Mack to join him. "That, my friend, is a story for another time."

PUBLISHER'S NOTE

We hope you have enjoyed the adventures of a Republic REC-Team presented in Callsign Valkyrie. Galaxy's Edge Press is currently considering whether to launch an ongoing series featuring Mack and REC-Team Pelican and would like to know what our Galaxy's Edge Leejes think. Please visit www.galaxysedge.us/valkyrie to find out more and share your opinion... and KTF!

HONOR ROLL

Jason and Nick would like to thank those who whose Galaxy's Edge Insider Subscriptions saw the conclusion of Galaxy's Edge, Season Two.

Cody Aalberg
Sam Abraham
Guido Abreu
Alex Acree
Chancellor Adams
Myron Adams
Daniel Adams
Chris Adkins
Garion Adkins
Ryan Adwers
Kyle Aguiar
Elias Aguilar
Dennis Aheard Jr.
Morgan Albert
Neal Albritton
Aleksey Aleshintsev
Willis Alfonso
Jonathan Allain
Bill Allen
Byron Allen
Jacob Forrest Allen
Justin Allred

Paul Almond
Larry Alotta
Chris Alston
Tony Alvarez
Christian Amburgey
Joachim Andersen
Jarad Anderson
Galen Anderson
Levi Anderson
Taylor Anderson
Pat Andrews
Caleb Angell
Robert Anspach
Melanie Apollo
Joseph Aranda
Benjamin Arguello
Thomas Armona
Daniel Armour
Omar Arroyo
Linda Artman
Jeff Asher
Nicholas Ashley

Jonathan Auerbach

Sean Averill

Nicholas Avila

Albert Avilla

Tisianna Azbill

Benjamin Backus

Matthew Bagwell

Christian Bailey

Marvin Bailey

Shane Bailey

Daniel Baker

Sallie Baliunas

Nathan Ball

Kevin Bangert

Christopher Barbagallo

John Barber

Caleb Barber

Brian Bardwell

Logan Barker

John Barley

Brian Barrows-Striker

Richard Bartle

Austin Bartlett

Sean Battista

Robert Battles

Eric Batzdorfer

John Baudoin

Adam Bear

Nahum Beard

Michelle Beaver

Mike Beeker

Randall Beem

Matt Beers

John Bell

Daniel Bendele

Royce Benford

Mark Bennett

Ryan Bennett

Edward Benson

Mark Berardi

Hjalmar Berggren

Matthew Bergklint

Carl Berglund

Brian Berkley

Corey Berman

David Bernatski

Gardner Berry

Tim Berube

Michael Betz

Kevin Biasci

Shannon Biggs

Gregory Bingham

Brien Birge

Brien Birge

Nathan Birt

Francisco Blankemeyer

Trevor Blasius

David Blount

Liz Bogard

James Bohling

Evan Boldt

Rodney Bonner

Rodney Bonner

Brandon Boone

Thomas Seth Bouchard

William Boucher

Aaron Bowen	Jeff Brussee
Brandon Bowles	Benjamin Bryan
Alex Bowling	Marion Buehring
Keiger Bowman	Wendy Bugos
Gregory Bowman	Wendy Bugos
Michael Boyle	Nicholas Burck
Clifton Bradley	John Burleigh
Chester Brads	Tyler Burnworth
Scott Brady	Noel Caddell
Alex Brady	Daniel Cadwell
Richard Brake	Brian Callahan
Ryan Bramblett	Joseph Calvey
Logan Brandon	Decker Cammack
Evan Brandt	Van Cammack
Ernest Brant	Mark Campbell
Daniel Bratton	Chris Campbell
Chet Braud	Danny Cannon
Chet Braud	Zachary Cantwell
Dennis Bray	John Cappleman
Robert Bredin	Spencer Card
Christopher Brewster	Brett Carden
Jacob Brinkman	Brett Carden
Geoff Brisco	Daniel Carpenter
Wayne Brite	Rafael Carrol
Joysell Brito	Brad Carter
Kevin Brock	Gabriel Castro
Spencer Bromley	Robert Cathey
Paul Brookins	Brian Cave
Raymond Brooks	Brian Cheney
Joseph Bross	Brad Chenoweth
Zack Brown	Caleb Cheshire
Matthew Brown	David Chor
RFC Brumley	James Christensen

Robyn Cimino-Hurt
Rebecca Clark
Rebecca Clark
Kelly Clark
Cooper Clark
Casey Clarkson
Andrew Clary
Ethan Clayton
Jonathan Clews
Beau Clifton
Sean Clifton
Morgan Cobb
David Collins
Robert Collins Sr.
Alex Collins-Gauweiler
Marcus Colwell
Jerry Conard
Robert Conaway
Gayler Conlin
Michael Conn
James Connolly
Ryan Connolly
James Conyers
Brian Cook
Devyn Cook
Dustin Coons
Terry Cooper
Kevin Cooper
Jacob Coppess
Michael Corbin
Alex Corcoran
Robert Cosler
Anthony Cotillo

Ryan Coulston
Seth Coussens
Andrew Craig
Adam Craig
Zachary Craig
Adam Crocker
Ben Crose
Justin Crowdy
Ben Crowley
Christopher Crowley
Jack Culbertson
Phil Culpepper
Scott Cummins
Ben Curcio
Tommy Cutler
Thomas Cutler
Christopher Da Pra
John Dames
David Danz
Matthew Dare
Hayden Darr
Chad David
Alister Davidson
Peter Davies
Ashton Davis
Ben Davis
Ben Davis
Brian Davis
Nathan Davis
LeRoy Davis
Ivy Davis
David Davis
Joseph Dawson

Andrew Day	Marc-André Dufor
Gabriel De Jesus	Cory Dufour
Ron Deage	Thomas DuLaney II
Nathan Deal	Brendan Dullaghan
Jason Del Ponte	Trent Duncan
Anthony Del Villar	Ryan Duncan
Tod Delaricheliere	Christopher Durrant
Wayne Dennis	Evan Durrant
Anerio (Wyatt)	Samuel Dutterer
Deorma (Dent)	Chris Dwyer
Douglas Deuel	Virgil Dwyer
Aaron Dewitt	Brian Dyck
Isaac Diamond	Brian Dye
Alexander Dickson	Nick Edwards
Nicholas Dieter	Travis Edwards
Christopher DiNote	Justin Eilenberger
Matthew Dippel	Brian Eisel
Gregory Divis	Jonathan R. Ellis
Brian Dobson	William Ely
Samuel Dodes	Michael Emes
Graham Doering	Paul Eng
Shawn Doherty	Brian England
Gerald Donovan	Andrew English
Ward Dorrity	Dakota Erisman
Dustyn Down	Stephane Escrig
Noah Doyle	Ethan Estep
Michael Drescher	Dakota Estepp
Adam Drucker	Colton Eubanks
John Dryden	Benjamin Eugster
John Dryden	Richard Everett
Josh DuBois	Jaeger Falco
Garrett Dubois	Nicholas Fasanella
Ray Duck	Christian Faulds

Steven Feily

Julie Fenimore

Meagan Ference

Brad Ferguson

Hunter Ferguson

Adolfo Fernandez

Rich Ferrante

Jonathan Fields

Austin Findley

Albert Fink

Ashley Finnigan

Alex Fisher

Lamar Fitzgerald

Rhys Fitzpatrick

Matthew Fiveson

Daniel Flanders

Waren Fleming

Kath Flohrs

Daniel Flores

Geoffrey Flowers

William Foley

Charles Ford

Steve Forrester

Skyla Forster

Joshua Foster

Kenneth Foster

Jacob Fowler

Chad Fox

Bryant Fox

Doug Foxford

Martin Foxley

Mark Franceschini

Dennis Frank

Tim Frantz

Greg Franz

Kris Franzen

Luke Frazer

Evan Freel

Erik Freeman

Kyle Freitus

Griffin Frendsdorff

Josh Frenzen

Timothy Fujimoto

Bob Fulsang

Elizabeth Gafford

David Gaither

Seth Galarneau

Matthew Gale

Zachary Galicki

Nicholas Galvez

Robert Garcia

Robert Garcia

Joshua Gardner

Michael Gardner

Alphonso Garner

Mackenzey Garrison

Cordell Gary

Nathan Garza

Marina Gaston

Robert Gates

Brad Gatter

Tyler Gault

Angelo Gentile

Cody George

Stephen George

Nick Gerlach

Eli Geroux
Christopher Gesell
Joshua Gibson
Kevin Gilchrist
Dylan Giles
Joe Gillis
Oscar Gillott-Cain
Jason Ginzkey
John Giorgis
Jodey Glaser
Johnny Glazebrooks
Bob Gleason
Martin Gleaton
James Glendenning
Seth Glenn
Jared Glissman
William Frank Godbold IV
Justin Godfrey
John Gooch
Tyler Goodman
Bryan Goodman
Zack Gotsch
Justin Gottwaltz
George Gowland
Thomas Graham
Gordon Grant
Mitch Greathouse
Gordon Green
James Green
Matt Green
Shawn Greene
Stephen Greene
Joe Greene

John Greenfield Jr.
Eric Griffin
Eric Griffin
Dan Griffin
Ronald Grisham
Paul Griz
Preston Groogan
Auguste Gumbs
Robert P. Gunter
Jeff Haagensen
Levi Haas
Joshua Haataja
Owen Haataja
Michael Hagen
Tyler Hagood
Kelton Hague
Levi Haines
Michael Hale
Leo Hallak
Norman Hamilton
Andrea Hamrick
Brandon Handy
Erik Hansen
Greg Hanson
Jeffrey Hardy
Ian Harper
Akoni Harris
Revan Harris
Jordan Harris
Shane Harris
Brett Harrison
Brandon Hart
Matthew Hartmann

Adam Hartswick	Craig Hiltbrunner
Reese Harvey	Lance Hirayama
Mohamed Hashem	Ty Hodges
Matthew Hathorn	Jonathan Hoehn
Ronald Haulman	David Hoeppner
Joshua Hayes	Aaron Holden
Ryan Hays	Brad Hollingsworth
Adam Hazen	Joe Holman
Brian Hazlewood	William Holman
Richard Heard	Clint Holmes
Colin Heavens	Jason Honeyfield
Ryan Heck	Charles Hood
Jon Hedrick	David Hoover
Jesse Heidenreich	Garrett Hopkins
Brenton Held	Tyson Hopkins
Kyler Helker	William Hopsicker
Jason Henderson	Justin Horton
Jason Henderson	Jefferson Hotchkiss
Anders Hendrickson	Aaron Hough-Barnes
Fynn Hendrikse	Caleb House
John Henkel	Ian House
Philip Heritage	Jack House
Daniel Heron	Ken Houseal
Bradley Herren	Nathan Housley
Felipe Herrera	Jeff Howard
Paul Herron	Nicholas Howser
Sven Hestrand	Mark Hoy
Kyle Hetzer	Kirstie Hudson
Korrey Heyder	James Huff
Matthew Hicks	Dante Hulin
Anthony Higel	Aaron Huling
Dustin Hill	Mike Hull
Samuel Hillman	Donald Humpal

Daunte Hunter
Bradley Huntoon
James Hurtado
Wayne Hutton
Gaetano Inglima
Antonio Iozzo
Randy Islas Jr.
Wendy Jacobson
Paul Jarman
Bobby Jeffers
James Jeffers
Michael Jenkins
Robert Jensen
Jacob Jensen
Tedman Jess
Eric Jett
Anthony Johnson
Gary Johnson
Josh Johnson
Eric Johnson
James Johnson
Cobra Johnson
Nick Johnson
Nick Johnson
Randolph Johnson
Timothy Johnson
Tyler Jones
Tyler Jones
Bryan Jones
Jason Jones
Jason Jones
Micah Jones
Paul Jones

David Jorgenson
Ryan Kalle
Chris Karabats
Ron Karroll
Timothy Keane
Cody Keaton
Tyler Keaton-El
Brian Keeter
Noah Kelly
George Kelly
Jacob Kelly
Caleb Kenner
Zack Kenny
Daniel Kimm
Kennith King
Zachary Kinsman
Tucker Kitchengs
Jesse Klein
Kyle Klincko
Brendan Klingner
Albert Klukowski
William Knapp
Marc Knapp
Robert Knox
Eric Koeppel
Andreas Kolb
Steven Konecni
Christian Koonce
Ethan Koska
Evan Kowalski
Byl Kravetz
Bodhi Kruft
Jacob Krute

Mitchell Kusterer	Lucas Lorentz
Nathan Laidlwe	Kyle Lorenzi
Clay Lambert	Joey Lorenzi
Jeremy Lambert	David Losey
Mark Landez	Doug Lower
Andrew Langler	Steven Ludtke
Travis Larsen	Johan Lundberg
Dave Lawrence	Caleb Lunsford
Chris Lawrence	Andrew Luong
Alexander Le	Jesse Lyon
Jacob Leake	Brooke Lyons
David Leal	Taylo Lywood
Andy Ledford	Collin Macall
Nicholas Lee	David MacAlpine
Furman Lee	John Machasek
Joseph Legacy	Brian Machimbira
David Levin	Sawyer Mack
Ruel Lindsay	Patrick Maclary
Luke Lindsay	Daniel Magano
Eron Lindsey	William Mahoney
Eric Lindsey	Richard Maier
Paul Lizer	Ryan Mallet
John Lloyd	Kevin Malley
Andre Locker	Chris Malone
Dominick Loele	Jake Malone
Michael Lofland	Adam Manlove
Maxwell Lombardi	Andrew Mann
Richard Long	Scott Mann
Oliver Longchamps	Aaron Manning
Litani Looby	John Mannion
David Lopez	Brian Mansur
Joseph Lopez	Brent Manzel
Matthew Lopez	Robert Marchi

Jacob Margheim

Deven Marincovich

John Marinos

Cory Marko

Jacob Marquis

Logan Martin

Edward Martin

Jason Martin

Lucas Martin

Bill Martin

Bertram Martin

Pawel Martin

Alexande Martin

Trevor Martin

Christopher P. Martin

Christopher Martin

Jeffrey Martin

Tim Martindale

Joseph Martinez

Phillip Martinez

Michael Martinez

Cory Masierowski

Michael Mason

Nicholas Mason

Tao Mason

Wills Masterson

Mark Mathewman

Michael Matsko

Justin Matsuoko

James Matthews

Ezekiel Matze

Mark Maurice

Simon Mayeski

Joseph Mazzara

Timothy McAleese

Sean McCafferty

Logan McCallister

Kyle McCarley

Mac McCleary

Timothy McCoy

Quinn McCusker

Matthew McDaniel

William Mcdaniel

Shane McDevitt

Alan McDonald

Caleb McDonald

Connor McDonald

Jeremy McElroy

Dennis McGriff

James McGuire

Hans McIlveen

Ryan McIntosh

Rachel McIntosh

Richard McKercher

Ryan McKracken

Jacob Mclemore

Jason McMarrow

Wayne McMurtrie

Colin McPherson

Daniel Mears

Christopher Menkhaus

Jim Mern

Dylon Merrell

Robert Mertz

Jacob Meushaw

Brady Meyer

John C. Meyers	Preston Morzelewski
Pete Micale	Nicholas Mukanos
Christopher Miel	Alexis Muniz
Mike Mieszcak	David Murray
Timothy Miles II	Bob Murray
Ted Milker	Jeff Murri
Corrigan Miller	Joseph Nahas
Daniel Miller	Vinesh Narayan
Patrick Millon	Colby Neal
Philip Mills	James Needham
Mark Mills	Ray Neel
Darren Mills	Merle Neer
Robert Milsop	Kristian Neidhardt
David Mitchell	Adam Nelson
Reimar Moeller	Tyler Neuschwanger
Ryan Mongeau	Timothy Nevin
Jacob Montagne	Ethan Nichols
Ramon Montijo	Travis Nichols
Dale Moody	Bennett Nickels
Sherry Moore	Trevor Nielsen
Mitchell Moore	Andrew Niesent
Maxwell Moore	Timothy Nixon
Josue Rios Morales	Sean Noble
Nicholas Moran	Otto (Mario) Noda
Matteo Morelli	Brett Noll-Emmick
Joe Morgan	Michael Norris
Todd Moriarty	Ryley Nortrup
Matthew Morley	Greg Nugent
Autumn Morris	Christina Nymeyer
Daniel Morris	Brian O'Connor
William Morris	Matthew O'Connor
Christian Morrison	Sean O'Hara
Alex Morstadt	Patrick O'Leary

Colin O'neill
Ryan O'neill
Patrick O'Rourke
Colin O'Rourke
Jacob Odell
Grant Odom
Conor Oehler
Quinn Oehler
Kevin Oess
Nolan Oglesby
Travis Olson
Gary Oneida
Max Oosten
Anthony Ornellas
Gareth Ortiz-Timpson
James Owens
James Owens
Christian Owens
Will Page
Nic Palacios
John Park
David Parker
Matthew Parker
Shawn Parrish
William Parry
Eric Pastorek
Anthony Patsch
Andrew Patterson
Trevor Pattillo
David Patzer
Yahya Payton
Thomas Pennington
Aaran Pereira

Hector Perez
Kevin Perkins
Daniel Perkins
Toby Permezel
Chase Barret Perryman
Zac Petersen
Trevor Petersen
Nicholas Peterson
Marcus Peterson
Chad Peyton
Corey Pfleiger
Peter Pham
Charlie Phillippe
David Phillips
Jon Phillips
Brandon Phillips
Sam Phinney
Tim Pickett
Dupres Pina
Michael Pister
Jared Plathe
Pete Plum
Luke Plummer
Matthew Pommerening
Stephen Pompeo
Jason Pond
Nathan Poplawski
Michael Portanger
Chancey Porter
Rodney Posey
Brian Potts
Jonathaon Poulter
Daniel Powderly

Matt Prescott
Thomas Preston
Matthew Print
Darren Pruitt
Aleksander Purcell
Joshua Purvis
Max Quezada
Adam Quinn
Justin Rader
Scott Raff
Shahik Rakib
Joe Ralston
Frederick Ramlow
Jason Randolph
Aindriu Ratliff
Michael Rausch
Joshua Ray
Beverly Raymond
T.J. Recio
Ron Redden, Sr.
Blake Rehrer
Ryan Reis
Cannon Renfro
John Resch
Nathaniel Reyes
Paul Richard
Cody Richards
Augustus Richardson
Robert Richenburg
Eric Ritenour
Paul Rivas
Tina Rivers
Michael Roach

David Roark
Grant Roark
Grant Roark
John Robertson
Walt Robillard
Joshua Robinson
Edward Robinson
Daniel Robitaille
Christopher Roby
John Roche
Adam Rochon
Paul Roder
Zack Roeleveld
Adam Rogers
Thomas Rogneby
Thomas Roman
Aaron G Rood
Elias Rostad
Rob Rudkin
Arthur Ruiz
Jim Rumford
John Runyan
Nick Rusch
Chad Rushing
Sterling Rutherford
Zarren Rutledge
RW
Mark Ryan
Justin Ryan
Matthew Ryan
Greg S
Zachary Sadenwasser
Emelliano Salas

Connor Samuelson
Lawrence Sanchez
Dustin Sanders
David Sanford
Joshua Sayles
Jaysn Schaener
Shayne Schettler
Jason Schilling
Daniel Schmagel
Andrew Schmidt
Ray Schmidt
Thomas Schmidt
Kurt Schneider
Peter Scholtes
Theodore Schott
Kevin Schroeder
Michael Schroeder
Alex Schwarz
William Schweisthal
Anthony Scimeca
Cullen Scism
Connor Scott
Ethan Scott
Preston Scott
Peter Scrivani
Andrew Scroggins
Robert Sealey
Aaron Seaman
Dan Searle
Phillip Seek
James Segars
Kevin Serpa
Dylan Sexton

Ryan Seymour
Austin Shafer
Mitch Shami
Timothy Sharkey
Kevin Sharp
Curtis Sharp
Christopher Shaw
Steven Shaw
Charles Sheehan
Wendell Shelton
Lawrence Shewark
Logan Shiley
Ian Short
Glenn Shotton
Emaleigh Shriver
Dave Simmons
Joshua Sipin
Chris Sizelove
Andrew Skaines
Chris Slater
Scott Sloan
Steven Smead
Jesse Smider
Anthony Smith
Daniel Smith
Ian Smith
Lawrence Smith
Cory Smith
Sharroll Smith
Tyler Smith
Michael Smith
Michael Smith
Caleb Smith

Timothy Smith

Robert Smith

David Smyth

Gregory Smyth

Tom Snapp

Andrew Snow

David Snowden

Alexander Snyder

Alain Southikhoun

Briana Sparh

Robert Speanburgh

John Spears

Thomas Spencer

Anthony Spencer

Troy Spencer

Jeremy Spires

Peter Spitzer

Dustin Sprick

Super Squirrel

George Srutkowski

Eric Stack

Cooper Stafford

Travis Stair

Travis Standford

Graham Stanton

Paul Starck

Jolene Starr

John Stephenson

Thomas Stewardson

Tanner Stewart

Maggie Stewart-Grant

Edmond Stone

Fredy Stout

Rob Strachan

James Street

Joshua Strickland

William Strickler

Shayla Striffler

John Stuhl

Brad Stumpp

Louis Styer

Ned Sullivan

Shaun Sullivan

Kevin Summers

Joe Summerville

Ernest Sumner

Randall Surles

Michael Swartwout

Aaron Sweeney

Bryan Swezey

Tiffany Swindle

Lloyd Swistara

George Switzer

Carol Szpara

Travis TadeWaldt

Allison Tallon

Daniel Tanner

Blake Tate

Joshua Tate

Lawrence Tate

Kyler Tatsch

Alyssa Tausevich

Dave Tavener

Justin Taylor

Robert Taylor

Tim Taylor

Christov Tenn
Jonathan Terry
Anthony Tessendorf
Stavros Theohary
David P. Thomas
Jacob Thomas
Marc Thomas
Vernetta Thomas
James Thomas
Chris Thompson
Steven Thompson
Jonathan Thompson
William Joseph Thorpe
Beverly Tierney
Yvonne Timm
Michael Tindal
Russ Tinnell
Daniel Torres
Justin Townsend
Matthew Townsend
Jameson Trauger
Dimitrios Tsaousis
Scott Tucker
Oliver Tunnicliffe
Eric Turnbull
Ryan Turner
Brandon Turton
John Tuttle
Dylan Tuxhorn
Nicholas Twidwell
Joshua Twist
O'brien Tyler
Nerissa Umanzor

Jalen Underwood
Barrett Utz
Paul Van Dop
David Van Dusen
Erik Van Otten
Andrew Van Winkle
Patrick Van Winkle
Paden VanBuskirk
Patrick Varrassi
Daniel Vatamaniuck
Jason Vaughn
Daniel Venema
Marshall Verkler
Abel Villesca
Cole Vineyard
Ralph Vloemans
Leo Voepel
Jeff Wadsworth
Anthony Wagnon
Wes "Gingy" Wahl
Christopher Walker
David Wall
Joshua Wallace
Justin Wang
Andrew Ward
Wedge Warford
David Warren
Scot Washam
Tyler Washburn
Christopher Waters
Zachary Waters
John Watson
William Webb

Bill Webb
Ben Wedow
Zachary Weig
Garry Welding
Hiram Wells
Matthew West
Jack Weston
William Westphal
Ben Wheeler
Paul White
Paul Wierzchowski
Grant Wiggins
Jack Williams
Taylor Williams
Christopher Williams
Joel Williams
Michael Williams
Patrick Williford
Justin Wilson
Dominic Winter
Scott Winters
Evan Wisniewski
Nicholas Withrow
Matthew Wittmann
Timothy Wolkowicz

Reese Wood
Tripp Wood
Ryan Wood
Robert Woodward
Sean Woodworth
Robin Woolen
Michael Woolwine
John Wooten
John Work
Bonnie Wright
Jason Wright
James Wright
Anthony Wulfkuhle
Elaine Yamon
Ethan Yerigan
Matthew Young
Phillip Zaragoza
Brandt Zeeh
Kevin Zhang
Pamela Ziemeck
Attila Zimler
David Zimmerman
Jordan Ziroli
Nathan Zoss